DARE
to
FALL

DARE

to

FALL

ESTELLE MASKAME

INK ROAD

First published 2017 by Ink Road
INK ROAD is an imprint and trade mark
of Black & White Publishing Ltd.

Black & White Publishing Ltd
Nautical House,
104 Commercial Street
Edinburgh
EH6 6NF

1 3 5 7 9 10 8 6 4 2   17 18 19 20

ISBN: 978 1 78530 108 7
Copyright © Estelle Maskame 2017

The right of Estelle Maskame to be identified as the
author of this work has been asserted by her in accordance with the
Copyright, Designs and Patents Act 1988.

A CIP catalogue record for this book is available from the British Library.

Typeset by Iolaire, Newtonmore
Printed and bound by CPI Group (UK) Ltd, Croydon, CR0 4YY

To you, Mum, my best friend and my everything. Love ya best.

Acknowledgements

As always, I am forever grateful to my readers, but especially those of you who have supported me from the very beginning. Thank you to everyone at Black & White for being the coolest, greatest team of people to work with, and for always believing in me even when I didn't always believe in myself. Thank you Megan for helping turn *Dare to Fall* into the book I wanted it to be, Janne for always being there to talk through my ideas with and Lina for reassuring me that everything was going to work out just fine. (It did.)

Thank you to my best friends Heather, Rachael, Kirsty and Morgan for making me laugh and letting me whine, which I always needed after a long week of writing. And for binge-eating chicken nuggets with me.

Thank you to all of you girls in the writers' group chat - there are too many of you to name, but you guys know who you are, and I am inspired by each and every one of you every single day. Thank you for always encouraging me, cheering me up and staying up late to write with me.

Thanks to Don MacBrayne at The Summit in Windsor for answering all of my questions, and to McKenna Gilloth and Caleb Bangs of Windsor High School for accepting my desperate plea to help me out with the more mundane, factual questions I had, including class schedules and carpets.

And finally, thank you to my entire family for putting up with me during the stressed, anxious months that I wrote this book. We are a big family, but your love and encouragement is even bigger. And most importantly, thank you Mum and Dad, for letting me live my dream and supporting me every step of the way. I love you so much.

1

I've never known why Monday gets all the credit for being the worst day of the week. I disagree entirely. Sundays are. There's just something so quiet and still about Sundays that I've really grown to hate. Maybe it's because half the town goes to church in the mornings while the other half attempts to cook a pot roast before giving up and finally ordering takeout. That tends to be the case in my family, at least. Or maybe it's because half the people we go to school with are at home rushing to finish all those assignments that have been left until the last minute, while the other half of us spends the entire day in Dairy Queen because there's nowhere else to go. We belong to the latter half.

"Do you want another?"

I didn't realize I'd zoned out until now. Tearing my gaze up from the table, I blink a couple times at Holden while straightening up a little from my slouched position in the booth. I didn't even notice him get up. "What?"

Holden looks down at me and nods to the remainder of my

iced coffee. There's only a small dribble left. "Do you want another?" he repeats.

"Oh," I say. "No thanks. I'm good."

As he turns around and heads up to the counter to order again for what must be the fifth time tonight, I rub my hand over my face, only remembering that I'm wearing two thick layers of mascara once it's too late. I curse under my breath and pick my phone up from the table, opening up my camera. My eyes are now smudged and rimmed with black. Reaching for a napkin, I try my best to clean up the mess I've made, but I only seem to make it worse.

Will lets out a laugh and I fire him a heavy glare across the booth. He's chewing on the straw of his chocolate shake, but he quickly ducks when I scrunch my napkin into a ball and hurl it at him. "You'd think you were hungover," he says as he sits back up, flicking his hair out of his eyes. I can't remember the last time he had a haircut, but he definitely needs another one.

"I'm just tired." I breathe a sigh and turn my attention to the trash that's amassed on our table. I swear, all we do on Sundays is eat because there's nothing else to do in this town. There are at least half a dozen empty cups, of which three are mine, and most of the food wrappers are Holden's. The ice cream tubs are Will's.

"Have you noticed who's here?" Will asks, lowering his voice. He tilts his head down and leans over the table toward me slightly, subtly giving a pointed glance over my shoulder. "I think this is the first time I've actually seen her out."

Slowly, I shift in the booth and steal a quick glance behind me, and I spot her immediately: Danielle Hunter.

Over in the booth right by the door, Danielle is sitting with her hands wrapped around a cup, her black hair falling over her eyes. She's with three other girls, all of whom are engaged in conversation, but Danielle is staring blankly at the table as though she is entirely tuned out of her surroundings. As I study her from across the restaurant, a lump forms in my throat. It's a surprise to see her here. She rarely goes out. No one ever sees Danielle Hunter anywhere other than school these days.

"Well," I murmur as I turn back around to face Will. "That's new." I steal another glance over my shoulder at Danielle, feeling strangely unnerved by the sight of her. I haven't spoken to her in a long time, so I am praying that she doesn't spot me over here, but I am intrigued by how alone she seems.

I only turn my attention away from her when Holden returns to the table with another burger, his third of the night, and slides back into the booth next to me. The football team lost the game against Pine Creek yesterday, so he's in a sulky mood, disappointed with his performance, and Will and I have agreed not to mention it. "Last one, I swear," Holden says as he takes a huge bite, and I shoot him a repulsed sideways glance.

"Sure it is," Will says with an air of sarcasm. I think he likes to push Holden's buttons sometimes, but it's always harmless, and I find it entertaining to watch. He leans back against the window, closes his eyes, and angles his head away from us.

I pick my phone up to check the time while Will snoozes and Holden devours that gross burger of his. It's just after 9:30PM, and pretty soon the manager will begin making her way around the booths to kick everyone out so that they can close up. I nudge Holden. "Let me out for a second." With his burger still clenched tightly in his fist, Holden begrudgingly

3

moves his legs aside just enough to let me slide out. Sighing, I gently whack his bicep. "And stop beating yourself up," I tell him, breaking the pact I made with Will. Football season has only just started; I can't put up with months of Holden being grouchy every time the team loses a game. He gets temperamental every single season, but even more so this year it seems. He's barely said two words to us all night. "You're playing Broomfield on Friday, right? You guys will win that game for sure!" I reassure him as I squeeze past.

Holden shrugs his shoulders. Reluctantly he flashes me a small smile. "I guess we'll see," he says.

"I guess we're still being monosyllabic," I retort, rolling my eyes.

Will heaves a sigh and opens one eye, though he doesn't move an inch. "Broomfield aren't that great though, right? So maybe you'll actually catch a pass this time." As he closes his eye again, he's smirking. Holden seizes the opportunity to throw his balled-up burger wrapper at Will, hitting him square in the forehead.

"Catch that, asshole," he grins. Idiots.

I leave the two of them goofing around and head off to the restrooms. The closer it gets to 10PM the more empty Dairy Queen becomes, though there're still some people from school hanging around. Once the manager kicks us out, that's it: There's nowhere else to go other than back home. I briefly give Jess Lopez a smile and a "hey" as I pass her table, but she's with some girls who I don't know all that well so I don't stop to chat.

I continue into the cramped restrooms instead and lock myself in one of three tiny stalls. While I'm there, I send my dad a quick text to let him know I'll be home within the next

4

hour, resigned to the fact that Sunday is almost over. I slip my phone back into the pocket of my jeans as I unlock the door, swinging it open. My heart stops for a split second when I glance up and there's someone there, standing motionless in front of the sinks. I hadn't heard anyone come in, and the moment I realize it's Danielle Hunter, I freeze on the spot. Her back is to me, but in the mirror's reflection her eyes meet mine.

I haven't said more than a few words to Danielle since last year. I've barely seen her, and when I have I've never known how to act or what to say. So I just don't say anything at all. What are you supposed to say to someone who's grieving the death of her parents? I don't know. No one does.

But right now, I can't just turn my eyes down to the floor and keep on walking like I would do otherwise. I'm suddenly aware of how small it is in here, and she's watching me with those blue eyes of hers. They are such a stark contrast with her newly jet-black hair that it just doesn't quite look right. Her entire face is blank, emotionless. I swallow and shift past her to the sink farthest away. I turn on the water, staring robotically at my hands as it cascades over my skin. Do I say something? I know I should, but I don't know what and I don't know how. My cheeks feel hot from the pressure bearing down on me while I deliberate over whether or not now is the right time to finally say something to Danielle Hunter. I have always wanted to talk to her again, but never could.

I glance back up at Danielle in the mirror, only to find that she's still staring at me. I am going to go for it. I am going to talk to her, and I am going to do it right now before I overthink it. With as much courage as I can muster, I force myself to look directly at Danielle. The smile I plaster upon my lips is supposed to be normal and sincere, but I'm trying too hard and she knows it. "Hi, Dani," I say. Saying her name gives me goosebumps. "It's really nice to see you out."

Danielle narrows her eyes at me, and I allow my smile to slowly collapse because I know she can see the reality behind my expression. I'm looking at her the way most people look at her: with pity. There is a hint of surprise in her blue eyes that I've actually spoken to her, though she doesn't say anything in response. Her frown doesn't so much as tremble as she looks back to her reflection in the mirror, pressing her hands to the edge of the sink.

Her silence is worse than any other possible reaction, because now I'm unsure how to navigate the situation. I've done what I should have: I've told her it's nice to see her out. That's what I'm supposed to tell her, but she doesn't seem to appreciate it. Her expression is so blank, so empty, that it is impossible to read.

It's been a rough year for the Hunters, and the entire town of Windsor knows this. I've witnessed how drastically Danielle has changed, how broken she's been, how big an impact her parents' deaths have had on her. I remember when her hair was triple its length, when it swayed down her back in blond waves, when her cheeks were always flushed, when she was known for having the loudest laugh in every single one of her classes. She's not the same girl she was a year ago, but who can blame her? No one has forgotten the Hunter tragedy, and no one knows how to deal with those left behind. Especially not me.

The thing is, I haven't just been avoiding Danielle for a year now. I've been avoiding her brother too. Jaden, the second half of the Hunter twins, who still smiles at me whenever he sees me. Jaden, who I'm not brave enough to stop and talk to. Jaden, who I don't know how to act around anymore. Jaden, who I'm terrified has changed just as much as his sister has. I can't bring myself to be around either of them. I can't deal with the constant fear of saying the wrong thing. I can't cope with the effects such a devastating loss will have had on them. It's not that I don't want to. *God, I want to.* But I just ... can't.

With water dripping from my hands, I turn off the tap and quickly dry them on my jeans. I try to look at Danielle again, though I can't exactly meet her eyes now. They look so much like Jaden's. She is still quiet and the time has passed for her to reply, so I know I have to say something else. I feel anxious at the thought of bringing him up, but I gulp back that fear and quietly murmur, "How's Jaden doing?"

I don't know how Jaden is doing, because I have never asked even though I know I should have. I am afraid the answer is anything other than "okay" or "fine". That's why I am waiting with bated breath, my eyebrows pinching together with sympathy.

Danielle immediately tilts her head and her bangs fall over her eyes. "Why do you ask?" she responds quietly, and I'm taken aback at the defensive tone to her voice. "It's not like you care."

I stare back at her, stunned by her words. A year ago, Danielle and I were friends. She used to joke that if Jaden and I ever got married, we'd technically be sisters, and she had always wanted a sister. What I never told her was that I had always wanted one too. "Dani ..."

"Because if you really did care," she says slowly, turning fully toward me, "then you would have asked that question a year ago when ... " Her sentence trails off, but I already know

7

what she was going to say. She was going to tell me that if I really cared, I would have asked how they were doing a year ago when their parents were killed.

"Dani … " I shake my head and take a step closer to her. The last thing I expected to do tonight was confront Danielle Hunter in the Dairy Queen restrooms. "You know I care."

"You have a funny way of showing it, MacKenzie," she says, her tone softer. She turns back to the mirror and moves her bangs back out of her eyes, then reaches for the door. However, she pauses and looks back at me over her shoulder before she leaves, mumbling, "I'll tell Jaden that you asked."

In that moment, as I stare after Dani, her words left hovering in the air around me, I feel like the smallest person in the world. I don't know why I am so surprised. It's not as though I expected her to treat me the way she used to, because I don't treat her the way I used to either, but I guess this is why I have been dreading this moment for so long. I knew from the second I pushed the Hunters away that things would always be different between us, but I had no choice.

I don't want Holden and Will to wonder where I am, so after a deep breath I leave the restrooms and head back to our booth. I notice that almost everyone has left apart from us and Dani's group, though they seem to be getting up to leave. I nudge Holden as soon as I reach him, urgently shoving him further into the booth so that I can slide back in next to him. My face feels hot.

My discomfort must be evident, because Will immediately sits up. "What's up with you?" he asks.

"I just spoke to Danielle," I tell them, my voice a whisper. "It's the first time I have since … " Even I can't say it out loud. Quickly, I glance back and forth between the two of them,

8

trying to gauge their reactions. Holden frowns and moves away from me, leaning into the window and turning his attention to the parking lot, whereas Will looks curious.

"You spoke to her?" he asks, clarifying that he did actually hear me correctly.

"I had to. She was right *there*." I prop my elbows up onto the table and throw my head into my hands, closing my eyes and releasing a muffled groan. The last person I expected to deal with tonight was Danielle Hunter, and I certainly didn't want the Dairy Queen restrooms to be the time and place where I did speak to her again for the first time. I wish I could have said something more, or at least something else. "She hates me, I can just tell," I mumble against my palms.

"Well," Will murmurs. His words are slow, his expression cautious, and I slowly raise my head again to look at him. "You can't exactly expect her not to ... After all, it's not like she knows *why* you cut her off."

"That isn't helpful," Holden cuts in, snapping his head around from the window again. "Sure, she's avoiding them, but everyone's kind of been avoiding them. It's not like she's doing it be cruel." He glances sideways at me, searching for confirmation. "Sometimes you just have to do what you have to do. Right, Kenzie?"

I can only nod.

Before either Holden or Will can say anything more, the manager pops up in front of our booth out of nowhere, politely asking us if we can get a move on because they want to start cleaning the place up before they close in ten minutes. When I look around, I realize we're the only ones still here.

We gather up our trash, then head outside to the parking lot where Will's bright red Jeep Renegade is waiting for us. He had it detailed this morning, so the glossy paintwork shines underneath the streetlights, and Holden is scowling as we stroll across the lot toward it. Will's parents are pretty rich, whereas Holden's are in debt. They sold his car last fall, so now he's forced to rely on Will the same way I am. Mom does let me borrow her car sometimes, but it's not the same.

I call shotgun and quickly clamber into the passenger seat and slam the door shut behind me before Holden can fight me over it. His scowl deepens, so I stick my tongue out to him as Will slides into the driver's seat. I automatically reach for the climate control and turn up the heat. Now that it's September, the nights are slowly beginning to grow colder as fall rolls in. Holden clambers into the back seat, but he is over six foot, so even in this huge car he still has to slump down a little. I always find it hilarious the way his head touches the roof.

There's not much to do in Windsor on a Sunday at this time. Most places are closed, most people are at home. The nights are darker, colder. There's school in the morning. Work to go to. We go for a drive anyway, a quick circle around the town, along the stores and fast food joints on Main Street and all the way out to the open fields at Windsor's outskirts, before Will asks if it's okay if he takes us home.

He drops me off first, just before 11PM, and I tell them both that I'll see them in the morning when Will picks us up for school. They don't drive off as soon as I've got out of the car, but instead wait until I've pushed open my front door and given them my usual wave, then they head off until I can't hear the sound of Holden's music anymore.

Instead, I hear the sound of my parents. Dad's voice, mostly. They're arguing in that gentle, soft sort of way that they do when they aren't mad, but concerned, rather. A quiet disagreement, something that is all too familiar in this house.

I kick off my flats by the door and lock up, then pad my way down the hall carpet and into the living room, where the NFL highlights from tonight are rolling across the TV at a lowered volume. Mom's sitting bolt upright on the edge of the couch, her eyes sunken and tired, her thin lips pressed firmly together. She's in a tracksuit, hair clipped back, makeup washed off—nothing new for this time on a Sunday. Dad's standing opposite her, on the far side of the room. The coffee table between them bears an empty wine glass, a smear of lipstick on its rim. I remember Mom pouring a glass of Chardonnay before I left earlier, fresh out of a new bottle. She promised it would be her first and last for today. But she always says that, and Dad has the empty bottle in hand to prove it.

"Oh. MacKenzie," he says, exhaling. As though I haven't already noticed the bottle, he moves his hand behind his back, hiding it. He frowns. "I didn't hear you come in."

I give him a closed smile, but I don't say anything, because I'm more focused on Mom. I take my height from my dad, but I take everything else from her. We have the same deep brown eyes. The same high, hollowed cheekbones, the same strong jawbone. "I'm going to bed, Mom," I tell her softly as I kneel down on the floor by her side, looking at her with a gentle expression. She's not drunk. No, not after one bottle, that's not enough now, but the ugly grimace on her face is one that only appears after a couple of glasses. "Maybe you should too?" I suggest, reaching for her hand.

Mom stares at the floor, motionless for a moment, before she lifts her heavy eyelids up to Dad, looking at him as though this is his fault, as though it was him who opened the bottle in the first place. Then she relaxes, heaves a sigh, and nods as her brown eyes meet mine.

I reach for her hand and stand up, pulling her with me, our fingers interlocked. Her hands are warm, some of her nails are broken. She doesn't care enough these days to fix them. Dad watches me with gratitude on his face, but his eyes tell a different story. They are apologetic, almost guilty. I wave him away with my free hand and lead Mom out of the living room and down the hall, into their bedroom. When I flick on the light, I grit my teeth when I see the mess that greets me. There's a pile of fresh laundry that has been carelessly tipped onto the floor and left there, the bed still unmade from this morning, drapes closed as though they haven't been opened all day. Usually, I consider it a good day if this room sees sunlight.

Mom sits down on the edge of the bed, but the watery smile of reassurance she gives me does little to appease my irritation. "I've only had a few glasses," she says, rolling her eyes. "Your dad is overreacting."

I don't think he is, and I don't think it was only a few glasses either. But I don't tell her this, only grab loose clothes from the floor, fold them back up and put them away. Atop the dresser—next to the framed photograph of Dad and me so many years ago, back when he still had hair and I had no front teeth—is another wine glass. Empty, on its side, abandoned from yesterday.

I draw my lower lip between my teeth and tilt my head down, slowly pushing the drawer closed. Mom's back on her feet now as she shuffles around their small room behind me, so I pick up the glass and turn around to look at her, hiding it behind my back. Masking the disappointment that tugs in my chest, I force a smile onto my face. "I'm super tired, so I'll talk to you in the morning," I tell her. "Will's picking me up at seven thirty."

Mom doesn't say anything else, but she does frown when she notices I've stolen the wine glass from her dresser. Her lips twitch and her eyes narrow slightly, yet she goes on to pretend that she hasn't noticed that it's gone. Instead, she slowly fluffs up her pillows, and I back out of the room, pulling the door shut with me, leaving her alone.

I stand in the hall and hold the wine glass up to examine it. My grip tightens so firmly around the glass that for a split second I think it may just shatter into pieces, but Dad interrupts me before I get the chance to squeeze any harder.

He's leaning against the frame of the living room door, his features ridden with guilt as he says, "I can take that." He straightens up and steps toward me, placing his hand over mine as he pulls the glass free from my rigid grip. The other glass, the one from the living room, is already in his other.

Dad's too young to be bald, and he's also too young to have so many wrinkles. But he *is* bald and he *does* have that many wrinkles, and I hate that saddened look in his eyes that appears every time there's another glass to wash because it makes him look even older still. He moves past me, making his way down the hall and into the dark kitchen, and I stand there, waiting, listening for the sound of the faucet.

As the water runs, as Dad scrubs Mom's lipstick from that wine glass, I find myself looking at the hall table. There's a framed photograph of Mom and Dad on their wedding day, and there's one of me on my first day of kindergarten with horrendous pink scrunchies in my hair, and then there's the frame

13

in the middle—the one that's a light pink and never gathers dust because Mom cleans it at least twice every day. Inside the frame there are five pink letters, cursive and delicate. Those five letters are all we have left of her, as simple as her name, our only memory because we weren't given the time to create any others.

Baby Grace, who we never got to meet, but who we will never forget.

Danielle Hunter may think I don't care about them, her and Jaden, but I do care, probably more than most people do, but the truth is, I'm scared to be around them. I'm scared because I know the impact losing someone can have; I know just how badly grief can affect someone; I know how much it changes people.

I know, because I've watched it change us too.

2

Whoever thought scheduling a Physics class for first period on a Monday is clearly sadistic. I enjoy Physics, I do, but not at 8AM, and although we're only into the fourth week of the semester, I already regret opting to take honors. Phrases like "static equilibrium" should not be used this early, when half the class is too tired to function.

I'm hunched over my desk, my head resting on my homework that Will rushed to copy this morning in the parking lot. I don't know why he struggled with it in the first place. He's a lot smarter than I'll ever be, and between us and Holden, he's the only one planning to actually leave Colorado for college. Holden and I will most likely end up at Colorado State, whereas Will's parents have the money to send him as far away from Windsor as he likes. Sometimes, I wish I could leave too.

I open my eyes but don't lift my head. At the desk next to me, Kailee Tucker has one hand in her lap, texting, the other hand taking notes, though I don't think she's even writing anything legible. Just beyond her, Will is chewing on the end of his pen, his head cocked to one side as he listens intently to Mr. Acker ramble on about the application of Newton's laws of motion once again. My lips curve into a small smile of their own accord as I watch the way his eyebrows gently pinch together with confusion every time Mr. Acker uses a term that's new. It feels like my stare has been boring into him for at least ten minutes before he finally notices.

"*What the hell?*" he mouths, pointing to the screen at the front of the room. I shrug back at him, because for the past thirty minutes I haven't exactly been listening. He sets his pen down as though he's giving up too, and he flicks his hair out of his eyes for what must be the hundredth time already this morning.

I remember back in freshman year, no one believed Will was *just* my friend, the same way they didn't believe Holden was either. I *had* to be dating one of them, people would argue. Will was cute in that messy-haired, always-grinning, good-sense-of-humor sort of way, while Holden was tall and athletic in the intimidating, brooding, hot sort of way. Two polar opposites, which *surely* must have meant that one of them was my type. Only no, they were my best friends, and the thought of seeing them as anything other than that was hilarious to me. Also, Will subtly announced over lunch one day back in sophomore year that he sort of batted for the other team, so that was that, and the possibility of us ever dating was finally ruled out for good.

Right then, the bell rings out across campus, jolting the class to life. I hadn't even realized that first period was almost over. There's the collective sound of chairs scuffing the carpet as everyone scrambles to gather up their books and make a swift departure.

"I'm pretty sure I slept through the first half of that," I tell Will once we're outside of Mr. Acker's class and heading to our lockers, skillfully maneuvering our way through the masses, dodging the new, wide-eyed freshmen.

When we reach my locker Holden is already leaning against it, empty-handed, with nothing but a pen behind his ear. He's one of those guys who likes to act as though he couldn't care less about school, like it's lame to be caught carrying a textbook, but in fact, he cares a lot more about passing his classes than he's willing to admit. He actually *wants* people to think the only thing he cares about is football, and I'll never know why.

"How was Physics?" He grins, stepping away from my locker to allow me to enter my combination. As I throw my textbook inside, I fire him a sideways look. Holden knows we hate having Physics first period, which is why neither Will nor I even bother to answer him.

I grab my Spanish book and slam my locker shut again. "I've got an off period last thing," I tell them, "so I'm just gonna head home after third period."

"And I have practice," Holden adds, looking at Will, because what we're really stating is that we don't need him to wait up for us after school to give us a ride.

Will opens his mouth wide in mock surprise. "Hold up. You mean I can actually go straight home tonight without being chauffeur to you guys? What did I do to deserve such luxury?"

We stop quickly at Will's locker so that he can grab his Biology textbook before the three of us split up to head for our next classes. I only have to suffer through an hour and a half of Spanish until I get to see them again at lunch, but as I make my way to class on my own, applying lip balm on the way, I suddenly dread the thought of walking into the room. Holden and Will may not share this class with me, but someone else does.

When I arrive outside Miss Hernandez's room, I slip into the class after Caleb from the football team, hiding behind his huge mass as I quickly scour the room. To my relief, Danielle Hunter hasn't arrived yet. I'm still a little wary after our exchange last night, so I end up sitting at a desk in the back corner, head down, staring obsessively at a random page in my textbook.

The bell rings a few moments later and I glance up, startled. Just as the shrill ends, in she walks, hugging her Spanish book to her chest. Her bangs are covering her eyes and I wonder if she can even see through them, but as the class quickly settles down, she weaves through the desks to take a seat at hers over in the opposite back corner. I'm staring at her without realizing, right until the second her blue eyes flicker up to look straight back at me.

I look away instantly and I almost knock my water bottle off my desk, but I catch it just in time. Miss Hernandez gets up from her desk to welcome us and ask how our weekend was in Spanish, but I'm staring at the back of Caleb's head, too distracted to listen to anything else she says after that. I can feel the throbbing of my pulse just below my jaw as I try my hardest to ignore Danielle's eyes on me, but it is impossible. It's too awkward and her stare is boring into me. I can feel it.

I hate that I am terrified of the Hunters. Usually, I'm not so weak. Over the years, I've faced up to a lot of people in this school, from the guys in freshman year who used to taunt me about my height, to the teachers who've graded my tests wrong and were adamant they didn't, to the girls I've found myself in arguments with. But when it comes to Danielle and Jaden Hunter, I just can't do it. I can't face them. They are the epitome of my biggest weakness; they are the embodiment of grief.

For the rest of class, I can't focus. I'm pretty good at Spanish and I enjoy Miss Hernandez's class usually, but everything she says today goes straight over my head because all I can think about is Danielle. At first, I linger on the idea of trying to talk to her after class, but I don't think there's anything I can say that'll smooth out the tension I'm feeling between us after last night, so I drop that idea and instead spend the rest of class wondering if she's told Jaden that we spoke. I haven't yet figured out if I hope she didn't or if I wish she did.

When the bell rings out again to signify the end of second period, I'm the first to stand, shoving everything into my bag as fast as I can and pushing past Caleb, my eye on the door, my heart pounding. I have English Lit after lunch, and then I'm homebound after that, so I should be in the clear.

And I'm almost there, almost out of the classroom door, so close that I can smell the sweat in the hallways, when someone gently barges past me from behind, nudging me forward a step. I stop to identify the culprit, and I don't know why I'm surprised to discover that it's Dani. She walks past me into the hallway before she comes to a halt, glancing over her shoulder, only a few feet between us.

Her expression is empty as she looks back at me, her arms folded across the textbook that's against her chest. Her lips twitch as though she is going to say something. She doesn't. Instead, she turns away and joins the lunch flow, disappearing into the mass of bodies. She really is mad at me. I can see it in her blue eyes, an anger that's deep-rooted and blazing. I try to remind myself that she's mad at a lot of things these days, not just me, but that doesn't make me feel any better. It makes me feel worse, actually, knowing that she's so disconnected from everything, so furious at the world, and that I haven't been there for her the way I should have.

A year ago, we curled each other's hair and tested out eye makeup on one another up in her room, and we sat side by side in Spanish last year rather than at opposite corners of the room. We were friends. Not anymore.

As I head to the cafeteria to meet Holden and Will, I decide en route that I'm going to do whatever I can at all costs to avoid Danielle not only for the rest of the day, but for the rest of the week. I can't deal with the guilt that rises in my chest when she looks at me. But Windsor High is a small school for a small town, so avoiding someone in these hallways can take a great deal of strategic effort. I keep my head down at lunch, not quite listening to whatever Holden and Will are talking about, and I stay focused in English Lit, which is easy enough because it's the only class where I don't *really* know anyone, and by the time the bell deafens me at the end of third period, I'm breathing a sigh of relief at the day being over.

Fourth period has already begun by the time I make my casual stroll to my locker, so the hallways are empty, silent, the only sound the faint echo of teachers' voices. I open my locker and stuff half its contents inside my bag, dreading the amount of homework I still have due this week. There's a small mirror on the back of my locker door, so I quickly pull a hairbrush through my hair before my walk home, but as I glance in the mirror one final time I catch sight of someone approaching.

And I really wish I hadn't looked, because it's him.

Hands in his pockets, bag slung over one shoulder, he makes his way down the hallway toward me. I immediately recognize his blond hair, shaved short at the sides but left heavier on the top. His shoulders are broad and his chest is firm. He *is* a linebacker on the football team, after all. I used to love running my fingers through his thick hair; I used to love how secure I felt whenever he pulled me to him. I'm starting to forget how it felt.

I pass him often in these hallways, though it's usually while we're both buried amongst everyone else battling their way to class, and I like that it feels more distant that way. I can always just look at the ground, keep my head down, and walk a little faster until he is out of sight.

But right now with no one else around, with nothing but silence consuming us, there's no distance, no students to hide behind, and my body feels tense as I struggle to look away. He wets his lips just as one side curves up to create his signature crooked smile, and then his eyes flicker to meet mine directly in my mirror. They're as blue as his sister's, if not brighter. He slows down, almost as though for a split second he considers stopping to say something. But he doesn't. His steps quicken again and he keeps on walking, looking away from me.

I click my locker shut and squeeze my eyes closed, pressing my forehead against the cool metal. My breath is caught in my throat. All I can see in my head is that smile of his, the same smile that I fell for last year. My heart is pounding when I open my eyes again. I stare after Jaden as he walks away, disappearing down the hallway. His stride is slow but confident. The nape of his neck is smooth and neat where his hair smoothly tapers off, and I find my gaze drifting from his broad shoulders down the curve of his spine where his T-shirt clings a little too

21

tightly to his torso, hinting at his toned physique. And then he turns the corner and he is gone, almost as quickly as he had appeared. The hallway is empty again and my shoulders sink with relief.

Because once upon a time, when Jaden Hunter smiled that crooked smile of his at me, I smiled back.

3

The fifteen-minute walk home from school is especially bad today, not only because of the amount of textbooks I'm lugging along with me, but because I can't focus. I have already been aggressively flicked off by an elderly man for stepping out into the road without looking—apparently I am so distracted by the Hunters that I am now a walking hazard.

Dani's emotionless stare last night, and today Jaden's crooked smile...I can't shake the thought of them. They are two people I was once close with. They were my friends, and Jaden was even more than that. A year ago, I was falling in love with him. From the very moment he'd grinned at me across the hallway after he'd kissed me for the first time the night before, I felt it. I don't know why I ever thought that shutting that feeling out would be easy if I tried hard enough. I don't know why I believed I could actually stay away from the Hunters, that I could push them out of my life entirely. Because I can't, and maybe it's time I stopped trying. I still think about the way Jaden smiled that morning and how my heart almost burst straight out of my chest. I still think about the way his lips felt against mine, and I still think about what it would be like to feel that again, just one more time.

Jaden and I were just like every other wannabe-couple back in sophomore year. There was nothing remarkable about the way Jaden and I came to like each other. Our story was just as simple as everyone else's. We knew each other from sharing some classes and we enjoyed each other's company. I thought he was sweet but cool, hilarious but also serious, and I knew I liked him more than a friend the day I noticed myself feeling giddy whenever I saw him. We had started hanging out together outside of school more often, just the two of us, until gradually, over the course of last summer, our friendship grew until we were no longer just friends. It was simple in the sense that it developed naturally over the months, and I enjoyed every moment I spent with him, and I can still remember that first time he kissed me in my bedroom as he was helping me with my homework, and I was ready to talk to him about what was going to happen next. I was ready to take it to the next level. I was ready to be with him. But all of that changed last August when I got a call from Will one morning and the first thing he asked was, "Have you heard?"

Jaden and I never spoke again after that day. The Hunter twins missed the first six months of junior year and when they returned, I couldn't bear to look at them. I didn't know what to say or how to act around them anymore, and I hated thinking about the Hunters because it made me nauseous. All I could ever wonder was whether they were coping or not, and if they were, then how? I know just how heartbreaking grief can be.

I'm breathing heavily as I turn into my quiet cul-de-sac and my pace quickens, desperate to get home and clear my head.

The moment I unlock my front door and step foot inside, I throw my bag halfway down the hall. The house is quiet, dull and cold. Dad works long, erratic shifts, so he most likely won't be home until 7PM at the earliest, and Mom'll be home around 4PM from her own shift at our local dentistry. She does the reception work there a couple days a week. Years ago she worked at a local preschool, but not anymore. She never went back.

With both of them at work, it means I've got the house to myself for a couple of hours until I start my own shift at 5PM over at The Summit, an entertainment complex over on the very outskirts of Windsor. Most of the time I like my job there and I've had it for just over a year now. I need to save up for my own car. And for college. *Ugh.*

The kitchen hasn't been cleaned up since breakfast, so before I sit down and do anything else, I clear the table and haphazardly stack everything into the dishwasher in a matter of minutes. I am a pro by now at keeping the house in order, though not by choice. When I have time to spare, like right now, I do make an effort to tidy up, because if I don't then who else is going to? Dad is forever working, and Mom isn't in the right state of mind at the moment. She hasn't been for a while now, so it's much easier just to relieve the pressure on her by helping out whenever I can. Sometimes I wonder if she ever asks herself how the laundry folded itself or how the dishes cleaned themselves, or if she just doesn't even notice at all, because she never acknowledges it. I have been doing it for so many years that I do it without thinking now. I vacuum the hall quickly before I finally collapse onto the couch with my Spanish homework and a box of strawberries, which I pick at for a while as my attention drifts back and forth between my homework and the TV.

I like having the house to myself. It means Mom's out doing something, and when she's out doing something, she's not moping around here with a glass of wine in her hand. That's only something she can do behind closed doors.

I focus on my homework and wait until after 3:30PM to give Will a chance to get home before I call him. Holden's at practice, but even if he wasn't, I doubt he'd answer my call. He's one of those people who solely believes in texting and nothing more, so he's never any use when I have gossip that's too good to spill over a text message or a rant that's too explosive to type. Will, however, answers right on the second ring.

"I was just about to call you," he says immediately upon answering. "I was driving home and I realized... You still haven't told me the color of your dress."

"What?" I say with a mouthful of strawberry, pausing the TV.

"Homecoming," he clarifies. "My bow tie. What color should it be?"

Ah, right. It's homecoming next weekend and although Holden is hyped up for the game on the Friday night, Will and I care more about the dance the following evening. We always go together, whereas Holden usually asks whichever girl he's got the hots for at the time. I think this year he's taking a girl from the marching band. I swallow and tell Will, "Blue."

"Can you be more specific?"

"Dark blue," I answer and I picture my dress in my room, hung at the very far end of my closet, protected by its plastic packaging. It's chiffon and knee-length, with a whole lot of silver diamante finishing around the bodice. Mom didn't like it at first when I brought it home. It revealed too much, she said in disdain as I flounced down the hall wearing it, but I figured it was the wine talking. "Cobalt blue or something."

"Cobalt blue?" Will repeats. He's quiet for a second, and then he asks, "So ... which is it then?"

"Um." I blink a few times and quickly snap out of the daze I'm in, shaking my head at myself before I confirm, "Cobalt."

"Got it," Will says, but then pauses yet again. "Are you okay? You sound a little ... off."

"Yeah, I'm fine," I reassure him—though I'm not, really. I have been distracted the entire day, more so than usual.

"Okay," Will says. "What were you calling for?"

When he asks me this, I realize I don't have an answer to give him other than I was bored of writing down paragraphs in Spanish and I was tired of the drama on *Jerry Springer* and I was sick of picturing Jaden Hunter's smile in my head all over again. It's all I thought about when I walked home, it's all I thought about while cleaning up the house, it's all I'm still thinking about. Jaden Hunter and his damn smile. I don't know how he manages to smile, after everything. I don't know how he can even bring himself to, but he always does. He smiles as he runs out onto the field at football games. He smiles when his friends joke around at lunch. He smiles when he sees me even though he doesn't have a reason to.

"Nothing," is what I tell Will.

It's just after 4:30PM when Mom finally arrives home from work and I'm sitting waiting for her in the kitchen, ready for my own shift. The red polo shirt I have to wear isn't the most attractive uniform in the world, given that I don't suit the color, but it could be worse. I could work somewhere where they make you wear a silly cap. I've got fresh makeup on too, half a bottle of perfume sprayed over me, and I've also tied my hair up into a high ponytail just in case I get put on the restaurant shift tonight. I prefer working the laser tag because I can't deal with bussing tables, but I do it if I absolutely have to because I need the money. That's why I'm cross-trained and work five shifts a week.

"Here you go," Mom says as she tosses me her car keys while entering the kitchen. I swiftly catch them with one hand but I remain seated, watching as she slips off her cardigan and brews up a pot of coffee. "Do you want some before you go?"

I shake my head and study her slow movements as the smell of coffee fills the kitchen. She opens up the refrigerator to examine what's there. Then she checks the freezer, then the cupboards, then she heaves a sigh. "Do you think your dad will mind if I tell him we're having takeout?"

"No," I lie. Mom's actually a good cook and can make a killer lasagna that we all love, but sometimes she just doesn't have the energy. When she suggests takeout, it usually means she's struggling to get through the day.

"Okay, then I'm ordering takeout," she says, then turns back to the coffee pot, pouring herself a cup while she stares absent-mindedly out onto our small backyard. The lawn is patchy and overgrown because Dad doesn't have the time to tend to it anymore.

Enclosing my fist around Mom's car keys, I get to my feet. I can't stick around to talk to her otherwise I'll be late. "I'll be back at eleven," I say, grabbing my jacket from the back of the kitchen chair. Mom doesn't say anything more to me, but just as I'm stepping outside onto the porch, I hear the splash of her coffee against the sink as she pours it down the drain, and disappointment fills me because I know exactly what she'll be replacing it with. But I can't run back and argue with her, so instead I shut the front door as quickly as I can and pretend that I didn't hear anything. Dad does that too, he ignores the things he doesn't want to deal with most of the time, so I've learned from him.

Mom's old Prius is parked on the driveway and I slide into the driver's seat, reversing out onto our quiet little cul-de-sac. Windsor is a small town, but its 20,000 residents are spread out across small neighborhoods on the outskirts of town. The Summit is a fifteen-minute drive along open roads and through expansive fields. There is nothing to see other than an endless roll of green into the distance, but I do enjoy the drive to work when it's still light out, mostly because on a clear day there's a view of the Rocky Mountains way off in the distance, a backdrop throughout the state that makes Colorado that little bit more special.

I park Mom's car at the back of The Summit's parking lot and clock myself in just before 5PM, then I hunt down my supervisor, Lynsey, who has me slotted in to work behind the counter at the bowling alley. Weekday nights are usually much quieter than the weekend, but tonight a large group of kids turns up as part of a birthday party, so it's manic.

I'm standing spraying the line of shoes along my counter with odor remover—my chin pressed to my chest, covering my mouth with my shirt to avoid the stench—when someone taps their hand against the counter to get my attention.

"Size twelve," he jokes, and I recognize his voice immediately, mostly from the cocky, obnoxious tone.

I drop my shirt from my mouth and turn to look at him. He's leaning against the counter with his hip, a smug smirk on his lips as he waits for my reaction.

29

"Oh. Hey Darren," I say, giving him a casual smile as I begin gathering up the line of shoes next to him and placing them back into their shelves on the wall behind me. I like Darren, I do. We are on good terms with one another, but sometimes I just don't have the energy to deal with him. I don't find his carefree attitude as attractive as I once did, and he can be a little overbearing sometimes. "What are you doing back in town?"

"Who doesn't love a trip back to little old Windsor?" he says with what I'm picking up on as sarcasm, his grin wide. He leans over the counter, edging in closer to me in an attempt to gain my full attention, rather than only half of it. "And," he says, "I wanted to see you. I figured there'd be a chance you'd be here."

"Yep, I'm always here," I joke with a quick roll of my eyes, slotting the final pair of bowling shoes into their shelf, and I slowly turn back around to face him. I press my hands to the edge of the counter and look up at him. "You can't just drop in on me while I'm working, you know ... "

"I just miss you, Kenz, that's all," Darren admits quietly, and he seems disappointed that his surprise appearance isn't appreciated on my end. Why does he insist on popping up like this without any warning? It's awkward and I'm not sure exactly sure what to say, so I turn back to organizing shoes.

Earlier this year, Darren and I were dating. We had been for over six months. He was a freshman at Colorado State and I was a high school junior, and I loved his confidence and the dimple in his left cheek and the *good morning* texts he made sure to send each day. He's an arrogant jerk most of the time, but never to me, and my parents even let me spend the weekends with him over in his tiny dorm room on campus in Fort

Collins. I loved hanging out with Darren, and we laughed a lot when we were together, and I liked that being with him made it easier to stay away from Jaden. I had something else to focus on other than my own guilt. But after six months of being with him, it dawned on me that I was only wasting Darren's time. I wasn't in love with him the same way he was in love with me, and I couldn't be. There, in the back of my mind, were my feelings for Jaden. Darren didn't look like Jaden, he didn't laugh like Jaden. Every moment I was with him, I kept imagining what it would be like with Jaden instead. So, back in May, I broke up with Darren because it was best for both of us. He just hasn't reached that conclusion himself yet.

"Darren," I say with a firm edge to my voice, nodding to the couple waiting behind him and offering him an apologetic frown, "can we not do this right now? I have people waiting."

With his shoulders slumped and his lips turned down, Darren sighs and steps to the side, but I'm dismayed to notice out of the corner of my eye that he doesn't actually leave. Instead, he waits until I've fixed the couple up with their bowling shoes, and I've barely had time to wipe the professional smile off my face when he steps back in front of me the moment they walk away.

"Kenz," he says again, this time more firmly, more desperately. "I'm serious. I miss you. I really fucking do." He tilts his head down, staring at my hands, and he whispers, "We were good together. You know we were."

I shrug. We *were* good together, but only sometimes. There were times when he was too clingy, too obsessive, to the point where I couldn't bear it anymore. I couldn't give him all of my time and I couldn't give him all of my heart, so it just wasn't meant to be. "I'm sorry, Darren."

31

Darren groans under his breath and runs his hand through his hair, then steps back from the counter and quickly looks up at me one final time. There's a slight crook in his nose from when he broke it during a fist fight many years ago when he was still in high school, and I used to find it cute when I was trying to convince myself that I loved him.

"I'm not going to stop trying," he states in a hushed voice, leaning back across the counter toward me, closing the safe distance that separates us. He looks deep into my eyes, his face only inches from mine, giving me a tight smile. Then, he turns around and walks away, disappearing across the bowling alley.

Darren may not stop trying, but I really, really wish that he would.

4

It's late Thursday evening when Mom taps gently on my bedroom door, opening it anyway before I've even answered her knock, and she peers around the door with a worn, weary expression on her face that makes her look ten years older. She's nervous. I can tell by the way she doesn't step inside my room, by the way she uses the door as a shield to hide her shame when she parts her lips and says, "Kenzie, I need you to do me a big favor."

It's almost 11:30PM and I'm sprawled out over my bed, lying on my stomach, my laptop in front of me. I'm in a pair of sweats and a tank top, my hair thrown up into a bun that tilts over to one side, and I already know that what Mom is about to ask of me will require a change of clothes, makeup and an A+ in acting.

"I need you..." she murmurs, rubbing nervously at her temple, "I need you to go to the store."

There it is, I think. I knew she was going to say that as soon as she knocked on the door. If Dad wasn't out on an emergency plumbing job, I know she wouldn't have had the nerve to ask me, but without his concerned glances to make her feel guilty she's bolder than usual.

"Mom ... " My voice is quiet and I trail off slowly, silently pleading with her not to make me do this again. I want to say no to her, I want to refuse to go. But she's my mom, so I know that, really, I can't. I don't have the mental strength to fight with her over this.

"Please, Kenzie," she begs, and the look in her eyes and the crack in her voice is enough to make me feel guilty, as though *I'd* be the one in the wrong if I did choose to argue over this.

That's why I don't. That's why I've already closed my laptop, that's why I'm pulling my hair out of its bun and grabbing a pair of fitted jeans from my closet. Because I just can't say no.

Mom slowly pushes my door open fully, finally stepping into the room with both relief and gratitude evident on her flushed face. She hands me twenty bucks, her driving license and her car keys. There's already a scent of wine in the air. "Just whatever's cheap," she adds, as though that makes the situation better.

I look away from her and remain silent. If I open my mouth, there's a chance my frustration could convey itself as aggression, and Mom'll do that awful thing where her features contort and her eyes fill with desperation, and I don't want to see her like that. That's why I say nothing at all. This isn't something I know how to fix.

Instead, I mutely get dressed, slipping into my jeans as Mom disappears out of my room and then returns again with one of her blouses. I pull it on and then sit down at my dresser, grabbing my makeup bag and rummaging through it. Mom's standing in the background, dithering by my door, watching. Although I'm not saying anything, I'm certain she can see the disapproval on my face. I'm sure she can feel my aggravation in the air around us, tense and stifling. I'm tired. I have school in the morning. I don't want to be putting on makeup at this time, I don't want to be driving to the store when it's this dark and cold outside, I don't want to be using my mother's ID to score cheap booze.

"I would go myself," she tells me, her tone shaky with guilt as I'm plastering makeup onto my face, "but I shouldn't drive."

For the most part, Mom hasn't been too bad this week. She had a glass or two of wine on Monday, and that's it, as far as I'm aware. She's not too bad in general. She doesn't drink all day every day or anything on that scale, but the amount she'll consume depends on her mood. Tonight, it seems she's not feeling too great. Mom disappears once again and comes back with a floral scarf of hers that I reluctantly wrap around my neck after I've pulled on a jacket. I look ridiculous and I'm highly aware of this, but there's nothing I can do about it besides complete the look by pulling on a hat. I'm grateful for my height, because I like to think it makes me look older, and once Mom sprays her perfume over me in five overbearing spritzes, I'm ready to go and break the law.

I've done it before, a few times actually, and only once did the cashier laugh their ass off at me, before giving me thirty seconds to drive off until he called the cops. I've never gone back to that store, and ever since, rather than looking like a confident middle-aged mother, I now look like a nervous wreck of a middle-aged mother.

Mom watches me from the living room window as I make a quick dash to her car, spending a few minutes messing with the heating. Windsor gets so cold during the night at this time of the year, and tonight is no exception. My knees are shaking as I drive, my body huddled over the steering wheel, the streets empty. Most houses are in darkness, with only an odd few with their lights still on, and I head straight up to Main Street and pull into the small 7-Eleven lot. It's the nearest place that's still open that I haven't tried yet, and I never go to the same store twice. Pretty soon, I will have no more options, and I will have to drive to the city.

There's no one else around, nothing but the sound of a car passing by, but I can feel the cashier's eyes on me as I make for the door. My acting skills are immediately put to the test, and I fake a determined stride with my hands in the pockets of my jacket, walking as though I've just finished a long evening shift at my job, and I'm here to buy some beers before I head home to my four children and husband. At least I hope I'm walking that way. If not, then I'm probably screwed already.

I push open the heavy glass door and step inside, and because I'm the only customer here and all of the cashier's attention is on me, I look at him and give him a tight smile. I've learned that keeping my head down and scuttling imme-diately down the liquor aisle is definitely not the route to take. "Temperatures are seriously dropping out there, huh?" I say, though the formal tone I've adopted makes me not only look like an idiot, but sound like one too.

"Yep," the cashier says. He's young, in his early twenties I figure, and he leans back against the screen displaying the footage from the security cameras, his arms folded across his chest, bored. He doesn't seem to be in the mood for chitchat.

I head down the first aisle, pretending to look around at

the candy as though I'm not in a rush, and then I stop by the bread. There's one loaf left and it's been reduced in price, so I grab it, because I've also learned that buying more than just the booze is another way to deceive the cashier into believing I'm thirty-eight. The kids need bread for their breakfast. This is going fine.

With the discounted loaf tucked under my arm, I stroll casually along to the small beer section in the back corner which I examine as I hear the door to the store open again, bringing a cold draft of air in. Quickly, I run my eyes over the price tags and the grab cheapest six-pack on display.

As I make my way to the counter, I keep my chin up and my eyes on the cashier despite the anxiety that's rising in my chest. With my feigned confidence, I place the bread and the wine down in front of him, and then I smile politely as I set down the twenty-dollar bill. I sense someone behind me, but I'm too concentrated on maintaining my shitty acting to even so much as glance over my shoulder.

The cashier's expression remains neutral as he scans the bread, and I think I'm clear, I think I've convinced him, but then he looks back at me and he says it, that dreaded question: "Can I see some ID, ma'am?"

"Oh," I say, and then force out a giggle the same way Mom would do if she got asked for ID, and then I add, "I'm flattered!" The cashier doesn't even blink, just waits expectantly with that same old blank expression on his face, and I swallow the lump in my throat as I pass him Mom's driving license. It suddenly feels this isn't going so well after all.

The cashier holds the license up to scrutinize it, his emotionless eyes shifting between the small photo and my face, comparing the two. People always tell me I look like my mom,

37

but we are by no means identical. The cashier furrows his eyebrows.

The person in line behind me clears their throat and steps around me, but I'm so terrified that I'm about to be caught that I only cast them a quick sideways glance. My heart drops into my stomach. My eyes flash back over to my right and my entire body feels numb when I realize I haven't just imagined it: it's really him, it's really Jaden Hunter.

I am rooted to the spot, unable to turn away from him. *No, no, no.* Jaden can't be here right now; he can't see me like this. I am completely mortified and my cheeks burn with humiliation, growing even redder beneath the inordinate amount of blush I'm wearing. Jaden's lips are curved into his signature crooked smile as he watches me in amusement. His hair is flattened and falls too heavy over his forehead without gel to keep it styled in place. He's wearing all black: black jeans that are torn at the knees, black sneakers, black hoodie. He's holding a carton of milk in his hand. Glancing down at the six-pack on the counter in front of me, his eyes meet mine again—though now his smile his developed into a teasing smirk.

"Nice try," the cashier remarks harshly with a laugh, and I suddenly remember where I am. He slaps Mom's ID down on the counter and grabs the beer, tucking the cans out of sight, shaking his head at me. My entire face feels as though it is blazing, and the cashier waves me away with the flick of his hand. "Get out of here," he tells me, then holds up the bread. "Unless you still want this."

Numbly, I shake my head and then rapidly shove the twenty-dollar bill and driving license into the pocket of my jacket and spin around, desperate to get out of this store. I keep my head down as I rush past Jaden and scramble toward the door, catching my breath as I step out into the cold. Tears prick at the corners of my eyes, but I fight hard against them, willing myself not to be overwhelmed by how pathetic I feel at this exact moment. I rush straight over to Mom's car and I am just about to slide into the driver's seat when I hear the door of the store slap shut.

"MacKenzie," Jaden says in a low voice, and I freeze again, one leg in the car, and I glance up at him as he advances across the small lot toward me, his face shadowy under the streetlights. "Please don't just drive off."

The pleading tone in his voice makes facing him all the more unbearable, especially right now. I look like a parody of a mom, and he just caught me attempting to buy booze at almost midnight on a Thursday. I'm so embarrassed, and the only thing I can do is quickly tear off the stupid scarf and throw it onto my passenger seat.

Jaden stops when he reaches me, with only the car door standing between us. His lips are pressed together as he studies me. Carefully, he lifts his free hand to move his hair out of his eyes, and then he gives a pointed glance toward my passenger seat with a cautious expression. Breaking the unbearable silence, he asks, "Can I hop in for a sec?"

I was not expecting that. I always knew I was going to have to talk to Jaden eventually. It's not that I don't *want* to talk to him. It's just that I feel as though I can't. Slowly, I nod back, and he smiles in a relieved sort of way as though he was expecting me to shut him down. It's like he's grateful just to have my attention for once, and it makes me feel awful inside. Guilty and ashamed, but also terrified. I'm numb, both from the cold and from his presence, but I know there's not

39

a single excuse I could give him right now that could justify saying no to him. So I nod. A single, clipped nod that lights up his expression. Relief, I think it is. I don't know what I'm supposed to say to Jaden, the same way I don't know what I'm supposed to say to Dani. Only it's much harder when it comes to Jaden. I'm tense as I sink down into the driver's seat and the cool night air fills Mom's car as Jaden climbs in on the opposite side. I swallow back that lump in my throat and turn the heating up so that it's on full, though I don't need it. My face is hot enough already.

"About what happened in there … " I murmur quickly before he can say anything, though I don't know how to explain myself. I'm still mortified and I can't even begin to imagine what he thinks of me now. I don't want Jaden to assume that stealing my mom's ID and sneaking out to buy alcohol is something I do all the time.

"Don't sweat it," Jaden says, then stifles a smirk. "What's up with the beers though?"

I fake a small laugh to give myself a few seconds to think of an answer that would fly, and I rack my brain as fast as I can. The truth is not an option right now. I quickly look back up at him and say in what I hope is a nonchalant voice, "My mom's having guests over tomorrow night. She gets super stressed if she's not organized the day before, and she forgot to get any beer when she went grocery shopping earlier, so she sent me out." And then, because I realize how bad it still sounds that my own mother would send me out to buy alcohol underage, I jokingly add, "Shameful, I know."

"Hey, at least your grandma didn't send you out to get milk," he says, holding up the carton. I laugh with him and for a split second I forget that we haven't spoken in a year.

40

There's no awkward tension, no wondering what I can and can't say, just laughter and ease, exactly like it was before. Until, that is, Jaden's laughter falters into a small sigh, and silence surrounds us.

Although I have seen Jaden around school, I have avoided bumping into him in public until now. The times I *have* seen him at school, I have kept my head down, and he has stayed away. He has never tried to talk to me, but I couldn't blame him. He had every right to be mad at me, and if anyone was to make the first move, it should have been me. But it seems he has given in, and I think I know why. "Did Dani tell you—"

"That she spoke to you?" he finishes. "Yeah, she did." He turns the heating down a couple notches so that the air isn't so loud. It's dark, but his eyes are so blue that they stand out in the gloom. "She said you asked about me? Gotta admit, I'm surprised. That's unlike you these days," he says laughingly, although when I look back at him a moment later there is a definite sadness in his expression. My insides lurch with the sudden guilt.

"Are you mad?" I blurt out. I know he must be, but I need to hear it from him. "At me?" I add.

Jaden turns to look at me now, the sadness that had been there now vanished. "Why would I be mad at you?"

My eyebrows knit together as I stare back at him for a second, wondering if he's acting clueless just to taunt me as punishment for being the girl who bailed on him when he needed me the most, for being the girl who distanced herself, for being the girl who never smiles back. He has every right to be mad at me. Yet I can't bring myself to answer him, because then I'd have to admit it out loud that I've done wrong, that I've been a coward—but also that I can't help it, that I can't be

41

around Jaden and Danielle Hunter because I can't be around grief.

I tried. Two weeks after the accident, I had jumped into Mom's car and driven over to Jaden and Dani's house. I had woken with courage that morning, having known for weeks that I should be there for them, to console them somehow, and that it was finally time. I can still remember the feeling I had as I pulled up outside the house. Complete dread. My hands shook against the steering wheel. I felt almost like I was floating as I walked toward the front door, numb, like I'd lost all control of my body. I remember standing there, trying my damn hardest to knock, but I just couldn't do it. I couldn't face what was on the other side of that door. I knew already, without seeing Jaden or Dani, what they would be feeling. I knew all too well. So I turned around and ran straight back to the car.

Jaden shifts in his seat and I realize I've gone silent. When I don't respond, he angles his body toward me, propping his knee up against the center console that separates us. "Okay. Yeah, I was a little mad. Well, a *lot* for a while," he says, and then turns the heating off entirely, plunging the car into complete silence. "But I'm mostly just disappointed. At the time, *everyone* took a step back, not just you." His gaze falls to the bare skin of his knee and he traces a pattern along the hem of his jeans with his forefinger. He doesn't have to say it, because we both know exactly what it is that he's referring to. "And then when you were with that Darren Sullivan guy, that's when I figured you hadn't just stepped back, but that you weren't interested anymore." He glances back up then, eyes bright beneath his eyelashes, but I can see the disappointment in them that he's talking about. "So yeah, that's all there is really. I just wanted more than that."

Jaden may think he has me figured out, and for the most part, he does. Only I took a much larger step back from the Hunters than most people did, and I've never stepped closer again ever since for reasons that I still can't admit to. So, having Jaden believe that I kept my distance because I was no longer interested in him is an excuse I'm willing to run with, even though it is far from the truth. *I kept my distance because I cared too much.* "Jaden ..."

"MacKenzie," he says in response, raising his voice a little, his tone light. "I didn't demand to hop into your car at midnight to talk about old news. I hopped into your car at midnight because you probably wouldn't stop to talk to me otherwise, and I've been thinking about talking to you for a while now."

I wish I'd had the courage to speak to him first, before now, but I didn't. "About what?"

"Anything," Jaden answers, and then shrugs as he runs his hand along Mom's dashboard, his eyes on the dust that rises into the air. "What did we talk about before?"

We talked about ourselves and we talked about each other. He talked about the freckles on my cheeks and I talked about his smile, and we talked about our plans for college and our goals in life, and we talked about the classes we were struggling with and the classes we were acing, and we talked about the things we loved most and the things we hated.

That's why I know that Jaden isn't sure which college he wants to go to, just as long as it's in Colorado. That's why I know that he wants to live in a house down in Water Valley with two kids, three at a push, and have a job that doesn't make him stare at the clock all day. That's why I know that he was failing Spanish but passing U.S. History. That's why I know

43

that he loves driving in the dark when the roads are empty and that he hates peanut butter.

At least he did a year ago.

I don't know what Jaden wants to do in the future anymore, or what his goals in life are, or what he loves. Maybe he wants to get as far away from Colorado as possible now, away from what happened here. Maybe he's failing *all* of his classes these days. Maybe he's passing them all, but I doubt it. All I know about Jaden Hunter lately is that I know nothing at all.

So, I ask the question that I'm supposed to, the question that's safe: "How have you been, Jaden?"

And he looks at me as though I've just asked the most offensive, intrusive question to ever exist. "Seriously, Kenzie?"

"What?"

"Ask me something other than: How are you? Are you okay? How's your sister? Are your grandparents doing well? Do you need to skip the assignment? Because I get asked those questions all the time and I'd rather I didn't," he explains, his voice a mixture of firmness and exasperation. Closing his eyes, he pinches the bridge of his nose with his thumb and forefinger, remaining quiet for a few seconds. "Ask me something you would have asked me a year ago. Ask me something *normal*. It's really not that hard."

His demands put me on the spot and I find myself taken aback, struggling to think of something. I don't understand what he's doing, what he wants from me. I thought I was *supposed* to ask him how he is. It would have been insensitive if I hadn't, wouldn't it?

I'm still trying to think of something "normal" to ask him when he opens his eyes again, watching me with an expectant gaze, and I quickly splutter the only thing that comes to me that's actually relevant. "Are you looking forward to the game against Broomfield tomorrow?"

"That's more like it," Jaden says. His face lights up with satisfaction and his features relax, the frustration replaced by a relieved smile. "And yes, actually. Are you coming?"

"Yeah," I say, trying to relax in my seat. "Holden expects us to come to every game."

"Good. After last weekend, we need all the support we can get."

"That's true," I say. "You guys sucked out there."

Jaden rolls his eyes and we exchange a laugh as though nothing has changed, as though we've rewound to last year when we would tease each other just like this, because that's what you did when you were crushing on someone. You flirted via insults, and Jaden and I were no different. We were always flirty. Always playful. Always laughing.

"I should let you get home," Jaden says after a moment. He taps his finger against the time displayed on the radio. It's almost 12:15AM, but that clock is a little fast. "School in seven hours. AP Stats first period is going to kill me."

"I'll bet." I smile. Quickly, I glance around the lot, and I realize that there are no other cars here. I look at Jaden, and as much as I feel out of place, I ask, "Do...do you need a ride?" I am gripping the wheel tight.

"Thanks, but I'm good. I don't mind the walk." He smiles then, but it's different than usual. It's not the kind of grin that forms on his face when he's laughing, or the type of crooked smile he gave me in the hallway at school. It's a small, lingering smile that's full of sincerity. His gaze flits slowly across my face, taking me in. Then he reaches for the door and pushes it open, shifting his body away from me. "I'll look out for you at the game tomorrow," he says quietly, his voice soft as he swings his legs out of the car. He steps out, straightening up and pulling his hood over his hair, shadowing his face further. "I always do."

5

It's approaching 7PM and I'm sitting in the bleachers with Will, a couple rows from the back, sporting my Windsor Wizards hoodie. It's the home game against Broomfield tonight, and there are high hopes for the Wizards to deliver a win after their lackluster performance last weekend against Pine Creek.

We are a collective mass of maroon and gold up here, looking across the field toward the Broomfield students in the smaller bleachers, a sea of blue and white, the Broomfield Eagles players already down on the sidelines. It's still light out, but the sun has disappeared and the sky is gradually growing duller and duller as the night rolls in. I love the fall solely for the football. There's nothing else to do in this town, so my Friday nights are filled with supporting the boys. Especially Holden.

The cheerleaders are already chanting their cheers below. The bleachers are rattling with the anticipation, loud and rumbling as a group of freshmen further along stomp their feet. The atmosphere is electric.

"If Holden doesn't catch a single throw again, I'm pretending I don't know him," Will murmurs into my ear. I turn to look at him as he shoves a handful of chips into his mouth, his eyes roaming the crowd around us.

"I think he'll play alright tonight," I say. Earlier, Holden was in a good mood, stoked for the game ahead, ready to pull off some killer runs. I just pray that he can deliver on his promises to himself, otherwise Will and I will have to cheer him up for the rest of the weekend.

The cheer squad finishes up its routine and moves into position at the far end of the field closest to the locker rooms, the girls climbing up onto each other's shoulders. Out comes the huge banner that's been made for the game, a giant white sheet of paper with "GO WIZARDS!" written in sloppy maroon paint. The excitement in the bleachers starts to build as our players emerge from the locker rooms in full gear. They gather behind the banner, forming a large huddle as they begin chanting, though it's hard to hear clearly from all the way up here. Then, moments later, the noise around the field amplifies and the bleachers explode in an uproar of cheering, whistling, and applauding as the Wizards come barreling out onto the field, tearing the banner apart. Will yanks me to my feet and I throw my hands into the air, cheering as loud as I can, carried on the wave of excitement rippling through the field.

As the players jog across the grass toward the bleachers to join the coaches on the sidelines, I search for Holden among them all, reading the jerseys until I find his number: nineteen. He may have been hyped up earlier, but when I spot him it's clear he's nervous now. He's pacing around in a small circle, his helmet swinging from his fingertips, his head down.

"Aaaand all hope is lost," Will remarks. I elbow him in the

ribs as we sink back down onto the bench. I roll my eyes, but then I quickly focus my attention back on the Wizards players. I'm not looking for Holden anymore. I'm looking for Jaden.

My eyes scan each player as they drift around the pitch, stretching their legs, jumping up and down, talking to the coach. I can't remember which number Jaden's jersey is, all I know is that he plays on defense, that he's a linebacker. Some players have taken their helmets off now, some still have theirs on, and so it makes it all the more difficult to actually see who's who. I keep searching until finally I spot him.

Standing rooted to the spot and facing toward the bleachers, Jaden has his helmet tucked under his arm, his eyes narrowed slightly as he searches the crowd. After last night, I'm pretty sure he's hoping to spot me, and his blue eyes move along the rows until he gazes in my direction. It takes a moment or two before his lips twitch into that crooked smile revealing his teeth, and he gives me a nod that's so small it's barely perceptible. I half expect him to wave, but he doesn't. Instead, he pulls his helmet back on, his features hidden behind his facemask, dark and competitive, as he turns his back to the crowd. I forgot just how hot he looks in his gear, with all his padding and the way his jersey clings to his body, enhancing the dip in his spine. He looks cute in his tight pants, but I wouldn't ever tell him that. The number fifty-one is emblazoned across his back.

I stuff my hands into the large, warm front pocket of my hoodie and lean against Will. "I'm keeping my eye on fifty-one tonight," I say. The referees and captains from each team are tossing a coin out on the center of the field to get the game started, but I'm still watching numbers nineteen and fifty-one over on the sidelines.

"You mean Jaden Hunter?" he asks, surprised.

"Yeah."

Whistles are blown and announcements are made, and suddenly the game is underway. I steal half of Will's chips as we watch Holden out on the field, trying his best. He has the physique of a wide receiver: He's tall and lean with a pretty mean sprint. He's fast and boy, can he run when he has the chance. Some of the passes thrown his way are incomplete, others he catches before immediately being tackled to the ground. Nothing significant so far, but at least he's playing better than he did last weekend. I rise to my feet as he catches a ball thrown down the field to him, and he's off running. We're screaming encouragement as he's gaining yards, and the end zone is near, and ... tackled. Never mind. I sit back down as Holden throws his fist into the ground. He'll be bruised after this game, but he won't care.

Jaden, on the other hand, plays entirely differently. Jaden's role is to tackle and block, and each time the defense is up I observe him closely. I've never noticed it before, but he plays the field well. He's a tactical blocker and has a fierce tackle. An Eagles receiver catches a throw and sets off running, but Jaden is close on his heels. There's one real reason Jaden is on this team: He's fast. He was never much of an attacker, but he's run his opponent down in no time and he promptly drags the player down to the ground. I find myself cheering loudly, much to Will's confusion. Every time I so much as clap my hands together, I catch him running his eyes over me.

Despite being the first to score a touchdown and get some points up on the board, by half-time we're trailing behind 19–7. Holden walks off the field toward the locker rooms, kicking at the grass, fists clenched. I don't think I've ever met someone as competitive as him in my entire life. I can never decide if it's a good trait to have, or if it's slowly destroying him.

"Question," Will says. He slides away from me on the bench a couple inches. "Why the sudden focus on Jaden Hunter? I thought you didn't want anything to do with him." People are moving around in the bleachers now as they edge along the rows to make their way down to the concession stands, and the marching band is performing on the field while the Wizards mascot prances around.

"I don't," I answer automatically as a force of habit. It's not true, though. Of course I want to have Jaden in my life, but I just don't know where he fits yet. I already have a lot to deal with, and until I know how to work through my own struggles, there is no room for him.

Will looks at me funny. "You're so weird, Kenzie." He runs his hand through his hair and stands, pressing his hand on my shoulder to push himself up. He looks cute tonight in his light jeans and white Converse. Will has never been one to wear any of the school merchandise, except for once a year at the homecoming game when he wears a maroon Wizards T-shirt. "I'll be back in a second. I'll grab us some water. Wouldn't want you getting too hot under the collar watching Jaden in tight pants."

I shake my head at him, smiling to myself as I watch him disappear into the flow of people and out of my sight. I look around for a few minutes, surveying the crowd to see who is here and who isn't. I've already waved to a couple of friends before I notice Danielle for the first time, sitting on the very front row of the bleachers. I'm not sure if she has been here

51

the entire time or if she has just slipped into the game halfway through.

It's the first time I've seen her at a game this year. Both she and Jaden missed the entire season last year. She's staring at her lap, repeatedly interlocking her fingers over and over again. The girls next to her are laughing amongst each other, wrapped up in a conversation, but I can't tell if Dani is with them or not. Either way, she looks lonely down there, sitting in silence, playing with her hands. It *is* nice to see her out again, but somehow she still seems so disconnected from everyone and I'm not sure that will ever change.

I hadn't noticed Will returning until he sits down next to me again, handing me a bottle of water. I blink a few times, trying to push Danielle out of my mind, and then Will holds up his hot dog and offers it to me. "Want a bite?"

I pull a face, repulsed at the yellow sauce that's dribbling over the bun. There's more sauce than there is meat, I swear. "Will, you *know* I hate mustard," I whine, pouting at him.

"Exactly," Will says. "That's why I asked for it." With a devilish grin, he takes a huge bite, and I nudge my shoulder against his, secretly hoping he drops it. But of course he doesn't.

While he consumes the rest of his mustard-drenched hot dog, my attention returns to Dani. I can't stop thinking about her. She's still sitting there, head still down, still mute. No one is talking to her, but I wonder if she realizes that no one knows *how* to talk to her. That after we ask her how she's doing, we don't know what to say next.

But Jaden knows, because he told me so himself last night.

I decide right then, in the split second that Jaden's words echo in my head, that I'm going to talk to Danielle Hunter. I'm not going to ask her how she's doing, because it's clear neither of the Hunters want to hear that question ever again. No, I'm going to ask her something normal that I would have asked her a year ago when we were still friends.

I quickly rise to my feet and Will glances up at me, confused, his mouth full.

"Danielle Hunter is down there," I say, nodding down to the front row of the bleachers. "I'm going to talk to her."

"You? *You* are going to talk to her?" he asks, smirking. Realizing I'm serious, he adds, "I thought you …I thought you couldn't be around them?"

"I can't," I say quietly, exhaling, "but maybe you have to face up to things sometimes." I turn around and begin my plea of "excuse me"s as I sidestep my way along our row. If I am to expect the Hunters to ever forgive me for not being there for them, then I need to do this. I need to earn their forgiveness. I *want* to.

And at first, my determined leap down the stairs toward the front row is eager, but the closer I get, the more my steps begin to slow down. I have Dani in my vision, my eyes fixated on only her. There's an empty spot by her side, and I awkwardly slide down into it. As soon as my body touches the bench, Dani's eyes flicker up from her lap to examine her new bench-mate, and when she realizes it's me, she looks baffled.

"Hey," I start, smiling despite my nerves. I can feel my guilt returning again too, but I feign confidence, because I actually think I know how to talk to Dani. I just have to talk to her the way I would have a year ago, and hopefully she will appreciate it more than she would sympathetic frowns and careful questions. "Jaden's playing great, isn't he?"

Dani's blue eyes soften and she is silent for few moments,

almost as though she's searching my expression for a hidden agenda. Perhaps she's wondering why I'm mentioning Jaden's name, considering I haven't done so in a long time. She must come up empty-handed, though, because she finally answers, "Yeah. I forgot how good he is." Her voice is quiet and a little cautious.

"Did you see him sack the Broomfield quarterback? Coach'll definitely be praising him for that tackle!"

Remarkably, I see a very vague hint of a smile as the corner of her mouth twitches. Her lips are dry and chapped. "I know," she says, then adds, "Holden's playing great too."

"Right? He'll be so pleased with himself for that forty-yard catch," I agree. "He didn't catch a single pass last week."

"Really?"

"Really," I say, then laugh. I'm surprised when Dani almost laughs with me. Almost, but not quite. I haven't heard her laugh since last year.

When we fall silent, I lean forward a little in order to look past Dani at the girls on the other side of her. Up close, I realize that they're the same people she was with last weekend at Dairy Queen. The three of them are still wrapped up in a conversation amongst themselves, leaving Dani excluded the same way she was on Sunday. It's nice that they invite her out with them, but it's sad that they don't know how to include her when she comes.

I lean back again and meet Dani's expectant gaze. "Do you want to sit with us? I'm near the back with Will."

Suddenly, her expression distorts and she defensively leans back, away from me. She stares at me with suspicion now and blankly asks, "Why?"

"Because I want you to." And it's true: I do. After talking

to Jaden last night and realizing that it wasn't as bad as I had imagined it would be, I am now making a conscious effort to talk to Dani too. Maybe the Hunters won't forgive me, but I have to try. It's the least I owe them.

Dani releases a long sigh and looks away, her black hair now covering half her face because she's lost the energy to push it back. "No thanks, MacKenzie," she mumbles, staring at the ground.

"Okay. We're going to Cane's Chicken in Fort Collins after the game, so how about you join us then instead?" I urge, trying to keep my tone light so that I don't sound desperate. I know I shouldn't push Dani into doing something she doesn't want to do, but I *want* her to see that I'm trying to make an effort for the first time, and that it's taking me a lot of damn courage to do so. Sure, it's easy enough to ask her a normal question, to talk to her the way we used to talk, but it's hard to ignore the fact that she's still suffering. I still have questions that I know I just can't ask, like: *How do you cope? How are you still breathing?*

"I'll let you know," Dani says, and I blink several times, surprised that she hasn't straight up told me no. I think she just wants to get rid of me, honestly.

"Please do," I say, standing up. The girls next to her stop their conversation to look up at me as though they hadn't noticed me until now. "If you need a ride, Will has space."

"Okay," she says, and when I give her a small wave good-bye and turn to walk away, I hear the girls finally begin to talk to her. Probably wondering why I was there, no doubt, but as long as they're talking to her for once, I don't really mind.

Half-time is over and the game is starting back up again

as the players from both teams make their way back out onto the field, hyped up and ready to go again. Everyone seems to quickly scramble back to their seats, and as I make my way back up to Will, he stares at me the entire time, slowly shaking his head as though he still can't believe that I actually made an attempt to communicate with one of the Hunters.

"So?" he says as I sit down, eagerly awaiting the verdict. "What did you say?"

I scoop up my bottle of water from the ground, glance sideways at Will, and I smile. "I invited her to come to Cane's with us."

6

Windsor loses the game. The final score is 37–25 for Broom-field, so the build-up of excitement in the bleachers meets an anticlimax as the game comes to an end. Holden kicks at the field in anger and tosses his helmet away, but Will and I only roll our eyes and pretend that we don't know him as we file out of the bleachers. The rest of the Wizards have their heads hung low, though they do shake the Broomfield players' hands before disappearing into the locker rooms as fast as they possibly can, most likely embarrassed by yet another loss. We're not doing so great this season.

I search for Jaden, but I can't find him out on the field, so I figure he's one of the guys intent on making a quick getaway.

I follow Will back to the student parking lot and over to his bright red Jeep. It stands out by a mile over everyone else's cars, but only because everyone else is more than grateful to drive a ten-year-old beaten-up Honda that they don't bother to wash. Will says he doesn't care that much about nice cars, but the amount of effort he puts into maintaining the gleaming bodywork of the Jeep begs to differ.

The parking lot is buzzing with noise as the crowd disperses and people drive off. It's not too cold, so Will and I stand by his Jeep, leaning against the hood as we wait for Holden. We always meet him in the parking lot, and he usually takes around twenty minutes to appear after the game ends, so he shouldn't be much longer. I did look for Danielle as we left the bleachers, but there were too many people moving around at once and I just couldn't spot her. I don't know if she'd already left, but I've figured by now that she isn't taking up my offer to come to Fort Collins with us.

As the lot empties out, leaving only a handful of cars, Holden finally comes storming across the concrete toward us. He's wearing a pair of jeans and a white T-shirt, and he carries with him the fresh scent of cologne now that he's showered. It's no shock to either Will or me that he is furious.

"What a joke!" he mutters, jaw clenched as he walks straight past us both. He opens up the trunk of the Jeep and throws his gym bag inside. Then he slams it shut again and spins back around, livid, wildly waving his water bottle around in the air. "Do you even *know* how many times that Broomfield asshole should have gotten a penalty for holding? At least five, that's for sure. Kid almost tore my jersey off!"

"But," Will says, stepping forward with a reassuring grin, "that forty-yard catch though. Pretty sweet if you ask me."

"Still not good enough," Holden mumbles, shaking his head. Sometimes I wish he wasn't so tough on himself. He played great tonight, but all he can focus on are the negatives. I guess it's because of the pressure he is under to bag himself a football scholarship. A bunch of guys on the team have already had multiple offers from colleges across the country to play for them. Most of those guys accepted their offers during the summer, and I think even Holden knows now that time is ticking by and if an offer was going to arrive, it more than likely would have already. Now he won't stop beating himself up about it, because with his parents' financial situation, an athletic scholarship is the ticket to college he needs so badly. He leans back against Will's Jeep and takes a long swig of his water, staring up at the dark sky.

"There's still some time, you know," I say, stepping toward him and tugging at the hem of his T-shirt. He glances down, his cheeks still flaming with anger. "You're a great player, Holden. Any college would be lucky to have you play for their team, so c'mon." I pat his chest and offer him a playful smile to lighten the mood. "Have some faith, huh?"

"I know what'll cheer you up," Will cuts in, moving around the hood of the Jeep and opening the driver door, standing on his tiptoes and peering over the roof at us. "Chicken. Now get in, guys." He's just about to climb inside when he pauses, hand on the top of the door, staring at something in the distance.

Slowly, I follow the direction of his eyes, craning my neck to look over my shoulder. Behind me, Jaden and Danielle Hunter are walking straight toward us, side by side. I can already sense Will's surprise at Dani actually showing up, and I have no idea what Holden is thinking, though I can't verify their expressions because I can't tear my eyes away from the Hunters.

I turn around and they stop a few feet in front of me. Dani looks uncomfortable and way out of her depth, whereas Jaden seems slightly more relaxed, his bright eyes on me, challenging me somehow. Dani states, "We'll come to Cane's."

My eyes travel back to her. "We?" I echo.

It's odd seeing them together after so long. It's not entirely obvious that they're twins anymore because of Dani's drastic change of hair color, though they do still share similarities, like their piercing blue eyes and sharp jawlines.

"Yeah," Jaden says. They may have lost the game, but he doesn't seem pissed off about it the same way Holden is. His hair still looks damp from his shower, and he's wearing all black yet again. Black gym shorts, black sneakers and that same black Nike hoodie from last night. He has his gym bag hooked over one shoulder, his hand on the strap, his other in his pocket. He looks over at Will and smiles. "You still got space in the back, Will?"

Holden looks from me to Jaden and back to me again.

I exchange glances with Will, watching as his surprise turns to confusion. I realize I haven't explained the situation to him very well, and now he looks like he has no idea what to say to anyone. Making up his mind, he finally says, "Yeah. Hop in."

"Great," Jaden says. "Thanks." He nudges Dani forward and she moves toward the Jeep with apprehension, playing nervously with her hands. He opens the door for her, and then the two of them slide into the back seat as Will clambers into the driver's seat.

Before we join them, Holden quickly fires me a questioning look, confused and bewildered, most probably because this is totally sudden and very random. He doesn't know that I spoke to Dani at the game, or that it was *me* who invited her to come, and I haven't told either him or Will about my run-in with Jaden late last night. All I can do is shrug back at Holden, because honestly, I still don't *really* know what I'm doing or what I'm hoping to gain from this. I decide to let Holden ride shotgun and climb into the back seat with Dani and Jaden. As soon as I close the door I realize just how close we have to sit.

Jaden is in the center, separating Dani and me, and there's not a whole lot of room back here. My arms are pinned to my sides, all of our elbows touching. I didn't expect Jaden to be here too. I close my eyes, reassuring myself that I can do this, I can be around the Hunters. I feel self-conscious, though, especially with Jaden so close to me after all this time. His knee touches mine, but I don't flinch away and I inhale the scent of his cologne. I wonder if he's even noticed that our legs are touching, or whether he's sitting this close on purpose. Holden slams the door hard behind him and my eyes flicker open again. He props his elbow up against the window, leaning his head on his hand, silent as he stares out of the window.

"I haven't been to Cane's in months," Jaden says, and I don't know if he notices or not, but his warm skin is rubbing against mine. My stomach lurches. I've never forgotten the way his touch felt, the way his hand felt in mine, the way his lips moved. I am tensed up next to him, trying to ignore the thoughts running through my head, but it is near impossible.

"I haven't been since last year," Dani adds, and although she says it casually, the atmosphere immediately thickens because I know exactly what we're all thinking. We're wondering if what she's really trying to say is that she hasn't been since her parents were killed. Just in case, none of us reply out of fear of saying the wrong thing, and the whole act-normal mentality I was trying to maintain goes out the window.

Luckily, Jaden speaks up to break the silence as Will puts the Jeep in drive. "Better game than last week, though, huh, Holden?"

I close my eyes and lean my head against the glass of the

61

window, wishing that Jaden hadn't brought up the game. It is not a conversation that ever goes down lightly in this vehicle. Holden doesn't even so much as glance over his shoulder at Jaden, just mutters, "Not really," and then proceeds to hook his phone up to the AUX cable.

"You don't think so?" Jaden asks, oblivious to Holden's frustration over the whole situation. I could jump in and change the subject, but honestly, I don't know what to change it to. I'd rather the car was filled with talk of the game than awkward silences. "We got a hell of a lot more points up on the board tonight than we did last weekend."

"What does it matter?" Holden fires back as he stares at his phone, scrolling through his music. Between his frustration at losing the game and being confused as to why the Hunters are with us, he is standoffish and cold. "We still lost, and at this rate, we're going to lose the homecoming game next week." He selects a song and throws his phone into the center console as his music consumes the car. Crappy electronic dance music beats in our ears. Half his music doesn't even have words in the songs, and although Will and I are used to it by now, both Jaden and Dani aren't. I even see Dani flinch.

Will has much better manners and he is quick to turn the volume back down a little, much to Holden's disapproval. As Will drives along Main Street I notice him eyeing us all in the rearview mirror. His gaze lingers on the Hunters, his expression curious but also cautious. "Are you guys going to the homecoming dance?"

They didn't go last year, but no one expected them to. Jaden and I were supposed to go together, and I was so excited for our first official homecoming dance together, but it never happened. Luckily, Will was happy to accompany me instead, the same way he had done every year until then, but I didn't enjoy last year's dance as much as I thought I was going to.

"Yeah. I'm looking forward to it," Jaden says, his face lighting up, and then he seems to almost blush as he quietly laughs under his breath. "Grandma has pressed my shirt like three times already. It's getting ridiculous."

I wonder what that's like, having your grandparents as your guardians, as parental figures. Growing up, I loved to have sleepovers at my grandparents' house with my cousins. Grandma would make us all hot chocolate before bed with mini marshmallows bought especially for us, and Granddad would tuck us in to the huge double bed in the spare room and kiss us goodnight. Although we loved staying with them, we also loved when our parents came to pick us up in the morning. I can't imagine what it's like knowing that your parents aren't ever going to come back.

Ugh. I'm doing it again.

I'm thinking about the death of Bradley and Kate Hunter and I'm thinking about the kids left behind, the two people sitting next to me right now talking about chicken and football and homecoming dances, and I'm wondering if I'll ever stop asking myself how they manage to cope. It amazes me. They must be in so much pain, and yet here they are in the back seat of Will's Jeep en route to Fort Collins to hang out after the game.

I don't hear what Will replies because I'm so zoned out, so I shake my head quickly to force myself back to reality. *Stop thinking about it.*

"I'm not going," Dani murmurs and I glance over at her. She's leaning back, arms folded across her chest, and I realize that perhaps she doesn't actually want to be here. Maybe Jaden is forcing her to come against her will, giving her a harsh nudge back into the world of social interaction.

"Why not?" Will pushes, and I fire him a glare in the rear-view mirror. My expression immediately softens when I realize that, actually, Dani might appreciate his lack of sympathetic caution.

"Because no one has asked me to go with them," she says with a shrug, and I'm surprised by her answer. I assumed she wasn't going because she didn't want to be around people, but it turns out she's not going because people don't seem to want to be around *her*.

"Can't you just go with your friends?" Will goes on.

"Don't really have any," she admits, which is sad, because she had a whole circle of friends before. But, like the friends she was sat with at the game, most of them don't really treat her the same anymore. She has distanced herself from a lot of people over the past year.

"Oh," Will says, his eyes on the road ahead. He's not sure what to say next, so instead he shifts his attention to her brother, and I'm so grateful that he's trying to keep a conversation going. "What about you, Jaden? Who are you going with?"

This question piques my interest, so I sit up a little as he tells us, "Do you guys know Ellie? The junior? Eleanor Boosey? I'm taking her."

"She's really nice," I force myself to say, although it comes out too loud. Eleanor *is* a really sweet girl, though now I have new questions. Are they dating? Just friends? *Please just be friends*.

"Yeah, she is. Harrison from the team is taking Ellie's friend, so I'm being a good wingman," Jaden explains, looking at me.

64

His eyes meet mine, his mouth already in a smile, and I feel my chest relax. So they're not dating. *Good*, I think. "Who are you going with this year?" he asks.

"That would be me again," Will cuts in, holding up one hand, the other gripping the steering wheel.

Jaden's smile falters and I wonder if he too is recalling that a year ago we were supposed to be going with each other. "Nice," he says, looking away.

It's after 10PM by now, and it's a twenty-minute drive to Fort Collins; fifteen if Will puts his foot down a little more. Denver is too far, over an hour's drive, so Fort Collins is the closest city that we have and it's certainly better than Windsor. It's always nice to get out of town every once in a while, even if it is only to buy a tray of chicken fingers.

At this time of night, the road is dark and almost entirely empty besides the occasional oncoming car as we pass through expansive fields. Colorado is known for its natural beauty, but sometimes the fields and the mountains and the greenery get a bit mundane when you have lived your entire life here. I sit back, close my eyes and listen to Holden's music as the Jeep falls into silence. It's not uncomfortable silence, thankfully, but we aren't entirely relaxed either. Will is focusing on driving in the dark, which I know he hates, and Holden is back on his phone, though I think he's only pretending to be texting.

As we advance across Fort Collins, heading north toward the center, the streets become much busier. It's a Friday night in the city, after all, and Fort Collins is home to Colorado State, so all of the college students will be around, out with friends or hitting up bars. Cane's is just down the street from the campus, and as we pull up it's already bustling with people, despite the fact that it closes in forty-five minutes. Will parks up in a spot and cuts the engine as we all sit up, and I'm not the only one who's relieved to finally get out of the car. A minute longer with Jaden's body against mine and I may have just torn the inside of my cheek open from biting so hard.

I throw open the door and slide out, hugging my Wizards hoodie closer around me, stuffing my hands into the front pocket. The night keeps on getting cooler and cooler, and now there's a breeze that seems to be picking up, but the fresh air feels amazing. Jaden follows out behind me, though I focus instead on scouring the parking lot. I can see Kailee's car over at the other end, and I just *know* she and Jess will be totally shocked when they see me stroll in through the door with not only Dani by my side, but Jaden too. Everyone knew I was friends with Dani, and everyone knew I had a thing for Jaden, and everyone knows I haven't spoken to them since last year, so this is going to be interesting.

Anxiously, I play with the ends of my hair as Holden gets out of the Jeep and slams the door shut again behind him, but then he doesn't wait around for the rest of us. Instead, he marches off on his own and heads inside. Will and I exchange a look. Holden and Jaden have never been best friends or anything, but they did used to get along. They're on the team together, after all, but ever since last year, he's been just as uncomfortable around Jaden as I have. A lot of people are uncomfortable around the twins.

"Is he alright?" Jaden asks, casting me a sideways glance.

"Yeah," I say, then feign a laugh as Will locks the Jeep. "He just loves his comfort food whenever you guys lose a game."

Will falls into step next to me as the four of us make our way to the door, Jaden and Dani behind us. As we walk, he leans in closer and whispers, "You okay?" And I really

66

don't know whether or not I am, so I just shrug and keep on walking.

I let Will push open the door, and the smell of grease and fried chicken is so overpowering that it's almost sickening in a good way. The restaurant is full and buzzing with noise, people sitting around tables, laughing and chatting. I try to search for Holden, but I find Jess and Kailee first, sitting with their boyfriends, Tanner and Anthony, near a booth by the counter. They've spotted me too, and as the door falls closed behind us and shuts out the cold, I feel Jaden and Dani lingering directly behind me.

Jess stares at us for a moment before whispering something to Kailee. She looks back and catches my eye, an accident I'd guess, but she gives me a cheeky, excited grin. Yep. They're definitely talking about us. But honestly, it really is rather simple. I am doing this because I have no choice, because I owe it to Jaden and Dani. But I can't tell Jess and Kailee this right now, so I just give them a small smile.

But it's not only them who have spotted my arrival.

At a rowdy booth by the window, with too many college guys hovering around one another and not enough space for them all, Darren is standing with his arm propped up against the booth divider, his eyes on me.

7

No, I think. *Please not now.*

Slowly, Darren's lips curve into a smile, revealing the dimple in his left cheek. He straightens up as though he's about to walk straight over to me and I quickly put my guard up, preparing myself. Darren is the last person I want to see right now. Even at the best of times, he is a douchebag whenever his friends are around, so I definitely can't handle him right now—not here in the middle of Cane's while I'm with Jaden Hunter.

Will begins to move and I stick to him like glue, following so close behind him that I almost trip over his feet, desperate to scramble away from Darren. Holden has found us an empty booth at the opposite side of the restaurant, which I couldn't be more relieved about. He's already sitting down, leaning against the window and counting the bills in his wallet as the four of us approach.

Will slides in next to him and, in my rush to avoid Darren, I quickly slide into the booth opposite them. Dani and then

Jaden follow in behind me, the three of us perfectly aligned opposite Holden and Will, and at this point, all nerves about being around the Hunters disappear. All I care about is Darren. I lean back and steal a glance past Dani, my eyes roaming the bustling restaurant in search of him. When I realize that he hasn't moved from his spot against the booth divider, I relax only a little. He's not looking at me anymore; instead he's chuckling as his group of friends explode into laughter. I exhale and turn back to face my own company.

"Should we just get a tray to share?" Will suggests, and we all agree on a tray of twenty-five and each toss some cash onto the table, which Will pools together as he stands, offering to get the food. I can see in Holden's face that he wishes he had offered instead.

"Is it just me or are Kailee Tucker and Jess Lopez staring at us?" Dani asks, speaking up for the first time. She keeps her voice low and her eyes on me, and she doesn't look too happy. I look past her, over Jaden, and find their table again. Sure enough, their curious gazes are boring straight into our booth, but the second my eyes meet theirs, they look away, embarrassed.

"I think they're just surprised to see you out again," I admit, looking back at Dani. I'm not going to lie, because it's not a cruel truth. They are surprised to see her. People are surprised in a good way. What I don't add is that they're probably more surprised to see them out with *me*.

"You know you live in a small town when people are surprised to see you outside of your house," Dani murmurs, pulling the long sleeves of her black T-shirt over her hands and then folding her arms across her chest, sighing.

"Dani," Jaden says, gently nudging her with his elbow. He

69

frowns at her and there's something in his blue eyes as he looks at her that I can't quite understand, something unspoken between them, almost like a warning.

"I just wish people would get over it already," she adds quietly, her expression sad as she leans back against the padded booth. "You expect us to move on and live our lives as normal and yet you don't make us *feel* normal."

Jaden glances between Holden and me with an apologetic sort of smile, sorry that Dani has made the conversation an impossible one. Now we're back at square one again, where neither Holden nor I have a clue how to respond.

"As you can imagine," Jaden says, forcing a laugh as he attempts to lighten the mood, "we can't wait to graduate."

Holden's expression is blank as he studies the twins, trying to figure them out, and with piqued interest he asks, "Why? Are you leaving Windsor?"

"Hopefully," Jaden says, nodding, though Dani rolls her eyes at him, seemingly annoyed. But I get it; I can understand why they would want to leave. Next year, when they start college elsewhere, no one is going to know their history; no one is going to know about "the Hunter tragedy"; no one is going to tiptoe around them like the way us folks in Windsor do.

At that exact moment, before anything more can be said, someone quickly slides into the booth next to Holden. It's Darren. Holden immediately exchanges a concerned look with me, and I part my lips, prepared to tell Darren that now isn't the time and to leave us alone. The guy I left him for is sitting right next to me.

"Hello, kids," he says with that annoyingly arrogant tone of his. There's a patronizing smirk on his face as he rests his elbows on the table and leans forward. If it were just the two of

70

us here, he would be his happy, sweet, gentle self. But when he has an audience, he changes. "So where have you guys been tonight?" he asks, glancing sideways at Holden.

"We had a game," Holden says, keeping his answer short. He doesn't ask anything in return, and instead pulls out his phone again and returns to fake texting. He's not Darren's biggest fan, and the last thing he wants to talk about right now is the game.

Darren's dark eyes flicker to meet mine and he smirks. "Were you there too, Kenz?"

There's irritation rising in my chest at the mere sight of his cocky expression. It is so frustrating watching his personality change so drastically depending on who he is surrounded by. I *know* that he is a nice person, really, but to everyone else, he is nothing more than Darren Sullivan the Asshole. I can't deal with this ridiculous act that he puts on.

"Yes, Darren, I was there," I say very slowly and very firmly, emphasizing my annoyance that he thought it would be okay to come over here. I sense Jaden shift uncomfortably at the end of the booth. He knows that Darren and I were together; however, Darren doesn't know that Jaden is the person I still had feelings for. And I do not want him to find out.

"Have you thought anymore about what we talked about?" Darren asks. I don't like the way he words this, as though it was a willing, casual conversation on my part when he ambushed me at work on Monday. It certainly wasn't.

Holden narrows his eyes suspiciously at me. I haven't told him and Will that I spoke to Darren on Monday, because I didn't think it was even important. Run-ins with Darren are a regular occurrence. He appears out of nowhere, claims he misses me, and then tries to get back together. I don't know how long he's going to keep trying until it finally hits him that it's never going to happen.

"No, I haven't," I answer, looking him straight in the eye. I am silently pleading with him to leave, and I can only hope my cold tone is enough to convince him that although we are friends, I don't want to be around him right now.

He cocks his head to one side as he reads my expression, that silly smirk still on his face as he studies me intensely, the gears in his mind shifting while he considers what to say next.

But he doesn't get the chance to say anything at all, because suddenly Will is back, apprehensive as he pushes the tray of chicken onto the table. His eyebrows are furrowed as he glances down to see who's stolen his spot in the booth, and the second he realizes it's Darren he fires me the same look of concern that Holden did.

"What are you doing here?" Will asks, defensive on my behalf. He's never really liked Darren either.

"I just came over to catch up with my old buddies," Darren says, grinning wide as he gets to his feet. He places his hand on Will's shoulder and, in the most patronizing manner possible, asks, "Anything new with you, Water Valley kid? Dad paid your way into Harvard already? Got a boyfriend yet?"

"Hilarious," Will deadpans, shrugging Darren's hand off him and stepping back. He stuffs his hands into the front pockets of his jeans and continues to hold Darren's taunting gaze, never looking away, never looking down. Darren is being more of a jerk than he usually is, and I'm pretty sure he's only acting this way because I shut him down on Monday. He's retaliating by putting up a front and hitting my friends with snide remarks, which he never would have done months ago.

"Darren," I say, shaking my head at him. He's not even worth the effort of grinding my teeth over, so I briskly wave him away with my hand. "C'mon. Go back to your own friends."

Darren's eyes flicker back over to meet mine. "But you haven't introduced me to *your* new friends yet."

I glance sideways at Dani and Jaden. They're both silent. Dani looks more uncomfortable than ever, her eyes on the table, expression blank, trying her best to not get involved. Jaden, however, is looking up at Darren with narrowed, curious eyes. I can already place a bet on what he's thinking. He's trying to figure out why I ever dated Darren. I sometimes find myself asking the same thing.

"Jaden Hunter," he says, then gently nudges his shoulder against Dani's as he motions toward her. "And this is my sister, Danielle."

Darren's expression softens for a split second as realization dawns on him. He looks at me again, but this time it seems he's searching for an answer. "Hunter?" he repeats, and I give him the smallest of nods to confirm his thoughts.

"Yep," Jaden says, plastering a smile across his face. Immediately, I can tell it's fake. It's not his real smile, the one he gives me, the one that's crooked.

"Right," Darren murmurs. He's lost his ego now and he awkwardly scratches the back of his neck, unsure of what to say next. Quickly, he glances over his shoulder, back to his friends, who are still the loudest booth in the joint. "I should go."

I don't even look at him again. Instead, I pull the tray of chicken fingers toward me and pay more attention to scouring the pile for the juiciest piece than I do to Darren. "Yeah," I say with a shrug. "See you."

No one says anything more as Darren turns on his heels and scuffles back across the restaurant to the safety of his friend-ship circle, who—for the record—are all pretty much morons. I used to think they were cool, but they're really not.

"No offense, MacKenzie," Dani says, finally looking up, her voice stronger than it was before, "but if I'm not wrong in figuring out that that's your ex, then you dated a douchebag."

"You got that right," Will says, nodding in agreement.

Jaden stays silent, but he catches my gaze. The warmth in his expression contrasts with the cool, ice blue of his eyes, and I wonder just what exactly, in that moment, he thinks of me. Maybe he thinks I'm an idiot for dating Darren. Maybe he thinks I'm smart for getting myself out of that relationship. Maybe he's glad that I did.

8

The drive home to Windsor is a lot more comfortable than before. Holden has eased up a little and he's slumped against the passenger seat, his head tilted to the side as he stares out of the window and into the darkness. He's still listening, however, and I hear him laugh under his breath every once in a while when one of us says something even remotely funny. Will's tired; I can tell by how quiet he's gone as he focuses on the road with strained eyes. I'm in the back seat again, but this time Dani is in the center, separating Jaden and me.

Just as we're driving along Main Street, Will casts a nervous glance at the Hunters in the rearview mirror. His eyes shine, glossy from the streetlights that glare in through the windshield. "Where do you live?" he asks slowly, his voice barely audible. It's an awkward question to ask and I realize as soon as he says it that I don't know the answer either. A year ago, Will would have been dropping the Hunters off at their house on the northern side of Main Street, on a quiet, small street that overlooked the lake. But a new family lives there now.

"Ponderosa Drive," Jaden answers without missing a beat. "It's by the ball parks."

"Ah," Will says after he thinks for a moment. "Got it."

Even though both mine and Holden's houses are closer, Will doesn't turn off Main Street to drop us off, and I know it's because he doesn't want to be left alone with Jaden and Dani. He'd rather waste his gas by driving back and forth than drop us off first, but I don't mind. I'm in no rush to get home.

Holden releases a yawn then, most likely exhausted after the game. He buries his head further into the passenger seat and runs his hand over his face, rubbing at his eyes. "I can't wait to sleep until noon tomorrow," he mumbles. He's lost interest in controlling the music, so we've all been listening to terrible chart remixes for the last ten minutes. The heating is on too, filling the car with warmth.

"Lucky for you," I say. I'm pushed up against the door by my shoulder, and it's not exactly the most comfortable of positions. My hand is in my hair, slowly massaging the back of my head. It has been a long week, and tonight has left me with a lot of questions, like: *What does Jaden think of me now?* "I have work at ten."

Out of the corner of my eye, I notice Jaden leaning forward only slightly, peering at me over Dani. Her eyes are closed, but she's awake. "Do you still work over at The Summit?" he asks.

I lift my head, shifting my tired gaze to look at him. He seems genuinely curious whether or not I still work five shifts a week. *Does he still feel the same about me as he did a year ago?* Probably not, and I can't expect him to after the way I let him down, but it still hurts to realize it. "Yeah."

"Long shift tomorrow?"

"Until six, so yeah."

Jaden pulls a face and leans back again, out of view behind Dani, so I sit back too, weaving my fingers back into my hair. I look out at the quiet streets of Windsor. It's not that late for a Friday night, but for the most part, the roads are still pretty empty. We pass the ball parks at Chimney Park, which I've never once used in my entire seventeen years of living here, and then Will pulls around onto Ponderosa Drive. It's a nicer part of town. It's not a wealthy area like Water Valley, but still the houses are of a nice size and better maintained than the houses on my side of town. Jaden quickly sits up again, sliding forward to the edge of his seat and hooking his arm around the headrest of the chair in front. He leans forward between Will and Holden, pointing out the windshield with his free hand.

"Just up there," he tells Will. "The one with the boat."

Will steps on the gas a little and we speed up toward the house on the corner of the intersection. He pulls up against the sidewalk and brings the Jeep to a stop outside Jaden and Dani's grandparents' home. The porch lights have been left on, but the rest of the house appears to be in darkness. The lawn looks overgrown, but it's hard to tell for sure, and the perimeter is lined with small shrubs. The house is much bigger and much nicer than my own, though smaller and less lavish than the Hunters' previous home. I spot the black Toyota Corolla in the driveway, the one that Jaden sometimes drives. Just behind it, however, tucked into the corner of the driveway on a patch of gravel is a small boat, hidden beneath a bright blue protective cover.

I remember that boat.

It belonged to Jaden and Dani's dad, Bradley. He and Kate used to take it out on the lake all the time. I went with them once but it feels like such a long time ago now, that first day in August out on the water with the sun burning down on us, Brad and Kate in the front, Jaden and I in the back, enjoying the refreshing splash of water as we cruised around for what felt like hours.

Two weeks later, Brad and Kate were killed.

It was never confirmed what exactly caused the accident. My uncle, Matt, was one of the first cops on the scene that night. He once told me it was one of the worst accidents he'd ever been called out to. They know for sure that Brad and Kate were on their way home from a late night at the office. They both worked for the Fort Collins Press. Kate was a journalist, Brad was an editor. Apparently, that's how they met. They would often stay behind to finish up new features, so their late drive home was nothing unusual. But on that night, sometime before midnight, their car flew off the dark, empty road. They hit a tree at such a high speed that the front half of the car was crushed instantly. They didn't stand a chance.

There were no witnesses to the crash, so the cause of the accident was determined through the process of elimination. There was no ice on the roads at that time of year. No mechanical faults in the car. No alcohol in Brad's system. All the police know is that something caused Brad to swerve that night, most likely an animal. Those fields are full of suicidal deer.

"Kenzie," I hear Jaden say, his voice loud and forceful, and immediately I snap back to reality. I hadn't even noticed that I'd zoned out, my mind in a completely different place, and as I quickly blink to bring myself back up to speed, I realize that Dani and Jaden are already out of the car. Jaden's hovering by the door, holding it open as he looks back in at me, perplexed. "I said 'I'll see you later'?"

Did he? I didn't even hear him, and now I'm slightly thrown off as I murmur, "Yeah," and give him a quick nod. Was it a real question, as in he really plans to see me later? Or just a casual goodbye?

Behind him, Dani has her arms wrapped around her shoulders, hugging herself to keep warm in the chilly air. Her blue eyes meet mine, and for a fraction of a second, she smiles. I don't know if I'm still zoned out or not, but I'm pretty certain it was a thankful smile, and then Jaden pushes the door shut with a thud, and it puts me fully back on track.

Will waits out front for a few seconds as we watch Jaden and Dani make their way straight past their parents' boat and up to the lit porch. They linger for a moment as Jaden fumbles in his gym bag for the keys, but as soon as he finds them and slides them into the lock, Will takes off.

"Okay," Holden says blankly, finally sitting up, more alert than before. He twists around in the passenger seat so that he can peer around the headrest, looking unhappy. "Way to catch us off guard! Some sort of warning would have been nice, you know."

"Nobody ever invites them anywhere," I tell him, defending my actions. I know I didn't get a chance to let Holden know that the Hunters might have joined us, but it's not *that* big a deal. I am the one who has an issue with the Hunters, not him, so if I can be around them without it being too awkward, then so can he. I invited Dani along to Cane's with us because I thought she might like some company, and judging by the smile I *think* she just gave me, I'm pretty sure she appreciates the gesture, so I feel slightly better about myself now.

"Um, nobody invites them anywhere because Dani looks as though she is going to burst into tears any second," Holden continues quietly, "and Jaden freaks me out because he acts like *nothing* happened, so I don't know who's worse. Some time to prepare would have been great. I thought you didn't want anything to do with them?"

Will removes a hand from the steering wheel and gently slaps Holden on the arm. "Dude, you're acting like Kenzie threw you into the damn lake," he says, rolling his eyes. "Now get out of your pissy mood and lighten up. Kenzie was just being nice."

Holden grinds his teeth and turns away from me, slumping back into the passenger seat. He's not the best at keeping his thoughts to himself, especially when he's already in a bad mood after losing the game earlier. Shrugging off his words, I turn back to the window, closing my eyes. Tonight might have been a bit of a shock; Jaden might have shown up and Darren might have been a jerk, but I still feel like I've done something good.

Will drives me home first, all the way back to the other side of town in the direction we just came from. It's 11:30PM, but I know my parents will still be awake. They often stay up until all hours of the morning at the weekend, watching Friday-night TV until they eventually doze off on the couch together. That's why it's no surprise when Will pulls into my cul-de-sac that I can see the flashing of the TV from the living room window.

"We're going golfing tomorrow, by the way," Will tells me. His gaze meets mine in the rearview mirror and he flicks his sandy hair out of his eyes. "Are you hanging with us tomorrow night after your shift?"

"I'll let you know," I answer, then reach for the car door. "Thanks for the ride. Again."

Will just laughs as I shut the door behind me. I receive no goodbye from Holden, so I don't say anything to him either. In all the years I've been friends with the two of them, I've had a lot more disagreements with Holden than I have with Will. It's never anything serious and it's usually not a big deal. We end up acting as though nothing has happened the very next day, so although he's pissed at me right now, I know by the time we're sitting in Dairy Queen again on Sunday we'll be back to normal.

I listen to the sound of Will's engine fade away into silence as I run across the lawn. I rarely use the footpath, and as soon as I step through the front door that's left unlocked for me, there's a strong aroma of spices in the air that wafts over me. There's laughter too, bouncing around the house from wall to wall, emanating from the living room. I kick off my shoes and make my way down the hall, pausing as I pass the small hall table. Grace's frame has been moved forward, positioned exactly in the center, the frame freshly cleaned. I run the tips of my fingers along the edge of the table, careful not to touch the frame. I knocked it over by accident a few years ago and Mom shrieked so loud I thought she was in pain. I don't touch it anymore.

The laughter dwindles as and I peer around the door, taking a single step into the room. My dad is on one couch, dressed in his nicest jeans and a decent shirt, a can of beer in one hand. Mom is down on the floor, sitting by the low coffee table, wine glass in her hand, the drained bottle of Chardonnay almost buried beneath the takeout containers and plates with leftover Indian food that takes up most of the table. Mom's dressed up too with jewelry to match her blouse, her hair styled in a nice blow-dry for once, her cheeks pink with too much blush.

"Kenzie!" she says, grinning wide as she holds up her wine glass to greet me. "You're home early."

I look back down at her suspiciously, trying to gauge whether or not she's still sober. "It's almost midnight, Mom ..." I state. My expression is blank and I know I must appear sullen, but I just can't hide my annoyance. Accusingly, I shift my narrowed eyes to Dad instead.

For once, he doesn't look worn out and exhausted. He is slumped back against the couch, relaxed and carefree. A bead of sweat runs down his temple. Normally, whenever Mom pours herself a glass of wine, he will frown and then swiftly leave the room, claiming he needs to shower, or he has a call to make, or a new job has just come in. Sometimes I think he *likes* being called out on emergency jobs just so that he doesn't have to stick around here watching Mom drink away her sorrows. He doesn't approve of it—definitely not—but I have noticed over the past year or so, as Mom has begun to work her way through more bottles each week, that it is easier for him to just ignore the problem. He can understand why she does it, so I don't think he wants to confront her about it. However, I am not pleased with him having a drink *with* her.

"Midnight?" Mom echoes. "Wow, we've definitely lost track of time!"

"We sure have!" Dad agrees with a laugh.

There's some cheap made-for-TV movie on in the background, though I doubt they've actually been watching it. It seems the pair of them have been having too much fun ordering takeout and drinking. For anyone else, this is a pretty average Friday night: a few beers and a couple glasses of wine to unwind and relax after a busy week. But in this house, the empty bottle of wine on the coffee table is a cause for concern.

"Dad," I say, folding my arms across my chest. He can probably hear the frustration in my voice, because I'm not even trying to hide it. I narrow my eyes at him. "Can I talk to you for a sec? In the kitchen?"

The smile on his face immediately disappears and he stares at me. Mom doesn't seem to notice that I've even said anything, because she has grabbed the TV remote and is now flicking through different channels. Dad glances over to her, and then pushes himself up to his feet, taking his beer with him. I am angry at him right now, but I'm trying to stay calm as he follows me to the kitchen. The lights are off, and I don't bother to turn them on.

"What are you doing?" I hiss at him, my arms still folded across my chest. I stare up at him as I wait for an answer. Recently, it feels as though every time I come home I find Mom either drinking or drunk. I don't know why I am still surprised every time. I should be used to it by now, but with each day that passes, the more concerned I become.

"We're just having a drink, MacKenzie," Dad says, heaving a sigh. He doesn't like to talk about Mom. We don't talk about anything in this house, and I hate that I'm the only one who seems to realize what's going on. And I'm the damn kid!

"Yeah, *you're* just having a drink," I mutter. Doesn't he get it? Doesn't he see it? "But Mom's not. You *know* it's more than that. You're just encouraging her."

"MacKenzie ... " Dad leans back against the counter and rubs at his temple, his beer still in his hand. "Not tonight. Please."

Not now, not ever, I think. "I'm going to bed," I state blankly, shaking my head at him. I don't have the energy to stand here and argue with him over this right now. I'm tired, and I will probably lose this battle the same way I always do. Slowly, I back out of the kitchen, fixing Dad with one final glare. It must be hard for him too. He doesn't get much of a break from all of this. But joining in is hardly the answer. There's nothing I can say now to change anything, so I bottle up my true thoughts and instead tell him, "Goodnight."

"Goodnight, Kenzie," he calls after me.

A minute later, just as I'm climbing the stairs to my room, I hear him and Mom laugh amongst themselves once more, and I decide that I'm not going to be mad at Dad tonight, because although Mom's been drinking, at least she seems happy.

9

For the first half of my shift, Lynsey lets me work the laser tag. The Summit is always at its busiest on a Saturday. The mornings are full of families as the young kids waste a hell of a lot of free change in the arcade, before battling it out over a game of intense bowling with the bumpers up and then finally finishing off their day in the restaurant. Then, as the afternoon fades into the evening, the kids are replaced by young couples on dates and older teens around my age. Luckily, I get to leave before they arrive. My shift finishes in fifteen minutes, and I know for sure that I'll be clocking out on the dot. I don't mind staying back and working longer if necessary, but on a weekend shift? Absolutely no way in hell. I'm out of here.

The second half of my shift has me back at the bowling lanes, behind the counter, spraying a row of bowling shoes yet again. It has made the past four hours go by excruciatingly slowly.

At the opposite end of the counter, Adam is working the register and assigning lanes. The bowling alley is so busy right now that customers have a ten-minute wait for a lane, so there's a small crowd of people lingering around the counter, just waiting. Adam is fun to work with in the sense that he blatantly doesn't care. He dropped out of college and has been here for a few weeks, though I don't think he'll be around much longer. He refuses to wear his name tag because apparently his name is no one's business.

"God," he mutters as he slams the register shut. There's a break in the flow of people which he takes advantage of by abandoning his post behind the register and walking over to me instead, sporting a deep frown. I know he's annoyed, but Lynsey wouldn't be impressed if she saw his lack of enthusiastic customer service. "Those guys on lane twenty are taking forever!"

I stop spraying the shoes along the counter in front of me and glance up at the lanes. It looks hectic from over here, all twenty-four lanes occupied as the bowling balls crack against the floor and pins shatter every single second. It's so loud. Over on lane twenty a couple are helping their two young kids push their bowling balls. I chuckle at his exasperation. "Their kids are, like, five. What do you expect?"

"I don't know—faster bowling, maybe?" Adam shakes his head, his eyes narrowed while he scratches at his buzzcut. "All these people are gonna go crazy if these lanes don't start freeing up soon."

"That's a Saturday shift for you." I smile teasingly at him as I throw the empty can of odor remover down into the trash can by my feet, then swoop up three pairs of shoes and turn away from him. Thankfully, Adam returns to the register, so I head into the back room.

I love the back room. I think *everyone* loves the back room,

86

no matter where they work. It's a nice place to waste five minutes of my shift without anyone noticing. I wait for the door to fall shut before I pull out the small stool from beneath a desk and sit down, sliding my phone out from my pocket. I have a text from Mom asking me if I want dinner after my shift, and if so, what do I want? It's a nice question to have her ask, because if she's in the mood to cook, then she hasn't been drinking. In my group chat with Will and Holden, there's nothing interesting besides the two of them discussing with each other hours and hours ago what time they wanted to meet up at to go golfing. Will has an annual membership and I don't know why, because he only uses it a couple times a year. I'll catch up with them after I clock out and see what's up, but I don't feel like spending the evening listening to them argue over who is better at golf.

The door to the back room swings open and I quickly scramble to my feet, almost dropping my phone as I stash it back into my pocket. I grab the first thing that comes to hand, which is simply an empty cardboard box, and I hold it up, pretending to look as though I'm actually doing something productive with it. I breathe a sigh of relief when it's only Adam who sticks his head around the door and not our boss.

"You're not sly," he tells me with a hint of smugness to his voice at having caught me slacking off. But it's okay, because I catch him out way more often than he does me. "I don't care, though. I just came to tell you that I need you back out front. You gotta hook people up with some shoes." He shrugs and then leaves again, so I immediately toss the empty cardboard box back onto the floor and follow after him.

I push the door open and the very last person I expect to

87

see the moment I step behind the counter is Jaden. *What is he doing here?* "Jaden?" I say. "Are you ... here to bowl?"

He's on the opposite side of the counter, blue eyes bright and smoldering as always. "I thought I'd take my grandparents out to do something fun for a change," he tells me, his voice soft and deep. Slowly, he nods over his shoulder in the direction of the older couple sitting down on the padded benches behind him.

I've never met Jaden's grandparents before. They still seem pretty young, perhaps in their mid-sixties. His granddad still has full, white, silky hair atop his head and a friendly smile as he watches me. Jaden's grandma is much smaller and she's awfully skinny too, but her cheeks are warm with pink blush, her eyes shining behind her glasses, graying hair perfectly permed. I offer them a tight smile back, lifting my hand to give them a small wave.

"That's nice of you," I say, shifting my attention back to Jaden. Why are his eyes so damn blue? They are pulling me straight in. "Where's Dani?"

"She didn't want to come," he answers, shrugging beneath the black leather jacket he's wearing. Underneath, he's wearing a black T-shirt with black jeans and black sneakers. Jaden always wears black and he has done for as long as I can remember. It's always been too drastic against his paler complexion and blond hair, but somehow it suits him. Or maybe I am just used to it. "Bowling is lame, according to her. Why ... why don't you join us instead?"

I blink at Jaden as he subtly leans forward over the counter toward me, though he seems anxious. His offer has come out of nowhere and I'm taken aback by it. A week ago we weren't even talking, and now he is asking me to join him for a game of bowling? I'm just thankful that he is asking me in the first place, because it means he may be willing to give me a second chance. If he was furious at me, if he didn't want to waste his time with me, then he wouldn't have climbed into my car on Thursday night. He wouldn't have to come to Cane's with us last night. He wouldn't be asking me to hang out with him now, but although I wish I could, I can't.

"I'm working," I point out with an awkward laugh, tapping at my name tag.

Jaden pulls back the leather sleeve of his jacket to reveal the silver watch on his wrist. He only glances down at it for a split second before he tilts his face back up to look at me. "But only for another seven minutes," he says. "You do finish at six, right? That's what you said last night."

I stare back across the counter at him and the hopeful little smile that slowly creeps onto his lips. I hope he's not going to pretend that it's merely a coincidence that he arrived just as I'm about to clock out, because it's pretty clear that he's planned this. "Yeah, I finish at six."

"Great!" he says, stepping back. He moves back down the counter toward Adam, who's drumming his fingertips impatiently against the register, his eyes on the clock on the wall by his side. He still has six more hours to go, so he looks over at Jaden with the same old disgruntled expression, and I can just tell he's holding back a groan when Jaden asks, "Can we add Kenzie to our game?" He pulls out his wallet and sets down a ten-dollar bill on the counter, exchanging a sideways glance with me. He's still smiling, though his expression seems more pleading than playful now. "Just one game, Kenzie. That's all. It'll be fun."

"One game," I agree, and when I smile, I am not forcing it.

89

Although being around him is still scary, it's not as bad as I had imagined it to be. In fact, it isn't bad at all. The only thing that makes it uncomfortable is my own damn guilt.

Just as Jaden's adding my name to the list of players, Amanda comes strolling over to the counter, ducking underneath the latch. She's here to take over from me now that my shift has come to an end, and she assures me I can leave five minutes early. I thank her, and then tell Jaden I'll be back after I've clocked out for the day, feeling excitement fluttering in my stomach.

"Don't take off," he jokes, wiggling the pen at me, and although he lets out a laugh, I sense a hint of solemnness to his words. My chest pangs with guilt once more as I turn away from him, questioning whether Jaden believes I *would* actually make a run for it. I'm not surprised he might think that. All I've done since last August is run from him.

I smile at his grandparents again as I pass them. They're sitting so patiently with those same warm smiles on their faces that for a second it breaks my heart. I'm not sure if they're Brad's parents or Kate's parents, but either way they've lost a child, and yet—just like Jaden—they seem so happy, so normal. In my house, it has been anything *but* normal, and we have had four entire years to recover.

The staff room is empty besides some new guy at the table against the wall, staring at the ceiling in silence and eating a sandwich. Normally I would introduce myself to a new employee, but my head's all over the place at the thought of bowling with Jaden and his grandparents that I simply ignore the poor kid. Instead, I grab my hoodie from my locker to disguise the awful red polo, and then, with two minutes to go until my shift officially ends, I waste the time by putting on some fresh makeup—trying to achieve the fine line between not wanting to look like I've made too much of an effort, but also like I haven't just worked an eight-hour shift. Finally, at 6PM on the dot, I clock out and brace myself to go back out there with Jaden.

I spot Jaden sitting down next to his grandparents, still waiting for a lane to open up. Now that Saturday evening is underway, The Summit is getting seriously busy.

"I'm back," I say, approaching Jaden from behind.

He twists around to look at me, and immediately the most perfect grin lights up his face. "Phew," he teases, getting to his feet. He extends his arm behind me, placing his hand on the small of my back, and he nods down at his grandparents who are already staring back up at me with their friendly faces. "This is Kenzie," Jaden tells them, his warm hand still pressed against me. "The friend from school who's joining us."

"The friend from school," his grandfather echoes, his throaty voice laced with sarcasm as he quickly winks at Jaden.

All Jaden and I can do is share a laugh at the misconception. I'm lucky to have even been called his friend from school, because honestly, we're not *really* friends anymore. And we're definitely not anything more than that either.

"I'm Nancy," his grandmother says.

"And you can call me Terry," his grandfather adds, pushing himself up from the bench. "Now, Kenzie, how long until we get a lane? I'll be as stiff as a board if we don't start bowling soon!"

I scour the bowling alley, running my eyes over the lanes to try and gauge if anyone is finishing up, but my search is quickly interrupted when Adam calls, "MacKenzie!" from behind the counter. "You guys are lane twelve," he informs us. "It's all set up."

"Great!" Terry says, clapping his hands together, the bright blue of his veins emboldened beneath his skin. "Let's go bowl." He reaches for Nancy's arm and pulls her up to her feet, hooking his arm around hers and directing her over to the counter to collect their bowling shoes. This couple is adorable.

Jaden rolls his eyes after them and then stuffs his hands into the pockets of his jacket as we follow behind them a little more slowly, side by side. "Thanks for not shutting me down," he murmurs as his arm brushes against mine for a fraction of a second. I move over slightly out of habit, increasing the distance between us, even though I like feeling his skin against mine. He's already looking at me, the expression in his eyes thankful, yet teasing all the same. "That's three times in three days. Progress, right?"

I'm surprised at how casually he talks about the fact that I've been avoiding him, looking down at the ground. But he's right, we're making progress. Or rather, *I'm* making progress.

The past three nights have shown me that Jaden Hunter hasn't changed at all from the Jaden Hunter I knew last year. And that's both a relief and a terrifying realization at the exact same time, because the Jaden Hunter I knew last year was the Jaden Hunter I was falling for.

10

Lane twelve is set up and ready for us when we reach it. We're sharing a booth with a group of young couples on lane eleven, though I'm pretty sure they're all tipsy given the amount of loud laughter and off-balance bowling that's going on. Back on our side of the booth, Terry is already over by the ball return machine, picking up different balls and testing them for weight, alternating between the two that he finally narrows it down to. There's a competitive grin on his face as he practices swinging with his bowling arm, and Nancy rolls her eyes and gestures for Jaden and I to come closer, so we sit down either side of her on the couch.

"Can we agree to let him win?" she whispers gently. "It'll make his week!"

Jaden and I exchange a glance, then snicker before we nod in agreement. His grandparents seem young at heart, and I don't mind messing up a few turns to let Terry win. It's just a game of bowling, after all, and Jaden's up first. Shrugging off his jacket, he grabs the first ball that comes to hand and positions himself in front of our lane, looking rather ridiculous in his white and red bowling shoes. He's definitely not pulling them off, but I decide not to point this out because I'm pretty sure he's already aware of it. I'm not one to laugh, though. I look pretty ridiculous myself, still wearing my awful work pants and a hoodie. I can't take it off, because the second I reveal my uniform beneath, customers will begin asking me to put up bumpers and fix stuck pins. And my eight hours of work here are *done*.

Jaden swings his arm back and hurls the ball down the lane, though it heads straight for the gutter. Terry points at him, cackling with laughter. "Give me a second to get into it," Jaden defends, flashing me a smirk. Dramatically, he rolls his neck from side to side until it cracks, and then he grits his teeth and grabs the ball again. He takes up position directly in front of the lane once more, hypes himself up for a few seconds, and then swiftly shoots the ball toward the pins. It careens left and only hits one.

I'm not sure if Jaden is trying to miss on purpose or if he just genuinely sucks at bowling. I can't remember if he's good at it or not. We did go bowling together once, just the two of us, back in the spring of last year. It feels so long ago now that we were last here together, constantly laughing as we battled it out to be the winner, enjoying the competition against one another. I can't remember which one of us won, because I was more focused on Jaden than I was on the scoreboard.

As Terry passes him with a smug grin, ready to take his own shot, Jaden pats him on the back. He doesn't seem to mind that he's messed up his turn, and he walks back over to the couch and sits down by my side. Nancy looks over at us, smiles, and then gets up to join Terry, leaving the two of us alone at the booth.

"Are you really that bad at bowling?" I ask Jaden.

"No!" he says indignantly, and then he tries to hold back a smirk as he adds, "I usually hit three pins on average." I pull a face and push his shoulder away from mine, laughing lightly. Jaden's always been one for cracking jokes, and it is such a relief to see that his sense of humor hasn't changed despite all that he has been through.

"You came here just before six on purpose, didn't you?" I ask him, nervous even though the answer feels obvious.

"Maybe," he says slowly as color rises to his cheeks. He drops his gaze to his hands in his lap just as Terry shatters all of his pins except one. "I thought I'd try my luck. You're actually talking to me for once this week, so I figured I'd take advantage of it before you cut me off again."

"Jaden ... " I swallow, no longer smiling. Even though his tone is friendly, his words feel as though they have a hard edge to them, and it's even worse because I know that everything he's saying is the truth.

"Don't worry about it," he says, holding up his palm to stop me from attempting to explain. He shoots me a tight smile. "I'm just glad you're playing with us, otherwise I'd have been playing alone with those two." He nods ahead to his grand-parents, who are celebrating Terry's spare with high fives to one another. Nancy's up next, and Terry helps her find a ball of the right size and weight. I suddenly feel a pang of envy at their closeness, their ease around each other. I wonder if my parents will ever get back to that place.

My eyes flicker back over to Jaden. He's staring straight ahead, watching Nancy take her first shot with a glossy expression on his face, his eyes shining with amusement as Terry stands behind her, helping her with her swing. I take the opportunity to study Jaden as he sits by my side. His hair is styled with gel again, and although shaved short on the sides, the top is tousled to create a sort of messy look. I can see his face clearly. What I always found attractive about Jaden was not only his long, dark eyelashes against the sky blue of his eyes, but the small, tan birthmark on his neck, right below the left side of his jawline. He once told me he hated it, but I think it's pretty cute.

Jaden turns back to me and I can't help but watch his full lips move as he says, "Kenz, you're up."

I tear my gaze away from his lips and glance up at the screen above our heads. Nancy only hit four pins, and now my name is highlighted on the screen as all of the pins are reset, so I quickly jump to my feet and head over to the ball-return machine in a daze, fumbling to grab a ball. I don't hang around searching for the ten-pound ball I like, and instead grab a six-pound ball that's far too light for me and so small that my fingers almost get stuck inside it as I numbly throw it straight into the gutter. Did Jaden just call me Kenz? Did he?

I love when people call me Kenz, but only a few do. My parents do, sometimes. Darren does, though I wish he'd stop. And Jaden used to, so it shouldn't come as a surprise that he still does, but for some reason, it sounds foreign hearing his voice say it after so long. Foreign, but strangely intimate.

Not even remotely focused, I toss my second ball down the lane and knock out a couple pins, and then I twirl around in the ugly bowling shoes that I just spent the past four hours staring at and make my way back to the booth, still asking myself if I heard Jaden right or not.

Jaden takes his shot as quickly as he possibly can, and then joins me back at the booth as Terry and Nancy get up to take their own turns, the pair of them giddy and enjoying this way more than Jaden and I are.

"So," he says, hunching forward. He cracks his fingers—a bad habit of his—and then looks up at me again from beneath those dark eyelashes of his. "Did I ruin your plans for tonight?"

"I didn't have any," I admit, shrugging. "And I like bowling, actually, so this isn't too bad. Better than falling asleep in the back of Will's Jeep, that's for sure."

"Really?" He sounds unsure. "Because if this sucks and all you want to do is leave and go home, then you can. You don't have to feel forced to stick around."

"I'm not leaving, Jaden," I reassure him with a laugh. He looks relieved to hear this, and it calms me to see him relax. I tilt my head down and throw my hair forward, gathering it up into a high, loose ponytail that I secure with the hair tie on my wrist. Then, I get to my feet and step forward to the ball-return machine as Terry is finishing up his turn. This time I'm feeling competitive and I need the correct ball to do my turn justice. "Now where's the ten-pounder?"

"That's more like it," Jaden says, standing up to join me.

We search through the balls already sitting in the machine, but they're all either too light or too heavy, and I even study the group next to us to see which balls they're using, but there isn't a ten-pound ball to be found. Most people don't care and just grab whichever ball they find first, but after working here for over a year, I've become fussy about my selection. Jaden turns to check the rack behind us, which contains several rows of backups, and just as I spin around to help him look, he says, "Here it is."

The neon blue ten-pound bowling ball that I love so much is on the bottom row of the rack and I spring forward, bending down to reach for it at the exact same time as Jaden does. He grasps it in both hands a fraction of a second before I do, and so my hands end up on top of his. His hands are large, his skin warm, and my breath catches in my throat. I am paralyzed for a fleeting second, unable to take my hands away, my cheeks flushing with color. I still remember the way he held my hand in his on long, late summer-night drives to the middle of nowhere, massaging his thumb in soft circles against my skin. Finally, I remove my hands from his, though I don't think I want to. I miss those times.

Jaden's eyes mirror mine and we both straighten back up, standing a little awkwardly in front of each other with only the bowling ball between us. Slowly and carefully, he places the ball into my hands. "There you go, Kenz," he says quietly, his eyes never leaving mine.

I can't even say thank you. *He did say Kenz.* I lower my eyes and tighten my grip on the ball, holding it close against my body and carrying it back over to the couch just as Nancy finishes her turn. There may be four of us, but at the moment, it only seems Terry and Nancy are actually playing. Jaden and I aren't even paying attention, but I'm up next, so I quickly shift my focus back to the game, congratulating Nancy on her great shot as I pass her. I don't even know if she hit any pins or not.

I take my turn, trying my hardest to give it my best shot because that's what we're here for, after all. I'm here to bowl and not to accidentally hold hands with Jaden. I line up, make a good run up to the lane, and then send the ten-pound ball whirling down the glossy floor. I hit eight pins, and then I knock out the final two for a spare. Now it's on.

After this, Jaden and I don't talk about anything else *other* than the game, which I'm grateful for because it's actually pretty fun hanging around him and his grandparents, all of us encouraging one another whenever we're taking our turns. It feels so normal bowling with them, and the entire time I don't even think about the fact that all three of them have suffered a tragic loss—because *they're* not thinking about it. We're sharing a laugh at Terry's competitive nature, and we're helping Nancy pick out a ball of the correct weight, and Jaden is making a fool of himself to entertain us by taking each of his turns using the most embarrassing technique ever, which involves an awkward run-up and throwing the ball into the air rather than along the ground. I'm just glad he's doing it on purpose, and the entire time, I'm laughing and rolling my eyes at him. I forgot how carefree he was, so secure within himself that he really doesn't care all that much about what others think of him. He's confident enough to embarrass himself in public, surrounded by all these people, just to make us laugh. I forgot how much I liked that about him.

By the end of the game, it's only really between Terry and me. Nancy and Jaden fell behind a long time ago, and I'm up last to make the final shot of the game, which will determine who wins. I only need to hit five pins to beat Terry, but I know I'm not going to let that happen, because I want him to win. He's standing behind me, hovering in anticipation as I line up. I'm not much of an actor, but I'm able to feign deep concentration as I prepare for my turn. I purposely send the ball flying to the right so that it's enough to hit a couple pins, but not five. And then, with Terry growing even more worked up, I promptly throw my second ball straight into the gutter.

"Yes!" Terry yells, throwing his fist into the air in celebration. Nancy shuffles over to squeeze his shoulder and she flashes me a gracious smile. The same goes for Jaden.

Picking up his jacket from the couch, he slips it back on as he walks over to me with his full-blown crooked smile. "Thanks for messing up your turn like that," he says quietly.

"No problem," I say. Above us, Terry's name is flashing on the screen, and then a moment later, the screen resets itself with a new list of names for the next group of players.

"Kenzie," Terry says, calling me over with a beaming grin. Teasingly, he says, "Great player, but not great enough to beat me. How about you join us for dinner?"

"What a great idea!" Nancy exclaims, and her face lights up. "We have barbecue ribs. Plenty of them! Enough for seconds each. What do you say?"

Jaden steps forward to join me in the circle that's formed, watching me carefully as he waits for my answer. "Yeah, Kenzie. Would you like to join us? I'm not being biased, but Grandma's barbecue ribs are something you just don't turn down."

The three of them are looking at me with hopeful smiles and my cheeks heat up with the pressure. "Thank you, but I can't," I murmur, and Jaden's face is the quickest to fall. "I mean, I can't come for dinner, because my mom's already made dinner for us. But I can come over later if that's still okay?"

Within a heartbeat, Jaden's smile is back, though now it's a wide, dazzling grin. He throws his grandparents a quick glance, searching for agreement. "That's okay, right?"

"Of course!" Nancy says, and the next group of players arrive before we have the chance to say anything more.

So far, my Saturday evening has—surprisingly—turned out alright, and now I've agreed to hang out over at Jaden's grandparents' house later, not because I felt inclined to take up the offer, but because I actually want to. All this time, I've been avoiding Jaden in fear of him acting differently, too overcome with grief to function as he used to, but he hasn't changed at all, not even one bit.

"Don't forget, we're on Ponderosa Drive," Jaden reminds me as we're walking out into the cool September air of the parking lot. It's only just gone 7PM, but the sun is slowly dipping behind the Rockies, creating streaks of orange and pink that light up the sky. Jaden's grandparents walk a few feet in front of us, hand in hand. I spot their black Toyota Corolla just ahead. "Do you remember which house?"

"The one with the boat."

Jaden smiles, giving me a small nod. "The one with the boat," he says.

His gaze drifts off into the distance and I wonder if he remembers that night in August out on the lake. I had my hopes up back then. I was hanging out with his parents, joining in on their family outings, and I felt like finally, *finally* Jaden and I were becoming serious. It was only a matter of time before we made it official, transitioning from sort-of-dating to Actually Together. Unfortunately, that never ended up happening. Two weeks later our priorities had changed. Jaden needed time and I needed distance.

He comes to a momentary pause and turns to face me directly. Mom's car is to my left and I reach into the front pocket of my hoodie to grab the keys as Jaden confirms, "So, see you later?"

"I'll be over in an hour," I tell him, and the words sound

odd as they roll off my tongue. I haven't told Jaden that in a while. "I'll text you when I'm on my way."

He shakes his head and laughs to himself.

"Errrm. What?"

"I'm just surprised you still have my number." He looks nothing less than elated as he turns to leave. "See you soon, Kenz."

11

Mom's sober when I get back to the house, which is a relief, though she's not impressed that I'm home an hour later than expected. Both her and Dad have already eaten the mac 'n' cheese she's actually made for once, but there's a plate left for me to heat up in the microwave, which I eat as Mom washes dishes in the sink, her back to me.

"I'm going out again," I tell her after I've filled her in on how my shift went, claiming that Lynsey asked me to stay back an hour. I don't want to tell her I went bowling with Jaden and his grandparents. She'll ask too many questions.

There's the squeaking of a wine glass as Mom cleans it thoroughly. "With Holden and Will?"

"No," I say. There's a small amount of pasta on my plate that I've given up on finishing, so I move it around anxiously with my fork, staring at the plate rather than at Mom. "I'm going over to see Jaden."

There's a pause. Mom sets the wine glass down on the drying rack and turns around, the soapy water dripping from her hands and onto the floor. "Hunter?" I nod and she reaches for a towel to dry her hands on as she studies me for a moment with confusion written across her face. "I didn't know you were talking to him again."

"Me either," I say with a forced, awkward laugh. My chair screeches against the floor as I stand up, picking up my plate and bringing it over to Mom. I stop just in front of her, shrugging. "I don't really know what's going on right now, but I figure there's no harm in finding out."

"Hmm," she says, taking the plate from me and turning back around again to scrape the leftovers into the trash can under the sink. Her hair is clipped back, but loose strands frame her face. There's no sign of makeup tonight. "He was a nice boy," she muses. "I always liked him better than Darren anyway."

"Who's a nice boy?" Dad cuts in, approaching from behind as he enters the kitchen. He opens up the refrigerator and scours its contents for a moment, before finally grabbing a can of Coke and cracking open the tab. He crosses his arms across his chest, staring at me with a teasing expression.

Dad's always been pretty laid back when it comes to guys. When I was thirteen, I had my first kiss with Ethan Bennett—who now sits behind me in AP Statistics, chewing gum way too loudly—in the parking lot after school when both our parents were late to pick us up. When Mom did finally collect me, I told her exactly what had just happened, confiding in her about such a crucial and, at the time, life-changing event. Six months pregnant and highly hormonal, Mom got so happy that tears broke free and she rushed home to tell Dad. I felt humiliated and terrified back then at the fragile age of thirteen, half expecting Dad to yell at me before he hunted Ethan down, so I ran upstairs in tears and hid under my comforter. A minute later, Dad knocked on the door and sat down on the edge of my bed.

"It's okay, Kenzie," he told me, pulling the comforter back to reveal my swollen, red eyes and damp cheeks. I still remember the smile of reassurance he gave me, back at a time when we were all so happy. "You're allowed to grow up. Soon, you aren't going to be the baby anymore!"

But three months later, I was still their baby. I was still their one and only. I didn't want to grow up after that. I wanted to stay young and innocent just for them.

"Kenzie's seeing Jaden again," Mom announces, and my eyes fire up from the floor, pulling my thoughts back to the conversation at hand.

"We're just friends," I quickly add when Dad appears surprised. "If even that. I don't really know."

Dad takes a sip of his Coke and then straightens up, scratching the back of his bare head. "I imagine they have a lot going on right now."

Like we don't? I think. I certainly don't say it out loud, though. Instead I just shrug. "I guess, but they were my friends."

Dad studies me for a moment longer, then presses his lips together. "Well, okay," he says, and then turns and leaves the kitchen, heading back to the living room, where the TV is blaring.

Mom has returned to finishing up the dishes, her hands back in the sink, glasses clinking together. "You can take my car," she tells me before I even have to ask. "But don't be too late. I've invited the family over for lunch tomorrow, so no sleeping until noon. I need you to help me with the roast."

"Okay." I spin around to leave so that I can head upstairs to change out of my work uniform, but before I even take one step forward, I spot a bottle of red wine on the counter by the coffee machine, pressed back against the wall as though that'll put it out of view. Mom hasn't had a single drink today, I can tell, but that doesn't mean she won't resort to it later.

I throw a quick glance over my shoulder. Her back is still to me, the dishes still splashing in the water. I stretch forward, swiping the unopened bottle from the counter and slipping it under my hoodie, holding it against my stomach.

I dart out of the kitchen and past the living room door without either Mom or Dad noticing, and I run up the stairs to my room so quickly that I'm surprised I don't break an ankle en route. The moment I get into my room, I stash the bottle under my pillows and then actively try my best to forget about it completely.

It's almost 8PM by now, but there's no way I'm going over to Jaden's place still looking the way I am. It was embarrassing enough having to bowl in my uniform after sweating off half my makeup during my shift, so I slip out of my red polo and pants and toss them into the corner behind my door that has become home to an ever-mounting laundry pile. I let my hair down and pull on my favorite black, ripped denim jeans, then quickly fix my makeup. I hate stepping foot out the front door with a bare face, not because I'm trying to impress anyone, but because I feel much more confident when the freckles across my nose and cheeks are hidden and when my eyelashes are much more defined. Concealer and mascara have been my best friends since freshman year. I throw in a pair of earrings and spray on perfume, and just as I'm slipping into a pair of black sneakers, my phone vibrates in my hand. Will's name lights up my screen, so I answer on the first ring.

"Hey, Will."

"Hey," he says. "We're going for a drive. Should I pick you up?"

I reach for Mom's car keys on my dresser and hook them around my index finger, flicking off my bedroom light. As I descend the staircase, I quickly mumble, "I'm actually just heading over to see Jaden."

"You're kidding?" I feel as though I have done nothing but surprise Will the whole weekend. "Really?"

"Really," I confirm. The thought of spending more time with Jaden sends warm shivers throughout my entire body, and not in a bad way.

"Good for you, Kenzie," Will says after a minute, and he sounds genuine and sincere, almost like he's proud of me. He knows how hard this is. "I hope it goes well."

"Me too," I say, and then we exchange quick goodbyes before hanging up the call.

Downstairs, I peer around the living room door to tell Mom and Dad that I'm leaving, and they wish me a nice evening. I inconspicuously scan the room at the same time, and I feel at ease walking out the front door knowing there isn't a single wine glass to be seen within a one-room radius of Mom.

I slide back into the Prius and I head off, feeling surprisingly relaxed. It's growing dark outside and the streetlights are slowly flickering to life, brightening up the streets of Windsor. I drive a little over the limit, and I'm across town and rolling along Ponderosa Drive within a matter of minutes. Small towns have their benefits.

I drive to the intersection, hunching over the steering wheel as I pull into the driveway behind the Corolla, studying the house through my windshield. The porch lights are on again, inviting me inside, and most of the lights inside the house are on too, creating a warm glow in the darkening night. I cut the engine and throw a final glance at myself in the rearview mirror. When I left for work at 9:30AM this morning, the last thing I expected was spend my Saturday night with Jaden.

As I'm walking up the driveway to the porch, I pass the boat again. It's still got its protective cover on and I wonder to myself if it's been sitting there for an entire year, untouched and abandoned. I try not to think too much about the day I got to ride in it, and instead, I hurry up to the porch. As I adjust my hair, I exhale a long breath of air, and then ring the doorbell. I hear it shrill around the house and I take a step back, waiting.

12

The door swings open and, of course, it's Jaden who's there on the other side of the threshold to greet me. He smiles as though he's relieved I've actually turned up. Still wearing his black jeans and T-shirt, the only thing that's different about him is his hair. It's flattened at the top now and it falls over his forehead. "Nice jeans," he comments, giving them a single nod.

Self-consciously, I run my fingers over the skin of my thigh that's exposed through the ripped, frayed edges of the denim. My anxious gaze falls to Jaden's own jeans, torn at the knees. "That's a coincidence."

"Or you did it on purpose because you're copying my style," he teases. Then, he cracks a smile and takes a step back from the door, ushering me inside. "Come on in."

I keep my head down as I brush past him. I kick off my shoes and tuck them to one side, feeling slightly out of my comfort zone.

The house radiates warmth, just as all grandparents' houses

should, with the hall lights dimmed low and a row of candles flickering from a shelf along the wall. The rich scent of cinnamon that fills the air is so delicious that I inhale deeply, taking a moment to appreciate it. I can hear the TV too, echoing from the back of the house.

"Granddad has been asking if you let him win earlier," Jaden says. "Can you do me a favor and reassure him that, actually, you suck at bowling and just got lucky, and that he's definitely the champ?"

I feign a dramatic gasp. "Are you asking me to *lie*, Jaden?"

"Only for a good cause," he says, grinning over his shoulder at me as he walks down the hall toward the sound of the TV, and I quickly follow. He pushes open the door to the kitchen and as we step into the room he says, "Kenzie's here."

The kitchen smells of barbecue and grease and Nancy is by the sink with water up to her elbows as she washes up the dishes. Terry sits at the table with his hands wrapped around a steaming mug of coffee and his eyes on the small flat-screen TV that's mounted on the wall. When we enter, they both crane their necks to look at us.

"Hello, Kenzie!" Beaming at me, Nancy swipes the towel off the counter and dries off her hands as she walks across the small kitchen toward us. She proceeds to take off her glasses, wipes them with the hem of her apron, and then sets them back on the bridge of her thin nose.

"Hi, Nancy," I say, mirroring her welcoming, friendly smile. I saw enough of Nancy and Terry during our game of bowling to decide that I like them both.

"Kenzie," Terry says. He leans forward, props his elbows up onto the table, then purses his lips. "Did you let me win

110

earlier? I don't trust these two." He flippantly waves his hand at Nancy and Jaden.

"Did I let you win?" I echo, widening my eyes at the accusation although he's exactly right. I can tell it's important to Terry and the competitive streak he possesses, so I quickly shake my head. "I tried my best on that last turn. It's a shame my luck ran out, otherwise I may have just beat you. I usually don't play that well," I lie, then exchange a sideways glance with Jaden. I can't bear the sight of his sparkling eyes for more than a fraction of a second, so I avert my gaze back to Terry and add, "That's why they keep me behind the counter!"

Terry smiles with vague smugness and then leans back again in the kitchen chair, reaching for his coffee and focusing his attention back on the TV. He's watching some cooking show.

"We're gonna head upstairs," Jaden says while carefully edging his way around Nancy. He heads to the refrigerator, pulls open the door, and quickly grabs two cans of soda. "Just yell if you need me."

"Alrighty!" Nancy grins and reaches up to pat Jaden's shoulder, though her eyes are on me as she does. I nod back as a small goodbye, then follow Jaden out of the kitchen and back out into hall, where the blissful scent of cinnamon hits me all over again.

"Thanks. Again," Jaden says with a laugh as he glances over his shoulder at me while we're ascending the staircase. "Maybe Granddad will actually stop talking about that game of bowling now. I swear, I take them out one time—*one time*— and suddenly he's like a five-year-old tripping on a sugar rush."

At the top of the stairs, there's a bathroom in the center directly in front of us, and then two doors either side. Jaden steps toward the door on the right, which I'm assuming is his room, but then he lingers for a second and I realize that, actually, it's not his. He frowns and then, with a can of Pepsi still in his hand, he taps his knuckles against the door. "Dani?"

"What?" Danielle immediately snaps back. I can sense her irritation from all the way over here on the other side of the door.

Although no permission to enter has been given, Jaden cracks the door open a few inches and peers around the frame. "Kenzie's here," he says quietly. Before he gets a reply, he swings the door open fully to reveal us both.

The first thing I think as I look around the room is that it's a hell of a mess. There're clothes scattered all over the floor, thrown carelessly around with no apparent attempt to organize them. The dresser is littered with used makeup wipes and empty cans of Sprite, and there's a bunch of textbooks stacked haphazardly on the chair. In her old room, Dani had posters of Zac Efron all over the walls. There are no posters in this room, only her schedule for her classes taped to the wall by the window, though it's torn around the edges.

On the double bed pushed against the wall, Dani is sitting cross-legged and hunched over a set of notes. She looks at us from beneath her eyelashes, barely bothering to lift her head. She's wearing a black tank top and gray sweatpants with her dark hair thrown into a high ponytail. Her intense gaze rests on me for what feels like forever until finally her eyes flicker back to Jaden.

"Why?" she asks with a hint of suspicion. I gather from her attitude that she had no idea I was coming over.

A sigh escapes Jaden's lips. "Because I invited her."

"We're just … hanging out," I quietly add. At least I think that's what we're doing. I'm not sure exactly. I've yet to figure

112

out where all of this is going and if I'm hoping to gain anything more than forgiveness. Maybe tonight I'll find out.

"Yeah," Dani says, "but *why?* Why now?" She places her pen between her teeth and cocks her head to one side, awaiting an answer. I feel like she's interrogating me. And honestly, I don't know what to say to her, because I really don't know why I have waited twelve months to do this. Made uncomfortable by her scrutiny, I stare at the Spanish textbook that's in front of her and keep quiet. Just last night, I was certain she smiled at me. I thought she was warming to me again, but apparently not.

"Goodnight, Dani," Jaden says firmly through gritted teeth, his voice raised. He fixes her with a look of both disappointment and anger, then nudges me out of the room, closing the door rather loudly behind him. "Sorry about her," he murmurs, frowning. For a moment, he appears exasperated, but then that warm, crooked smile of his returns. "By the way, here." Extending his arm, he passes me a can of Diet Pepsi. I take it from him, careful not to brush my fingers against his again after already grasping his hands earlier at The Summit. I'm pretty sure it took at least ten minutes for the color to fade from my cheeks, and although I enjoyed it, I'm not sure how Jaden felt about it. Maybe he only wants us to be friends again and nothing more than that.

"Thanks."

He pushes open the door to his room, allowing me to enter before closing it again behind us with a soft click. "It's a little smaller than before," he says. He lingers by the door as I look around the room.

I was hardly ever in Jaden's old room in his parents' house, but I do remember that it was pretty big, and the design was pretty much identical to the room I'm standing in now. Unlike Dani's room, Jaden's hasn't changed at all. Still the same flat-screen TV atop the dresser. Still the same Xbox next to it with a stack of games, including a copy of *Grand Theft Auto* that we once played together. Still the same mini football perched on a shelf against the gray walls. Still the same black furniture. Still the same framed Peyton Manning jersey hung on the wall. Still personal, still Jaden's. I don't know why, but it comforts me.

"It hasn't changed much though," I comment. There's the fresh scent of cologne in the air, and as I continue to study the room, Jaden shifts past me.

"Yeah, I tried to keep it the same," he admits. He grabs the TV remote from his bed and turns it on, flicking through channels until he finds something, then lowers the volume until it's almost muted entirely. I'm grateful for the background hum to avoid any silences that may arise. "It totally bugs me that the window is at the opposite side now," he adds when he turns back around. He tosses the remote back onto his bed and then points to the window on the left, shaking his head.

"Yeah, I bet." I glance back at the shelves on the walls. There's that mini football again, and a calculus textbook, a couple bottles of cologne, and a set of keys. But there's also a photograph, and I know what it is before I've even leaned in closer to have a look.

Of course, it's the Hunters. Back when the family was still whole, back when there were four rather than just two. The photo is from several years ago, from a time when Jaden had a full, messy head of blond hair before he took interest in styling it, from a time when Dani was still blond with her long hair flowing down her back. She looked like a different person back then, but not just because of the drastic change in appearance. She looked like a different person because she was smiling, and she rarely does that anymore. The twins are young, maybe around ten or eleven, and they're sitting on the grass in what appears to be their old back yard. Jaden's sprawled out, squinting through the sunlight at the camera, and Dani is cross-legged and grinning wide.

Behind them are Brad and Kate. They're there, right in front of me, lounging on a pair of deck chairs, smiling their perfect, sincere smiles. Brad was tall and handsome, with sharp features and neatly shaped stubble. The twins get their warm complexions and blond hair from him. On the other hand, Kate was young and beautiful, and her dark hair contrasted with her pale skin in the most elegant of ways. She looked a lot like Dani does now. I force myself to look away from them. There's something unsettling to me about seeing Brad and Kate while knowing that they're gone, perhaps because I'm not used to seeing photographs of someone I've lost. I'm only used to seeing their name and nothing more. There is nothing more.

There's a small sticky note stuck to the top of the frame, only it's old and the glue has dried out, so it's taped to the frame instead. The bottom edge has curled up, so I carefully reach forward and gently grasp it between my thumb and forefinger. I hold it down and squint at the faded cursive writing. It's only three words.

Be good! Dad

"They left us notes every morning," Jaden tells me quietly.

I quickly let go of the sticky note as though I've been caught manhandling something precious and fragile. I sort of forgot he was even here. I glance back at him, but he's looking straight past me at the photograph and the note.

"They would stick them to the refrigerator every morning before they left for work," he explains. "Dani used to keep them all and I thought she was so lame for doing that." His lips curve into a small, sad smile and his eyes flicker over to meet mine. "I ended up being grateful that she did," he admits. "I managed to steal that one from her, but she hoards the rest."

"I . . ." Words evade me. I just don't know what to say, so I swallow and drop my gaze to the carpet. After a brief moment of silence, I finally say, "I'm sorry."

"Oh, God, not again," Jaden says. Confused, I glance back up and stare bewildered at him as he rolls his gorgeous blue eyes and turns away from me, shaking his head. He collapses down onto his bed and props up his pillows, getting comfortable. "You don't have to say that. Seriously. I can talk about them. I *like* talking about them. I've accepted it, so stop tiptoeing around me," he explains, laying flat with his arms folded behind his neck, his head tilted toward me, eyes locked on mine. His words are fast and his tone is sharp, and I feel as though he is losing his patience with me. "*Please*, Kenzie. This is the last time I'm going to ask you."

How can Jaden be so positive? It's unbelievable, and learning what to say around him is quickly proving to be a tough process. "Okay," I say, nodding. I'll try again. I'll try harder to talk to him the way I used to. I'll talk to him about all of the things we used to talk about together. That's what he wants, I hope. *It's what I want too.*

Jaden's still watching me, his eyes boring into mine as though he's analyzing me. Slowly, I move closer and sit down on the edge of his bed next to him. My eyes find Jaden's again, and he's waiting patiently for me to say something. And I do have some questions that I want to know the answers to. I feel like I don't know him anymore, even though in the back of my mind I *know* that I do.

"Have you applied to colleges yet?"

As soon as the words leave my mouth, Jaden sits up. We're at opposite corners of the bed, with several feet separating us, yet I still feel so close to him. "Yeah," he answers after a moment. "I still have a couple more schools to apply to and then I'm done. Have you?"

I shake my head and shrug. "I really need to get started, but I'm so undecided. I settled with Colorado State because it's a safe bet, but now I'm not so sure." The last thing I want to do is go to the same college as Darren, but I don't mention this to Jaden. "I'll probably just end up applying to half the schools in the state. I visited the Boulder campus in the summer and it was pretty nice."

"I've applied for a couple out of state," Jaden tells me. A year ago, he didn't want to leave Colorado. He was happy to go to school here, but it seems his mind has changed. He said yesterday that he was planning to leave Windsor, but I didn't realize he is hoping to leave Colorado too.

"Where?"

"Notre Dame and Florida State," he says, running a hand through his hair to push it back off his forehead as he drops his gaze to his lap, his legs extending in front of him. "I probably won't get in, but it's worth a shot. I can't imagine spending the rest of my life in Colorado, you know?" He glances back up again. "Especially Windsor."

"I know what you mean. I can cope with living in Colorado, just as long as it's not *here*." I glance around the room again, drawn back to the mini football on the shelf just above Jaden's head. "Didn't you want to try for a football scholarship?"

"No. Honestly, I'm not even into football that much. I only signed up because I was trying to be cool back in freshman year," he says with a laugh, covering his face with his hand in embarrassment. "I wasn't even that good of a linebacker," he continues as his eyes flicker back to mine, "and the only reason I've actually been a decent player this season is because I discovered I tackle a lot better when I've got something to be angry about. I get to hit people and not be arrested for it, so yeah." A pleased smile appears on his face and then he glances away again, grabbing the TV remote. I know what he is referring to, but I don't want to ask about it.

"Holden tried for one," I say as he flits through the channels once more. "He needs one *so* badly, but he started messing up his chances last year. He's not been playing as well as he used to, grades started dropping, all that shit. He gets in the worst moods about it, so don't take the way he acted last night personally."

"Yeah, I noticed," Jaden says. He settles for an old *SNL* rerun with Jonah Hill and tosses the remote back down again as he turns to look at me. I can see the birthmark on his neck again, but I don't dare tell him out loud that I think it's cute. "At practice you can tell he's stressed out. Coach is losing patience with him. He's got a hell of an attitude, doesn't he?" I roll my eyes and nod in agreement, and a small smirk plays at his lips. "Funny thing is, we used to get along pretty well. He stopped talking to me last year. Have you got anything to do with that, MacKenzie?"

Color immediately rises to my cheeks and I find myself turning red with humiliation. "I may have ... " I mumble, but I'm too embarrassed to admit it. Out loud, it makes me sound like the worst person in the world, but Jaden deserves the truth. Not all of it, not yet, but I at least need to make a start. "Holden and Will have stayed clear of you because I asked them to," I admit. "I'm sorry." My face feels so hot, and I throw my head back and cover my face with both hands, unable to look at him. Even though he's only messing around with me, I still try my hardest to hide the shame in my eyes.

"That's not cool, you know," he says gently, his tone changing. Suddenly the mattress beneath me shifts and a moment later, Jaden's hands are gently grasping mine. Carefully, he moves my hands away from my face, his skin calloused but warm against mine. My breath catches in my throat as my eyes flicker open again. Jaden is on his knees in front of me, his blue eyes smoldering down at me. My gaze mirrors his as I look up at him, then glance down at our hands, and back up. "I just want to ask one thing ... " he murmurs. "Why? I ... I needed you, Kenz, and you weren't there." He shakes his head at me, letting go of my hands.

I feel my heart breaking and cutting through my chest when he says this out loud. I knew he needed me, which is why I have felt so guilty and so awful that I couldn't be there for him, but actually hearing him tell me this himself is gut-wrenching. All of the oxygen in the room seems to disappear. I knew eventually I would have to answer this question, but I'm still struggling to put it into words.

How do I tell Jaden that I was scared everything would be different? How do I tell him that grief terrifies me? How do I tell him that it was easier to step back than to step up? How do I tell Jaden that I know what it feels like, in my own way, and that I didn't even know how to make my own mom feel better, let alone him?

A lump rises in my throat and I swallow hard. I reach for Jaden's hands again, feeling desperate now, and intertwine our fingers tightly, then squeeze, searching for reassurance. Our eyes are still locked and Jaden doesn't break the intense contact, but he does rub his thumb over mine as he waits. Finally, I exhale and with great trepidation, I whisper, "I didn't know what to do or what to say to make it okay. I didn't know how to make you feel better. I didn't know if you would still be ... I didn't know if you would still be Jaden. *This* Jaden." I give him a small nod, but my voice feels weak. Admitting what I've done wrong is hard. "It was easier to just stay away. I'm so sorry. I shouldn't have avoided you for so long."

"Kenzie," Jaden murmurs. He lets go of one of my hands again and then moves his to my shoulder, delicately brushing his thumb against my neck as he tilts his head down toward me, looking back at me. "It's okay. I get it," he reassures me, though I'm not entirely convinced that he's forgiven me. "You're here now, right? That's what counts, so please don't disappear on me again. I can only deal with the girl I like cutting me off once." He laughs a little to lighten the mood, then he retreats, releasing his hold on my hand and my shoulder. With his back to me, he slides off the bed and walks over to his TV. "Hey, I know," he says, grabbing one of the games from next to his Xbox. Spinning back to look at me with a playful grin on his face, he holds up the game and winks. "How about a good old traditional game of *Grand Theft Auto* since you love stealing cars from innocent civilians?"

I laugh out loud and it feels so good to laugh alongside Jaden again. Quickly, I nod in agreement and shift forward into position on his bed as he sets up the game. It feels just like old times, sitting in Jaden's room, staring at the emboldened vein that runs down the side of his neck as he slots the *GTA* disc into the console. I've missed how carefree everything felt with Jaden, how playful and spontaneous and easy everything was, and the only thing running through my mind as I watch him right now are the words that escaped his lips only a minute ago.

I can only deal with the girl I like cutting me off once.

Present tense, and enough for my lips to curve into a smile.

It's after midnight by the time Jaden and I quietly sneak back downstairs and he shows me out. I didn't intend to stay so late, but it's not exactly like we were watching the time. One game rolled into another, and then another, and then another. It wasn't until Jaden's phone vibrated with a text from Dani asking us to shut up because she was trying to sleep that we realized just how late it was, and that I should probably get going.

The house is in darkness and the candles in the hall have been blown out, but the scent of cinnamon remains. There's complete silence too, and it seems Terry and Nancy have turned in for the night, so I follow quietly behind Jaden down into the hall. When we get to the foot of the staircase, Jaden reaches back to gently grasp my wrist, and then his hand slides down into mine. He leads me over to the front door and the glow from the streetlights outside shines through the glass, illuminating his face as I turn to look at him one last time before I go. He lets go of my hand again and I have to force myself not to care too much about it.

"Thanks for today," I murmur in a hushed voice as I step

into my shoes. "The bowling and everything ... I had fun."

"You're welcome," he replies, and I'm reminded of just how raspy and attractive Jaden sounds when he whispers, especially when he's smiling his signature crooked smile at me the way he is now. I can appreciate it again now that I've realized it's as sincere and real as it's always been, and not just some fake grin he's putting on to fool everyone into believing he was okay. He *is* okay.

We stand opposite one another for a moment. Everything is so still and quiet that I'm afraid to move, afraid to shatter this silent connection between the two of us. I can just about make out all of his features as I wonder what I'm doing here, standing in front of Jaden Hunter in the dark. I thought I came here because I felt guilty. I thought I came here because I owed it to him. I thought I came here because I was wrong about him being different. I thought I came here because I enjoyed being around him earlier.

But I don't think that's why I came. I think I came because somewhere at the back of my mind, I'm wondering: *What if?* I'm only realizing that now as I find myself unable to wipe the smile off my face simply because Jaden is staring back me with those damn blue eyes. I can almost *feel* the weight of the question pressing down on me.

What if we could still be something more?

I'm feeling reluctant to leave, a wave of confidence hits me and I just can't hold myself back. Reaching up, I place my hand flat against the warm skin of Jaden's neck, slowly brushing my thumb over his birthmark. "Cute," I whisper.

Embarrassed, he quickly places his hand on top of mine and moves it away, blushing. He tilts his chin down in an effort to hide the birthmark, then he looks back across at me as silence forms around us. My pulse begins to race as the gaze we're sharing intensifies and I swallow, parting my lips slightly. I wonder whether or not Jaden is going to make a move.

But he doesn't. He lets go of my hand and steps back, then quietly murmurs, "Goodnight, Kenz," as he unlocks the front door and pulls it open. The cold night air immediately drifts over us and the sudden chill brings me back to reality.

"Goodnight, Jaden."

We exchange one final smile and then I head outside onto the porch with Mom's car keys jingling in my hand. The wind has also picked up and it blows my hair across my face, so I keep my head down and half jog to the car, but I stop as I'm passing Brad's boat. I look at it for a second, but it looks even sadder abandoned out here when it's dark, and then I turn back around to face the porch. Jaden's still at the front door, leaning against the frame, watching me as I leave.

"Do you ever take the boat out these days?" I call out to him across the lawn, holding my hand over my eyes to shield my face from the wind.

Jaden's quiet for a second as he glances over to the boat in the corner. Expression blank, he stares at it for several seconds before his eyes move back to me. "Not anymore," he says with a small shrug.

I nod once and then turn back to Mom's Prius, running down the driveway, throwing the car door open, and sliding into the driver's seat. I start up the engine, desperate to turn on the heating. I'm not wearing a jacket, so I'm pretty cold. I just want to get home, so I give Jaden one final wave. I don't want to leave, but I know I have to.

And as I drive home, I can't decide whether I'm disappointed or relieved that he didn't make a move, because I'm not sure whether or not I would have allowed him to.

I think, just maybe, I would have.

13

I wake suddenly to the sound of Mom banging her fist against my door, calling my name and threatening that this is my last chance to get out of bed before she drags me out on her own. I'm confused at first as I try to peel open my eyelids, but I've slept with my makeup on and my mascara has clumped together, sealing my eyes shut. I force them open and sit up, squinting at the sunlight that's streaming in through a gap in my blinds. I feel more tired than usual, and when I rake my hand under my comforter in search for my phone to check the time, I'm shocked to see that it's almost noon.

Groaning, I tilt my head back and run my hands through my hair, but I immediately feel a painful strain in the back of my neck. I carefully massage the area, wondering what the hell I've done to myself, until I remember ... I twist my body around and grab my pillow, lifting it up to reveal the bottle of red wine that I hid there last night. *Ugh*. The bright side is that Mom hasn't discovered it, but the downside is that I slept on it.

Sliding out of bed, I stretch my legs, and then my neck in an attempt to relieve the strain. I can already smell Mom's cooking wafting upstairs and I know I should be downstairs helping before the family arrives so I quickly grab the bottle of wine and carry it over to my window. I lean out and dispose of it by pouring the liquid out onto the roof. It dribbles down the roof tiles, into the gutter, down the drainpipe and is gone forever. It's not something I do often, but I do it whenever I get the chance. Mom would be furious if she knew, not only for wasting her wine, but for throwing away money. But so far she hasn't ever caught me.

I pull my window shut again and hide the empty bottle at the back of my closet, then make a quick dash next door to the bathroom. I'm trying to be as quick as I can before Mom truly gets fed up, so I throw my hair up into a messy bun and jump into the shower.

I end up being in there for way longer than I plan on, because I spend the entire time thinking about last night, thinking about Jaden. We spent the evening together, just the two of us, for the first time in a year, and it was amazing. The awkwardness was gone. It was exactly like it used to be, and I am full of hope now that we can do it again. I miss him already. I feel giddy when I do finally get out of the shower, making my way downstairs, following the smell of ham into the kitchen, where Mom is frantically flitting between dishes. There is also a whiff of wine in the air, but I pretend not to notice it.

"Can I help with anything?" I offer, feeling a little sheepish that I'm only now arriving to help. Usually I give her a hand with the vegetables, but by the look of the mess in here, it seems she's already done it all on her own.

"It's fine. I've got it," she fires back over her shoulder

without missing a beat. As always, she's a little stressed out, and she exhales loudly and rubs at her temple while stealing a peek inside the Crock-Pot. "Just set the table, please."

I do as she asks, heading for the cupboard to search for the placemats that were last used a month ago when we had the family over. For as long as I can remember, it's been a tradition in my family that we all get together one Sunday each month. Mom always goes all out and cooks a big meal, so it's a nice change from our usual burgers or takeout.

With our backs to each other, I set the table for eight while Mom continues to prepare the meal behind me, and just as I'm arranging all the knives, she clears her throat and asks, "How was your night with Jaden?"

I don't answer her immediately, and I definitely don't turn around to look at her. Truthfully, last night was a lot better than I ever expected it to be. "It was good," I answer casually. I don't want to tell Mom *everything,* and luckily she doesn't ask anything more on the matter, so I finish up setting the table in silence.

Once I'm happy with my neat arrangement of the utensils, I shift over to Mom's side and open the top cupboard to fetch eight glasses, but as I'm setting them down along the countertop in front of me, I spot the wine glasses and champagne flutes up on the top shelf. Frowning, I glance sideways at Mom, but she's too busy staring into the oven to notice. "Can I ask you a favor?"

"Which is?" she says without looking over. She tilts her head to one side as she studies the tray of sweet potatoes she's trying so hard not to burn like last time, but her balance sways a little.

"Please don't drink today," I say, though I think it's too late.

The moment the words leave my mouth, Mom heaves a sigh and slams the oven door shut, straightening up and spinning around to face me. Her features tighten in disapproval. "I can have a glass of wine with my food, Kenzie," she tells me in a stern, matter-of-fact voice. "The same way your dad will have a beer with his."

"But it's never just one, is it?"

Mom stares at me with widened eyes as though I'm verbally attacking her, but the truth is, I'm just telling it like it is. It's a simple request for her own good. I'm getting real sick of her sneaking into the kitchen to pour herself another glass late at night, sending me to the store to buy another bottle, and for sincerely believing that there's nothing wrong with drinking as much as she does. It's even worse when the rest of the family is here, because I see the pitiful looks they give her across the table whenever she reaches for the bottle to top up her glass.

"I don't have time for this right now," she says, waving me away as she turns back to the oven, bending down to peer inside it again. "You know it's just a comfort thing."

Frustrated by how oblivious she is, I grab all eight glasses and carefully carry them over to the table, but not without muttering, "I think it's getting a little *too* comfortable," under my breath.

Of course, Mom hears me. "What was that?"

"Nothing." Giving up, I set the glasses in place and then leave the kitchen. I love Mom to death, but trying to get through to her is nearly impossible. Dad tried at first, but he gave up a long time ago, and I can't bring myself to blatantly ignore it the same way he does.

As I make my way down the hall, I smile at Grace's frame,

and then keep walking to the front door. I can hear the sound of the lawnmower growling and vibrating outside, so I pull open the door and step out onto the porch, barefoot. Dad's tracing a pattern around the lawn with our rusty old mower as he wipes a bead of sweat from his forehead. It's warm enough outside today, so I stand and watch Dad for a few minutes until he finally notices me, but only once he's done and once he's switched the machine off.

"So you're finally awake!" he calls across the lawn.

Shrugging innocently, I smile and then joke, "Last-minute maintenance before Grandma gets here?"

"Exactly," Dad says, laughing as he begins to drag the mower around to the back yard. Just before he disappears around the side of the house, he adds, "We don't want her to call us trashy for having an overgrown lawn again!"

I roll my eyes and am just about to head back inside when I hear the sound of a car turning into our cul-de-sac. Stepping out further onto the porch, I spot my uncle Matt's old Corvette approaching. It makes a hell of a sound, and even though it's at least three decades old, he loves the damn thing. He pulls up and parks behind Mom's Prius, then pushes open his door and steps out, waving over to me.

"Hey, Uncle Matt," I say as he crosses the freshly cut lawn, locking his car behind him. It's not often that we see him in a pair of jeans and a flannel shirt I always find it strange whenever I see Matt wearing anything other than his uniform. He's much less intimidating when there isn't a gun and handcuffs strapped around his waist.

"What's up? I thought I'd come by early and catch the end of the Panthers game," he says once he reaches me. He's Dad's youngest brother, and unlike Dad, he still has his hair. He runs a hand through it and smiles as he dramatically inhales. "Mmm. Smells good."

I follow him back inside the house, closing the front door behind us, and we make our way toward the kitchen. We walk in at the same time as Dad walks in through the back door, so I'm mostly ignored for a few minutes as the adults talk between themselves. I linger at the door until Dad excuses himself to go shower before everyone else arrives and Mom returns to organizing the food.

"C'mon then, Kenzie, let's get this game on," Matt says, walking over and throwing his arm around me. We head into the living room, and I sit down on the couch, pulling my legs up to get comfy, as he stands in front of the TV and gets up the second half of the Panthers game. They're winning against the 49ers, and Matt fist pumps the air. "Hell yeah!"

He walks backward, his eyes locked on the TV screen, and sits down on the couch next to me. I really like Matt, mostly because he's only nine years older than me and easy to joke around with. We get along well, and even though I couldn't care less about the Panthers game, I don't mind chilling out and watching it with him while he offers a running commentary. I listen to him for about five minutes before I tune out and my mind drifts to Jaden.

I had a great time last night with him, but now I find myself wondering just exactly how many good times we may have missed out on over the past year. If I had just been stronger, if I had just been braver, then I wouldn't have distanced myself for so long. I wouldn't have thrown away so many opportunities, but I did. All I know right now is that I *do* like being around him, and now that I'm aware of this, I *want* to be around him. Nothing may ever come of it. We might just be friends, but right now, I have nothing to lose. I'm curious about the possibilities.

I look over at Matt for a few minutes as I wait for a commercial break, and as soon as one begins, I swallow and say, "Can I ask you something?"

"Sure," Matt says, quickly glancing sideways at me with a flash of worry and then back to the TV. "What is it?"

"Do you remember the Hunters?" I ask quietly. "That accident last summer?"

Matt glances back at me, but this time his gaze remains locked on mine. He's quiet for a moment as he attempts to read my expression, confused by my question, before he finally answers, "Sure I do. Trust me, there ain't no forgetting that. The car didn't even look like a car anymore. Why?"

"Just wondering," I mumble, then glance down at my hands in my lap as I add, "I'm hanging around with their kids again."

"Really?" Matt sounds surprised. "How are they doing? God, what were their names again?"

"Jaden and Danielle," I tell him, looking back up. I don't know why I feel awkward discussing them, but all I can picture in my head right now is the car that didn't even look like a car anymore and it makes me feel a little nauseous. "Jaden's doing great, actually. But Danielle ... I mean, she's getting there."

"Man, poor kids." Matt shakes his head and exhales loudly, looking past me at nothing in particular as though he's reflecting back on that fateful night last August. "That accident totally had me fucked up for a couple days afterward," he admits. "Like, if they'd just left their office a minute later, or if they'd just taken a different route home, then they would have missed whatever the hell ran out in front of them. Sad, really, the way that the right timing can make things so wrong, ain't it?"

As the game resumes and Matt turns his attention back to the TV, I think about his words over and over again in my head. It's a terrifying thought that so many tiny things had to perfectly align in order for that accident to even happen in the first place, and if one of those things had been different, then the outcome may have been different too. But I quickly realize that it works both ways.

Bumping into Jaden at 7-Eleven while posing as my mom was most definitely the wrong timing, yet we both ended up at that register at the exact same moment, and talking to him that night seemed to kick-start something between us again. The right timing *can* make things go wrong, but the wrong timing can also make things go so right.

I focus back on the game, listening to Matt's commentary again as he groans and cheers, though it's a struggle to actually concentrate. In between his "aw c'mon!"s and "hell yeah!"s, all I can think about is Jaden. *Jaden Hunter.* Even just saying his name in my head is enough to give me goosebumps.

"Kenzie," Dad says, peering around the living room door after ten minutes. He has just gotten out of the shower and changed into a nice dress shirt, and the rest of the family should be turning up any second now, which explains why he looks anxious. "Can you help me out with the food?"

Matt is so engrossed in the game on TV that he doesn't even pay attention to me as I get up and walk over to join Dad in the hall. He looks as though he is about to break out into a sweat any second. "Where's Mom?" I ask. Dad *never* cooks. He sucks at it, so I'm concerned that he is asking me to help him out.

Dad gives me a tight, apologetic smile and squeezes my shoulder, guiding me to the kitchen. Mom isn't here anymore. "She's just ... just getting some fresh air," he says.

I knew it. I knew Mom was already tipsy, I knew she'd already been drinking today. She does this *all* the time, and it's getting embarrassing now. I shake my head at the ground in anger, and then I glance out of the window above the sink. Mom is sitting outside in the yard on her own, huddled over our old wooden table with both her hands pressed to her forehead. In front of her, there is a glass of water. It pains me to admit it, but she looks pathetic out there. I wish I could just shake her. I wish she could just look at herself and see what the rest of us see.

"Your mom might need to go and lie down for a few hours, so looks like it's you and me doing the dinner!" Dad says to me with false cheer, snapping some kitchen tongs in my direction. I turn away from the window and join him by the oven, and I grind my teeth together while I pretend that I haven't noticed the empty bottle of wine that's peeking out from the trash can.

14

By Thursday afternoon, I'm struggling to stay awake and focused in AP Lit. I've been working eight-hour shifts every night this week in exchange for getting both Friday and Saturday off for homecoming, and the late-night finishes are beginning to take their toll on me. Mr. Anderson has been discussing our answers to the questions on our summer reading assignment, and I've pretty much been snoozing during the majority of it. The only thing that's keeping me sane today is that I have an off period next, which means I have an extra hour to spare before my shift at 4PM.

My head is resting on my crossed arms on the table, my eyes are half shut, and I'm wondering how I've lasted in this position for so long without being yelled at. It's probably because I'm at the back, hidden behind other students, completely out of view. Just as I begin to yawn, the bell rings out and startles me. Voices rise and chairs scuff against the carpet as everyone races to the door. It's Spirit Week, the week leading up to homecoming weekend and the only week of the year where being at school isn't hell on earth. Each day is filled with activities to get us all hyped up for the game tomorrow night. And generally, everyone *is* pretty hyped up and excited, but I'm too exhausted to be one of them.

I don't have a class to rush to next, so I pack up my stuff slowly and keep my head down as I pass Mr. Anderson. He doesn't say anything as I leave, so I breathe a sigh of relief as soon as I'm in the hallway. It's loud and packed as everyone switches classes, the hallways nothing more than a sea of colors for today's Spirit Week theme, and I swiftly weave my way through the crowd as I make my way to my locker. En route, I spot Holden and Will approaching from the opposite direction. There's no room to stop and chat without being knocked to the ground during passing period, so I quickly throw my hand up and wave over to them instead. Only Will waves back as he sticks his tongue out at me. Holden has his hands in his pockets and his eyes on the ground, but he does glance up for a split second and gives me a small smile.

It feels like I haven't seen them in forever, because it's only here at school during lunch that I've been able to catch up with them this week. I miss hanging out with them, so I'm excited for the game tomorrow night and the dance on Saturday. I still haven't told them the full details about my night with Jaden on Saturday, other than that it went well. Until I know just what exactly is going on between Jaden and me, I'm going to continue keeping it on the down-low.

My steps are slow as I continue to head for my locker, and even though I try my best to stay as close to the wall as possible, everyone barges into me anyway. The rush dies down after thirty seconds or so as they begin to split up into their classes, and by the time I finally reach my locker, there's only me and a few remaining stragglers left. The hallways are almost silent again apart from a guy cussing to himself as he runs past me, late for class, but I ignore him and pull open my locker. Casually, I begin switching textbooks around and stuffing the ones I need to take home with me into my bag.

Suddenly, someone presses their hand against the metal locker next to mine, and I instantly jump. I don't even have to look to know that it's Jaden. I haven't seen him too much this week besides the occasional exchange of smiles as we pass each other in the hallways, which is always exciting every time it happens, given that a week ago I never did smile back. Other than that, I haven't had much of a chance to actually talk to him, so I'm thrilled to have him standing in front of me now.

"Hey you," he says, grinning widely, eyes smoldering. I can tell he's in a good mood by the expression on his face, and although he's wearing black jeans as usual, he's also sporting a bright orange hoodie in support of the senior color. "I figured I'd catch you here."

So he came looking for me? After last weekend, this is a good sign. I feel giddy, but I try to play it cool. "Yeah, I have an off period," I tell him as I step back and shut my locker, swinging the strap of my bag back over my shoulder. I don't own a single piece of clothing that's orange, so I'm not as committed to today's theme as he is. "Do you?"

"Nope," he says, popping his lips on the "p". He leans his shoulder against the lockers and then he shrugs. "I have calculus, actually. None of my teachers want to yell at me if I'm late. It used to piss me off, but then I just decided to start taking advantage of it, like taking a quick detour past your locker just in case you're here." Sheepishly, he glances down at the ground. "Luckily, you usually are."

Until now, I always believed it was just a coincidence that Jaden and I ended up passing each other every time I was at my locker after AP Lit. Apparently, it's not as random as I thought it was, and there's something endearing to me about the thought of Jaden walking past my locker to see me, even when I kept my head down and couldn't bring myself to smile back. His honesty has me smiling from ear to ear as my cheeks heat up. I'm blushing, I know it, but at this point, I don't care if Jaden notices or not.

"Yep, always here!" I joke, then nod to his attire, still smiling. "Nice hoodie. Ready for the game tomorrow?"

"Don't lie," Jaden says, shaking his head in disagreement as he glances down at the bright orange fabric. He rolls his eyes and tugs at the drawstrings. "It's the ugliest thing I've ever worn, but you gotta do what you gotta do, right?" He straightens up again and pretends to brush dirt off his shoulders, and I laugh, forgetting that although Jaden is incredibly attractive, he's also extremely playful and a little goofy at times. "I'm as ready as can be! Greeley West's offense better watch out. Are you coming?"

"To the homecoming game?" I repeat blankly. "No, I think I'll pass." As I shrug my shoulders, Jaden's smile begins to falter, but before it disappears entirely, I quickly drop the act and laugh loudly, rolling my eyes at him. "Of course I'm coming!"

"You had me there," he admits, chuckling. Mindlessly, he brushes his thumb over his birthmark as he checks the time on his phone. I watch him, slightly mesmerized. "I should get to class," he says, frowning. I'm enjoying our quick exchange, so I really wish he didn't have a class right now, but unfortunately, calculus is calling his name. "I'll see you tomorrow night."

"I'll be in the stands," I tell him with a small, awkward wave. *God,* I think. I've never gotten nervous around guys before. Hell, I didn't even get nervous around Jaden a year ago, but for some reason, I'm awkward and embarrassed around him now.

Jaden turns to head off to his class, then smirks over his shoulder and quips back, "I'll be looking for you." He gives me a small wink and pressure builds in my chest as I watch him walk away. I don't want him to leave.

We're the only two people in the hallway now, and with my hand on the strap of my bag, I enjoy watching Jaden wander down the corridor. Just as I'm noticing how perfectly broad his shoulders really are, he pauses and swivels back around to face me. That crooked smile that I can't get enough of appears, and, with a mischievous glint in his eyes, he calls, "Win or lose, will you wait up for me after the game?"

I part my lips to answer him, but no words seem to find their way to my mouth. Instead, I smile at him and nod. Of course I'll wait for him after the game. I have to wait for Holden anyway, but even if I didn't, I'd *still* wait.

Satisfied, Jaden nods back and then turns again. I watch him for a few more seconds until he rounds the corner and disappears out of sight completely, leaving me desperate for tomorrow night to arrive.

Sighing, I decide not to hang around any longer, so I turn in the opposite direction, ready for the dreaded walk home while my shoulder bears the weight of my bag. Walking past the front office toward the main doors, I notice a familiar face up ahead, turning into the library. It's Dani, who has pretty much blanked me the entire week during Spanish class, despite saying hey to her several times. She is always quiet and reserved, but that's not going to stop me from continuing to make an effort with her. I know she's skipping the homecoming dance on Saturday, but that doesn't mean she has to skip the game tomorrow night. I want her to go to the game. I want her to have fun. I want her to get involved. I want her to hang out with me again.

Speeding up, I make for the library door and enter after her. The library is silent with only a few juniors and seniors scattered around, some at the computers, some at the desks, one searching the shelves. I spot Dani settling down at a table in the center of the room, opening up a book and hunching herself over it.

Mrs. Bolan, our librarian, smiles to greet me as I pass her desk. I don't use the library at all, so I doubt she even knows who I am. Nonetheless, I smile back and keep on walking toward Dani. She doesn't seem to notice me approach, because she doesn't look up from her book. Either that, or she just pretends not to.

"Hey," I whisper as I slide into the chair next to her. I reach into my bag and grab the first book that comes to hand—my Physics textbook—and set it down on the table in front of me, opening it to a random page so that it looks like I came here for a purpose other than cornering her.

Dani glances sideways at me, exhales deeply, then looks back down at her book and continues reading. She doesn't say anything, but she doesn't have to, because hostility is radiating from her. She is impossible to figure out. She says she is sick of no one treating her the way they used to, but when we do, she seems to assume our efforts are fake or out of pity. They're not. I care about her.

Feeling awkward, I stare blankly down at my own book,

pretending to read a few pages for a couple of minutes in the silence that surrounds us. I spend the time mentally hyping myself up before I attempt to talk to Dani again. She makes it extremely difficult, and this uncomfortable tension is exactly what I was afraid of. I'm trying my best to break through it, but it's a hell of a challenge. "Are you going to the game tomorrow?"

"No," she says without looking up.

"You should come," I urge, even though she isn't paying me any attention. Trying to reason with her, I prop my elbow up onto the table and bend forward, trying to invade her line of sight. "It's homecoming, Dani. You can't miss it. I'm sure Jaden would love to see you there again."

Out of nowhere, Mrs. Bolan pops up by my side and scares the hell out of me when she hisses, "Shhh." Her eyebrows are furrowed with disapproval.

"Sorry," I whisper, holding up my hands in surrender and giving her a polite, apologetic smile until she turns and walks back over to her desk. As soon as she sits down, I quickly twist my body back to face Dani, who still has her eyes fixated on her book. "Please come with Will and me," I whisper, careful to keep my voice down this time. "I really, really want you to come. I don't want you to miss out."

Heaving a drastic sigh of defeat, Dani slaps her book shut and fires her gaze up to meet mine, folding her arms across her chest. Like me, she isn't wearing any orange today. "Kenzie, I get it. You're trying to make amends, and I appreciate that, but I like being alone, and I'm not going to the game." She says her words with such firm finality that I realize instantly that there's not much of a fight here. As she opens her book again and returns to reading as though I'm not even here, I grab my Physics textbook and ram it back into my bag.

"Actually," I say, rising to my feet, "I'm asking you to come to the game because I *want* you to, not because I'm trying to be a Good Samaritan, or because I feel like I have to, or because I'm trying to earn your forgiveness. It's as simple as that," I tell her truthfully. I'm not even whispering anymore and I don't care if I sound harsh, but I'm quickly learning that some tough love is sometimes necessary when you care about someone. "You have friends, Dani," I continue, looking down at her. She's still staring at the pages of her book, but I know she's listening. "I know I haven't exactly acted like one the past year, but I'm your friend. And friends do stuff together, like go to the damn homecoming game."

Feeling exasperated, I swing the strap of my bag onto my shoulder and am about to march off when I remember something. I drop my eyes back to Dani, studying her intensely while I recall the photograph of her parents in Jaden's room. "By the way, I didn't notice it before, but with your dark hair you look just like your mom," I say gently, and with that, I turn and walk away.

"Kenzie," Dani says after a few steps. I pause and turn back around, my lips pressed together into a thin line as she stares at me. "You really think so?"

"Yeah," I say with a small shrug. I hope I haven't upset her. "I saw a photo the other night in Jaden's room."

"It's gone a little darker than hers," Dani says quietly, glancing down at the ends of her hair as she runs her fingers through them. "I couldn't find her shade, and I cut it too short, so it sort of backfired, but thanks." Her eyes meet mine and remarkably, she gives me a sincere smile full of gratitude. I'm surprised by her words, because like everyone else, I assumed

141

Dani's drastic change in appearance was the result of emotional trauma. Only now do I realize that, actually, there was a reason behind it.

Still smiling, Dani tucks a loose strand of her dark hair behind her ear and pulls her book onto her lap, getting comfortable. Just before I turn to finally leave, she glances up one last time. "I'll meet you in the parking lot before the game."

15

The student parking lot is almost completely full by 6:30PM, so Will and I spend the greater part of ten minutes slowly rolling around the lot, navigating around the flow of people walking all over the place, until he finally finds a spot wide enough to squeeze his Jeep into. It's as far away from the field as we could possibly get, but it's homecoming, so it's no surprise. Our school campus is always at its busiest during homecoming weekend, with cars filing into the lot one after another, with students chanting and yelling as they march proudly to the bleachers, with the smell of grease emanating from the food carts. It's hectic and loud, but I love the buzz.

"So where exactly are we meeting Dani?" Will asks as he shuts his door behind him and locks the Jeep, walking around the front of the hood to meet me. He'd kill me if I said it out loud, but he looks super cute in his washed-out denim jeans and Converse, with his maroon Windsor Wizards T-shirt to match. Homecoming is the only time he wears it.

"Over at the entrance," I say. Yesterday, Dani agreed to

meet us here in the parking lot at around 6:30PM, and when I told Will that she would be joining us, he was pretty happy about it. I'm just glad she decided to come after all, because the atmosphere alone is totally worth coming out for.

Side by side, Will and I make our way across the lot, dodging cars and following the flow of students toward the football field. Everyone tends to make an effort for the homecoming game, so everyone is decked out in their Wizards merchandise. I'm wearing my usual hoodie, because the temperature is dropping fast tonight and I like to keep my hands warm in the front pouch while Will freezes to death. There are a lot of young freshmen milling around too, excited for their first homecoming experience, grinning widely and walking in small packs. It's one of the best weekends of the year.

We continue to navigate our way through the cars and the people for a minute or so until we reach the entrance to the field, where the parking lot narrows off to lead to the bleachers. Students are spilling through, eager to snatch themselves a good spot, but I grab Will's arm and pull him to one side so that we can find Dani. I don't immediately spot her, so I tilt myself up onto my tiptoes to get a better view as I scour the area. When I still don't see her, I begin to panic that perhaps she's bailed on us at the last second.

"Where is she?" Will asks, but as soon as he says it, someone taps me on the shoulder.

Dani is behind us, with a small, nervous smile playing at her lips. Although she looks uncomfortable, she doesn't look as sad and fearful as she usually does, so I consider this an improvement. "I'm here," she states. There's a sense of pride in her voice as she announces this, like it took her a whole lot of courage to come. Her short hair is curled slightly at

144

the ends rather than straightened for once, and she's wearing more makeup than usual. She looks amazing. Not only that, but she's also wearing a maroon Wizards sweatshirt, though it's too big for her, so it reaches her thighs and the sleeves cover her hands.

"Look at you!" I say. I'm so glad she's turned up and she's getting involved. I really didn't expect her to. "Supportive and all!"

"I know," she groans, glancing down at the baggy sweatshirt with a sheepish laugh. She tries to push the sleeves up her arms, but they immediately fall back down again, so she gives up. "I stole it from Jaden's room, because my T-shirt from sophomore year doesn't exactly fit anymore."

"The oversized sweater look is totally in season, so you look great," Will comments, and when I glance sideways at him, I can tell he isn't saying it just to be nice, he's saying it because he means it. When I look back across at Dani, she is blushing and, for once, she doesn't hold back her smile.

"C'mon then," I say, taking a step backward toward the field. "Let's go!"

The three of us head for the bleachers, with me leading the way as Will and Dani flank me. It's still light out although it's growing dull, but the field is alive with activity as the marching band and color guard perform. Drums and trumpets ring in my ears as I try to scan the bleachers for a free spot, but with so many people milling around and so many things going on at once, including the cheerleaders prancing around, it's virtually impossible.

"Kenzie!" someone yells, and the three of us glance up into the bleachers. I can't seem to figure out who called my name until Jess rises from a couple rows back, flailing her arms around to grab my attention. "Up here!" she yells down at us over the sound of all the other noise. "We have space!"

She's sitting with Kailee and their boyfriends, Tanner and Anthony, and even Tanner lifts his hand to motion for us to join them, so I head for the steps with Will and Dani still trailing behind me. I'm not sure how comfortable Dani will be sitting with Jess and Kailee, but I know that a year ago she wouldn't have minded, so I don't give it a second thought. If the Hunters want normal, then this is it.

"Hey, guys!" I say once we reach them after side-stepping our way along the fourth row and stomping on half a dozen people's feet. Both Jess and Kailee stand up, but although they're smiling to greet us, I can also see the questioning looks they keep trying to send me. I know exactly what they're wondering, but I decide that I really don't even need to explain why Dani is here, because I can't see why it matters. She's here for the same reasons the rest of us are, and I don't feel as though any further explanation is necessary.

Jess leans forward and pulls me into a tight hug, but she buries her face into my hair and murmurs, "You brought her to the game?" into my ear, impressed, as though I'm some sort of miracle worker. I nod back against her and then we quickly separate again as Tanner and Anthony scoot over a little on the bench to make room for the three of us. There's a series of mumbled "hey"s as we all try to arrange ourselves, until eventually we have the three guys on the left and us girls on the right. I have Will on one side of me, talking casually with Tanner and Anthony, and then I have Dani on the other, silent as ever, staring at the bottom of her sleeves as we all get settled in.

"Are you guys going to Cane's again tonight?" Kailee

asks, leaning forward to look at me as she tucks her blond hair behind her ears, revealing an entire collection of studded earrings. "It'll be packed."

I shake my head. Will, Holden and I have already decided to give Cane's a miss tonight. I think Holden's afraid I'll invite the Hunters along with us again, and I'm afraid Darren will be there to terrorize me. "Not tonight," I answer, then I jokingly add, "We'll decide what we're doing after the game once we determine what kind of mood Holden's in."

We share a laugh and Jess says, "Oh, please. They've got this game in the bag!" She edges forward to look at Dani, and with a warm smile, she asks, "Are you here to support your brother?"

Dani glances up from her hands and is silent for a moment as she stares back at Jess, as though she's trying to figure out if she's being patronizing or not, and when she realizes that Jess is only being friendly and making conversation, she smiles back. "Sort of," Dani says with a small shrug. "I didn't want to miss out on the homecoming game. I've missed too much already." She quickly glances at me and her glossy lips curve into a teasing smirk before her gaze shifts back to Jess. "That and the fact that Kenzie didn't exactly give me a choice."

"God, Kenzie," Jess says with mock disbelief, shaking her head in disapproval. "You bullied the girl into coming? And all this time, I thought you were *nice*."

I roll my eyes as we all laugh together again. Although a little uncomfortable at first, Dani is easing up and joining in. The simplicity of the situation seems to be enough for her, and I'm so glad Jess and Kailee are being themselves and treating her like any other girl.

There are at least a thousand people here, and although it's homecoming, there's nothing too spectacular about the game itself other than the fact that more people turn up than usual. Everything else is pretty much just the same as any other game, so it's not *too* exciting, apart from the half-time break, when the homecoming royalty are announced. Right now, however, it's pretty standard as the team gathers behind their huge banner, pumping themselves up for what feels like forever, before finally crashing through the paper, tearing it apart and running out onto the field to a chorus of cheering, whistling and applauding. We rise to our feet in sync with everyone else, and even Dani is on her feet clapping her hands.

Just like with every game, I begin searching for Holden. My eyes roam the field in search of the jersey bearing number nineteen, until finally I spot him huddled around the coach. His helmet is already on, so I can't see his face, but I have a feeling he's pretty stressed out right now. After another loss last week, it would be a complete tragedy if the team lost the homecoming game, so he'll be feeling the pressure.

I switch my attention to Jaden, and standing down on the sideline with his helmet tucked under his arm, chin tilted up, eyes scanning the bleachers, he's fairly easy to spot. I know he's looking for me. He told me so himself, and exactly like last week, he scours each row until his gaze finally meets mine. As soon as our eyes lock, his face lights up with the widest of grins. There are butterflies in my stomach as we wave at each other across the field. He mouths something, but it's impossible to read his lips, and then his eyes widen in surprise when he seems to notice Dani by my side. He points a finger at her, and she laughs and throws him a thumbs-up back. He seems so pleased to see us both here, and with his grin still plastered upon his face, he turns around and walks back over to join the rest of the team, throwing glances over his shoulder at us. I don't even care about the game anymore, I just want to see Jaden as soon as it's over.

"Did you tell him you were coming?" I ask Dani, turning to look at her. He seemed surprised to see her.

"Yeah," she says with a small laugh, and then adds, "but not that I was coming with you."

16

Windsor wins the homecoming game. After a lousy first half with no points up on the board, they turned it around in the second half with four touchdowns, including one made by Holden, to seize the win they so desperately needed. The bleachers went wild. Everyone was on their feet, cheering so loudly you could feel the stand rumbling as the Windsor players celebrated down on the field. The look of pure relief on Holden's face was priceless. He played great, and so did Jaden.

"God, it's so cold," Will murmurs through chattering teeth as he hugs his arms to his chest. It's dark and extremely windy, with the temperatures continuing to plummet as the night wears on, and he's shivering in his T-shirt as we wait around for Holden and Jaden.

It's nearing 10PM and the parking lot is emptying out. Most of the crowd has already left, but there are still a few groups of people lingering around, waiting for friends. Will, Dani and I have been waiting for what feels like forever, pacing in circles to pass the time. Will is freezing to death out here, so I step in front of him, pressing my body against his and wrapping my arms around his back in an attempt to radiate some warmth. He immediately shoves his hands into the front pouch of my hoodie.

"Tonight wasn't actually that bad," Dani muses. She's sitting on the ground, hugging her legs and wrapped up warm in Jaden's huge sweatshirt. She's staring at the ground, tracing patterns on the concrete with her middle finger. She pauses and glances up. "Thanks, Kenzie. I'm going to try and come to every game for the rest of the season."

"Really? That's awesome."

Right then, someone lets out a long, low whistle, and when I crane my neck, I see Holden confidently striding toward us. Unlike the past couple of weeks, he's smiling for once, even though his expression is more smug than anything else. I love when Holden's in a good mood, and after his touchdown tonight, I think he'll be happy and content for the rest of the week.

"Don't tell me that touchdown wasn't incredible, because it was," he boasts, fueling his ego as he runs a newly busted hand through his hair. "That Greeley West kid had no chance of catching up to me!"

Rolling my eyes, I step back from Will and turn around, rushing over and pulling Holden into a hug. "Well done!" I say, and he briefly hugs me back, although not as tightly. Cocky Holden is much, much better than grouchy Holden.

"You did alright," Will says with a shrug. Holden steps around me and fixes him with a menacing glower until Will cracks into laughter and tells him, "You played great, man."

"Thanks," Holden says, and in effort to get back at him, he condescendingly pats Will on the head. "I know I did." Sliding the strap of his gym bag further up his shoulder, he stuffs a hand into the pocket of his shorts and asks, "So what's the plan?" But before either of us can reply, he finally spots Dani, who's still sitting on the ground a few feet away and watching us carefully. He blurts out, "Dani? What are you doing here?"

"Kenzie invited me to the game with her," Dani answers. She pushes herself up from the ground and straightens up in front of us, and the wind blows her dark hair across her face.

Holden immediately twists his neck to look at me, his eyes wide as though he can't believe I have invited Dani out again. I can understand why he looks so confused, given that *I* was the one who asked him and Will to stay clear of the Hunters, and he looks down at the ground, stuffing his hands into his pockets.

Luckily, I don't have to explain myself *again* like last Friday night, because behind me, I hear Jaden's voice call out, "Hey!" and Dani quickly runs past me, most likely desperate to get away from Holden, who's mumbling, "Him too?"

I decide to ignore Holden completely, because his reaction is unwarranted. Somehow he has managed to dampen the mood within the space of four seconds, just from the look he has given me. I force my smile back onto my face as I turn around to look at Jaden instead. To no one's surprise, he's dressed in black jeans again and a maroon Windsor Wizards hoodie, the exact same one as mine. His attention is all on Dani as she quickly approaches him, congratulating him on the team's win, and it's so adorable how pleased he is to see her. That's two weeks in a row now that she's come along to the game.

"Isn't this mine?" he asks suspiciously, grabbing a fistful of the sweatshirt she's wearing. Dani just shrugs, and he jokingly shakes his head at her while letting go of the fabric. That's when he finally glances over Dani's shoulder, settling his bright eyes on me. "Not gonna lie," he says, motioning between Dani and me, "I really didn't expect to see you two together."

"Me either," Dani admits quietly, briefly looking over at me. "But I thought I'd give her a chance."

I playfully nudge her, then give her a little cuddle as I look back at Jaden. Really I want to hug *him*, but I know it would be too forward in the current situation, so I stuff my hands into the front pouch of my hoodie instead to stop myself from involuntarily touching him. "Well done on the win," I say, our eyes locked. "Those tackles? Pretty badass if you ask me."

"Not so badass when you fuck up your shoulder," he points out, placing his hand over his hoodie near his collarbone and massaging the area for emphasis, his warm, playful eyes never leaving mine.

Out of the corner of my eye, I can see Will and Holden watching me closely. Will's head is cocked to one side as he studies us, whereas Holden has his fist pressed to his mouth, blinking rapidly, his cheeks still red from the adrenaline of the game. He drops his hand, steps forward and mumbles, "Kenzie, we're leaving." Then, he frantically nudges Will in the ribs. "Will, c'mon, get your keys out," he says quietly.

"Where are we going?" I ask, folding my arms across my chest. Last I heard, we hadn't made any plans yet, but Holden seems to be in a rush to get out of here. He probably doesn't want the Hunters tagging along with us again, but I do.

"I don't know. McDonalds," Holden answers. Will hesitantly reaches into his pocket for the keys to his Jeep, glancing between Holden and me, unsure if we're leaving or not. "C'mon, I'll buy you your Big Mac."

153

I look to Will for help, but he just shrugs, holding his hands up, refusing to join the debate. Then I look back at Jaden and Dani, who seem uncomfortable. I hate being stuck in the middle like this, being forced to decide whether to leave with my friends or stay with Jaden. I did promise Jaden I would meet him after the game, and I really don't want to bail after a couple of minutes, not just because I keep my promises, but because I really want to spend time with him.

"Why don't we ... why don't we all go together?"

"Kenzie," Holden whines, poised to make a dash for the Jeep. "Can't the three of us just hang out?" he asks, his voice quiet as he reaches for the keys and steals them out of Will's hand.

"Holden," Jaden calls out, and Holden immediately glances up with a flash of bewilderment on his face at the sound of Jaden saying his name. But Jaden's not smiling anymore. He looks really pissed for once. "What the hell is your problem?"

"Let's just go," Dani mumbles, reaching for him and tugging at his arm. Despite the relaxed, happy mood she was in a few minutes ago, she's now suddenly back to her wary, reserved self. She keeps her head down a little, a deep frown etched into her face as she tries to get Jaden to leave with her. It's clear she doesn't want to be here anymore, and I can't blame her.

Holden tightens his fist around Will's keys so hard that his knuckles pale from the pressure, and he narrows his eyes at Jaden. "I just wanna hang out with Kenzie and Will, man," he mumbles, barely audible.

Jaden looks even more baffled as he stares back at Holden. I think he is losing his patience now. "Dude, just say that then. If you're so desperate to leave, then leave already. You're putting a downer on everyone's good mood anyway."

Holden is glaring at him now, looking pissed off at Jaden having dared to talk back to him. I doubt he was expecting it, and for a few seconds he looks as though he is contemplating replying, but he doesn't. He keeps quiet and instead turns to me. "Kenzie, are you coming with us?"

"No. Jaden can take me home," I state. I don't know why Holden is behaving like this. He can't keep acting like a petulant child whenever it suits him, and I'm not leaving with Will and Holden if Jaden isn't welcome to join. I'd rather Jaden just took me home himself. Holden releases a long, heavy sigh and then simply shakes his head at me.

"Let's go," he mutters, nudging Will forward, forcing him to leave with him. Will rolls his eyes at me as we exchange a small nod of agreement, and then he and Holden turn around and begin to walk away, headed back toward the Jeep.

"Just because you scored a touchdown for once doesn't mean you can act like a dick!" Jaden calls after them, raising his voice to ensure Holden hears. He rolls his eyes, and it is clear he is annoyed. I can't blame him: Holden wasn't exactly subtle about the fact that he doesn't want Jaden and Dani around.

Holden almost twists back around, but Will grabs him and forces him to keep moving forward until they disappear around the corner of the school building. I'm left alone with Jaden and Dani, and if this was a month ago, I'd be sprinting halfway across town by this point. But not anymore. It feels more like Holden is the one who's unpredictable to be around now.

"What's wrong with him?" Dani asks. She looks aggrieved

and upset as she waits for me to offer an explanation for Holden's erratic behavior.

Unfortunately, I don't have one, so all I can do is apologize on his behalf. "I'm sorry about him. I don't know what his issue is, but I'll talk to him about it." It really is starting to get cold, so I pull my hoodie tighter around me, yanking the hood up over my head. My eyes find Jaden's and he's already staring at me, though he still looks full of residual anger. "You really don't mind taking me home?"

"Kenzie," is all he says as he rolls his eyes, and then he reaches into the pocket of his jeans and pulls out the keys to the Corolla, nodding across the near-empty lot. "Let's go."

The three of us stroll across the cold lot toward the car, though Dani walks slightly ahead of us, and she even lets me ride shotgun. As she climbs into the back seat, she peers around the back of Jaden's headrest and says, "You can drop me off first." She leans back and pulls on her seatbelt, and when I glance over my shoulder at her, she gives me a small, knowing smile. It reminds me of the way Dani used to be before, back when she would teasingly kiss the air in front of me whenever Jaden's back was turned, back when she would wink and offer to give us some space, back when she would ask when we were going to hurry up and get together already.

"I was going to dump your ass back at the house first anyway," Jaden tells her with a hearty laugh as he starts up the engine. Dani promptly stretches forward and flicks the back of his ear, and I smile as I watch the two of them bickering.

Sometimes I really hate being an only child. I've grown up missing out on the fun of a playful sibling rivalry and the sharing of deep secrets and the feeling of knowing someone was always going to have my back. I thought that I was finally going to have all of that, but then I never did. I try not to think about it too much as Jaden pulls out of the school grounds, heating on full blast, radio on low, and heads toward his grandparents' house to drop Dani off so that we can be alone at last. Just the thought of it has my heart beating that tiny bit faster.

17

Dani waves to us from the porch, the small light above her illuminating her features, before she disappears into the house, closing the door behind her. I'm still sitting in the car with Jaden by my side, the two of us watching her in silence with only the sound of the heating whirring in the background. The boat at the back of the driveway looks old and dismal.

One hand on the steering wheel, Jaden reaches up and turns on the small light so that he can see me better. His eyes meet mine. "Do I really have to take you home right now?" he asks quietly, wetting his lips. "Because I don't want to."

I don't want him to take me home, either. Not now, not when we're alone finally. My house is only a few minutes away, and a few minutes aren't enough, so I give him a small smile as I shake my head. "Take me for a drive."

He nods and turns the light back off, putting the car into reverse and craning his neck to look out of the back windshield as he backs out of the driveway. I sit in the passenger seat with my hands inside the front pouch of my hoodie and my full attention on Jaden while he heads out of Ponderosa Drive again, retracing the way we came from. I like watching him drive, especially in the dark. His face is shadowed and I stare at his hands on the wheel, at his tight knuckles, at the emboldened veins that disappear under the sleeves of his hoodie, and I sigh, shaking off the urge to touch him.

"Are you ever going to take your dad's boat out again?" I ask carefully. I would never, ever have brought up Jaden's parents before, but on Sunday he told me that he likes talking about them, so I figure it's okay to mention them, despite the fact that I find that hard to understand. In my family, mentioning Grace is unbearable. Maybe it's because we have nothing to talk about. We only have a name, and even that is enough to send Mom cascading into tears and enough to silence Dad for the rest of the day. Maybe that's why we've never been able to move forward: We haven't confronted the past yet.

Jaden looks at me, surprised that I've mentioned his dad, and then he turns back to the road. "I don't think so," he admits. "We own it, and I wanted to sell it, but Dani wants to keep it. I don't know why. It's just been sitting there, rotting away for the past year. The insurance ran out and neither of us has a permit to drive the damn thing."

"I don't think you should sell it," I tell him. "I think you should keep it. Your parents loved that boat, and I'm pretty sure they'd want you to use it."

"I know." The streetlight briefly sets his face aglow, and I see that, for the first time, he looks sad. He props his elbow up against the door and rests his head on his palm, absentmindedly playing with his hair as he drives. "Do you remember when they took us out on it last summer?"

"Yeah." I stare out of the windshield at the dark, near-empty streets of Windsor. "That was pretty fun. It was my first ever time on a boat." Growing up in Colorado, it's slightly insane that I'd never gone boating until then.

"They really liked you," Jaden murmurs quietly, and my gaze finds its way back to him again. He's staring rather blankly at the road ahead as we turn onto Main Street, a small, sad smile on his face, lost in thought. We have to stop at the traffic lights right outside of the 7-Eleven where we bumped into each other a few weeks ago. Jaden chuckles and nods towards it. "I bet they'd be real pleased that we spoke that night. I think they'd be happy we're together right now—though Mom would probably tell me to keep both hands on the wheel." Rolling his eyes, he takes his arm down from the door and places his hand back onto the steering wheel. Waiting for a green light, he stares down at his hands and brushes his thumb against the wheel in soft strokes. I watch in comfortable silence, wondering if he's thinking about them. I know that he is.

The lights switch and Jaden takes the right exit off Main Street, heading northbound. "So why were you *really* buying that booze?" he asks. He says it playfully so I think he's trying to lighten the mood, clearly unaware that the subject matter is just as dark. "I once successfully bought beer, so I swear I'm not judging you. Although posing as your mom is an interesting method to use ... "

Clearly, my excuse at the time didn't convince him. I groan and press my hands to my face, partly wanting to avoid the discussion and partly out of my total embarrassment.

"Don't worry about it," he says, sensing my discomfort, and I flinch when he gently wraps his hand around my wrist and moves my hand away from my face so that he can look at me. He glances quickly between the road and me, trying to pay attention to both, and with his warm fingers still wrapped loosely around my wrist, he grins and teases, "Aren't you glad I was the one to witness it and not anyone else?"

I just nod quickly at him. I am very aware of his skin against mine and the fact that he isn't letting go. I adore the feeling of Jaden's touch after so long, and I love the sense of comfort and anticipation that comes with it. "I'm actually glad you were there," I murmur after a while, "because otherwise we might not be talking right now."

"And what a shame that would be," Jaden agrees. He lets go, his fingers disappearing from my wrist, and moves his hand back to the wheel as he takes a turn. Suddenly, I know where we're going.

At the end of the street is a small parking lot, and behind it, Windsor's prime attraction: Windsor Lake. It is the hallmark image of this town, something that we all love. It's absolutely huge, and it's surrounded by a trail that loops around the entire perimeter. People come here for walking or biking, and there is nothing better than the view of the Rockies in the distant background. In the winter you can even see the snow on the caps. It's always busy in the summer, with kids playing on the small beach and people swimming, kayaking, fishing. When I was little, my parents used to take me to the lake a lot. Dad would swim with me in the water while Mom anxiously watched from the sand in panic, even though it wasn't that deep. I used to hang out a lot with Holden and Will here too, though not so much anymore. We used to ride our bikes around the lake when we were twelve. And, of course, I still remember the long walk Jaden and I took last summer, back before everything changed, when the sun was setting over in the horizon as we walked hand in hand, talking about anything and everything. Every time I come back here it reminds me that Windsor isn't all that bad.

Right now, however, it's late and it's cold. Jaden pulls into a parking bay in the empty lot, facing out over the shoreline. At this time of night it's just a huge, dark pool of water and the only thing to see is the moonlight glinting off the still surface. We can imagine the view in front of us, because everyone who grew up in Windsor has it ingrained in their minds. It feels nice to be here, knowing there's so much right in front of us that we can't see. Peaceful, somehow. Windsor Lake always has been.

Jaden shuts the engine off, and we become part of the silence. I feel almost afraid to breathe. Jaden leans forward and rests his chin on his crossed arms, staring blankly out of the windshield at the darkness in front of us, watching the gentle ripples of water roll around, lit up by the moonlight.

"I come here a lot," he tells me quietly, his soft voice cutting through the silence. "Mostly at night, because I prefer it when it's empty. I sometimes just park up right here, or I'll go for a walk around the trail."

"To think?

"No," he says, then inhales deeply, holds it for a seconds, and releases it again. His eyes reflect the dark water. "Sometimes I think *too* much and my head feels like it might explode, so when that happens, I come here *not* to think. To just focus on something else, to clear my head."

For as long as I've known Jaden, my favorite thing about him has always been how honest and open he is with me. That, and his adorable little birthmark. I've always taken comfort in the fact that he trusted me enough to share things with me and it's reassuring to know that he still trusts me now, even after all that I've done. He can't say the same for me, though.

There are a lot of things I've kept from him, things that hold me back from telling him that sometimes I think too much too, that sometimes I wonder if Mom will ever laugh the way she used to, that sometimes I wish I had the answers as to why I never got to meet Grace.

"I know exactly what you mean," I whisper, my voice barely audible. Releasing my seatbelt, I cross my legs on the seat and pick at the material of my jeans, staring blankly down at my hands. I swallow hard and glance back up at him, my voice shaky as I ask, "What do you do when you miss them, Jaden? Your parents?"

Slowly, Jaden sits back from the steering wheel, pulling one knee up onto the edge of the seat as he looks at me. "I think about the time Dad accidentally hurled a football at my face in the back yard," he begins, rolling his eyes, "and I think about the time Mom once accidentally food-poisoned us all. And it makes me laugh, because I'm so lucky that those crazy fools were mine." He shakes his head as he reflects on this, smiling to himself. My heart is breaking in my chest as I listen to him, unable to understand how he can possibly be smiling right now. "But most of the time," he says, smile faltering, "I try to think of everything they taught me and everything I've learned since."

"And what's that?" I urge, my voice cracking. Hearing him talk about this is almost unbearable, but I *need* to hear it. I need to understand him, and I need him to help me understand myself.

Jaden must see the heartache in my eyes, because he leans across the center console and takes my hand in his, interlocking our fingers the same way he did on Sunday. He squeezes his hand tightly around mine and gives me a reassuring smile

163

and a nod to let me know that everything is okay before he answers my question. "They taught me to be a good person," he says, "and to believe in myself, and to work hard to get to where I want to be, and to look out for Dani, and that it's okay to mess up along the way because they were always there to forgive us."

With his free hand, he reaches for the pocket of my hoodie and gently pulls me closer. There are only a few inches separating us as we hover over the center console, his gorgeous blue eyes piercing mine, overflowing with an emotion that I can't quite decipher. Delicately, he moves his cheek to mine, his lips by my ear. "But most importantly," he murmurs, and my entire body shivers from the breathy huskiness of his voice, "all of this has taught me not to waste time, because there might not be time. It's taught me that if I want to do something, then I need to do it right now." His breath is warm against my cheek, and his lips brush my skin as he lightly trails his mouth along my jawline. "Exactly like this," he breathes, and then presses his lips to mine.

It's been a long time since I last kissed Jaden, so it feels like the first time all over again, soft and gentle, slow and long. My eyes are closed, my entire body shivering beneath his touch, until I gradually relax into it, losing myself in the movement of his mouth against mine. Our hands are still interlocked, and his other finds its way to the back of my neck, his fingers weaving into my hair. Slowly, he leans back, tearing his lips away for a split second. Our eyes flicker open at the exact same time, and he's so close that I can see the detail in his glossy eyes, his lips parted right before mine.

We look at one another for a long moment and I try to process why I've been lucky enough to have Jaden Hunter forgive me, to have him give me a second chance, to have him wait all this time for me to come back to him. I may not know why, but I do know that I'm so, so glad that he did.

Smiling, Jaden exhales against my mouth as he closes his eyes again, leaning back in, capturing my lips once more.

18

Sitting on the corner of my bed, I carefully bend forward to slip on my silver, sparkling heels. I move my feet around, rolling my ankles until they fit as comfortably as possible, and then I stand up, balancing myself. I love the shoes, I do, but every time I wear them, I'm left suffering from painful blisters. That's why there's a stash of Band-Aids in the matching silver clutch bag on my dresser. I reach over to grab it, opening it and sliding in my phone, some cash and some body spray. I've been getting ready for the past couple hours, and I enjoy the process, mostly because there's hardly ever an excuse in Windsor for dressing up nice. I love having the chance to change from a pair of jeans to a dress.

Right as I'm clicking my clutch shut, the doorbell rings, and Mom yells my name from somewhere downstairs. Will's early. It's not even 7:30PM yet, so he shouldn't be here for at least another fifteen minutes, but I don't panic too much since I'm pretty much ready to go as it is. We'll have plenty of time for photographs, where I'll have to do my annual awkward crouch down so that I'm not towering over him.

I gently fetch my glitzy, dangling earrings from my dresser and move over to my full-length mirror, leaning in close as I insert them. I remove my helix piercing while I'm at it, but only for tonight, only for homecoming. And then, taking a step back again, I pause and take a moment to run my eyes over my reflection.

My hair falls over my shoulders in loose, bouncy waves with the front swept to one side and pinned back. I don't do it very often, but I love wearing my hair curly, all bouncy and shiny. The knee-length chiffon, cobalt-blue dress I'm wearing fits almost perfectly, cinching my waist and making my legs look longer. It's light and airy, floating around me whenever I move. The bodice is decorated with sparkling, silver beading and diamanté gems—it's low, heart-shaped, and maybe too revealing, but I like it. My nails are painted to match and my fingers display a small collection of silver rings. My makeup is more natural for a change, so the freckles that dust my nose and cheeks are more noticeable than they usually are. They're the only thing I would change about myself if I could. I have high, hollowed cheekbones, carefully bronzed and defined to perfection for the occasion, and I like my bright eyes—a deep, warm shade of chocolate just like my mom's. I have her strong, sharp jawline too.

"Kenzie!" Mom yells again, though this time it's much louder as she calls up from the foot of the staircase.

I give myself one final glance, and then turn away from the mirror, grabbing the first bottle of perfume from my dresser that comes to hand and spraying myself with a couple spritzes of the luscious, sweet fragrance. I run my fingers through the ends of my hair as I leave my room, making extra sure I don't trip over my own feet as I step out onto the landing.

Mom is waiting at the bottom of the stairs for me with her dark hair clipped back and an eyebrow teasingly raised. To my surprise, there's a large box of gorgeous flowers in her arms, so big that she has to tilt her chin up in order to look over them. The budding flowers are a beautiful collection of different shades of pink that spill over the edge of the glittery box they're in and already I can smell the floral, fresh scent in the air. My heart beats a little faster than it should. I've never received flowers before.

"These were left on the porch," Mom tells me as I descend the stairs, "and I doubt they're for me." She smiles wide as I reach her, nodding down at the flowers and urging me to read the small card that's attached. She peers around the box and her gaze sweeps over me, then she straightens back up and says, "You look gorgeous." Her eyes are bright with pride but, for a fleeting moment, I see sadness. I know exactly why. This is the last ever time she'll be watching her daughter head off to the homecoming dance when, in a perfect world, she was supposed to do this four more times with Grace. Mom appreciates these moments a lot more than I think she would have if the circumstances had been different.

I give her a reassuring smile back and tell her, "Thanks, Mom." I glance down at the flowers again, inhaling their freshness. My cheeks flood with warmth as I pinch the small card between my thumb and forefinger, squinting at the tiny handwriting.

After last night, I'm entirely convinced these flowers are from Jaden and I'm grinning at the thought of the kiss we shared. My skin is still tingling from his touch and my stomach

168

flutters in anticipation for tonight to arrive just so that I can see him again.

However, my heart immediately sinks in my chest when I read the words that have been written:

I'm sorry about last weekend. I'll wait for you, Kenz. Enjoy the dance. —D

Darren. My smile quickly falters and I squeeze my eyes shut. The gesture is sweet, and I know the flowers must have been expensive, especially for a broke college student like Darren, but it frustrates me all the same. When I open my eyes again, Mom is frowning back at me, confused by my lack of excitement, so I give her a minute shake of my head and then finally take the box from her.

"Darren," I mumble, and that's all she needs to know. Rolling my eyes, I shift past her and carry the box of flowers down the hall and into the kitchen, heels clicking against the floor. I slide the flowers onto the counter and stand back, thoughtfully studying them with my arms folded across my chest, the detailing on my dress scratching against my skin.

I know Darren is trying his best, but there is a line and he keeps crossing it. I know he cares about me, and I know just how desperately he wants us to get back together. I keep trying to remind myself that he was a good guy when we were together, and I do appreciate the effort, but it is becoming overwhelming now. I just want to be friends with him and nothing more—I wish he understood that.

The doorbell rings again, echoing down the hall, and it has to be Will this time. I spin around on my heels and make my way back out of the kitchen just as Mom's swinging open the front door to reveal Will's enormous grin. He's standing on the porch, sandy hair perfectly flicked into position just out

169

of his eyes, dressed smartly in his light dress pants and shoes, white shirt neatly pressed and, of course, his blue bow tie.

"You look great, Will!" Mom tells him with a beaming smile, reaching for his arm and gently pulling him inside. She's already reaching for her cell phone, desperate to take pictures of us together just like the previous three years. "Very handsome."

"Thank you," Will says, bowing his head once and reaching up to adjust his bow tie rather dramatically. It's a couple shades lighter than my dress, but it's close enough. He smiles goofily at me. "Look at you," he comments. "Looking good *and* ready on time!"

"Pictures!" Mom orders, flapping her hands in the air to motion us into position. She's sober and content, something that rarely ever happens simultaneously, so I let her have her moment of pride.

"Oh God," Will jokes, feigning despair as he glances up at me. I'm several inches taller than him, but with heels on the height difference is even more noticeable. I like to tease him so I straighten up and prop my elbow on his shoulder, leaning casually against him as Mom snaps some pictures.

We head into the front yard to take our official, Instagram-worthy photos. The lawn is still freshly cut from last weekend, and Will and I take up our position on the grass just in front of his Jeep, with the sun setting just off in the distance to create a warm, golden glow. Will subtly tilts himself up onto his tiptoes and I even more subtly bend down a little so that we don't look so silly next to one another. Mom takes enough pictures to last a lifetime, sending some over to Dad, who's out on a job, and then waves us goodbye from the porch with teary eyes.

170

"So," Will says as we're pulling on our seatbelts, "last ever homecoming. Emotional yet?"

"Not really, but ask me again when prom comes around," I say. He really does look adorable in his bow tie. It's only a short drive to school and there's something on my mind that I'm desperate to talk about before we get to the dance, so as Will starts up the engine, I clear my throat and ask, "What was up with Holden last night?"

Will's smile fades and then he shrugs. "He told me after we left that the Hunters make him uncomfortable. Oh, and he thinks you're a hypocrite."

"A hypocrite?"

"Yeah," Will says, keeping his eyes on the road as he pulls out of my cul-de-sac. "Because you asked us to stay away from them, but now suddenly you're with them all the time."

Holden's right; I did ask them both to stay away from the Hunters because I couldn't face seeing them. But that was a long time ago, back before I realized that I was wrong, back before I discovered that being around them doesn't scare me as much as I thought it would. Frowning, I murmur, "Are you kidding me? He's annoyed about that? I'm allowed to change my mind, and he should be glad now that he doesn't have to avoid them on my behalf."

"I know," Will says. "I'm glad you're hanging out with them again." He pauses for a brief moment. "When are you going to tell us what's actually going on with you and the Hunters? And by the Hunters, I really mean Jaden." He glances over at me once more, a smirk forming.

My eyes fall to my lap and I gently brush my fingers over the chiffon of my dress. I know my friends aren't oblivious to

171

what's going on between Jaden and me, but I still feel nervous to have to admit it.

"I don't know *exactly* what's going on between us yet," I begin, playing anxiously with my hands, "but I think we're finally getting back to the place we were in a year ago." Even just saying it out loud sends relief through me. I never thought this would happen. I never believed I still had a chance with Jaden. I suddenly feel giddy and I bite down on my lower lip in an attempt to hide the smile that's spreading across my face.

"Damn, oh damn," Will says after a few seconds, elbowing me across the center console with a teasing grin. "It's Jenzie: Round Two!"

19

Windsor High's homecoming dance takes place in a giant marquee set up in the courtyard of the school, and the atmosphere is electric. Cars pull into the parking lot under the warm glow of the setting sun and groups of friends huddle together, posing for pictures. It's warm out, and the buzz of excitement that fills the campus is nothing short of special. The young freshmen look adorable as the girls teeter along in their shoes and the guys look around wide-eyed, but the rest of us play it cool. Will and I stroll along casually, chatting to some of our fellow classmates as we wait for Holden and his date. He's taking Olivia Vincent from the marching band, and although I don't know her all that well, I do know that she's a sweet girl. He's had his eye on her for a while and it took him an entire week to build up the courage to ask her to be his date tonight, but Holden's crushes are often short-lived. By the time prom rolls around, he'll have the hots for someone else.

As we wait, I keep an eye out for Jaden. I know he's coming tonight and there's a part of me that wishes we were going together. I still wish we'd had the chance to go together last year, and a not-so-small part of me is already thinking about prom. Just the thought of it has me smiling as I peer over Will's shoulder, eyes roaming the parking lot.

Holden is the one I end up spotting first. It's impossible *not* to, given his sheer height and brooding expression. He's wearing all black, except the white tie that hangs loosely around his neck. He walks with his hands in his pockets as though he's too cool to be here, but both Will and I know that, in fact, Holden does secretly enjoy the homecoming dance each year. By his side, Olivia Vincent is busy shoving her car keys into her bag as she totters across the parking lot, restricted by the excruciatingly tight-fitting white dress she's wearing. When she glances up and fixes her hair for the third time, she smiles and waves to let us know that they've spotted us too.

"Last ever homecoming!" Will announces yet again as they near us, stepping forward and bumping fists with Holden, who really doesn't look all that thrilled to be here and who has yet to make eye contact with me.

Olivia, on the other hand, seems over the moon. We exchange a warm, friendly smile and I tell her, "I love your dress."

"Thanks!" she says, gesturing back at me. "I love yours."

I glance over at Holden and he is fiddling awkwardly with the buttons on his jacket even though they are already all done up. I am still annoyed at him for the way he behaved last night, and I think he feels bad about it, because now he has his tail between his legs. "You look nice, Kenz," he mumbles, glancing up briefly. He gives me a small smile before returning to the issue of his jacket buttons, but I'll take it.

"Right back at you," I reply, and then leave it at that. I can

174

question him another time about last night's events—a time that *isn't* our final homecoming dance.

"C'mon," Will says, "let's head inside." Flicking his hair in a way that lets me know he's ready to make an entrance, he reaches for my wrist and interlocks our arms, escorting me across the school grounds toward the courtyard as Holden and Olivia follow on our heels.

It's just after 8PM and already I can hear the music pumping all around the campus. The atmosphere is a complete buzz as the last remaining stragglers, including us, get in line to enter. I still haven't clocked Jaden yet, so he must already be inside. I adjust and readjust my dress as I consider what exactly I will say to him when I see him. Last night, we finally kissed. I know I just have to act normal, but I'm really starting to hate the fact that I become shy around him, nervous and blushing beyond belief. It's so not me.

Tickets exchanged, Will leads me inside to the dance. The marquee is large enough to hold the entire student body, with huge circular tables lining the walls—most of which are claimed already—and the DJ set up over by the dance floor. The main lights are dimmed, with strobe-lighting rather frantically emitting from the DJ booth, and I complete a full scan of the tent in search of Jaden, only to be disappointed when I *still* can't find him. I really hope he hasn't bailed, but I haven't caught sight of his date, Eleanor Boosey, yet either, so perhaps they're just late.

"I love this song!" Will yells, and before I've even had a chance to soak up the atmosphere, fetch myself a drink or even sit down, his hand is in mine and he's pulling me to the center of the dance floor. There are only a few others up already, mostly because everyone else is still settling in and feeling too awkward to start busting out their moves just yet. But not Will. I'm not the best dancer by any means, but Will is really something. He's the kind of dancer that gives it so much enthusiasm that you forget your own inhibitions and just get involved, so I've learned to stop worrying about how I look and to just enjoy myself. I glance over my shoulder to check if Holden and Olivia have followed, but they haven't. They disappear into the cafeteria to grab some drinks, probably because Holden is an even worse dancer than I am.

Will reaches for my hand again and twirls me around twice, causing my dress to fan out around me, and I find myself laughing as I crash back into him. He catches me against his chest and steadies me, but that's when I finally see Jaden over his shoulder.

He and Eleanor have just walked in. They linger to the side for a moment as they look around, though I think Ellie may be searching for her friends. However, my attention isn't on her but on the boy standing next to her. Jaden looks extremely handsome in his black pants, white shirt and black bow tie. It's a change from his usual black jeans or football jersey, and his hair is perfectly styled, gelled back into a tousled quiff like something out of a movie. He has one hand in his pocket and his blue eyes carefully move around the marquee until they eventually land on me. Jaden's small smile stretches into a grin and I swear he may have blushed, or maybe it's just me. I smile back at him, anxiously biting my lower lip. I can still feel his touch from last night. We exchange a smile for what feels like forever before I finally lift my hand and wave. He gives me a tiny wave back, right before Ellie reaches for his wrist and pulls him off to one of the tables where her group of friends is sitting.

"Looking like a dead fish *isn't* a dance move, Kenzie!" Will yells into my ear, grabbing my arms and forcing me to dance. I do begin to move again, now feeling increasingly self-conscious about my dance skills. Every once in a while I look back over to Jaden. I catch glimpses of him and Ellie sitting together, and try to guess what they're discussing. I check for any signs of flirtation, but can't see anything to worry about. Still, I can't help but wish he was with me.

Will and I stay up dancing for a long time. The music is actually pretty good—a mixture of current chart music and iconic pop songs from our childhood. Gradually more people come up to join us, including Jess and Kailee, and before long there's a big group of us jumping around together. I don't dance with Holden, not just because I imagine it will be awkward, but because when he does finally drag himself onto the dance floor he just stands at the very edge, chatting to some of the guys from the football team. Will is showing no signs of giving up, but it's getting so hot that I think all my makeup must have melted right off by now. I can already feel the blisters forming on my feet and the dryness in my throat.

"Time out," I tell Will rather breathlessly. I've been laughing and singing for the better part of two hours, and if I push it any longer, I might just collapse. I don't know how Will has so much stamina.

"Fine," Will says, rolling his eyes. "Amateur." He locks his arm around mine and guides me through the heaving crowd to an empty table. I pull out a chair and sit down, facing the dance floor so that I can keep a lookout for Jaden, and Holden and Olivia quickly stroll over to join us. Holden slides into the chair three along from me, leaving a safe distance between us.

"I'll grab us some drinks," Will says, and adjusts his bow tie then wanders off.

"I'll come with you," Olivia says, and I really wish she hadn't offered, because as she heads off with her hand on Will's shoulder, I'm left alone with Holden at the huge table.

Both of us are silent as we stare at anything but each other. I don't want to speak first, because I know I wasn't the one who was wrong last night, so I pull out my makeup from my bag and begin to powder my face and top up my lipstick.

Holden finally looks over at me, his dark eyes reflecting the bright, neon flashes of color from the strobe lights, and then shakes his head. He pushes his chair back and slides along the row until he's finally sitting in the chair next to me, reaching up to loosen his tie although it's already hanging freely. He has to lean in close to me so that I can hear him clearly over the music as he says, "I'm sorry about last night." He's only a few inches away from me, so I can sense him swallow his pride as he admits, "I was being a jerk, and I didn't mean to make Jaden and Dani feel bad."

"Yeah," I agree, shoving my makeup back into my bag, "you were." I know it's hard for Holden to admit when he's wrong, so I appreciate his apology, though I want more from him. I want an explanation. "You think I'm a hypocrite, don't you?"

Holden leans away from me and clenches his jaw. He'll be pissed at Will for telling me what he said, but I don't care. "You did ask us ..." he mumbles after a moment of silence.

"A year ago, Holden," I cut in firmly, fixing him with a look. I wish he would just let it go. "I asked you a year ago, and you know exactly why I did. You *know* why I couldn't be around them, and I can't thank you and Will enough for taking my side, but you don't have to avoid them anymore." I fold my arms across my chest and lean forward, forcing Holden to look at me. "So why are you being so rude whenever they're around?"

"Because I..." he begins, dark eyes narrowed and a frown forming. "I don't know how to act around them."

"You... you just act normal, Holden," I say quietly, then heave a sigh as I sit back against my chair again. It's easy to say, but it's so much harder to do. I know that from experience. "If I can be around them without freaking out, then I'm pretty sure you can."

Holden props his elbows up on the table and runs his hands through his hair in frustration, leaving it ruffled. He stares blankly ahead at the bustling dance floor, watching everyone bust out their best moves. "I can't," he says finally.

It's then that I spot Jaden again. He's at the very corner of the dance floor, right by the DJ booth, awkwardly side-stepping back and forth and nodding his head to the music as Ellie dances around him. She's a great dancer and she is putting him to shame. He has a drink in his hand that he sips at every few seconds. "You're going to have to," I murmur, tearing my gaze away, "because you might be seeing a lot more of them."

"What?" Holden's eyes immediately flash back over to meet mine and he straightens up, staring at me in panic. "Kenzie, *what?*" he pleads.

"I've missed hanging out with them, and I am trying to make up for lost time," I tell him. I figure it's better to be straight-up than to pivot around the subject. I didn't want to do this here, but if I have the chance, then I'm taking it. I have already told Will, so it's time to tell Holden the truth too. "And, believe it or not, I like Jaden all over again."

Holden's face contorts with an entire range of different emotions. "What the fuck, Kenzie?"

I look back at him, surprised yet again by his attitude, wondering if I'm missing something. Holden didn't mind when I was dating Jaden a year ago. "What, Holden?" I urge, leaning toward him.

"*Nothing*, Kenzie," he says, shaking his head. Eyes still wide, he swallows hard and his gaze bores aimlessly into the crowd on the dance floor, zoned out as though he isn't even here anymore. I can't tell if he thinks I'm fickle, or if he's annoyed out of some weird sense of protectiveness.

As if the devil himself had planned it, Jaden emerges from the crowd on the dance floor and stops in front of our table, oblivious to his awful timing. He flashes me his signature crooked smile and then shifts his gaze to the spaced-out Holden that's sitting next to me.

"Hey, man," Jaden says, leaning forward and pressing his hand flat down on the table. "Last night was something, huh? How about we forget about it?" He stretches across the huge circular table and extends his hand to Holden.

Holden tilts his chin up, his expression blank, and he doesn't shake Jaden's awaiting hand. "What's taking them so long with the drinks?" he mumbles under his breath, quickly rising to his feet and striding off across the dance floor, cutting through the mass of bodies, most likely elbowing a few of them on his way.

"Ignore him," I tell Jaden, who, for some reason or another, seems surprised by Holden's odd behavior. By now, he should be used to it. "He's being a jerk again, though I don't think he realizes."

"I can tell," Jaden says with a small chuckle, straightening back up. He walks around the table and pulls out the chair next to me, sitting down sideways and propping one arm up on the edge on the table. His smile is addictive and contagious as his gaze sweeps over my entire body, and I blush under his scrutiny. His glossy blue eyes come to rest on my mouth and he swallows hard. I know what he's thinking about, because I'm thinking about it too: We're thinking of last night. I wouldn't mind repeating it. In fact, I'm dying to.

He leans in closer and for a split second I think he's about to kiss me, but instead he places his hand on my knee, his touch soft, and glances up from beneath his dark eyelashes. "Every time I catch a glimpse of you," he murmurs, "all I can think is … wow."

My eyes fall to my lap and I break the eye contact, because I'm unable to look at him without my cheeks flaming with color. Nervously, I run my fingers over the material of my dress and stare at Jaden's hand on my knee. I reach for my bag and look back up at him, finally meeting his eyes again. I nod to the dance floor and smile. "Dance with me?"

Jaden's touch disappears from my knee as his hand finds mine. He interlocks our fingers firmly together and then stands up, carefully pulling me with him. Even though my feet hurt, I'm willing to dance my way through the pain so long as it's with Jaden, and with my hand in his, in front of the entire school, we make our way to the very center of the dance floor.

20

Jess and Kailee are giving me curious, funny looks. They're dancing not too far away with Tanner and Anthony, though their attention is more on Jaden and me than their boyfriends. They're desperate to know what's going on and I can tell by the teasing winks that they've already figured it out for themselves, so I just roll my eyes at them and look back to the boy in front of me. Never in a million years did I expect to be dancing with Jaden Hunter at homecoming.

However, we're not exactly dancing. We're swaying around in front of one another, singing along to the music and laughing in sync, just like everyone else is. Hands are in the air, voices are raised. We're all crammed in tightly, brushing up against one another, but it's enjoyable.

With the music loud and the entire marquee vibrating from the noise, I have to step closer to Jaden and lean in so I can speak to him, but I don't mind, because it gives me an excuse to touch him as I press my hand to his jaw, my mouth by his ear. "Do you remember that we were supposed to go to homecoming together last year?"

As I drop my hand from his jaw, he places his on my shoulder and edges back in closer to answer me. "Yeah," he says, his breath warm against cheek. "It would have been fun."

Again, the two of us alternate between listening and talking, touching one another and leaning in. "But hey, we're here now, right?"

"Right."

The current song dwindles to an end, but the opening beat of "Closer" by The Chainsmokers echoes around the tent and results in a uproar of cheers. The song has been dominating the charts for weeks now, especially here in Colorado because of that damn Boulder reference, and every single person on the dance floor is yelling the lyrics and becoming more rowdy. The energy in here is at its peak as the end of the dance to draws closer, and Jaden and I are no exception. I find myself singing along at the top of my voice while moving closer and closer to Jaden until our bodies are touching again.

Reaching up, I place my hand around the nape of his neck and I can feel the soft trim of his hair beneath my fingertips. I'm not known for being shy, but I have an unusual amount of confidence all of a sudden as the song rolls into its chorus, and I move my lips to the edge of Jaden's jaw, right below his ear, and dare to murmur, "*So, baby, pull me closer in the back seat of your Corolla.*"

He immediately steps back from me so that his gaze can meet mine, and he's clearly surprised by my personalized rewrite of the lyrics, because he studies me intensely as he tries to gauge whether or not I'm only kidding or if I'm being serious. It's a mixture of both, really, and I can feel the rush of excitement throughout my body as I wait for his reaction.

Finally, his lips curve into a mischievous smirk. "Is that a request, MacKenzie Rivers?"

"Maybe."

Everyone around us is still dancing, still singing, still laughing, but we're no longer interested in the dance. At this point, the only thing I'm interested in is Jaden and the warmth of his skin as he subtly slips his hand into mine and squeezes our fingers together. I stay close behind him with my free hand on his bicep, following him through the crowd toward the exit. Already, my skin is tingling in anticipation of what's to come. I want to kiss Jaden again. So badly, so desperately, and right now.

We break out of the heat of the marquee and into the cool night air outside. It's dark and it's nearing 11PM. There are already a few others mingling around outside, mostly for some fresh air, but for the most part, Jaden and I appear to be the only students making a swift, early getaway. We stride out of the courtyard, but as we pass some of the guys from the football team, leaning against the school building and chuckling amongst themselves, Jaden comes to an abrupt stop and I bump straight into the back of him.

He spins around to face me with our hands still interlocked, and I feel him brush his thumb over my skin in soft circles while his flirty gaze captures mine. "Since we don't have an official homecoming picture together," he says, "let's take one right now. It's our last chance." He releases his hold on my hand and reaches into the pocket of his pants to fetch his phone. Opening up the camera, he glances around at those standing by and then calls over one of his teammates. "Can you take a picture of Kenz and me?"

Caleb, who sits in front of me in Spanish class and often cheats off of me, nods. He takes Jaden's phone and holds it up, flashing us a grin.

Jaden and I move closer to one another and I angle my body into his, wrapping one hand around his back and placing the other on his chest, tilting my head toward him. His hand rests gently on the small of my back, and when I quickly glance sideways at him, he's already staring straight ahead at his phone, that gorgeous, crooked smile toying at his lips. I look back at Caleb and I don't even have to force myself to smile, because I've been grinning the entire time already. I do tone it down to a more subtle smile in an effort to look more elegant than goofy, and there's a bright flash that almost blinds me as Caleb snaps the picture.

"Thanks," Jaden says, breaking out of our pose and stepping forward to reclaim his phone. He doesn't even check to see if the picture has turned out okay; he simply shoves the device back into his pocket and then turns and reaches for my hand. His skin feels cooler now as a result of the chilly breeze, but with our hands locked again, warmth seems to quickly radiate between our skin.

"Jaden," Caleb says, and we pause after a few steps, glancing back over our shoulders. Caleb shoves his hands into the front pockets of his pants and shrugs. There's a small, awkward smile of trepidation on his lips as he says, "It's cool that you didn't miss homecoming this year. You played great yesterday."

I glance at Jaden to check his reaction, and I can tell by the gentle softness to his smile that he appreciates the comment, despite Caleb's unsure, cautious tone. Unlike when I use that tone with Jaden, he seems to let it slide with Caleb, and simply says, "Thanks, man."

We finally set off again, this time making it out of the court-yard and into the parking lot with no more interruptions. It's full of cars, yet clear of students. There are still another twenty minutes of the dance left and we can hear the music and the collective singing from all the way out here. It continues to fade as we near Jaden's Corolla parked over by the football field until the noise is nothing more than a distant buzz. The only thing that's louder in the silence of the parking lot is the thumping of my heart.

I swallow the lump in my throat as we stop just in front of the car. Jaden leans back against the passenger door and I hover a few inches in front of him, so we're facing one another with our hands still connected. "So," he breathes, voice slightly husky after raising his voice for so long back inside the dance. My voice hurts too, mostly from all the singing I've done, and I'm really hoping I can pull off the cracked, raspy voice as attractively as he can. "Kenzie."

"Yeah?"

"Nothing," Jaden says. He looks down, studying our inter-locked hands for a moment. He separates our fingers and then realigns them. "I just like saying your name," he murmurs, still looking down, still moving our hands back and forth. "MacKenzie ... Kenzie ... Kenz ... "

"You know you can just call me Kenz," I tell him. I reserve that nickname for those I care about the most, and I love the way it sounds on Jaden's lips the best.

"Kenz," he says firmly. His eyes flash up to meet mine and he exhales into the cool night air. "Can I tell you something?"

It's not as cold as it was last night, but a shiver surges down my spine. My chest feels heavy with nerves as one million and one possibilities run through my mind. Jaden makes me so, so

186

nervous and I'm still trying to decide whether I love it or hate it. I'm beginning to think it's a good thing, because it means Jaden is doing something to me that no one has ever done before. I can't speak, so I just nod, my eyes never leaving his.

Jaden straightens up and pushes himself off the car. He hovers in front of me for the longest of moments, his eyes taking in every single part of me while I remain frozen under his stare. He lifts his free hand and places it against my jawline. "I really love these," he says, brushing his thumb delicately over the freckles on my left cheek. The blue of his eyes seems lighter somehow, almost gray in the darkness of the night. They meet mine and the corners of his lips curve into the most adorable, sincere smile that forces his eyes to crinkle at their edges. "Or as you would say ... 'cute'."

I press my cheek into the soft palm of Jaden's hand and release a small laugh, closing my eyes and placing my hand over his, holding it there and enjoying the sensation that his touch gives me. "Your birthmark *is* cute," I tease as I open my eyes again, my eyelashes flickering.

He sweeps his thumb over my cheek again, over all of the freckles that I hate so much. "If you say that one more time, Kenz, I swear ... "

"You swear what?" I challenge, wrapping my hand around his and teasingly removing it from my face. I bite down on my lower lip, drawing Jaden's attention to my mouth, and then I purposely part my lips and raise an eyebrow, waiting.

"Then I swear I'll do this," he whispers.

He breaks free and eagerly reaches for my face, cupping his hand beneath my jaw again. His mouth crashes against mine at the same time as his body does, and he releases my other hand so that he can also grab my waist, pulling me against him until we fall back against the car with a thud. My hands find their way into his hair and the kiss becomes rougher than it was last night. Faster, deeper, longer. I follow Jaden's lead for the most part, though I exercise control at points, and the two of us alternate back and forth, showing one another what we've got to offer. My fingers are tangled into his tousled hair, his hand is along my jawline, his fingertips on the back of my neck, holding me near. I can't get enough of him and I wish I could kiss him all night long, but I have to stop eventually in order to catch my breath. As I pull away, I take his lower lip between my teeth, teasing him.

Jaden releases a long breath of air as he drops his hand from my jaw and runs it through his ruffled hair instead. It's lost its style, but I don't think he cares, because he just stares at me in admiration or disbelief. I'm not sure which, but I know that I'm breathing heavily as I tuck lose strands of my own hair back behind my ear. Behind me, I hear the distant echo of voices, and when I cast a glance over my shoulder, I spy a group of young freshmen strolling through the parking lot further down. When I turn back around, I nod once over Jaden's shoulder to the Corolla behind him.

"Unlock the car, Jaden," I whisper.

Jaden's eyebrows shoot upward as it dawns on him that I'm not finished yet, and he quickly feels around in the pockets of his pants for the car keys. He pulls open the passenger door to allow me inside, but I shake my head while smirking at him. I purposely rub against his body as I head for the back door instead, pulling it open and carefully sliding into the back seat. I move right along to the other side, kick off my shoes, and then lean forward to glance up at Jaden.

"Come here," I tell him, motioning him inside.

It's endearing the way color floods his pale cheeks as he glances all around, scouring the parking lot to see if the coast is clear before he settles into the back seat beside me, pulling the door shut behind him. It cuts off the faint thumping of music from the dance so that we're left in complete silence, just Jaden and I.

"I should point out that this is my grandparents' car," he mumbles nervously, glancing back and forth between me and the headrest in front of him while fidgeting with his hands, "so this could be weird, but I'm down with being disrespectful."

A laugh escapes my lips and I can't stop myself even as Jaden stares at me in confusion. He really is such a sweet, charming guy and I can't believe I almost threw away my chance with him last summer. I'm so happy to be here now with him. "We're not going to do anything disrespectful, Jaden," I manage to tell him through my fit of laughter.

Immediately, Jaden realizes his mistake and begins to laugh too, embarrassed. He reaches up to pull off his bow tie and open the top few buttons of his shirt, then angles his body toward me. "Ever?" he teases.

"Not here," I correct, playing along with him. I lean forward and briefly press my lips to his, then sit back again to look at him fully. "Can I be upfront with you?" I ask, adopting a more serious tone rather than playful. I need to tell Jaden something. I don't like keeping secrets unless I absolutely must and if I want to say something, I'll say it. I like to think of myself as being rather straightforward, yet so far with Jaden, I've been anything *but* straightforward. I still haven't told him the full truth as to why I avoided him for so long, but starting now, I want to be completely open and honest with him, because like he said last night, we don't know when our time will run out.

Jaden dramatically pretends to get comfortable, sitting up straight and giving me a nod. "Yes. Be upfront. If I'm a bad kisser, tell me. I will gladly let you teach me."

I roll my eyes at him and then exhale, allowing enough time to pass for him to realize I'm not about to joke around with him, that I'm trying to be sincere. When he finally wipes the grin off his face, I tell him, "I really liked you last year," though I'm pretty sure he already knew that. We spent a lot of time together last summer. We knew we liked one another. Everyone knew; everyone could see it. But a lot of time has passed, so I feel as though some clarification is needed, which is why I reach for Jaden's hand and trace the lines on his palm with the tip of my index finger and say, "And I really like you now."

Jaden closes his hand around mine and edges across the back seat toward me. His smile is small but crooked as our eyes meet. His are smoldering and the blue within them is electric and beautiful, striking and enchanting. He leans forward and brings his lips to the corner of my mouth. "Well, Kenz, isn't it a coincidence that I really like you too?" he whispers, and before he can close the distance between us, I reach for his jaw and press my lips to his first.

21

As I stand on Holden's porch, I'm nervously twisting my hair around my index finger while I wait for someone to open the door. It's Tuesday evening and I've just got off work. It's just after 10PM and I know Will was coming over to hang out, so I drove straight here as soon as my shift ended. Holden hasn't spoken to me since the homecoming dance on Saturday, all because of our disagreement over the Hunters, and Will has been stuck in the middle, awkwardly tiptoeing around the two of us, trying to remain neutral. Although it's Holden's fault for overreacting over nothing, I can't bear not talking to him. Being around the Hunters again really isn't a big deal, but he is making it one.

"Kenzie!" Holden's mom, Mel, says cheerfully when she swings open the front door. Even though it's late, she doesn't seem to mind me showing up at her house. "They're upstairs," she tells me, stepping back and opening the door wider to allow me inside. "Just head on up!"

"Thanks." I quickly kick off my shoes in the hall and make

my way upstairs. I'm determined to clear the air and I'm not leaving until I have. It will be impossible to hang out with Jaden and Dani if Holden is going to become grouchy every time that we do.

I can hear cursing from Holden's room before I've even reached it, from both him and Will. I stand outside the door for a minute, breathing deeply and mentally preparing myself in case Holden decides to argue with me over the matter, and then I push open the door. Holden's room is rather cramped and messy. There's not a lot of space in here, and there's a lot of trash and dirty clothes scattered all over the floor. He and Will are glued to the small TV screen with PlayStation 4 controllers in their hands and their backs to me. Will is perched on the adjustable computer chair, while Holden is sitting on the edge of his bed. Neither of them seem to hear me enter.

"So this is how you guys hang out when I'm not here," I say loudly, causing them both to flinch.

Holden scowls as he pauses the game and throws the controller down onto the floor in frustration at the interruption. "Kenzie," he says, rising to his feet, "What are you doing here? Aren't you supposed to be at work?"

"I just got off," I tell him, stepping further into the room. I exchange glances with Will, but he keeps his mouth shut as he sinks down in the chair. It's so typical of him not to get involved, even though I know he is on my side. "So I thought I'd drop by and see if there's anything I can do that'll help you learn how to be nice to Jaden and Dani." I fix Holden with a firm, challenging look and cock my head to one side.

Holden releases a long sigh and closes his eyes, rubbing at

his temple. "Not this again," he mumbles. He knows I'm here to confront him and exasperation is written all over his face, but I just don't want him acting out again the next time we are around the Hunters.

"Yes, Holden, this again," I tell him, folding my arms across my chest. I don't raise my voice, but I do keep my tone firm. I'm not going to back down on this. "What is your problem with the Hunters? I know it can be hard figuring out what to say around them, but c'mon."

Holden groans under his breath. "Can't you just let it go?"

"Let it go?" I repeat, blinking at him in disbelief. "Will," I snap, firing my eyes over to him. "Who's wrong here?"

Will swings awkwardly back and forth on the computer chair, clearly uncomfortable from the pressure I'm putting him under. He thinks for a moment while Holden and I stare at him expectantly. Finally, Will shrugs and sits up. "You *are* taking this a little too far, Holden," he says quietly. "So what if we talk to the Hunters? I don't see why there's a problem."

"Okay, fine! *Fine,*" Holden snaps. He shakes his head and then heaves a sigh, collapsing back down onto the corner of his bed, staring at the floor in defeat. His nostrils are still flaring in anger. "It's awkward, but fuck it, I'll just deal with it."

"Now was that so hard?" I ask with a small smile, but Holden completely ignores me. I know he's uncomfortable around Jaden and Dani, but he'll ease up the more he's around them, I'm sure. He's pissed off at Will and me ganging up on him, so I sit down on the bed next to him and playfully wrap my arms around his lean body. I bury my face into his chest and forcefully hug him. Even though he doesn't reciprocate, he doesn't push me off, either. He'll come around soon, but for now, I'll take what I can get.

"Since you guys are friends again," Will says, sitting forward in the chair and dangling the game controller from his fingertips, "you'll both be at the party I'm throwing next month, right?"

"You're throwing another party?" I ask. I remain wrapped around Holden, refusing to move. "Didn't someone smash a mirror last year?"

"Yes," Will says, rolling his eyes. "But it was only a cheap one. Mom hated it, anyway. Dad's out of town again on the fifteenth, so she says I can throw another party if I want to." He pauses only to give us a devilish grin. "And I sure as hell want to," he says. "Invite whoever you want."

"We can still drink, right?" Holden mutters. He's still being grouchy, though I can tell by the curious glances he gives Will that the thought of a party has piqued his interest. He just doesn't want to show it.

"Yeah," Will says with a laugh. "Just don't go throwing up in my back yard or anything. Now can we get back to the game?" He waves the controller at the TV screen and pulls a face at Holden, urging him to unpause it. "Two players max, sorry, Kenzie. You can watch."

"That's okay," I say, finally releasing my grip on Holden and standing up. In one final attempt to lighten the mood, I squeeze his shoulder. "I'm not staying. I have homework."

"Sucks to be you," Will says. "See you at school."

As I head to the door, Holden grabs his controller from the floor again and unpauses the game. He doesn't acknowledge the fact that I'm leaving, but I don't worry too much about it, because at least Will gives me a quick wave over his shoulder before he tunes in to the game.

My house is only a five-minute drive from Holden's place,

so I'm pulling into my quiet cul-de-sac in no time at all, though I find it odd that the house is in complete darkness. There's not a single light on, not even the porch light, which is unusual given that the porch light is *always* left on for me coming home late from work. I pull up by the sidewalk and turn off the engine, puzzled. As far as I'm aware, Mom wasn't supposed to be going anywhere tonight. There's a possibility Dad may have been called out on an emergency plumbing job, but there's no reason why Mom shouldn't be here.

Stepping out of the car, I sprint up to the porch, fumbling around in my bag for my keys. There's a sense of worry at the back of my mind. I jam my keys into the lock, but for some reason they don't end up working. I grab the door handle and shake it around, then try again. It takes me a few seconds of frantic struggling before I realize that the reason my keys aren't turning in the lock is because the door is already unlocked. So someone *is* home.

Holding my breath, I slowly push the door open and peer around the frame into the darkness of the house. My eyes take a minute to adjust while I silently step inside. The house feels eerie in the cold, quiet stillness that surrounds me. There's the distant dripping of our leaky faucet echoing down the hall from the kitchen, but I hardly even notice it, because my attention is drawn to Mom.

She's sitting on the bottom of the stairs, still and unmoving, her knees hugged to her chest. Loose strands of dark hair frame her face, the rest clipped back, and her strong features don't look the way they usually do. Her lips seem thin and frail, her cheeks more hollowed. What really, truly terrifies me is the lost, broken look in her dark eyes as she stares aimlessly at the small, pink frame she's clutching in her hands: a look of complete and utter devastation, her still gaze raw with hurt. On the floor beside her, a glass of wine that's full. Next to it, a bottle that's almost empty. In front of her, the name of the child she lost.

There's a lump in my dry throat that I painfully swallow as I take a tiny, cautious step forward. "Mom?"

"She would have been four today," Mom whispers, her voice cracking with pain. Her eyes don't move from Grace's frame and she seems entirely disconnected from reality as she lifts the glass of wine to her lips, taking a long sip. She swallows and lowers the glass again, but as soon as she does, her bottom lip begins to quiver. "What would she have liked for her party?" she asks into the silence while I listen. "What kind of cake would she have liked? What kind of ice cream would she have wanted there to be?" As she asks the questions we both know we will never know the answers to, her pained eyes well up and a single tear breaks free, rolling down her cheek and dripping off her chin. And then another, and another. "Would she have liked chocolate like you? Or vanilla like your dad?"

"Mom," I murmur, trying to soothe her, but my voice sounds almost as broken as hers. I can't bear to see her like this: this low and this heartbroken when there is nothing in this world that anyone can do to fix it. My cheeks grow wet as I try to wipe away my own tears. I step closer to Mom and lower myself down onto the stairs next to her. A wave of sickness hits me when I glance over to Grace's name and it stares straight back at us.

Mom's right. My baby sister would have no longer been a baby by now. Today, she would have been four years old. She would have been learning new things in preschool. She would have developed her own interesting little quirks by now that we would have adored.

Mom and Dad had always thought of Grace as a miracle. After years of complications, they never thought they'd be able to have a second child, and so they settled with having just one. Just me. But their hopes were raised back when I was thirteen, when they sat me down in the living room one evening with big, beautiful grins on their faces and delivered the news they'd always dreamed of sharing: I was going to have a sibling, and we were going to be a happy family of four. We were so excited back then. I would press my hands to Mom's stomach and feel the baby's kicking feet, and Dad would sing along to the radio while cleaning out the spare room upstairs in order to convert it into a nursery, and Mom would buy tiny pink little outfits to fill the new chest of drawers they'd bought.

It's been four years, but we still don't know why we lost Grace. She was healthy, yet she didn't make it. Many still-births are often unexplainable, and unfortunately, we were never given a reason. The doctors could only tell us how sorry they were, that they couldn't determine the cause, and I think not having a reason is why it's been so hard to move on after all this time. Mom has nothing to pin the blame on other than herself.

"Four years old," Mom whispers, shaking her head slowly, tears still rolling down her cheeks. She is refusing to tear her eyes away from the frame despite the pain it's putting her through. "We were supposed to have two beautiful girls," she murmurs, and then she finally seems to crack as she breaks out into a sob, her emotions pouring out of her. She drops her gaze and presses her hand to her mouth, trying to muffle her own wails. "Two," she weeps, and I'm sobbing along with her as I shift closer, reaching for the glass in her shaking hand, prying it from her stiff fingers. I set it down on the floor of the hall and then turn back to my mother, wrapping my arms tightly around her trembling body. Her eyes are squeezed shut and an endless flow of tears cascades down her cheeks. She collapses against me in overwhelming defeat and I hold her as tightly as I can as she buries her face into my polo shirt, soaking the material.

Suddenly, the front door is pushed open and I glance up through blurred vision, only to see Dad stepping into the house, worn out, hands dirty from work. Mom is still sobbing and so am I, and Dad looks down at us in both fear and concern. He glances sideways at Grace's frame, and when his eyes meet mine again, his own expression breaks into one of heartache. Dumping his tools on the floor, Dad falls to his knees in front of Mom and me and immediately pulls us both into the safety and reassurance of his strong arms. He clings onto us both so tightly, and I squeeze him back even harder, desperate for him to do something, to make this all better so that we don't have to go through pain like this ever again.

But there is nothing Dad can do to make it all stop. He doesn't know how, the same way I don't, the same way Mom doesn't. We are broken, and no one knows how to fix us.

22

I'm riding shotgun in Will's Jeep on the drive home from school on Thursday, just the two of us because Holden has football practice, when my phone vibrates in the back pocket of my jeans. I tune out of Will's rant about how much of an asshole his Biology teacher is and fish my phone out of my pocket, glancing down at the lit-up message displayed on my screen. It's from Jaden, and although the message is rather blunt and vague, my heart does skip a beat or two when I read the words he's written.

Meet me at the lake at five. Same spot as last time.

Jaden and I had no plans together tonight, but luckily I don't happen to be slotted in for a shift at The Summit, so I'm free and more than willing to spend time with him, even if I don't know what exactly he has in mind. I like the demanding tone to the message, however. I like that it's not a question. I like that he knows I'll be there. We haven't seen each other outside of the school walls since last weekend, so I'm more than desperate to hang out with him anywhere other than by my locker for once.

"What are you smiling about?" Will asks, eyeing me suspiciously. He moves one hand from the steering wheel to lower the radio and then teasingly wiggles his eyebrows at me. "Talking to your *boyfriend?*"

I roll my eyes at him and look back down at my phone, quickly typing a reply. "He's not my boyfriend," I say. At the same time, I hit send, letting Jaden know that I'll definitely be there.

"Whatever you say," Will continues to tease, and then as he pulls into my cul-de-sac, he adds, "Are you inviting him to my party?"

I slip my phone back into my pocket and straighten up in the passenger seat as my house comes into view. I grab my bag from the floor and pull it onto my lap, then release my seatbelt and get ready to jump out, my hand resting on the door handle. I look over at Will and nod. "Yeah, if it's okay with you."

"Why wouldn't it be?" he asks. Pulling up outside my house, he unlocks the doors and tilts his head to look at me, hair flopping into his eyes. He should really get his hair cut. "You know me, I go with the flow. Invite Dani too. She's nice and she could use it."

"Sure thing," I say. I was planning on inviting Dani, anyway. She most likely won't come, but at least the offer will be there. "Catch you later!" I tell Will as I slide out of the Jeep and slam the door shut behind me. He doesn't wait around for me to get inside my house, and within a matter of seconds, he's gone.

Swinging my bag onto my shoulder, I run across my lawn

and onto my porch. Mom and Dad are both at work, so I have the house to myself, though I hardly notice that they're not here. They've been so quiet this week. Last night, I found Dad sitting at the kitchen table in silence, staring at a cut on his palm for almost an hour. He didn't hear me when I asked him if he wanted coffee. Yesterday morning, Mom skipped work and was still wrapped up in bed with water and painkillers on the bedside table when I got home from school. She was ill, she told me. But I knew better: She'd drunk her way through three full bottles of wine the night before.

I rush upstairs to my room and throw my bag down on my bed. I have an hour and half to spend getting ready before I meet Jaden, and I definitely need it. I ran track third period, so my makeup has more or less sweated off and my hair is stuck in a messy ponytail. There's no way Jaden can see me like this, so I hop in the shower, get dressed, straighten my hair and apply fresh makeup.

I'm drowning myself in body spray and perfume when I hear Mom finally arriving home from work.

I get everything together: my phone, my keys to the house, some cash. If I'm meeting Jaden at the lake, then I most definitely don't want to be late, so I make my way downstairs. When I reach the hall, I catch Mom walking into the kitchen and kicking off her shoes with a sigh of relief. I head into the kitchen to try and get her attention, but she's standing in front of the counter, her hands gripping the edge, breathing deeply.

"Mom?" I say carefully, trying not to startle her. "Can I borrow the car?"

Mom glances sideways at me, the exhaustion in her eyes evident. She can't even bring herself to open her mouth to ask where I'm going or who I'm going to be with, most likely because right now she simply doesn't care. Her mind has been elsewhere the entire week. She lethargically reaches into her purse, grabs the keys and then dumps them down on the counter in front of me. She turns away then, walking over to pull open one of the top cupboards. There's a clink as she fetches a glass, and then nothing but silence as she pulls a fresh bottle of white wine from the rack next to the flowers Darren sent last weekend. I keep forgetting to water them, so they're withering already.

I watch in silence as Mom screws the cap off the cheap wine and pours a full glass with no energy whatsoever. Never looking at me, she carries both the glass and the bottle over to the kitchen table and sets them down. She pulls out a chair, drops down onto the edge of it, and focuses her blank stare on the window. I don't want to be around to witness her take that first sip, and I know there's nothing I can say that will prevent it, so I grab the car keys from the counter and walk away, turning my back to her. It is easier to do that, to just walk away. I can ignore it that way.

When I pull into the lake's parking lot exactly four minutes before 5PM, it's only half full. There are some parents and their kids playing at the Boardwalk Park playground and a woman strolling by with her dog, but it's relatively quiet compared with the summer months. Suddenly, I spot Jaden standing in the middle of the road only a few feet away from my car, and I brake harshly. He jogs over, wearing his favorite black, ripped jeans and a red flannel shirt that's too big around the sleeves. As he approaches, I roll down my window and he presses both hands against the door, leaning down to look at me.

"I got a permit," he announces immediately, grinning widely from ear to ear. It stretches all the way up his face, capturing his glistening eyes. "And the boat is finally registered again and fully insured, so park and let's go!" He thumps his hand excitedly against the metal of the car door, playfully urging me to hurry up. "We're taking her out to see if she still runs as well as she did."

I can't believe it. I lean forward in my seat so that I can peer around Jaden. Behind him, his grandparents' Corolla is reversed onto the launch ramp with Brad's boat perched on the trailer that's attached, already half-loaded into the water. Terry is in the car with a beaming smile on his face, and when he sees me, he sticks his arm out of his rolled-down window and waves.

I look back up at Jaden, still blinking in surprise. I thought we were going to go for a walk around the lake or sit on the beach, not take his parents' boat out onto the water together for the very first time. "You're really taking the boat out?"

Jaden nods, glancing over his shoulder to steal another look at it. "You were right," he says when his eyes meet mine again. His grin transforms into a more sincere, grateful smile. "Dad wouldn't want it sitting on the driveway. He'd want me to take a girl like you out on it, so what do you say? Are you coming with me?"

"Of course I'm coming with you," I say, placing my hand on top of his on the door. I know how big a moment this must be for him. He wanted to get rid of the boat, after all, so it must be difficult to take it out on the water again, given how special it was to his father. With my eyes never leaving his, I gently squeeze his hand. "Give me a second to pull up."

Jaden nods again and steps back from the car, pulling his

hand free from beneath mine, and I roll the window back up and drive into the closest free parking spot. I'm not sure if I'm dressed appropriately for going boating, so I grab an old hoodie of mine from the back seat and take it with me just in case it's colder out on the water. I lock up and then sprint over to join Jaden and Terry on the launch ramp as they release the boat from the trailer, and I follow Jaden as he walks along the edge of the dock while the boat drifts into the water, tying it to the dock with thick rope.

"Got it?" Terry yells out of the car window, and Jaden throws him a thumbs-up. "Alright, be careful and have fun! Call me when you're done." He rolls the window up and drives forward, pulling the trailer out of the water and back up the launch ramp. Then he drives off, disappearing out of the parking lot much to my surprise.

I drop my gaze to Jaden, who's still crouched down, pulling the boat against the dock. "He's not coming?"

"What?" he says, glancing up at me. He pulls a face and then laughs a little, straightening up in front of me. "You thought my granddad was gonna join us?" He shakes his head, still laughing as I shrug sheepishly, and then points to the boat. "Okay, jump in. We're only allowed to stay out on the water until sunset."

"Okay," I say, and step closer to the edge, running my eyes over Brad's boat now that it's finally back in the water where it belongs. It's the first time I've seen it without its cover on, and I'm amazed by the pristine condition that it has been kept in. There are no signs of corrosion or scuffed paintwork, no dirt or dampness on the seats. Although it looked abandoned and uncared for in the driveway, it clearly has been shown some attention over the past year so as not to let it deteriorate. Along the bow, in perfect, large letters, it says: *Hunter*.

The water is calm, so the boat doesn't bob around too much as I step one foot inside it, and then the other, carefully climbing in. There are only four seats: the two in the front where Brad and Kate had sat that summer's day last August, and the two in the back where Jaden and I had been, exchanging flirtatious glances with one another behind his parents' backs. My stomach lurches as I stand in the center of the small boat, glancing around, imagining Brad and Kate here now, still smiling, still living.

The boat jerks slightly as Jaden steps in next to me, and he pauses in front of me when he sees my expression and gently grasps my arm. "Are you okay?" he asks, concerned. "Don't tell me you've developed motion sickness within the space of a year. Kenz?"

I press my lips together and try to force the bile that's rising in my throat back down, shaking my head slowly. "Do you know how to ... how to drive this?" I ask through ragged breaths, trying to focus on something else, *anything* else.

"Sit down," Jaden urges. With his hand still on my arm, he gently guides me into the front passenger seat, the same seat where his mom once sat. "And yes, I know how to drive this thing. Dad taught me," he explains as he slips into the seat next to me behind the controls. He rests one hand loosely over the steering wheel and presses the key into the ignition, turning it with concentration until the engine splutters to life, forcing the boat to shudder beneath us. "Now tell me," he says, looking back over, "are you okay?"

I still feel as though I might throw up all over the white leather seats, so I keep my mouth firmly clamped shut and breathe deeply through my nose, giving Jaden a small nod. He doesn't look entirely convinced, but he stands up and moves back to the boat's edge to untie us from the dock. I close my eyes and grab a fistful of my hoodie in my lap, desperate for the overwhelming sense of sickness to disappear. I just can't shake Brad and Kate from my mind. I can see their faces, their beautiful smiles. I can hear their voices, their lively laughter.

I sense Jaden walk back over so I force my eyes open, keeping them trained on him as he settles into the driver's seat. The boat is slowly drifting away from the dock with the gentle flow of the lake. "If you want to get off, just tell me and I'll take you straight back, okay?" Jaden says. There is still worry written across his face, but I don't want to ruin this experience for him, so I promise myself that I'll stick it out. This is supposed to be a special moment.

Leaning back against the leather seat, I watch as Jaden rests one hand over the control levers and adjusts them. The boat increases in speed, spewing out water in our wake as we head across the open lake. Apart from a small sailing boat far off at the other side, we have the place to ourselves, and Jaden seems to use the space to its full potential. We speed through the water, engine growling, bow rising up. Splashes of water lightly spray over us and my nausea begins to wear off after a few minutes when I switch from thinking about Brad and Kate to thinking about how much fun this actually is.

I laugh a little as the wind relentlessly blows my hair across my face and I steal a glance over at Jaden. His face is aglow with pure joy as he races the boat around the full perimeter of the lake. "I told you I knew how to drive this thing!" he yells over the sound of the engine and the crashing of the water, and with a satisfied smile, he begins to slow the boat down.

We come to a stop in the very center of Windsor Lake. The boat sits idly on the water, drifting back and forth only barely, and there is no one else around. In the distance, the stunning peaks of the Rocky Mountains are visible in the clear, light sky. There is nothing other than complete silence out on the lake and I like how alone we seem out here, so far from everything else, just Jaden and me.

"Mom would have yelled at me for driving like that," he says, propping his elbow up on the back of the leather seat and lazily slumping against it. His smile is warm as he looks over at me, his gaze content. "Dad would have told me to go faster."

I stare back at him, but my eyes don't mirror his. My gaze is full of confusion, my mind full of so many questions. I really like Jaden. I do, but sometimes I just can't understand him. I don't understand how he can possibly talk about his parents so casually, so playfully, without even so much as a flicker of pain and longing in his eyes. He has been so open and so honest with me about them and about himself, yet I still don't understand any of it. How can he possibly be so happy?

Jaden has let me straight back into his life, every single part of it. Taking this boat out again for the very first time after the death of his parents is a big moment for him, but he still brought me. He fully trusts me, I can see it, but I know that he shouldn't, because I haven't been telling him the truth. I've been evading it, keeping secrets and holding up barriers this entire time. I've been lying to him. I haven't told him the full truth as to why I couldn't bear to be around him for an entire year. I have never told him about Grace.

I want Jaden to truly understand me, the same way I want

207

to understand him. I need to be honest. I need to tell him the truth, every single tiny fraction of it.

My chest feels heavy and I drop my eyes to my hoodie, my hands trembling slightly as I fumble anxiously with the material. I've never been good at this. "Jaden," I murmur, "there's something I need to tell you."

Jaden must tell from the terrified look in my eyes and the quietness of my voice that whatever I'm about to tell him isn't going to be light, because he immediately wipes the smile from his face and sits up. "Kenz?"

God, where do I even begin? There is so much to say, and I don't know how to say it. It's impossible to look at Jaden right now, so I keep my head down and my eyes on my hands. "That night at the store ... I wasn't buying the beer for myself," I admit. My breathing is shallow and I feel ashamed to have to tell him about Mom, but I know that it's necessary. "I was buying it for my mom. There were no bottles in the kitchen, so she gave me her ID and sent me out for some more."

I swallow hard and force myself to bravely steal a sideways glance at Jaden to gauge his reaction. He's watching me, listening very carefully, his expression calm but focused. He's waiting for me to continue, but it's so hard to say these things out loud. I've never told anyone about Mom's self-destructive behavior, not even Will and Holden. I always found it easier to just push it to the back of my mind, but it's time I admit it not only to Jaden, but also to myself.

"She's been drinking for four years now," I continue, shifting my nervous gaze to the Rocky Mountains over in the distance behind Jaden. I focus on their peaks as the sun gradually lowers. "Every year, it seems to get worse and worse. It started with a couple glasses during the week. And then a glass every night. And then several glasses a night." I try to relieve some of the pressure that's building in my chest by pausing to exhale, but it makes no difference. "And now we're counting how much she drinks in terms of bottles rather than glasses."

Jaden is silent for a moment. He slides forward to the edge of his seat and places his hand on my knee. "Kenzie, I'm sorry," he says.

"There's a reason why I avoided you," I splutter abruptly, choking out the words that are stuck in my throat. My eyes flicker down to meet Jaden's. My entire body is trembling, not because it's cold out on the water, but because nerves are consuming every inch of me. I hate this, but I have to push through it. "A real reason. I didn't tell you everything that I should have."

"What is it, Kenz?" Jaden urges. His eyes dilate with a mixture of both panic and intrigue as he searches my terrified expression for answers. "What didn't you tell me?"

The pressure in my chest only continues to build, growing more painful with each moment that passes. Telling Jaden the truth means opening up about everything that I have spent so long repressing in order to move on. For four entire years, I have done a relatively good job at keeping Grace out of my mind. I see her name in our hall every day, but apart from those fleeting seconds when the thought of her crosses my mind, I rarely think about her. It has always been easier that way. Thinking about Grace and everything she would have been would only send me into a downward spiral exactly like Mom. That's why it is so difficult now to force Grace to the front of my mind. To talk about her. To tell Jaden about her.

I angle my head away from him again, turning to face the

calm water that surrounds us. All I can hear is my ragged breathing and the pounding of my heart against my ribs. I squeeze my eyes tightly shut and focus on the darkness. I have been silent for too long. "My sister would have been four this week," I whisper. My throat is so dry, my voice cracked, my words pained. I refuse to open my eyes. I like it better in the darkness. "Her name was Grace, or at least it would have been. She was stillborn when I was thirteen, so we never got to meet her."

I hear Jaden release a long breath of air as his hand tightens on my knee. His other hand finds mine and he grasps both my hands under his in what I can only sense as empathy and reassurance. Warmth radiates between our skin and I'm thankful for his supportive touch as he remains silent, allowing me time to continue when I'm ready. My eyes are still closed, though now I'm squeezing them even tighter, fighting back the tears that I feel forming. I feel so vulnerable having to expose myself bare like this, and I've only just begun.

"My parents ... They've never gotten over it. They've never been the same since. I've watched how it's changed them. They don't laugh as much as they used to, and there's always this sadness in their eyes even when I think they're happy. Mom's one and only pastime is sitting with a glass of wine in her hand, and Dad works around the clock now just so he doesn't have to be home to witness it," I tell him in a trembling mumble. The words are spilling out of me and so are the tears. Now that I've started, I can't stop. "Grace is the only person I've ever lost in my life, and even though I never had the chance to meet her, the grief is unbearable," I whisper, and there's a pang of hurt in my chest that finally bursts the pressure that has been mounting. My tense body seems to collapse and my shoulders sink as I force my damp eyes open, looking over at Jaden through a thick, blurred layer of tears. "That's why I couldn't be around you, Jaden," I confess in a choked sob. The tears are streaming down my cheeks in hot, stinging rivers. The relief of finally letting the truth out of my system is painful, yet the pain is satisfying, as though I can *feel* it filtering out. I've been holding it in for too long. "Because you ... you had it even worse," I continue, still crying out my words. He's never seen me like this, because this isn't usually me. There's understanding and compassion in his eyes as he squeezes my hands even tighter, letting me know that he's still there, still listening. "You *knew* your parents. You knew what kind of people they were, you knew what they loved and what they believed in and what they stood for. You have memories with them, so how do you possibly move on from that? How do you cope when you lose someone you truly *knew*? How do you keep on living without them when you have already experienced what life is like *with* them?"

Jaden and I may have both lost someone in our lives, but I can't even begin to imagine what he's been through. Unlike Jaden, we didn't have Grace in our lives. The only thing we had was the *idea* of Grace. The thought of her. We only lost what could have been, whereas Jaden lost so, so much more.

I look down at my hands in Jaden's and only then do I realize that it's not him who's tightening his hold on me, but rather I am tightening my hold on him. I'm squeezing my hands around his so tightly that my fingers are rigid from the tension, my knuckles pale. If I'm hurting him, he doesn't show it. "I couldn't be around you when you were figuring that out, Jaden," I admit, frantically shaking my head at him, ashamed.

I wish I was stronger. I wish I could handle grief. "I'm so sorry. I just couldn't, because I thought you would never find those answers. I thought you would be a different person. I thought you would never be happy again, and I couldn't bear to watch that happen all over again."

"Kenzie," Jaden whispers, sliding off the seat and dropping to his knees on the tiny floor of the boat in front of me, looking up at me from beneath his eyelashes. He moves his hand from my knee and cups my face, brushing away my burning tears with the soft pad of his thumb. "I cope *because* I have memories," he tells me firmly. "I got to live sixteen years of my life with my parents, and I feel lucky for having every single one of those years. I knew they were happy, and although their time here was cut short, they had a good ride. They loved each other and they loved Dani and me, and I know them well enough to know now that they wouldn't want me to spend the rest of my life hung up over them. They would want me to be as happy as they were, they would want me to keep on *living*. That doesn't mean that I don't miss them, because God, I really fucking do." He exhales and glances up to the sky full of clouds, blinking several times and then looking back down at me. "But I cope because they will always live on in the memories I hold of them, so you were wrong. It's not worse. It's bearable, because I can't imagine how it would feel to lose someone without having a single memory of them. Kenz," he says, tilting my chin down toward him so that his eyes can meet mine. The sympathy within them is true and sincere. "I'm sorry."

"Tell me something normal," I whisper, a tiny hint of a smile cracking through my pained expression. I feel lighter now, less weighed down somehow now that I have everything off my chest. I understand Jaden, but I may also understand myself. Now that I've said it out loud, I understand *why* I feel the way I do.

"Okay," Jaden says with a small smile. "I like you even more than I did an hour ago, and I thought that was pretty impossible," he admits, "so thanks for proving me wrong."

He glances out over the water, back in the direction of the dock. With his hand still in mine, he straightens up from the floor of the boat and then places his free hand to my cheek, feeling the dampness of my skin. I know I'm a mess right now. A complete, utter mess. My mascara stings my eyes, so I roll my hoodie up and use it to dab at them.

"Kenz," Jaden says softly, and I pause, glancing up at him. He leans forward, hand still pressed to my cheek, and gently places his cool lips just above my temple. "Thank you for telling me everything that you just did."

23

I drive over to Jaden's grandparents house separately, following behind Jaden and Terry in the Corolla as they tow the boat back. The few minutes I have to myself are desperately needed. I drive with one hand on the wheel and with the other I furiously scrub my makeup off with a wipe as I glance back and forth between the road and my rearview mirror. My eyes are still red and puffy.

As I drive, I feel light with a sense of relief, but there's something more. I have an overwhelming feeling of pride that I don't quite know how to process. I'm not sure why I feel proud of myself for breaking down in front of Jaden. If anything, I should be embarrassed, but for some reason I'm not. I think, just maybe, I'm proud of myself for building up the courage to finally let everything out.

We turn onto Ponderosa Drive and I continue to follow Jaden and Terry back to the house. I've been invited over to spend the rest of the evening with Jaden, and I'm glad. I don't want to go home yet. It's still early, just after sunset, and after laying myself bare in front of him, I want to be with Jaden more than ever. They pull up into the driveway with the boat, and I park up by the sidewalk, killing the engine. Before I climb out of the car, I cast one final glance over myself in the small rearview mirror. My skin is blotchy and uneven, my eyes still swollen and my freckles on full display. I heave a sigh. There is nothing I can do about it now, and although I feel much more confident when my eyelashes are coated in mascara and my skin is perfected with a layer of foundation, it's not the end of the world. I feel completely naked in front of Jaden today, but it's okay. I grab my hoodie from the passenger seat and pull it on over my head, then step out of the car and lock up just as Jaden and Terry are hovering around the back of the Corolla. They're trying to detach the boat's trailer, most likely so that it can be pushed back into the corner of the driveway. I just hope it doesn't get left there untouched for another whole year. That would be a shame.

"Just head on in!" Terry calls over his shoulder. He's kneeling down on the ground, pulling at something that I can't quite see. "Nancy should be in the kitchen."

Jaden is lingering, waiting for his help to be called upon, and he glances over at me with a small smile of reassurance. He gives me a nod, encouraging me to go inside. "We'll just be a minute."

I nod back and stuff my hands into the front pocket of my hoodie, turning toward the porch. The sky is a gorgeous painting of pink and orange streaks, but the darkness is slowly filtering through, cracking it. I pause on the porch, rub at my eyes one last time, and then cautiously open up the front door. That glorious scent of cinnamon wafts straight over me and I step inside the warm, cozy house. It's much more welcoming

215

than mine. I respectfully take off my shoes and follow the trail of candles down the hall, awkwardly peering around the open kitchen door. I almost feel as though I'm intruding.

"Hello, Kenzie!" Nancy says. She looks surprised but pleased to see me when she glances over from the TV. She's sitting at the table with a steaming cup of coffee, her glasses perched on the bridge of her nose, her cheeks rosy as always.

"Hi," I say, stepping fully into the kitchen. I point behind me at nothing in particular. "They're just unhitching the trailer," I explain.

"Great!" She sets the coffee down and pushes herself up from the table with a beaming smile on her small face. "Can I get you anything? Something to drink?"

"Some water would be perfect right now," I say. My throat is still so dry that my voice sounds raspy, so I really could do with a drink. Nancy gently squeezes my elbow with her warm, frail hands as she brushes past me on her way to the refrigerator.

"I thought it was you," someone mumbles from behind me, and I crane my neck to find Dani padding into the kitchen. I'm still not entirely sure where I stand with her yet. She smiles at me in Spanish class now. Even says hello sometimes. But it's still nothing like the friendship we had before. "Did you have fun out on the boat?" she asks. She flops down onto one of the kitchen chairs and begins to gather her dark hair up into a ponytail, her gaze still fixated on me. I'm not sure if she's being passive-aggressive or friendly.

"It was great to see it back out on the water," I answer to play it safe. Fun? For the most part, yes. The rest of the time I was either nauseous or in tears.

"Right?" she agrees, and her eyes light up. She secures her

216

hair and then leans back against the chair, rolling her eyes. "I've always thought we should use it." As Nancy walks back over from the refrigerator and hands me a bottle of cool, fresh water, Dani looks up at her. "I think we're all going to take it out on Sunday, aren't we?"

"We sure are!" Nancy says.

There are footsteps in the hall as Jaden and Terry come inside to join us, chatting between themselves until they enter the kitchen. Nancy turns around to put the coffee on, and over her shoulder, she cheerfully asks, "Did you enjoy taking the boat out, Jaden?"

"Yeah," he says, but a moment later, he presses his lips into a small, closed smile and releases a long, slow sigh. "It's just weird, you know? I kept thinking it should have been Dad behind the wheel and not me."

A strangely long moment of silence follows. The only sound is the quiet whistle of the coffee machine as Terry slumps down into a chair at the table, directly opposite Dani, who stares blankly at her hands. Nancy frowns. I think it's the first time I've actually witnessed a glimmer of sadness, but I'm not too surprised by it. I would be naïve to believe that they *didn't* still have these moments where a brief reminder of what they have lost comes rushing back to them.

Jaden cracks his knuckles and the irritating sound is enough to break the silence. Exchanging a sideways glance with me, he gives me a knowing smile and then announces, "We'll be upstairs."

I follow him out of the kitchen and into the cinnamon-infused hall, sipping at my bottle of water all the way upstairs to his room. It's ridiculous how dry my mouth is, most likely from all the tears I've wept, so I gulp the water down until

217

it quenches my thirst. Once inside Jaden's room, he closes the door behind us and then scrambles to quickly arrange his unmade bed, though I remain rooted to the spot at the door, my eyes fixated on the floor. There are too many thoughts running through my head right now. Jaden turns back around and closes the distance between us, stopping directly in front of me. With deep concern, he quietly asks, "How are you feeling now?"

I drop my eyes to the floor again and give him a small shrug. I don't know how I feel, because right now, I am feeling too many things at once.

Jaden's piercing eyes study every part of my face for a while. It's as though he's seeing me for the very first time all over again, though right now I must look ten times worse. "I've never seen you like this," he says.

"I know. I'm sorry," I say, self-consciously turning my head to one side, away from him. "Close your eyes."

"Or," he says, placing his thumb gently to my chin and angling my face back toward him, "I can keep them open, because I get a nice view of these." He moves his thumb from my chin to my cheeks and brushes it over my exposed freckles the same way he did at homecoming. I don't know why he likes them, but I figure my freckles to him are the same as what his birthmark is to me. Something cute and unique, something special.

"A nice view?" I echo, reaching for his hand and moving it away from my cheeks. I raise an eyebrow and then grasp the collar of his flannel shirt, folding it down to reveal that oh-so-adorable tan birthmark on his neck. "Shouldn't I have a nice view too?"

"Oh God, no!" he whines, grabbing my hand and trying

218

his absolute best to stop me, but I keep on persisting, keep on messing with him until we end up wrestling with one another. I keep trying to pull back the collar of his shirt as he tries to push my hand away, but eventually he bursts into laughter. "Kenz! I swear!"

"Yes, Jaden?" I say, but I'm still fighting back against him, still pushing. He's grabbing at my hands and I'm grabbing at his, the pair of us laughing at how pathetic this is until we eventually collapse backward onto his bed. Jaden falls first, and I land on top of him, my chest against his. I might just be crushing him, but I don't care, because I seize the opportunity to finally reveal that birthmark of his. Quickly, I hook my fingers over the soft material of his shirt and pull it back, planting a kiss directly on the birthmark. "Cute, cute, cute," I murmur when I lean back to meet his eyes. I look down at him and we stare at one another, lips parted, breathing slowly.

"Same to you," he whispers. His strong arms snake their way around my body until I'm fully wrapped in his embrace. He pulls me down against him and touches his forehead to mine. The corner of his lips curve into a smirk, and I have no choice but to close the distance between us by leaning forward and pressing my mouth against his. Right now, all I want is him.

Silence pounds in my ears as I close my eyes, utterly enthralled by the movement of Jaden's lips against mine. He kisses with just the right balance of softness and roughness, and this time, I let him take full control while I sink into the spine-tingling sensation. His arms are still wrapped around my body, holding me down against him, and my hand is resting on his neck, still touching his birthmark. He doesn't seem to mind anymore, because he's too busy kissing me, and I'm too busy kissing him back.

He rolls us over so that's he's hovering over me now, pinning me between his body and the bed. One hand is holding himself up, the other is wrapped into my hair. Our movements become more eager, more urgent, more intense. After confiding in Jaden back on the boat, there's a sense of immense trust between us. He trusts me and I trust him, and our kiss is fueled by our emotions. It's both playful but meaningful, rough but caring. I can feel his gentle nature in the way his lips softly capture mine, but also his seductive-ness in the way that he takes my lower lip between his teeth. I don't remember him ever doing this before, but God, it's driving me crazy. It only makes me want more from him, more of him.

Reaching for the collar of his shirt again, I move my fingers to the top button, but I don't undo it yet. I'm not sure how far Jaden will want to go, so instead, I break the kiss, tearing my lips away from his. My eyes flicker open and so do Jaden's. Both of us are breathing heavily, his glossy, lustful eyes mirror mine, and he runs his tongue over his lower lip, surprised by my sudden disruption.

With a small smile, I glance down at the buttons of his shirt and then back up. "Okay?" I whisper.

Jaden nods once and leans back in, only this time, he presses his lips to the edge of my jaw. He plants kisses along my skin, fingers still tangled into my hair, while I undo the top button of his shirt, and the second, and the next. I slip my hand under-neath the material and run my fingertips across his chest. His skin is smooth but is radiating blazing heat, and I press my palm flat against his chest, feeling his heartbeat. It thumps erratically beneath my hand, but it reminds me that he's still here, still breathing after everything he has been through, the exact same way that I am. I thought Jaden was strong, but maybe I am too.

I pause for a minute as Jaden trails a path of kisses along my jawbone and down to my neck. My eyes flutter shut and I tilt my head to one side, slipping my hands back through his hair and enjoying the pleasure that spreads throughout my body in warm waves as his moist lips work against the soft skin of my neck. I shiver beneath him and drop my hand from his hair back down to his half-opened shirt, blindly fumbling around for the remaining buttons.

That's when I hear the click of the door as it opens.

Jaden's lips disappear from my skin at the exact same time as I release my hold on his shirt, and he pushes himself up and scrambles to his feet. Quickly, I sit up and automatically press my hand to my neck, where Jaden's kisses are still fresh.

Dani is standing at the door, looking both surprised and amused by the sight in front of her. "Oh God," she says, pulling a face. "Grosssss." She folds her arms across her chest and leans against the doorframe. "Grandma wanted me to let you guys know that there are fresh cookies downstairs, but I doubt you'll be interested. You seem a little ... well, busy."

"Thanks for fucking knocking," Jaden mutters as he rushes to do up every single one of the buttons I've just opened. His cheeks are flushed red the same way mine are, and he walks across the room toward Dani, pushing her out into the hall. "Get out of here, Dracula."

"Not cool," Dani says, pursing her lips and shaking her head back at him. She peers around his broad shoulders in

221

order to look at me, though there's a teasing glint to her eyes. I can't look at her, so I drop my gaze straight to my lap. This is embarrassing.

"I said *get out*," Jaden repeats more firmly this time, stepping in front of Dani to cut off her view of me. He gently pushes her back another step, and then he slams the door shut. As he turns back around to look at me with irritation written all over his features, he releases a groan and sits down on the edge of the bed next to me. "I'm sorry about that," he says, running a hand back through his hair. His cheeks are still tinted with a rose hue and the color deepens when I place my hand on his knee.

As I'm looking at him, I notice the photograph on the shelf behind his shoulder. It's the photograph of Jaden, Dani and their parents, Brad and Kate. The photo that was taken back when Dani's hair was still naturally blond and the same shade as Jaden's.

"Did Dani dye her hair to look more like your mom?"

"What?" Jaden follows my gaze to the frame behind him. He looks at it and then shrugs several seconds later. "She really misses her," he tells me, glancing back over. His cheeks are finally returning to their natural color. "She said she wanted to look in the mirror and see Mom, but she dyed her hair way too dark, and now she looks like Dracula." He laughs a little under his breath, and I figure it must be a running joke between them.

I nod to the photograph. There's an idea forming in my head and I'm not sure whether it's a good one or not, but at least I know that my intentions are. "Can … can you take the picture out of the frame?"

Jaden looks perplexed again, but he does as I ask anyway.

He stretches over his bed and swipes the frame off the shelf, then turns it over in his hands and removes the back. He pulls out the photograph and holds it up to me. "Why?"

"Because," I say, gently taking the photo and rising to my feet, "we're going shopping."

24

"You know, Kenz," Jaden murmurs, "when you started taking my shirt off, this wasn't exactly where I imagined the night going." He slides out of the passenger seat of Mom's Prius and shuts the door behind him, looking over the roof of the car at me. He purses his lips innocently, but I only roll my eyes and turn away from him before he can see me blush.

It's dark out and we're standing in the parking lot of Walgreens. Admittedly, it's not where I expected the night to go either, but when an idea like this hits, I don't have a choice other than to follow through with it. It could backfire entirely and may not be appreciated the way I'm hoping for, but I feel as though it's at least worth a shot. I could do with something to focus on right now.

I lock up and walk around the front of the car to meet Jaden, and in his hand he's holding the photograph from his room, the one of him and his family. I'm grateful that he was willing to not only take it out of its frame, but to also take it out of the house and all the way to Walgreens, of all places.

"It's not what I had in mind either," I admit, glancing sideways at him. I slide my hand down his arm and interlock my fingers around his as we head across the small lot toward the entrance. "But I think Dani will thank us for this."

It's quiet at this time of night and it should be closing up in an hour or so, so the store is relatively empty when we get inside. There aren't many people shopping at a drugstore at this time on a Thursday night. Windsor may be small, but there *are* better things to do than this.

"She sure as hell better thank us," Jaden grumbles. I can tell he's irritated, but he's being playful about it, which I appreciate. He traces small circles on the back of my hand with his thumb as I pull him along by my side, and he nudges his shoulder into mine to get my attention. When I glance over at him, he teasingly narrows his eyes and adds, "Especially since I'm giving up kissing *you* for this."

"We have all night," I remind him. It's just before 9PM, so we do have a couple hours before I head home. There's still plenty of time to kiss him tonight, and tomorrow, and the day after that. "Up here," I say, and speed up my pace toward the beauty aisles. Jaden reluctantly follows me, mostly because he doesn't have a choice. With our hands interlocked, I'm pretty much dragging him with me all the way down one of the aisles until I come to an abrupt halt in front of the shelves full of hair dye. "Can I see that?" I nod to the photo in Jaden's hand.

"I really don't think you're gonna find the right shade," he says as he passes it to me. He seems doubtful as I step forward to examine the large selection of hair dyes, releasing my hold on his hand. He remains behind me, heaving a sigh. "If the right one existed, Dani would have found it by now."

I glance over my shoulder at him. "But has she tried mixing shades?"

"I don't know. You can do that?"

Laughing, I turn back to the shelves. Under the store's fluorescent lighting, I hold the photograph up slightly and squint at Kate's hair. She was a natural dark, warm brunette. Exactly like chocolate. At the moment, Dani is too dark, more of a soft black than a dark, rich brunette. I kneel down on the floor in front of the shelves and hold the photograph up against all of the different shades in front of me. There's not a shade here that's identical to Kate's shade. After five minutes of searching and comparing, I finally settle on a natural, soft black shade and a warm, dark brown shade. Mixed together, I'm pretty sure they'd create a shade that comes as close to Kate's as possible. I can only hope that Dani will be willing to give it a shot.

"These ones," I announce, straightening up and holding out the two boxes of different hair dyes to show Jaden. He looks extremely bored by this point, and with his arms folded across his chest as he leans back against the shelves of shampoo, he quickly glances at the boxes and nods.

"Can we please go now?" he says, slipping his arm around my shoulders. He pulls me in close and nuzzles his face into my hair, pressing his lips to my temple. "Buying hair dye for my sister isn't exactly my favorite thing to do, you know."

"We're going," I reassure him, shrugging his arm off me. I carefully pass him back the photograph, relieved that I haven't creased it.

With the boxes of hair dye in my hands, we make our way back down the aisle toward the cash registers, but when we reach the end of the aisle we abruptly come to a stop. So does the person in front of us, and when I glance up, my shoulders sink.

"Darren?" I blink at him in surprise. I do bump into him occasionally, but never as frequently as I have these past few weeks. It's easy to assume that he's stalking me somehow, but I need to remind myself that he's not. It's Windsor, after all. Every third person I pass is someone I know. "What are you doing here?"

"Grabbing some eye drops." Darren holds up the small box as proof. He seems surprised to see me too and, true to his word, his eyes do seem a little red and irritated. "My eyes are dry as hell."

"What are you doing back in town, though?" I ask. Darren never used to come home this often, and I never could blame him. I wouldn't either. "Shouldn't you be back in your dorm chugging beer or something?"

Darren laughs as he rubs at his left eye. "I'm trying to come home more often," he says. "Mom misses me, so I'm trying to keep her happy, and my classes tomorrow got canceled, so here I am. Home again." Shrugging, he rolls his eyes and then seems to finally notice Jaden for the first time. His smile falters a little as his brown eyes study Jaden, looking him up and down slowly until he forces a tiny smile back onto his face. "Jaden Hunter, right?"

"Right," Jaden says, shifting his footing. He looks uncomfortable and it is clear he is finding this awkward. He knows that Darren is my ex.

Darren gives him another quite obvious once-over. His eyes sharpen with something like confusion as he analyzes Jaden, and he glances between the two of us for a few seconds. I can almost see the gears in his mind turning as he pieces together the obvious. The muscle in his jaw twitches as he looks me in the eye. "Did you get the flowers that I left for you?"

"Yes," I tell him, stiffly. I appreciate the fact that he is trying, and the flowers were a sweet gesture, but I just wish he would stop putting in the effort. He is wasting his time, and the harder he tries, the more I want to push him away. "They were nice. But you should really stop doing stuff like that."

"I don't mind. You're welcome," he says. His lips curve into a smile to reveal the dimple in his cheek. With great emphasis, he glances at the watch on his wrist. He doesn't want to stick around to chat, and neither do I. "Well, I guess I'll see you around, Kenz."

I give him a small farewell smile back as he brushes past me. I hate that he just called me *Kenz,* and I already know for a fact that Jaden has noticed too, because as soon as Darren is out of earshot, he steps around in front of me looking distinctly perplexed. "He sent you flowers?" he demands.

"Last weekend before the dance," I admit, shrugging. I don't really think it's that big a deal. Darren started asking me to take him back long before Jaden and I started talking again, so it's not anything new. However, the flicker of anger that crosses Jaden's face tells me that he disagrees, so I quickly add, "But it doesn't matter, because I'm not really much of a flowers type of girl, anyway." To lighten the mood, I force out, "He should have just sent me a box of Hershey's."

Jaden doesn't even so much as crack a smile as we begin to walk, falling into place by my side. "Is he bothering you?"

I roll my eyes. "I can handle him, Jaden," I tell him firmly. It's actually pretty attractive that Jaden is trying to look out for me, but Darren really isn't a problem.

Jaden remains silent all the way to the cash registers. He doesn't say anything more on the matter, but he has a face like thunder. We pay for the boxes of hair dye, have them bagged up, then leave the store in silence. He kicks at the ground as we cross the parking lot to the car and I watch him, surprised by his reaction. I try to figure out why he's suddenly gone so quiet. Jealousy, maybe? I don't know why he's so irritated, but I do know that he has nothing to be jealous about. He was the one I was kissing thirty minutes ago, not Darren.

"How long left?" Dani asks.

She's sitting on the toilet seat, legs crossed, hands in her lap. There's a towel draped around her shoulders and a shower cap on her head. Underneath it, her hair is gathered into a damp, sticky mound. Nancy and Terry's bathroom reeks of chemicals, but it doesn't smell as strong as it did when we first started.

I'm perched on the edge of the bathtub. I reach for my phone and check the timer that's running. "Five minutes," I tell her.

Dani was reluctant at first. After the surprise of having me thrust two boxes of hair dye in front of her wore off, she was skeptical that mixing the two shades I'd chosen wouldn't get her any closer to the color that her mom was. It did take some convincing before she agreed to let me potentially ruin her hair, and even now she still has doubts. "You really think this will work?"

I set my phone back down on the sink's counter and give her a shrug, though there's a small smile on my face. "It's worth a shot, isn't it?"

I'm glad she agreed to let me do this. Sitting here together, chatting casually while the dye in her hair develops reminds me of how we used to be last summer. We would often hang out, and when we did we were always gossiping, always laughing. Being friends with Dani was something that filled the void that Grace left. Being friends with Dani allowed me to see what life with a sister would have been like, and I've missed these kind of nights with her.

"Thanks for this, Kenzie," Dani says after a moment. She reaches up for the towel around her neck and pulls it closer around her. She looks ridiculous right now, but I'm just glad she feels comfortable enough to even do this with me. A smile full of gratitude lights up her face but her bright, blue eyes grow sad. "I've tried so many different shades, but they're always too dark," she admits. "I never thought about mixing colors, so hopefully this will work."

"If it doesn't," I begin slowly, my voice cautious, "then you could always just go back to being you. I don't think your mom would mind."

Dani's gaze meets mine as she thinks about my words. She seems to subconsciously chew on the inside of her cheek at the same time and I'm surprised by the fact that she appears to never have considered it before. She doesn't get the chance to answer me either, because Jaden appears at the door.

"God, you look horrific," he tells Dani. I roll my eyes at him. He was in the kitchen eating the cookies Nancy made and then he went upstairs to his room to watch TV, but it seems he's growing impatient now. I've forgotten how it feels to have to balance out my time between the pair of them.

"Shut up," Dani says. She stretches over to grab a towel from the rack so she can whip him with it, but he successfully dodges the attack.

"How much longer are you guys going to be?" he asks,

carefully traversing the bathroom floor and all of the newspapers that cover it. He sits down on the edge of the bathtub next to me and, on purpose or by accident, places his hand on top of mine as we grip the edge.

"A couple minutes," I tell him. The closer the time to rinse out Dani's hair gets, the more nervous I begin to feel. This is my idea, so if it backfires then I'll be the one to blame. I really hope the color turns out the way I'm praying it will.

Dani, however, has something on her mind other than her hair. She gently narrows her eyes and studies Jaden's hand on top of mine on the edge of the tub. She arches a brow and then glances between the two of us. A smirk toys at the corners of her lips. "So, just in case the two of you making out earlier wasn't already enough evidence, are you guys, like, a thing now?"

Is it obvious? Do we look like we're a thing? I instantly pull my hand free from beneath Jaden's and turn my face away, hiding my blushing cheeks. I really don't know what to tell her, even though I'm pretty sure I *do* know what the answer is. I like to hope Jaden and I *are* something, and luckily, he's the one to muster up a reply.

"I think so," he says, but there's a tinge of uncertainty in his words. He casts me a sideways glance, eyes glossy, waiting patiently for my agreement. My cheeks already feel hot again, and I'm unable to truly meet either of their gazes, so I just nod quickly at the floor. *Yes,* I think. *We* are *a thing.*

And then, because I'm so desperate to change the subject, I quickly blurt out, "Will's throwing a party on the fifteenth. You're both invited."

"Me?" Dani says, blinking a few times. It's sad, really. A lot of people would have invited Dani to a lot of places a year ago.

"Yeah. Will personally reminded me to ask you, so what do you say?"

"Count me in," Jaden says from beside me. He leans forward and cocks his head to one side, exchanging a glance with Dani. "What about you, Dracula? You haven't been to a party in forever. You should come."

Dani frowns as though she's fighting a mental battle with herself. She spends a few seconds pulling a face and then finally heaves a sigh. "Okay, I'll come. Just as long as it's not a pity invite."

As soon as the words leave her mouth, the timer that's been running on my phone rings out around the bathroom. I rise to my feet and grab it, switching it off and turning back around to look at Dani with nervous anticipation. She looks equally anxious, and she stands up, stretches her legs, and huddles over the sink. I get the water running and give it a second to heat up.

"Kenzie, I swear to God, I'm trusting you ..." she mumbles, hugging the towel tighter around her shoulders as she bends down and lowers her head to the edge of the sink. "If this turns out—I don't know—blue or something, then I'm going back to ignoring you."

"It'll be fine!" I promise her with a laugh, but I'm not all that confident. The water is warm when I stick my hand under it, so I begin to slowly massage my hands through Dani's hair, rinsing out all of the hair dye. The stream of water turns black as I do so, and I can only continue to pray that Dani's hair will now be as close to her mom's shade as possible.

"I still can't believe my night has turned into *this*," Jaden complains as he hovers behind me. He leans in closer and slips his hands around my waist from behind, his chin resting

232

on my shoulder and his body hugged tight against mine as he watches me rinse Dani's hair. I like that I'm spending time with both of them together, and I find myself laughing out loud when Jaden says, "I'm literally standing here watching the girl I like dunk my sister's face into a sink."

25

It's just after 6:30PM on Sunday. I'm sitting in the living room with Dad, not too long home from my shift at work, trying to pay attention to the Broncos game on TV, but I'm unable to focus. I'm too nervous. This morning, Mom insisted that I invite Jaden over for dinner. It's nothing special, just burgers and fries, but she was adamant that he joined us. She wanted to meet him again because it's been so long since the last time Jaden met my parents. I did put up a fight for a mere five minutes or so, but eventually I had no choice but to give in. Usually, I don't like having friends over. I can't remember the last time I actually hung out with Will and Holden here at my place, mostly because I'm afraid Mom will end up drunk. I couldn't handle that embarrass-ment, and if I hadn't already told Jaden the truth, then I definitely wouldn't have given in so easily. But although I don't have anything to hide anymore, I still feel anxious as I wait for him to arrive.

I glance sideways at Dad. He's next to me on the couch,

eyes glued to the TV, totally invested in the game. He's not accepting any emergency calls today, so without the stress of work looming over him he looks more relaxed than usual. "Can you do me a favor?"

Dad looks over at me only briefly before he turns his eyes back to the game. "Yes, Kenzie, I promise I won't tell your boyfriend that you still sleep with Mr. Cuddles the bear," he says with a quick roll of his eyes.

"*I don't!*" I throw my hands up in frustration, my tone indignant.

Dad chuckles under his breath, and as the game goes to a commercial break, he turns his neck to look back at me again, this time more solemnly. "What's the favor?"

"Please don't ask Jaden how he's doing," I tell him, and my voice sounds almost pleading, because I know just how much Jaden would loathe those sympathetic, pitying questions. "Just ask him normal questions. Talk about football or something. He's on the team, remember? And they won the game against Grand Junction on Friday, so ask him about that."

"Football, you say?" Dad takes a sip of the beer in his hand and nods. "I'll give it a go!"

Mom walks into the living room, heaving a sigh and collapsing onto the couch opposite Dad and me. She's been in the kitchen preparing dinner, but she seems to have also taken the time to dress up nice. She's changed into a fresh pair of pants and a new beige blouse. She's left her hair down and loosely curled it at the ends, and she's even added some silver jewelry. It's great to see her make an effort for once.

"You look nice," Dad comments, nodding across the room at her. "By the way, we're on strict orders not to talk about Mr. Cuddles."

235

"Oh, really?" Mom says, shifting her gaze to me. Her smile is teasing. "Jaden can't know about Mr. Cuddles?"

"Oh my God. Stop!" I pull out the cushion from behind me and toss it across the room at her, then throw my head back and cover my face with my hands. If they embarrass me tonight in front of Jaden, I don't think I'll ever talk to them again. They didn't embarrass me last time.

"Here comes a car!" Dad announces, leaning forward on the couch and straining his neck to peer out of the living room window.

My heartbeat rockets and I quickly lean forward too, looking out the window onto our quiet cul-de-sac as a car rolls down the street. Of course it's Jaden. My palms feel sweaty as the black Corolla slows to a stop outside of our house, pulling up behind Mom's car. It's still light out and I can see Jaden in the driver's seat, though he doesn't step out of the car immediately. Instead, he spends a minute or so touching up his hair and spraying cologne, and I watch him all the while, smiling at how adorable he is. He's met my parents before, so I can only hope he isn't as nervous as I am. Luckily, he looks confident when he gets out of the car and makes his way up our footpath.

"Time to scatter!" Dad says, ducking away from the window and pushing himself up from the couch. Taking his beer with him, he shifts around the coffee table toward Mom and gently reaches for her hand, pulling her to her feet. Mom's expression is teasing as the two of them head for the door, and Dad says over his shoulder, "We'll be hiding in the kitchen."

As they disappear out of sight, I quickly give myself a once-over in the huge mirror that's hanging on the wall behind me. I run my fingers through the ends of my hair, check the lipstick on my lips hasn't smudged, and then rush out into the hall, headed for the front door. I don't want Jaden to have to knock, because that feels too formal, so I abruptly swing the door open.

Jaden is only a few steps away from reaching the porch and his face lights up with a smile when he sees me. He's wearing a pair of black jeans that *don't* have rips in them and a white shirt, though it's not buttoned all the way up. The heavier top half of his hair is perfectly gelled and styled into a slight quiff again, and he stops directly in front of me on the porch, blue eyes capturing mine. "Hey, Kenz."

"You know you didn't have to wear a shirt," I point out. I do like the fact that it's clear he has made an effort for meeting my parents tonight, but he really didn't have to.

"I wanted to look respectable," Jaden says. He puffs out his chest and pretends to smooth out the creases on his shirt, then exhales, allowing his shoulders to slump back down again. "Besides," he whispers as he takes a step closer, smoldering his eyes at me, "you'll get to tear it off me later."

My knees feel weak, but I quickly swat him away with my hand. "Jaden!" I don't remember him being as confident as this a year ago. He was always more reserved before, or at least more subtle, but I have to remind myself of what he told me not too long ago, about not wasting time. If there's something on his mind, he'll say it. If there's something he wants to do, he'll do it. However, there are some exceptions, and I'm quick to remind him by saying, "*Please* don't repeat that in front of my dad."

"Repeat what?" Dad echoes, and I instantly flinch, spinning my head around to look at him. He walks down the hall toward us, gesturing us inside. Thankfully, he just cracks a grin. "Stop hovering by the door and come on in!"

I step back and pull the door open wider, encouraging Jaden to come into the house. He steps in, flashing Dad his best smile. It's more charming than his usual playful, crooked one, and I like it just as much, if not more.

"Hello, Jaden," Dad says. The tone of his voice is slightly off when he's trying too hard to play it cool. He steps forward to shake Jaden's hand. "It's great to meet you." Jokingly, he adds, "Again."

Jaden laughs and firmly shakes Dad's extended hand. "You too, Mr. Rivers."

"It's just Howard," Dad tells him, patting him on the shoulder. "Now I hope you're hungry, because the food is ready." With his hand still on Jaden's shoulder, he guides him down the hall, leaving me to trail along behind them both. Jaden doesn't seem to notice Grace's frame as he passes the hall table, but I'm not surprised. Most people never do.

In the kitchen, the table is set with four placemats and Mom is drifting between counter, trying to dish up the food. When the three of us walk in, she takes a minute to pause and turn around, plastering a wide smile onto her face. Her gaze falls on Jaden. "Hello!" she says. "Isn't it nice to have you back here again?"

I'm quick to notice that in the past few minutes she's poured herself a glass of wine, which sits on the counter behind her. It's unsurprising. This week has been rough, and now she's pouring glasses out of habit rather than for comfort, but I'm not going to point this out. She seems relatively happy today, so I don't expect her to have any breakdowns tonight.

"Yeah," Jaden agrees with a nod. Although he is smiling, I

do catch his eyes move and I realize he's spotted the glass of wine too. "Thank you for having me."

"Our pleasure," Mom says. "Now have a seat!"

Jaden glances sideways at me and I reach for the cuff of his sleeve, brushing my thumb over the warm skin of the back of his hand. Now that he's here, blue eyes and bright smile and all, I don't feel as nervous as I did before; however, I can't help but be aware of that damn glass of wine. It's going to irritate me for the rest of the evening, but for now I push it to the back of my mind and try my hardest to ignore it as I lead Jaden over to the table.

"You're sitting next to me." I wink as I run the tips of my fingers under the sleeve of Jaden's shirt and over his wrist, batting my eyelashes at him. I slide down into my usual seat and pull him into the one next to me, touching my knee to his under the table. "Aren't you lucky?"

Jaden's grin widens. He scoots his chair closer to the table, places his hand on my knee, and mouths, "*Yes.*"

"So," Dad says, walking over to the table with plates in his hands as he helps Mom dish up the food. They're loaded with fries and huge homemade burgers overflowing with fillings—Mom's signature meal—and Dad sets the plates down in front of Jaden and me. "I hear you guys won the game on Friday night."

"Yeah, we did," Jaden tells him, his hand still on my knee beneath the table. "We were playing Grand Junction, and they didn't stand a chance."

Dad returns to the table again, this time with his and Mom's plates, and he sinks down into the chair opposite me. "Are you planning on playing college football?"

"No," Jaden answers, shaking his head. With a small shrug

he admits, "I'm not that serious about it. I just love tackling people."

Mom joins us at the table then and, of course, she carries with her the freshly poured glass of wine. She sits down on the seat next to Dad and places the glass on the table, though she doesn't let go of it. It's as though she's afraid it'll disappear out of her sight. "Tackling people? Should I be worried?"

I'm watching Jaden out of the corner of my eye. He quickly shakes his head and laughs again. "No, it's not like that. I love tackling people, not hurting them. It's just a great stress-reliever."

Mom nods in agreement. "I can imagine," she says. "Gotta let off some steam somehow." Her grip on the glass tightens as she raises it to her lips and takes a sip. Most people wouldn't even notice, let alone give it a second thought, but I do. And Dad does. And I think Jaden does. And none of us can do anything but frown. I'm relieved when Mom sets the glass back down again and smiles, glancing around the table at the three of us. "Anyway, eat up!"

Jaden's touch on my knee disappears as he straightens up and reaches for his cutlery. I don't like having him right next to me but not feeling his body against mine, so I scoot my chair a few inches closer to his and place my hand on his thigh. With a fry in his mouth, he tilts his head down and studies my expression out of the corner of his eye, but I only smirk down at my food. I don't move my hand, and it feels secret and exciting with my parents sitting directly opposite us.

"So, which colleges are you thinking of applying to, Jaden?" Dad asks, and it kicks off an entire discussion about the colleges

Jaden has already applied to and the ones he's thinking of applying to, and of course, my parents subtly reminding me that I still need to decide.

Even with Jaden here, I dig into my food. Life is too short to worry about getting sauce on the side of my mouth in front of the boy I like, though I don't focus on Jaden all that much, because I'm concentrating on monitoring Mom's wine consumption throughout dinner. I keep witnessing her take sip after sip, and halfway through eating she rises from the table to fetch what she says is more salt. Only she brings back more than just the salt to the table; she brings back the bottle of wine and fills up her empty glass.

"Kenzie said the two of you took your father's boat out on the lake yesterday," Dad says, glancing up from his plate to look at Jaden with wary eyes. I wish Dad knew that he doesn't have to be cautious around Jaden, or watch his words, or tiptoe around subjects.

Jaden stops eating, swallows and then nods back across the table to Dad. "Yeah, we did. It had been sitting in the corner of the driveway for way too long, and Kenzie reminded me that my parents would have wanted us to use it."

Dad's eyes widen slightly in surprise. I don't know why, but when he looks at me, I'm certain there's pride flickering across his eyes. I wish I could offer my parents advice the way I can offer it to Jaden. "She did, did she?"

"Yeah," Jaden says. Lips curving into a smile, he turns his head to look at me while he drops one hand below the table. A moment later, I feel his hand on my leg, running from my knee to my thigh. "Thanks, Kenz," he says, and then fixates his eyes back on my parents, though his hand remains where it is.

241

Both Mom and Dad are watching us closely, and Mom pushes her cleared plate away from her so that she can rest her elbows on the table. The glass of wine is in her hands, hovering by her lips, half empty already.

"I'm trying to do things my parents would want me to do," Jaden admits quietly, slowly rubbing his hand over my thigh in circles. "They'd want me to be nice to people. They'd want me to do well in school. They'd want me to look out for my sister. They'd want me to treat Kenzie right. They'd want me to live my life. They'd want me to be happy." Jaden pauses, leaving silence to fill the air as he glances back and forth between Mom and Dad. His gaze is soft, but somehow there's an intensity to it that I can't quite figure out, and it finally comes to rest on Mom. Jaden meets her eyes, and he parts his lips and asks, "The people we lose in life wouldn't want us to be *unhappy*, would they?"

Mom leans back against her chair, presses the glass of wine to her lips and exchanges a knowing glance with Dad. A new panic fills me and I try to catch Jaden's eye, but he won't look at me. I need him to stop, because whether he knows it or not, his words make sense to us too.

"No," Dad finally answers, tearing his eyes away from Mom so that he can look back at Jaden. "They wouldn't," he agrees, though he mumbles his words.

Mom looks on edge now and she tilts the glass of wine against her lips again, promptly finishing the glass off with one gulp. Exhaling, she shakes her head, clearly affected by Jaden's words. Grace wouldn't want *us* to be unhappy, and she knows that.

Already two glasses of wine down, Mom's mood has plummeted quickly. She's no longer as bubbly and upbeat as she was when Jaden first arrived, and over the course of dinner, she's gradually become more morose. But she clearly can't see the difference, because she roughly sets the empty glass down on the table in front of her and snatches the bottle of wine. With her face set in a scowl, she unscrews the cap and begins to pour. We all watch. None of us dare to say a word, and I am grateful when Jaden clears his throat and continues talking. "So yeah," he says with a small shrug, as though he's struggled to articulate what he means. "It's not to say I don't miss them. I miss them *so* much. Every day. But there's no point wasting my life being unhappy, because what good would that do? My parents wouldn't want me to sit around moping, like Grace wouldn't want you to sit around drinki—" He immediately cuts himself off and turns pale with horror.

My mouth falls open in disbelief. Mom releases a sharp gasp as her eyes go wild, and she looks as stunned as I do, if not more. Furious, I grab Jaden's hand and throw it off my thigh. My chair loudly screeches against the kitchen flooring when I abruptly angle myself to face him, everything inside of me erupting with rage. I told Jaden the truth because I trusted him, and now he has only gone and put his foot in it. I grit my teeth and hiss, "What the *hell?*"

"Excuse me?" Dad says through stiff lips, his voice low and rumbling. Almost in slow motion, he presses his hands down flat against the table and pushes himself up to his feet, rising tall until he towers over all of us. He steps closer to Mom, protecting her behind his height as her lips begin to tremble.

Jaden's expression twists with panic as he tilts his chin up to look at Dad. He is silent for a second, and then he looks back over to me. Suddenly, there is guilt in his cool blue eyes, but he doesn't stare at me for too long, because his gaze flickers back over to Mom. "I'm ... I'm sorry, Mrs. Rivers. I really didn't mean to say that. Kenzie told me," he stutters, pointing to the bottle of wine on the table in front of her. I feel paralyzed in my seat as I watch him push his chair back and stand. He is digging himself into an even bigger hole, and now he is dragging me down with him. The look of betrayal my parents give me is hard to ignore. Jaden presses his hands to the edge of the table and clears his throat. Out of the corner of his eye, he glances down at me in panic once more, then back to Mom. "She ... she's just worried about you. And that wine isn't going to make you feel better. You might think that it does, but I don't think ... " He is stumbling all over his own words, and despite his obvious horrified alarm, I am furious at him right now. *What the hell is he thinking?* He pauses to catch his breath and he shakes his head, almost as though he can't believe what he has just said. "God, I'm so sorry, I—"

Mom lets out a muffled sob and bursts into tears, and that's all it takes for the rage in me to explode. I jump to my feet, knocking over my chair, and push my hands hard into Jaden's chest, shoving him back a few steps. "LEAVE!" I scream. My voice rings out around the entire house and my cheeks are burning red with anger. My body is trembling.

Jaden's eyes meet mine, exasperated. Quickly, he tries to reach for my wrist, but I push him away again. "Kenz—"

"Leave, Jaden!" I yell, pointing toward the front door. I'm breathing heavily now. I don't lose my temper often and it's rare that I'll raise my voice, but he's crossed the line here. No one gets to talk down to my mom like that. No one gets to reduce my mom to tears. Jaden is no exception, no matter how badly I am falling for him.

When Jaden still doesn't budge, Dad moves around the

kitchen table and grabs him by the shoulder, his features hard and unforgiving. He casts a glance back over his shoulder at Mom as she is breaking down, and then he turns back to Jaden. "I need you to leave."

Jaden surrenders then. He holds up his hands and meets Dad's blazing eyes, slowly nodding once as he backs up a step, retreating toward the hall, realizing that he has done wrong. All I can hear is the sound of Mom crying behind me and the painful throbbing of my pulse, and my glare only continues to sharpen the longer Jaden is in my sight.

He tilts his head down toward the floor as he turns away from us, and his broad shoulders are slumped low as we watch him walk down our hall toward the front door. He pulls it open slowly and then freezes, angling his jaw down toward the small hall table. The atmosphere is thick with tension, and I know what he is looking at. He has spotted Grace's frame. Carefully, he lifts his hand and lightly brushes his fingertips over the glass, over her name behind it.

Jaden glances back at me. The guilt is almost dripping from him now and I can see that he's sorry; it's written all over his features, it's in his eyes. But it's too late for apologies, because I don't know how I will forgive him for this.

26

I am dreading school today. I'm sitting at my dressing table, mindlessly brushing my hair, still half-asleep. There are several text messages from Jaden on my phone that I have yet to open. But while it's easy to ignore his messages, it's a lot harder to dodge Jaden in real life.

It's just before 7:30AM, and Will should be outside waiting for me soon. Resigned to my fate, I grab my bag and my Physics textbook, then head downstairs feeling bleary-eyed. Usually, the house is pretty quiet in the mornings. Dad's at work and Mom sleeps in a lot. Today, however, there isn't the usual silence. I'm halfway down the stairs when I hear the clink of a bottle echoing from the kitchen. I immediately pause, listening.

Another clink.

I stand there, stuck in limbo on the staircase as disappointment floods through me. Mom will be feeling guilty this morning whenever she thinks about Grace, which only gives her another excuse to pour herself a glass or four. And that's exactly what she's doing now: pouring wine.

Hugging my textbook closer to my chest, I force myself to continue downstairs and toward the kitchen. I can see Mom already, hovering in front of the counter with her back to me. I creep forward, mentally preparing myself to deal with her this early in the morning, when I notice Dad sitting at the kitchen table.

"Good morning, Kenzie," he says, glancing over to me. He's hunched over an untouched cup of coffee and is twiddling his thumbs. He should be at work by now. And the last I knew, *our* pipes were fine.

Mom looks at me over her shoulder. Although she looks deflated, there's a sense of determination in her eyes, a strength that I haven't ever seen before. Her thin lips form a small smile and I realize then that there's a collection of different bottles of wine on the counter in front of her. There's a bottle already in her hand, opened, and she turns her attention back to it. Then, she leans over and promptly pours the entire bottle of wine down our sink.

"What's going on?"

Dad straightens up in his chair and his eyes meet mine. "Jaden was out of line."

"But he was right," Mom finishes for him without missing a beat, spinning around to face me. She has the now empty bottle in her hand, and she drops her eyes to study it, as though now she's only seeing it for the first time. "What he said is what I needed to hear," she murmurs, gaze still lowered. "I didn't like it, but it was the truth. I mean, look at this!" She motions to the bottles behind her and shakes her head, the self-defeat evident in her voice. "What would

Grace say?" For once, she says her name without flinching. She grabs another bottle, unscrews the cap, and pours that down the drain too.

I blink at her in disbelief as she *willingly* gets rid of the one thing that has been her crutch for the past four years. I try to process what I'm seeing, but nothing is registering.

Mom sets the two empty bottles down on the counter at the other side of the sink, and then leans back over to grab a third bottle, twisting its cap off. "I didn't realize what I've been doing all these years," she admits. Still, she pauses with the opened bottle of wine in her hand for a few seconds before she forces herself to pour its contents out. "Neither of you said anything," she murmurs, placing the empty bottle down. She leans back against the counter and looks at Dad and me. That strength in her eyes is quickly replaced with a flash of hurt. "Why didn't you say anything?"

I exchange a glance with Dad, and he gives me a small nod, encouraging me to answer her. But I don't have an answer. Not really. It was always easier *not* to say anything. I remain silent as I really try to think about the reason why I never said the words Jaden said last night, why I never told her that the wine wasn't helping her, that it was unfair of her to send me out to buy it, that Grace wouldn't want this for her.

"Because you're my mom," I say, finally. This isn't what I expected to wake up to, but I'm glad that it is. "I didn't want to upset you, or argue with you, or make you feel even worse. And I guess we never wanted to admit that it was an actual problem."

Mom's eyes mirror mine and she studies my expression, analyzing every single one of my features. Slowly, the corners of her eyes begin to crinkle with both pain and love all at the same time, and she nods as though in acceptance. She shifts her gaze to Dad. "And you?"

"I didn't say anything," Dad begins, eyes locked on Mom, "because I understood. I couldn't blame you."

The tiny smile Mom gives Dad is full of sadness, but then she turns back to the counter and scoops up the five empty bottles of wine into her arms. "No more drinking," she announces with fragile determination. She moves across the kitchen and dumps the bottles by the back door. "I'd like a drink right now, but it looks like we don't have any wine left in this house anymore," she says. She walks over to Dad and places her hand on his shoulder, looking down at him. "I will try this on my own for now, but if it becomes too difficult, I will get help. Okay?"

I hear the honking of Will's Jeep out front, but I don't care. Overwhelmed by a mixture of emotions, from pride to relief to joy, I dump my bag and my textbook down onto the table next to Dad and throw myself at Mom. Wrapping my arms around her, I pull her against me and hug her tight. I didn't realize how badly I wanted to hear her say these things until now. She buries her face into my hair and hugs me back even tighter as though she's afraid to let go, and she whispers, "Sometimes I forget that I'm still lucky enough to be a mom."

During Physics, I find it impossible to concentrate. I try, I really do. But no matter how hard I try to focus my full attention on Mr. Acker as he discusses vectors, my mind always wonders elsewhere within a matter of seconds. I'm thinking about Mom, hoping she's managing on her own. I'm also thinking about Jaden. I have yet to see him, but it's only first period. I'm still angry, but now it feels like it's more out of a sense of hurt pride. His truthful words were harsh but necessary, and they seem to have gotten the message across to Mom that she has been grieving the wrong way for four years now. But Jaden still did not have the right to talk to my mom the way he did. He didn't have the right to get involved. It could have backfired. Luckily for him, it didn't. So I forgive him, but not entirely.

I glance sideways to Kailee at the desk next to me. Her elbow is propped up on the desk, her chin is rested in her hand, her face blank as she stares at nothing in particular. I reach for my notebook and tear off a small section of a page, popping the lid off my pen and scribbling down a quick message.

Party at Will's on the 15th. By the way, I'm sort of, kinda, maybe dating Jaden Hunter again. I'll fill you in at lunch!

I steal a glance up at Mr. Acker to double-check that he isn't looking, and when he turns his back on the class to point to the screen, I lean over the aisle and set the piece of scrap paper down on Kailee's desk. She jumps at the movement and her hand falls to her chest, suggesting that I've given her a heart attack. We exchange a grin and then she picks up the note, holding it up in front of her face and squinting at my seemingly illegible handwriting. Seconds pass before she fires her wide-eyed gaze back over to me. Her jaw hangs open.

"*I knew it!*" she mouths, and I roll my eyes, biting back a smile. I can't gush about Jaden to Holden and Will, and it would be too awkward to talk about Jaden with Dani, so I ought to fill Kailee and Jess in on all of my news from the past few weeks. There's a lot to tell, and I *want* to tell it.

I shift my gaze from Kailee's surprised excitement to Will. He's busy listening to Mr. Acker and taking notes, and I'm just about to toss my eraser at him when the bell rings out. The abruptness of it startles me and I close my books, getting to my feet.

Almost immediately, Kailee steps in front of me. There's a shine to her eyes as she tells me, "I always wondered if you guys would ever get back together!"

I laugh and push my chair in. "We're not really *together*," I admit with a small shrug. It almost feels strange talking about Jaden and me so casually like this again after so long. I used to talk about Jaden all the time, most likely to the point where I would frustrate people, but I couldn't help myself back then. "I'll tell you about it later, okay?"

"Okay. I gotta tell Jess," Kailee says, then grits her teeth and releases a small squeal under her breath. I can always count on Kailee to get excited for me. "See you at lunch, Kenzie!"

She heads for the door, following the rest of the class out into the bustling hallways, throwing me a tiny wave before she disappears. A smile has taken over my lips and it won't let go. Seeing Kailee so excited has massively boosted my mood. Rather than being full of dread and anger, I'm feeling hopeful. Hopeful that Mom will be okay, hopeful that Jaden and me will be just fine.

"I don't have all day, you know," Will remarks playfully, grabbing my attention. He's standing by his desk, textbook against his chest, his hair in his eyes as he waits for me. The class has emptied out, and we're the only two people left besides one other guy who is chatting to Mr. Acker.

"Sorry," I apologize. He looks at me with suspicion, and all I can tell him is, "I'm a little distracted today."

"Yeah, I can tell," he says. Side by side, we make for the

251

door and join the flow of students in the hallways, forced to raise our voices. "What's up?"

"Uh, nothing really," I lie. *Such an understatement.* But Will doesn't know about Mom's growing alcohol consumption, so I know I can't tell him about what happened last night with Jaden. That's why I quickly change the subject. "Jaden and Dani are coming to your party, by the way," I inform him. I keep half of my attention on Will and the other half focused on keeping an eye out for Jaden. I'm nervous about seeing him again.

"Really? Dani said she'd come?" Will asks, surprised. He looks pleased when I nod. "That's cool. I thought she'd say no. Holden's invited some of the guys from the team, so it's shaping up to be a good crowd."

We split up in different directions then. Will heads off to his next class, and I make for my locker. I don't have much time left to get to class, so I quickly switch my textbooks around and then steal a glance at myself in the tiny mirror on the back of my locker door. My heart completely stops when the reflection shows Jaden behind me. I spin around to face him, my hair whipping around my shoulders.

"Kenz," Jaden murmurs, stepping closer to me. His eyebrows are furrowed, his eyes wide with guilt, his forehead creased with worry. His hair is flat today and he's wearing a black hoodie again, his hand gripping the strap of his backpack. He's squeezing so tightly, his knuckles are paling, and he looks at me in apologetic desperation.

"Don't," I tell him. I slam my locker shut, and the bell echoes throughout the school building once more. I'm late for class, and there are only a few other stragglers that remain in the halls.

"Kenz, I'm sorry," Jaden tries again, reaching for my hand. He shakes his head fast and I've never seen him look so anxious before. With his fingers still grasping my hand, he continues, "I didn't mean to say what I did. I couldn't stop myself, and I was wrong, but it just…came out. I guess I thought it might help."

I pull my hand free from his and place it flat against his chest, forcing him to stop. In the silence that forms, I look straight back into his eyes, recognizing the same guilt that I saw in them last night. It's sincere, and I'm glad he feels guilty. He should. However, my anger is gone. After several seconds have passed, I finally say, "Thank you."

Confusion crosses Jaden's eyes. He stares back at me, head tilted to one side, puzzled over my reply. I don't think it was the one he was expecting. "What?"

"You said exactly what we've wanted to say for a while now," I admit, dropping my hand from his chest and shifting my gaze to the floor. "We just didn't have the guts to admit it, let alone say it, and it hit Mom right where it needed to. So thank you." I glance back up at the boy in front of me, knowing that it would have been impossible to remain angry at him. He's too caring, too loving. I know his intentions were good. He just went about it the wrong way. "Jaden," I say firmly, my tone solemn, "don't *ever* do anything like that again, though."

"Never," he says quickly. "*Never.*" He exhales loudly in relief, his broad shoulders sinking as he wraps his arms around me and pulls me against his body. He's full of warmth and he holds me tightly, and I feel safe and secure in his arms. Burying my face into the crook of his neck, I inhale his scent, and against my ear, Jaden whispers, "I thought I'd really messed up." He squeezes me tight and then releases his hold on me, taking a step back. His features have softened again and he slides his bag off his shoulder and fumbles around inside it. "Since you're not a flowers type of girl," he murmurs. Glancing back up, he gives me a smile and pulls out a small cardboard box from his bag. He hands it to me, brushing his fingers over mine.

"What's this?" I ask, holding it between my hands and studying it.

"Not flowers," Jaden answers with a laugh. He nods to the box. "Open it."

I do as he asks, pulling open the folds of the box. When I look down at what's inside, I laugh out loud in the hallway. There's a pile of Hershey's chocolate bars, and it seems Jaden really does listen to every word I say. He's smiling sheepishly at his sweet gesture, slightly embarrassed.

"This is *way* better than flowers," I tell him. And, because I'm late for class anyway, I step forward and press my lips to the corner of his mouth, leaving a lingering kiss there. "Thank you."

"It's no problem," Jaden says. He zips his bag up and slides it back onto one shoulder, stealing a glance at the watch on his wrist. "Looks like I'm taking advantage again of the fact that I don't get yelled at for being late. I should get to class."

"Yeah, me too."

Meeting my eyes, he reaches up and presses the pad of his thumb to the edge of my jaw. His gentle smile is forever warm and sincere. "See you later, Kenz," he says, and he turns and walks away, drifting off down the hallway along with the final remaining stragglers.

There's a giddy smile on my face as I turn back to my

locker and open it up all over again, sliding the box inside. Jaden really is sweet in the most attractive way possible. He's endearing and strong, charming and flirtatious. I get everything in one with Jaden, and it's the absolute perfect mixture.

"Kenzie," someone hisses, and I instantly recognize the voice as Holden's. I crane my neck to the right and see Holden sneaking up next to me. We've been on good terms the past few days and he has said nothing more on the whole Jaden matter; however, it doesn't seem to have lasted. Now, his expression is cold and he stares down at me, giving a pointed glance in the direction that Jaden has just walked off in. "What was that?"

"I'm late, Holden," I tell him, rolling my eyes at the question. He knows what the answer is: I was talking to Jaden, I was hugging Jaden, I was kissing Jaden, because I like Jaden. I've told him this already, so I don't know why he almost looks surprised, and I'm not prepared to discuss it all over again. "I need to get to Spanish, and I'm pretty sure you've got a class to get to, too."

"Tell me one thing, Kenzie," Holden blurts out quickly, grabbing my elbow so that I can't push past him. He looks down at me with those dark eyes of his. The expression within them is different, something that I've never quite seen before, and I find myself trying to decode it as I look back up at him. Quietly, he finally asks, "Are you serious about Jaden Hunter?"

I pull my elbow free from his grasp and push my locker shut, sending an echo bouncing throughout the hall. "Yes, Holden," I answer with confidence, looking him straight in the eye. "I am."

A flash of fear tears across his face and his eyes crinkle at their corners, his frown growing more prominent. He looks down to the ground, shaking his head slowly. "Oh, Kenzie," he whispers under his breath. "I really, really wish you hadn't said that."

27

I'm sprawled out across the living room floor, lying flat on my stomach, staring aimlessly at my AP Statistics homework in front of me. I have the night off work, so I'm using it to my full advantage by catching up on all of the homework I've let stack up over the past week. I'm not quite focused, however, mostly because I keep glancing up at the TV and over to Mom.

She's sitting stiffly on the couch, chewing on her lower lip as she tries to concentrate on the episode of *Scandal* she's watching. But I can tell her mind is elsewhere, and it doesn't take a genius to figure out where exactly. It's been less than twenty-four hours since she announced her decision to cut out the wine, and already she appears lost and unsure of herself. I can see it in her eyes. She's struggling.

Setting my pen down on my notebook, I prop myself up onto one elbow and look up at her. "What are you thinking about?" I ask her quietly, my tone gentle.

Her dark eyes flicker from the TV down to me. As she looks

at me with a blank stare, it becomes clear that she is fighting a mental battle with herself. I can see it in her expression, in her frown, in her warm brown eyes. "Everything," she admits. She interlocks her fingers and then releases them, only to repeat the action all over again. She's more fidgety than usual, most likely because her mind won't rest. There is no wine in her system to numb it.

"Maybe you just need to find a new hobby," I suggest with a hopeful smile. I push myself up completely and cross my legs on the floor, leaning back against the couch. I rack my brain for possible ideas, and blurt out the first ones that come to mind. "How about knitting? Scrapbooks? Drawing? You were arty in college, weren't you? Why don't you create something?" The tight smile that Mom gives me in reply does little to mask her frustration and desperation, so I quickly add, "Or you can do my homework, if you'd like?"

That gets her to laugh, and she rolls her eyes and relaxes back against the couch, breaking out of her stiff posture. "Nice try," she murmurs.

Heaving a sigh, I push my homework to one side and get to my feet. If Mom is going to be successful with this, she's going to need a new distraction. She'll drive herself insane otherwise. I leave the room and head into the kitchen, pulling open drawers and fumbling around them in search of scrap paper. It's just after 9PM, but the evening has felt long and the time has dragged, so I can only imagine that it feels much longer to Mom. She needs something to keep herself occupied, so I grab some old sheets of paper and a couple pencils, close the drawers and head back into the living room.

"Draw something," I tell Mom. I set the paper and pencils down on the couch next to her, giving her a nod of encouragement when she glances down at them. I'm not exactly sure where I'm going with this, but I press my palms flat on the arm of the couch and lean forward, looking at Mom from beneath my eyelashes. "None of this is really about the drinking," I state quietly. My words are slow and cautious as I continue. "It's about Grace. It's about accepting it, and if you don't think you can, then maybe you *should* talk to someone who isn't me or Dad. But first, there's a habit you need to break, so please, draw something."

Mom frowns at the paper on the couch by her side. She picks up a pencil and holds it delicately between her fingertips, then glances back up at me. "When did you get so smart?"

Smiling, I tell her, "My mom raised me."

At that exact moment, the doorbell rings out around the house with a bouncing echo. It's followed by several loud knocks against the front door, and I exchange a glance with Mom. Neither of us is expecting anyone.

"I'll get it," I tell her. Pushing myself back from the couch, I leave Mom with the scraps of paper and head down the hall toward the front door. It's dark out, so it's impossible to peer through the door's glass panels to see who's on the porch. I unlock the door and swing it open only by a few inches just to be safe and then peer around the frame.

"Holden?"

What is he doing here? Holden is the last person I expected to turn up on my porch unannounced like this. Even Will doesn't just show up without warning, so I slowly edge the door open wider, wondering why he's here. Holden is standing a few feet back from the door with his hands in the pockets of his football jacket and his chin tilted down to the ground. The small porch light above him flickers every few seconds, illuminating his shadowed face. He glances up at me, swallows, and asks, "Can we talk?"

"If it involves you giving me an explanation for the way you acted this morning, then yes," I answer, folding my arms across my chest and stepping to the side. "Come on in."

Head still down, hands still in his pockets, Holden slowly shuffles past me over the threshold and into the hall. He lingers by my side as I close the door and lock up again, but there's tension radiating from him. I try to catch his eye, but he only continues to stare at the floor as he follows me down to the hall, back toward the living room.

Stepping into the room, I meet Mom's awaiting gaze and inform her, "It's only Holden." As I say his name, he places his hand against the doorframe and leans forward enough to let Mom see him. However, he doesn't come into the room.

"Hello, Holden!" Mom greets him with a warm smile, and she appears grateful for the distraction. Holden showing up is apparently better than my suggestion of having her draw something.

"Hey," Holden murmurs with a small nod. He doesn't smile back at her or look at her for longer than one second. He drops his hand from the frame of the door to my elbow, and carefully but quickly he tugs me back out into the hall with him. This is weird, and I'm not exactly sure what's going on. Holden towers over me, dark eyes on mine, his cold fingers still on my arm.

"Can we ... can we go out back or something?" he asks, his voice nothing more than an anxious whisper.

There's something hugely off about him right now, but I'm not sure what and I don't know why. Holden can be moody, sure. Hell, he's grouchy most of the time, anyway. But this tense? This nervous? This isn't Holden.

"Um. I guess."

I shake his grip off me and turn for the kitchen. It's in darkness, but I don't bother to switch on any lights, and instead I head straight for the back door while Holden follows close on my heels. I hear his breathing deepen as I unlock the door and pull it open, allowing the fresh, cool night air to hit us. I walk over to the old wooden table and set of chairs in the center of the yard. It's not too cold out tonight, but there is a small breeze in the air that blows my hair across my face.

I press my hand against the back of a chair and turn around to face Holden. He has stopped a few feet away from me again, almost as though he's afraid to come any closer, and his dark eyes have grown wide and fearful. "Is everything okay, Holden?"

Holden's eyes close. Slowly, he shakes his head back and forth, hands balled into fists inside his pockets. "No," he whispers. Even though it's not cold, his breath is visible in the air and it seems his breathing has become shallow. His eyes flicker open again and he reflects my panicked stare, then exhales deeply and states, "There's something I need to tell you."

"What?" Holden is never, ever like this, and the panic that is quickly sweeping through me sends me into a fit of desperation when he doesn't immediately reply. Stepping forward until I am standing directly in front of him, I beg: "Holden, what is it?"

Swallowing hard, he sinks lifelessly into a chair and I quickly sit down next to him. I'm worried now, and I need him to say something. I need him to answer me.

"If you're serious about Jaden Hunter," he murmurs, "then you need to know. I have to tell you." He tries his best to meet my eyes, but I can see it's difficult for him. "You need to know why I can't be around him and Dani, not unless you want me to explode. I can't…I can't bear it." He shakes his head fast and drops his gaze back down to the grass again, unable to look at me. "It's too much."

"What are you talking about?"

"Being around them makes the guilt unbearable," he says to the ground, voice quivering. He releases his interlocked hands and throws them back into his hair, roughly running his fingers through the ends. Why won't he look at me?

"Guilt?" I echo. I don't know what he's talking about. "Holden?"

"The Hunter crash, Kenzie!" he blurts out. I still don't understand, so I only stare blankly back at him with my heartbeat thumping against my ribcage. Holden leans forward, his dark eyes full of terror as he continues. "Do you remember the final report? They swerved off the road because they think an animal ran out on the road in front of them." He pauses for a brief moment to take a deep breath, and it's only then that I notice he is trembling—and it's not because he's cold. "But the cops were wrong. There were no animals on the road that night," he whispers, voice cracking, face paling. "But I was."

28

I can feel the weight of Holden's words crashing down on me. They repeat over and over again in my head until I can make sense of them, until I can figure out what exactly it is that he's telling me. Seconds of suffocating silence have passed by the time I process it all, and this new information is like a punch in the gut.

"You were *there?*" I hiss in disbelief, blinking repeatedly back at him.

"It was back at the time of football camp," Holden blurts out, his words spilling from his mouth so fast that I can hardly keep up. He is shaking even harder than he was a moment ago. "It had been such a long, long, shitty day and I was so *tired*. I wanted to go out for a drive just to clear my head. God, I thought I'd take the country roads, because I knew they'd be quiet."

With his arm still propped up on the table, he presses his forehead into his palm and squeezes his eyes shut again, his face angled away from me. I can't bring myself to speak. All I can do is listen in frozen horror, willing Holden not to tell me what I think he is going to tell me.

"And the roads *were* quiet," he murmurs. "And I was just... just driving. And it was dark, and my music was playing, and I don't really... I don't really remember anything." He throws his head back to the sky and parts his lips, blowing air out of his lungs while slowly opening his eyes again. His chest is rising and falling with his heavy breathing, and now his lower lip is quivering. He tilts his head down so that his pained, terrified eyes can meet mine, and my stomach twists even more as bile rises in my throat.

"I was so damn tired, but I was only gonna drive to Fort Collins then head straight home," he continues. His crushed expression is laced with guilt. "I guess I... I guess I dozed off." His entire face is so pale that it makes him appear sick, and he freezes, locking his eyes on a spot somewhere over my shoulder. The corners of his eyes crinkle as the guilt consumes him and he presses his hand over his mouth, as if to keep in the truth that is falling out of it. "And all I remember is the sound of this car horn cutting straight through me and opening my eyes," he whispers against his palm. He begins to shake his head again in disbelief, faster and faster, as though he doesn't *want* to believe it. "I was just so tired. I shouldn't have got in the fucking car!" he yells, but his voice is so weak that his words are nothing more than a coarse squeak. He moves both his hands to the top of his head, interlocking his fingers through his hair. "I didn't even *realize*," he breathes. "I slowed down a little and checked my rearview mirror, but I couldn't see anything, just blurry tail lights."

He looks up at the sky again, but I still notice him blinking fast in an attempt to hold back the tears that are fighting to

264

break free. "I just carried on going. I wasn't thinking straight, I just ... " His words dwindle into silence, hanging unfinished in the night air. "I heard about the crash the next morning. But the Hunters didn't swerve to avoid an animal, Kenzie," he whispers. "They swerved to avoid me."

A long, numb silence follows. For what feels like hours, I watch Holden's tears drop onto the grass across the chasm that has suddenly opened up between us. Neither one of us is brave enough to speak.

My entire chest feels as though it's collapsing. What was Holden thinking? Why is he only telling me this now? There is so much running through my mind that it is impossible to think straight. All I can do is press my hand to my chest and whisper, "Oh, Holden."

The bile in my throat continues to rise and I quickly slap my hand over my mouth to stop myself from throwing up. Opposite me, Holden is trembling. He can't bring himself to look at me right now, and he presses both hands to his face and hunches over, burying his head between his knees.

I can't look at him either, so I force myself onto my feet and walk away from the table, my hands pressed to my temples. There is a throbbing, agonizing pain at the back of my head. I don't want to believe this. I *can't* believe this. Suddenly, I become lightheaded, and the back yard begins to spin around me as an awful dizziness takes over my body. Fearful that I might collapse, I quickly drop down onto the lawn, pressing my hands against the grass to steady myself. "Why didn't you say anything?" I ask Holden, but my voice is a whisper. The back of my throat hurts as I fight back the tears. *How am I going to tell Jaden and Danielle?*

"Because I didn't want to get into trouble," Holden admits

through a muffled cry against his hands. He doesn't sound like himself anymore. He sounds like a child, weak and vulnerable, everything that Holden usually isn't. "I didn't know what would happen to me," he says quickly, lifting his head slightly. He looks at me beneath his damp eyelashes, his eyes swollen. Suddenly, he begins dry-heaving. He stands up from the chair and bends over the table, one hand pressed against it for support, and retches so many times I'm surprised that he *doesn't* throw up. I feel frozen stiff as I look up at him from the grass. A pained numbness begins to take over as the reality of the situation sinks in.

"Holden ..." I whisper. "They need to know."

"No!" Holden yells. He immediately straightens up, breathing so heavily that it's almost panting, and he wipes away the tears from his cheeks. "No," he says again, this time quieter, softer. He stares down at me with desperate eyes and I can't bear to look. "Please, Kenzie," he begs. "It was an accident."

"You can't expect me to keep this from them ..." I trail off, blinking up at him. *Did he expect me to do that?* Holden can't burden me with this secret. I refuse to carry the weight of it, and he can't expect me *not* to tell Jaden. It's *Jaden*. I have to.

He runs his hand back through his hair again, taking several cautious steps across the lawn toward me. When he reaches me, he crouches down and reaches for my wrist, his dark eyes mirroring the panic in mine. "Kenzie, listen to me," he says. "I'm going to ride this out. Once we all head off to college, we can start over. We'll have separate lives; it'll be easier then. Once we all leave this place, it'll be over. I can still have a future."

"Holden," I whisper, "I don't know what to say. I don't know what to tell you."

He reaches for my other wrist and pins them both against his chest. I can feel his heartbeat thumping erratically beneath his skin, even faster than mine. "I'm your best friend. You have to keep quiet about this. Please, I am begging you, Kenzie. I can still get into college, I can *make* something of myself."

I look straight back into his eyes, analyzing the pain and the hurt within them, the guilt and the fear, the dread and the nerves. I don't know this Holden. "I ... I don't know if I can," I finally say, shaking my head at him. Do I keep this secret to protect my best friend, knowing that I'm keeping the truth from Jaden? Or do I tell Jaden, but destroy Holden? I feel a single tear rolling slowly down my cheek. *No*. This isn't about who I want to protect. This is about what is right, and what Holden asks of me is too much. I can't keep this quiet. Jaden needs to know.

Holden physically deflates in front of me, his shoulders sinking, his chest falling. Gently squeezing my wrists, he releases his hold on me and stares into my eyes in silence. He doesn't say anything, he only nods once and begins to walk away, dragging his feet across the lawn.

I can't believe it was *my* Holden who was there that night. *My* Holden who was on that road. *My* Holden who is responsible. And despite all of this, I can't help but feel like he *is* still my Holden. He is upset right now, and the last thing I want is for him to feel alone.

"Holden," I say gently, following him. I don't want him to leave, not when he's like this, not after everything he just told me. I want him to stay, but he ignores me completely and continues into the house, his pace quickening as he shakes my grip off him. He is now desperate to get out of here as quickly as he had arrived.

When he reaches the front door he throws it open without hesitation, but then immediately flinches backward, bumping into me. On the other side of the threshold, Uncle Matt is standing with his hand in mid-air, ready to knock. He steps back in surprise, and he glances between Holden and me before cracking a smile and saying, "Hey, Kenzie! Is your dad around?"

I steal a sideways glance up at Holden. He is even paler than he was outside, his eyes locked on my uncle. Matt is standing before us in full uniform, his Windsor Police badge on full display, his free hand resting on his duty belt right above his set of cuffs. The sight of a cop is seemingly enough to make Holden's blood run cold, and his movements are jittery. "Kenzie, I'll ... I'll see you around," he mumbles, and then, without waiting a second longer, he rushes past Uncle Matt and down the driveway.

"Is everything alright?" Matt asks. He cranes his neck to look over his shoulder at Holden, who is striding across the lawn and throwing open the door of his dad's truck. He slams it shut behind him. "What's wrong with him?"

"Nothing," I answer without missing a beat. I'm surprised I can even speak at this point, though I can barely look at Matt as the sound of Holden's dad's engine roars to life. The tires screech against the ground as he speeds off, and with my head as all over the place as it is, I can't stick around here. I need to be alone to process everything, so I quickly spin around and take a few steps back down the hall. "Dad's out on a job," I tell Matt, snatching Mom's car keys from the hall table next to Grace's frame, "but can you please keep Mom company until I get back?"

Matt scours me intensely with a solemn expression. I hate

it when he goes all professional on me, and in a more formal tone, he asks, "MacKenzie, where are you off to?"

With Mom's keys gripped firmly in my hand, I swiftly step into a pair of flats that are lying by the door and make a dash outside onto the porch, headed for the car. Over my shoulder, I tell him, "Anywhere!"

29

I don't know where to go. I don't know what to do, what to think. I just drive.

There is a weight bearing down on me that is forcing me to question everything. I am torn between my best friend and the boy I am falling in love with. I am torn between protecting Holden and telling Jaden the truth. He and Dani deserve to know what truly happened that night back in August. They need to know *why* their parents were killed.

But Holden ...

I don't know what sort of trouble he could get into. I don't know what would happen if the truth was revealed. I imagine there would be a new investigation into the accident, but then what? I keep telling myself that Holden was at fault. Holden is the one who fell asleep at the wheel. But it was an accident. An accident that happened partly because he'd been working so hard to secure a future for himself. And now I'm the person who has to decide whether or not to take that future away from him. When I looked into his eyes, it almost seemed like the guilt that's been eating him this last year is punishment enough. And will it even help the Hunters to have someone to blame?

There is no one I can talk to about this, no one to ask for advice who isn't already connected to the Hunters, no one to turn to. I don't want to chase after Holden, mostly because I can't look at him right now, and I can't call Will. Mom already has too much going on in her head to bombard her with this, and usually I feel pretty comfortable confiding in Uncle Matt, but I obviously can't tell him about Holden and the Hunter crash—he's a cop! I don't want to keep this secret to myself; how am I supposed to figure out how to deal with it? I only have two options: Keep the secret a secret, or tell it. Both of them are going to hurt someone.

Stifling a groan, I hunch over the steering wheel, gripping it tightly with both hands and blinking fast to hold back the tears. I wish Holden hadn't told me the truth. I wish I didn't now know what I do, because I don't know how I'm supposed to face him tomorrow after this. And how am I going to face up to Jaden? To Dani? How do I face them when I know something as important as this?

I don't know where I'm going, but I don't want to be in Windsor, so I drive and drive and drive without planning any particular route. I head along Main Street and westbound out of the town, driving just below the speed limit while I focus on controlling my breathing. There are a lot of other cars out on the roads right now, but I try to imagine that they're not here. That the road is empty apart from myself. I try to imagine myself as Holden, driving out of town to clear his head the same way I am now, and try to understand how quickly everything in your life can change.

Wiping away my tears, I take the exit and merge onto the interstate. It's busier here. More cars around, more lights. I keep on driving, following the interstate north toward Fort Collins. I don't know where I'm going or if I'll stop. I just drive, watching the glow of the streetlights.

Standing in the hallway, knocking gently on the dorm room door, I find myself shivering. It's growing colder outside and these dorms aren't exactly the warmest in the hallways. I'm not wearing a jacket, because I left the house so fast that I didn't have time to grab one. I didn't have time to even brush my hair either, but right now, I don't care that I'm in an awful state. I don't care that there are streaks of mascara running down my cheeks. I don't care that I've had to throw my hair up into a tangled bun atop my head. I stand with my arms wrapped around me, hugging my body tight while I wait patiently for the door to open. I hope he is here.

It feels as though an hour has passed by the time I hear the door unlock, and then, slowly, it cracks open a few inches. Darren peers through the tiny gap at me. "Kenz?" he says. I'm pretty sure I'm the last person he would expect to see tonight, but nonetheless, he swings the door open wider. It's not all that late, but he looks half asleep as he stands there in nothing but a pair of boxer shorts and a T-shirt. "What are you doing here? What's wrong?"

"I need to talk to someone," I sniff. I can't remember the last time I was in Darren's dorm. It feels like forever ago since we were dating. Time has passed, things have changed, but right now he is the only person I know who is entirely neutral to the situation I have found myself in. He is the only person I can talk to about this, because although Darren is too clingy and too protective, there was a time when he knew how to comfort me. He always listened, he always offered advice, and he *does* give tight, reassuring hugs. He doesn't know the Hunters. Holden isn't his friend. And he keeps saying he still wants to be there for me, so here's his chance to prove it.

"Come in," he says quickly, stepping back and ushering me inside. As I walk into the small, cramped dorm room, his brown eyes remain fixed on me. He looks concerned, and when he closes the door again behind us and locks it, he follows me across the cluttered floor. I'm relieved that his roommate isn't here, and I sit down on the edge of his unmade bed and anxiously fumble with my hands. "Is this about Jaden Hunter?"

I look up at Darren. "What?"

"It was him, right? He was the guy you still had feelings for?" he asks quietly, lowering himself down onto the bed next me. He stares back at me, intensely. The dimple in his left cheek doesn't show when he isn't smiling, and I used to hate when it wasn't on display.

I heave a slow sigh and shoot Darren an awkward, apologetic glance. I guess he figured it out over the weekend when he saw me and Jaden together at Walgreens. I suppose it was obvious. "Yeah. He's the one," I murmur. There is no point in denying it now.

Darren nods once and then tilts his head down, looking up at me from beneath his eyelashes. "So is this about him?" he asks carefully, his voice gentle and caring. "You know I don't like seeing you cry, Kenz. Just say the word and I'll beat his ass."

"No, Darren," I say, placing my hand over the top of his enclosed fist. Slowly, he flexes his hand beneath mine, and I glance around the room. The pressure of my headache keeps on building, so I move my hand from Darren's and press my fingers to my temple instead, gently trying to massage the pain away. "Do you remember what happened to Jaden's parents?" I ask him, my eyes fixed on an empty beer bottle that's been dumped on the floor. I stare at it in an effort to keep myself steady, because the ground is beginning to sway beneath me again. "That crash last summer?"

Out of the corner of my eye, I see Darren nod. "What about it?"

A small hiccup escapes. I think I have cried the entire drive to Fort Collins, and now there are no tears left. All I can do is sniff and try to swallow the painful lump in my throat. I can't keep Holden's revelation to myself. I need advice, and Darren is the only person who can give it to me right now. Taking a deep breath, I force my eyes away from the beer bottle and back up to look at Darren. "It didn't happen the way the police said it happened," I tell him, and as soon as I say it out loud, my stomach twists. *How did all of this happen? Why Holden?*

Darren is silent while he takes a moment to consider what I'm telling him. He cocks his head to one side, ready to listen carefully. "What do you mean?"

Holden doesn't want me to tell anyone, but I just *have* to. And at least it's only Darren I'm telling, not Jaden. Yet. Running my hands back through my hair and heaving an agonized sigh, I attempt to piece together everything that Holden has told me. In my head, the facts are all over the place, so I spend a minute trying to realign them again. The longer I take, the more confused Darren becomes. "Jaden's parents didn't swerve to avoid an animal," I finally say, my voice weak and

274

nothing more than a croaked whisper. "They swerved to avoid Holden."

"*What?*" Darren physically recoils from me for a moment. "Was Holden on the road?"

"He fell asleep and he must have forced them off the road or something," I splutter, my words fast. Right now, I am helpless. There is nothing I can do to change what happened that night, no matter how much I wish I could. *If Holden hadn't been on that road then Bradley and Kate Hunter would still...* No. I can't bring myself to imagine it. I can't think that way, not unless I want to end up enraged at Holden. The last thing he needs right now is for me to be angry at him. Shaking away the thought of it, I fix my attention back on Darren, throwing my head forward and burying my face into my hands. "He's kept this a secret for over a year! He only *just* told me! *Now* what am I supposed to do?"

"Let me get this straight," Darren says, and he places his hand on my shoulder. The mattress creaks as he scoots closer to me until his leg is against mine. "Your best friend caused the car crash that killed your new boyfriend's parents?"

"Yes ... And the worst part is that Jaden doesn't know."

"That's fucked up," Darren says. He doesn't even so much as flinch at the thought of Jaden being my boyfriend, even though he isn't *officially*. Instead, he only frowns and tightens his grip on my shoulder. After the lengths he has been going to lately to win me back, I thought he would have been more annoyed, but he doesn't seem to be. In a way, I am thankful. Now isn't the time to argue about our failed relationship. "Is that why you're crying?" he asks. "Because he doesn't know?"

"Because I'm going to have to be the one to tell him." Dread fills me and there's a pang in my chest that constricts my breathing. *How am I going to tell Jaden and Dani? How am I supposed to say it?* I thought telling Jaden about Mom and Grace would be the hardest thing I ever did, but apparently not. Now I have to tell the boy I'm falling for that my best friend may have been the reason his parents are no longer alive. The nausea returns again. My knees feel week, my head is spinning. "It feels like the Hunters have finally gotten over it, are finally moving on, are finally happy again," I murmur. "And now I have to crush them all over again."

Darren begins to massage my shoulder now in what I can only assume is an attempt to comfort me, though it's far from soothing. "Shouldn't Holden be the one to tell them?"

"Yes, but he won't," I answer. I look to the ceiling and run my hands through my hair, exasperated. Goddamn Holden. "And I can't keep this a secret, so it's going to have to be me who breaks the news. I just don't want anyone to get hurt."

"You don't *have* to tell them, Kenz," Darren says. Scratching at the back of his neck, he uses my shoulder for support as he pushes himself up. He walks across the cluttered floor and swipes a near-empty bottle of water off his desk, then watches me closely over the rim as he takes a long swig. "If you tell Jaden, aren't you hurting both him and Holden? Like you said, the Hunters have moved on." He tosses the empty bottle toward the overflowing trash can, but it misses and lands on the floor with a bounce. "Why bring it up again?"

"Are you serious?" I blink at Darren several times while I try to gauge if he's kidding or not, and when I realize he *is* being serious, I shake my head at him in horror. "Imagine if Jaden found out I had kept this from him! He would never forgive me."

"If you weren't with him, then you wouldn't feel obliged

276

to tell him," Darren mutters under his breath. He turns his back to me and fishes around inside his dresser drawer until he pulls out a pair of black sweats. I watch in silence as he slips them on, then he heaves a deep sigh and sits back down on the bed next to me. The light hits the crook in his nose, drawing my attention to it. I used to find a lot of things about Darren attractive, like that damn dimple in his left cheek that is slowly beginning to appear as the corners of his lips curve into a small, gentle smile. His soft brown eyes meet mine and a silence forms around us. We are sitting so close together that it is easy for him to lift his hand and press the pad of his thumb to my chin. He tilts my head only slightly, forcing my gaze to meet his. "You know, Kenz," he murmurs quietly, leaning in toward my face, "you wouldn't be in this situation at all if you were still with me."

"Darren!" Instinctively, I smack his hand away and retreat from him. A new sense of fury washes over me and my cheeks burn hot with sudden rage. I am already emotional enough as it is. *How dare Darren make this about us?* "This isn't the damn time for this!"

There's a flash of hurt in Darren's eyes at my abrupt rejection, but he seems to quickly get over it, because it turns to anger as he rises to his feet. "Fine," he retorts. He strides across the small dorm, unlocking the door and swinging it wide open. He spins around and fixes me with a firm, challenging look. "Leave, Kenz."

"Fine!" I yell. Breathing heavily, I stand up and enclose my fist around Mom's car keys so tightly that it'll leave an imprint in my skin. I shouldn't have come here. I shouldn't have expected Darren to help. My palms feel sweaty as I reach the door, barging past him into the hallway. I turn around one last time, and despite my swollen eyes, the swirls of mascara on my cheeks and my dry, chapped lips, I am brave enough to look Darren straight in the eye. "For the record," I tell him, "your advice *sucked*."

"Then don't come looking for it again," he states monotonously. Without letting another second pass, he steps back and slams the door shut, leaving me standing in the cold hallway by myself.

30

"Am I missing something here?" Will asks the next morning as he pulls into the school parking lot. As he navigates the lot, avoiding the freshmen who are jaywalking all over the place, he glances sideways at me and then over his shoulder at Holden in the back seat. There is suspicion in his eyes. "What is up with you guys?"

"I'm just tired," I mumble, staring aimlessly out of the Jeep's windshield through the shaded lenses of my sunglasses. It's a dull, cloudy day and there is a darkness lingering over Windsor that probably has as much to do with my mood as it does with the clouds, but I refuse to take the sunglasses off.

"Yeah, me too," Holden says quietly from the back seat. I cast a look over the back of the passenger seat at him, but his face is angled toward the window, his jaw tight. He has been quiet during the short drive to school, and so have I.

In fact, I didn't even want to go to school today. I wanted to avoid Holden and I wanted to avoid Jaden and I wanted to avoid Dani. Skipping school and staying home, wrapped up in bed with a handful of snacks on the pillow next to me would have been much better use of my time than this. I even feigned sickness when I woke up, dramatizing a fever by drinking glasses of hot water before feebly crawling downstairs to the kitchen. I think that maybe, for a single split second, my parents were fooled. But then Dad only laughed and headed off to work. Mom shook her head and stole the chance—for the hundredth time—to ask me what happened last night. That was enough to send me running back upstairs, pulling on clothes as fast as I could and stuffing my backpack with everything I would require to get through the day, like the sunglasses I refuse to remove so that I don't have to make eye contact with Holden.

"Are you *sure*?" Will asks, his tone skeptical as he pulls into an empty parking spot. He puts the Jeep in park, kills the engine, and then swivels around in his seat. There is silence in the vehicle, but I can hear the muffled voices of a group of sophomores who walk past. Will rests his elbow over the edge of his seat, staring into the back seat at Holden with a frown. "Is this about the Jaden thing? Because I thought you guys were over that."

In the tiny mirror of the pulled-down sun visor, I watch Holden snap his head around to fix Will with a sharp glare. After his confession last night, it is clear he does not appreciate Will's innocent question. Will doesn't know that there is a lot more to Holden's discomfort around the Hunters than we first thought, and I hate not being able to talk about it with him. For Holden's sake, I am keeping quiet this morning.

"*No*," Holden spits firmly. It's not very convincing, but it's aggressive enough to stop Will from asking anything more.

Grabbing his textbook from the floor, Holden reaches for the car door and shoves it open. He has to duck as he slides out of the Jeep, and then he turns around and leans back in to tell us, "I'm skipping practice today, so wait up for me." Without waiting for a reply from either of us, he slams the door shut and strides off across the parking lot, disappearing into the flow of other students. The three of us usually walk to our first classes together, so if it wasn't obvious already that there is something wrong, then it sure as hell is now.

Will cranes his neck to watch Holden until he's out of sight, and then he looks to me for an explanation. "God, what the fuck is his problem lately?" He shakes his head in bewilderment. Will rarely curses, so it seems he is losing his patience.

"I don't know," I lie with a shrug. I push my sunglasses farther up the bridge of my nose to disguise the fact that I'm hiding something, then quickly scoop up my bag from the floor and climb out of the Jeep. I can't do this every day. I can't look at Holden every morning before school without thinking about him driving along that road last August. I can't lie to Will every day. I can't hide the truth from Jaden and Dani every day. I will only end up feeling as guilty as Holden does, and that guilt would be enough to consume me.

"Are you sure you don't know?" Will asks, meeting me in front of the hood of the Jeep. With the swift flick of his wrist, he swipes my sunglasses straight off my face and holds them away from me. "Because you're being pretty weird, too."

"I told you. I'm tired," I mutter. I snatch the sunglasses back out of his hand, but now that Holden is gone, I don't bother to put them back on. Instead, I throw them into my backpack and begin to walk. There is a breeze in the air that chills my face. "Is that such a crime?"

Will holds up both his hands in surrender and dramatically takes a sideways step away from me, increasing the distance between us. "Alright, so now I have *two* moody best friends," he jokes, but I don't laugh. If only he knew what the situation *really* was, then he definitely wouldn't be rolling his eyes at us.

I keep my head down as we head for the school's main door and I stuff one hand into the front pocket of the huge oversized hoodie that I'm wearing. We still have five minutes or so until first period begins, so just enough time for the usual locker trip and hallway gossip. If there was ever a day that I could sincerely say I would rather do *anything* else than go to my classes, it is today.

Will and I are walking through the courtyard in silence when I hear my name faintly being called from somewhere in the distance. Not MacKenzie, not Kenzie, but *Kenz*. That's why I know that it's Jaden before I've even turned around, and I stop dead in my tracks, bracing myself. No matter how much I want to avoid him today, I just *can't*. In my heart, I know that I want nothing more than to be around him. I just have to remain calm and collected, strong and in control until I make a decision. I take several slow, deep breaths and then finally turn around. So does Will. Walking straight toward us are, of course, Jaden and Dani.

I can still remember the first day they returned to school after the accident. They had slowly walked across the courtyard, side by side with their eyes on the ground, Jaden's arm around Dani's shoulder. Hardly anyone recognized Dani that day. She had cut her hair and dyed it black, and by second period she had already burst into tears and gone home. Jaden, however, stuck it out for the entire school day. There were a lot of hushed whispers that day. A lot of sympathetic glances and commiserating frowns. No one knew what to say, and if anyone did say something, it was nothing more than a few words of consolation. That entire day, I kept quiet. I kept my head down in class, didn't linger in the hallways, went home for lunch. I was so afraid of bumping into Jaden Hunter that day. I was so scared that he wouldn't be the same boy I was in love with six months before.

Now, however, it is a different story. Jaden and Danielle Hunter are strolling across the courtyard with confidence in their stride, their heads held high, their blue eyes brighter than ever. Jaden gives a nod of acknowledgment to one of the guys from the team as they pass each other, and Dani can't stop running her fingers through the ends of her hair. She doesn't look the same as the girl with the long blond hair, but she also doesn't look like the girl with the blunt black hair anymore either. There is an exuberance to Dani that I haven't seen in her for a long time. A bounce in her stride. A smile on her face that is sincere. Her hair is now a rich, dark brunette and it really does suit her. It's not *exactly* the same shade as her mom's, but it's so much closer than it was before. Yesterday in Spanish class alone, I counted compliments from three different people about how great she looks.

"Hey guys!" Will says, raising his hand to give them a small wave. Will is friends with almost everyone, so he looks pleased to see Jaden and Dani as they reach us, especially now that we are no longer keeping our distance from the two of them. "Kenzie says you can make my party this weekend. You're still coming, right?"

"Yes, we are! What's the dress code?" Dani asks. The ends of her hair are curled and she is *still* running her fingers through them, unable to stop herself. In all of the years that I have known Danielle, I have never seen her look so happy and content. "No dress code," Will tells her. "Just wear whatever is comfortable."

The party this weekend is the last thing on my mind right now. Both Holden *and* the Hunters will be there, and a party puts the three of them within much closer proximity than school does. It will be a lot harder for Holden to avoid the two of them in the confinement of a house. Right now, I try not to think about the problems that will cause, so I tune out of Will and Dani's conversation and look over to Jaden instead. His focus is already on me, his smoldering eyes burning into me.

"Hey you," he murmurs, stepping forward. The smile playing at his lips is genuine and there is a glossy shine to his blue eyes that is so sincere that it's beautiful to look at. After everything that Jaden has gone through, he has found his way back to being content and happy. Dani is on that same road, though her journey is slightly slower, but as the two of them stand before me now, reality hits me all at once—the Hunter twins are happy.

It is in that exact moment that I realize just how much courage I am going to require in order to tell them the truth about what happened that night last August. Jaden and Dani have had an extremely rough year, but month after month they have slowly but surely recovered from the grief they have suffered. Months ago, Dani never smiled. Months ago, Jaden and I didn't talk. I don't want to ruin this. I would never forgive myself for breaking their hearts all over again, but could I forgive myself for keeping the truth from them? Could I live with myself, knowing what I know now, but not telling them?

I keep reminding myself that Holden isn't a criminal. He's

not a bad person, he just made an awful mistake. But he's wrong, and I don't know if my loyalty to him is enough to prevent me from doing the right thing. If it was any other secret, *anything* else, that loyalty would stand. But this? This is too much, and I know within myself that I have to tell the Hunters, however hard it may be. I have to do the right thing.

I feel so overwhelmed by everything, and now that Jaden is standing in front of me, all I can do is collapse straight into him. Wrapping my arms around his body, I bury my face into the crook of his neck and absorb his warmth. I think he's surprised at my sudden affection, but he is fast to lock his arms around me, pulling me closer. He squeezes me tight and I feel so at ease in his embrace, despite knowing that soon I am going to be the one to crush him with this news. After last night, comfort and reassurance from Jaden is all that I need, even if he doesn't know what exactly it is that he is comforting me for.

"And so the PDA begins!" Dani teases with a laugh, but I ignore her and only hug Jaden even tighter. I can imagine she and Will rolling their eyes at us, but I don't care.

After a minute, Jaden leans back from me, though he keeps his arms around my body. His eyes mirror mine and he studies my features, searching for an explanation for my behavior. The distress I'm feeling must be obvious. "What's up, Kenz?"

"Nothing," I lie, dropping my eyes to his chest. I place my hand over the material of his jacket and trace a pattern over his chest, unable to look at him. I'm trying my best not to show how guilty I feel, and I lower my voice and tell him, "I just care about you a lot."

Slowly, Jaden's frown transforms into a smile and he moves his hand to the back of my neck. The soft skin of his palm radiates heat. "I know you do," he murmurs, and he leans forward, pressing his lips to my forehead. I squeeze my eyes shut and place my hand on Jaden's wrist, tilting my head forward and exhaling, breathing out all of the pressure that has been building since last night.

I am going to tell the Hunters the truth, but not now. I need to find the right time, the right moment.

31

The music is pumping throughout Will's huge house via a set of speakers that has been placed directly in the main entryway by the front door, the loud thumping greeting everyone who arrives. There is a buzz of energy in the air and everyone is in good spirits. It's not often that a party is thrown around here, so when one *does* come up, everyone has a good time. Will's Mom has gone out for the evening to let us have the house to ourselves, so Will's guest list has become a little bigger than it was at his last party almost a year ago. There are maybe forty or so people here, mostly fellow seniors, and there are only a few others who have yet to arrive. Like Jaden and Dani.

I'm leaning against the kitchen counter, resentfully sipping from a can of beer. I don't even like beer and I'm not much of a drinker, but I'm trying to appear more sociable as I scan the house over the rim of the can. It's just after 9PM, so it's still pretty early, but so far everyone is on their best behavior. No one is throwing furniture around. No one is spilling drinks.

Everyone is just chilling out, mingling and chatting with one another, or singing along to the pounding music and dancing clumsily in the lounge. We'll probably have to turn it down soon, before Will's neighbors come knocking.

For the past half hour or so, I've been pacing around the huge kitchen, circling the center island and talking to anyone who walks in while keeping my eye on the front door. Every time anyone other than the Hunters walks in, I grow a little more impatient. Jaden texted me five minutes ago to let me know that they were just about to leave to come over, so at least I know they haven't bailed.

My attention shifts from the front door over to Holden when I spot him walking into the kitchen out of the corner of my eye. Cautiously, he glances around for a few seconds before deeming the coast clear. I've watched him closely tonight so far. He has been hanging with some of the guys from the team and some of his friends from his classes, but it is so obvious to me that there is something off about him. His movements are jittery, his laugh sounds forced, he keeps his eyes down. There has been something different about Holden all of this time, ever since last August; I just have never noticed until now. I wasn't paying enough attention.

Anxiously, he makes his way across the kitchen toward me, his dark eyes lowered, and then leans against the counter by my side. His arm brushes against mine and we exchange a sideways glance. We are in this together now. "Are they here yet?" he asks under his breath. He doesn't have to clarify; I know who he is talking about.

"No," I tell him, "but they're on their way." I am trying to enjoy tonight, I really am, but nerves are getting the better of me. I am too worried about Holden lashing out at Jaden and

Dani again for no reason other than his own guilt, but at the exact same time, I can't wait for them to arrive. I'm excited to see Jaden. Holden glances up at the high ceiling and then takes a sip of his beer. He can't stop biting the inside of his cheek. "Thank you, Kenzie," he says firmly, eyes meeting mine. They show a mixture of sincerity and gratitude. "For not ... for not telling them," he adds. "I'll just lay low tonight, okay?"

"Yeah. I get it," I say quietly, frowning. Of course, I understand now why Holden doesn't want to be around the Hunters, but no one else does. Will doesn't know where Holden's awkwardness is coming from, and I'm sure Jaden and Dani have been wondering what the hell they have done to make Holden act so odd toward them. "If you do talk to them, though, don't be a jerk. At least be nice." I push myself away from the counter and step in front of him, adding, "It *is* the least you could do, after everything."

Holden gives me a small nod, then sidesteps away from me and tosses his empty beer can into the trash. He doesn't grab another one, and I keep my eyes trained on him until he disappears into the bathroom. I heave a sigh and throw the remainder of my beer in the trash too, even though the can is still half full. I don't know who I'm trying to impress, so I finally leave the kitchen and join the rest of the party through in the living room, where an intense game of Truth or Dare is underway. Will isn't drinking tonight, but he looks wasted as he shakes with laughter. I try to catch his eye, but he is too preoccupied to notice me walk into the room, so I linger by the door, watching the game unfold. Kailee and Jess are giggling between themselves over on the expensive leather couch against the far wall, so they don't notice me either, and

I decide to remain by the door in fear of being dragged into the game. I watch as Caleb from the football team takes a trio of shots, as Olivia Vincent admits to hooking up with Holden after the homecoming dance, as Will performs the quirkiest dance routine he can pull off on the spot.

I'm stifling a laugh when a pair of firm hands slides around my waist from behind, gripping my hips. My entire body stiffens and I tense up with bated breath. I know it's him before I've even turned around, and he rests his chin on my shoulder, his lips lightly grazing the soft spot just below my ear. "Kenz," he murmurs, breath hot against my skin.

The shiver that surges down my spine is pleasurable and I spin around to face Jaden. "Finally!" I exclaim, exhaling with relief. It feels as though I have spent hours waiting for him to get here, and I am so glad that he has finally arrived. There is a delicious scent of cologne clinging to him and he is wearing his favorite black jeans again with a baby-blue dress shirt. It complements his eyes well and the first few buttons are undone, so I can see the birthmark on his neck, which I definitely appreciate.

"Sorry we're a little late," he says with a sheepish shrug, then rolls his eyes toward Dani by his side. "*Someone* was taking forever."

Dani gently swats his bicep and shakes her head at him, then sets her gaze on me. She is seriously rocking her new hair. She's curled it into bouncy, loose waves. For the first time in a while, she is also wearing a full face of makeup, but it's not her bronzed cheekbones or darkly lined eyes that make her look gorgeous tonight. No, it is everything else. It is the brightness that lights up her face, the glimmer in her eyes. Seeing Dani happy is what is truly beautiful. "I haven't gone out to anything like this in a while," she admits quietly, and I barely hear her over the sound of the music.

"Don't worry about it, there's no pressure. It's all pretty chilled out," I reassure her, then motion over my shoulder to the game that's taking place behind me at the same moment that laughter erupts. "Truth or Dare in here, drinks in the kitchen, bathroom down the hall. Upstairs is out of bounds."

"Got it," she says. Slowly, she peers around me and scours the huge living room, analyzing who is here and who isn't. After a moment, a smile lights up her face. "Oh, Kailee and Jess are here! I'll catch up with you guys later," she says, and, much to my surprise, she confidently strolls into the living room without so much as a hint of apprehension. She looks like an entirely different person, and I watch in disbelief as she traverses the living room and slides down onto the couch next to Jess and Kailee as though they have been best friends their whole lives. *There's* the old Dani.

"Kenz," Jaden says. My gaze immediately flickers away from Dani and back to him. There is a a suggestive smirk on his lips as he says, "Come and grab a drink with me?" Without waiting for a reply, he slips his hand into mine, interlocking our fingers. Despite how normal this has become lately, my heartbeat does speed up a beat or two whenever Jaden takes my hand and a satisfying warmth spreads through my body.

We cross over the hall and into the kitchen together, and apart from the odd few individuals wandering around the house, most people appear to be in the living room together. The kitchen is empty apart from Eleanor Boosey, who is fetching herself a glass of water from the faucet with her back to us.

Letting go of Jaden's hand, I step toward the large center island that is entirely covered with cans of beer and soda, and bowls of chips and dips. Pressing my hands flat against the counter, I pull myself up onto an empty spot and sit on the edge, my legs dangling below me. I have lost track of Holden, so tonight is going to involve some tactical dodging skills. That's why I keep one eye on Jaden in front of me and one eye on the hall over his shoulder. "I was wondering when you'd get here," I tell him.

"Is that so?" Jaden asks, grinning devilishly. He moves around the island, grabbing himself a can of beer. He cracks open the tab and takes a sip while eyeing me over the rim. "I was wondering something too," he says. Setting the can down by my thigh, he steps forward and presses his body against my legs, grinding his hips against me. He runs his fingers over the rips in my black jeans, over the exposed skin of my thighs, his tongue trailing over his lower lip. Glancing up at me from beneath his dark eyelashes, his mouth forms a seductive smirk and he dares to whisper, "When do we get to be disrespectful again?"

"Jaden!" My mouth falls open with surprise and my eyes dart rapidly around the kitchen, ensuring no one has heard, but only Eleanor is still here. She walks past us with her glass of water, exchanges a small smile and a "hey" with Jaden, and then leaves the kitchen.

Jaden fixes his attention back on me and, for once, he is the one blushing in front of me. "I'm sorry," he says quietly, "that was too forward. I had some drinks while I was waiting for Dani to get ready." He steps back and his hands disappear from my body, though I wish that he hadn't. I find it incredibly attractive when Jaden is flirtatious, and after the week I've had,

292

I seriously appreciate this side to him right now. "Are you having fun?"

"Not yet," I say, but now I am smirking straight back at him. All I want to do right now is kiss the hell out of him, but in the middle of the kitchen it seems too much. I glance around again, and when I am confident no one is within earshot, I place my hand on Jaden's shoulder and lean forward, moving my lips to his jaw. "Jaden," I murmur in a breathy whisper, "do you want to go upstairs?"

"I thought no one was allowed upstairs," he says blankly.

Leaning away from him again, I roll my eyes at his innocence. "Exactly."

It takes a moment for him to realize what exactly it is that I'm suggesting, and I am quickly learning that Jaden is rather slow when it comes to picking up hints. It's cute, though, and I really can't stop myself from giggling when his expression completely transforms within a heartbeat as soon as it hits him. His pale cheeks flush with color and he nods eagerly.

"Um, *yes I want to go upstairs*," he blurts. He holds out his hand and I take it, sliding off the counter and landing on my feet. Our hands are tightly interlocked again as he leads me back out of the kitchen, and I grab his beer for him and carry it with me out into the hall.

In the living room, Truth or Dare has come to an end and everyone is simply hanging out. Will is nodding his head in sync with the music. Dani is wrapped up in a conversation with Jess and Kailee. I don't see Holden in the living room though and I know that he could appear at any moment, so I step around Jaden and take the lead so that we can get upstairs as quickly as we can. I can already imagine the teasing winks

Kailee would give me in Physics class next week if she spotted Jaden and I disappearing upstairs together.

That's why I run up the staircase two steps at a time, dragging Jaden and his beaming grin along behind me. A lot of Will's parents' expensive vases and artwork have been moved into the upstairs hall to protect them from any potential damage that may occur downstairs, so the dark hall is cluttered with booby-traps that we are forced to maneuver around. It is an intense creep down the hall to Will's room at the far end, and my heart is pounding fast with anticipation by the time we get there. I can hear Jaden's breathing close behind me and he remains patient, his hand still in mine, as I push open the door.

Will's room is in darkness, but I don't turn the lights on. I don't want them on. I tug Jaden into the huge room behind me and quickly dump his beer down on the dresser, then I use my free hand to fumble around in the dark, using furniture to guide us while my eyes take a minute to adjust. Holden and I are spending the night here, and I almost trip over the blow-up beds lying on the floor.

"Mm, Kenz?" Jaden says in a low, husky voice, squeezing my hand and pulling me back. I stop walking and turn around to look at him. Through the darkness, his outline slowly comes into focus and I can see the glint in his eyes, but not their color. There is silence up here in Will's room. The music from downstairs is faint and the only other sound is our anxious breathing. Unlocking our intertwined hands, he steps forward and presses his hips against mine, both his hands softly cupping my jaw. My heart is racing as he leans in, but he only lightly brushes his lips against mine, and then he pauses. "I spent an entire year wishing I would get the chance to kiss you again," he murmurs.

"I spent an entire year wishing that too," I whisper. I know he is going to kiss me, I know he *wants* to kiss me, and my breath catches in my throat as I wait. I can see his chest rising and falling in the darkness before slowly, very slowly, his lips capture mine.

My eyes flutter closed and I sink into that thrilling sensation of his mouth against mine all over again. The kiss begins soft and caring, tender and loving, but then, within a matter of moments, the desire becomes overwhelming and the kiss becomes faster, deeper, rougher. His hand is on my jaw, his fingertips tangled into my hair, and I hook my arms loosely around his neck, desperately pulling him closer against me. The lustful energy running through my veins fuels my eagerness and I begin to push against him instead, blindly guiding him backward until he hits the bed.

Without breaking his lips away from mine, Jaden sinks down onto the edge of the bed and pulls me with him, his arms wrapped around my body as he guides me down onto his lap. I cross my legs around him and take his lower lip between my teeth when we break to catch our breaths, and my hand falls to his shirt. This time around, I undo the buttons in swift movements and rake my fingers down his chest. At the same time, Jaden's warm hands slide under my shirt, over the skin of my back. When I undo the final button of his shirt, I move my hand to his belt.

I cannot get enough of him. I try to kiss him deeper, but it's impossible. I need more, and in the heat of the moment, a new revelation hits me at full force. I am not just falling in love with Jaden Hunter anymore. I *am* in love with Jaden Hunter.

Tearing my lips from his, my eyes flash open and I press both my hands to his bare chest, holding him back so that I can absorb the love and passion in his sparkling blue eyes. In the silence, his gaze mirrors mine while his chest rises and falls beneath my touch. "Jaden..." I whisper, then swallow hard. "I lo—"

I am cut off when the door is thrown open without so much as a knock first, and my head snaps around so quick it almost gives me whiplash. Will is at the door, sticking his head around the frame and peering into the room. "Kenzie?"

"*What*, Will?" I snap. I can't think of a worse time to be interrupted, and at this point I'm beginning to believe that Jaden and I are *always* going to get walked in on. It was embarrassing the first time with Dani, but now it is just frustrating. Especially when I was about to tell Jaden something important.

However, Will doesn't look annoyed that we're upstairs, or that we're making out on his bed. In fact, he doesn't even seem to care, because he looks more concerned than anything else. "Did you invite Darren?" he asks.

"What? No." I drop my hands from Jaden's chest and stare back at Will, confused. "Why the hell would I invite Darren?"

"Because he's here."

32

I storm down the staircase at lightning speed with Will racing after me. My cheeks are red with fury; my pulse is racing. I most certainly did not invite Darren and considering I am the only person in this house that he can even be considered friends with, I know that I am the reason he is here. It is my job to ask him to leave, not only because he wasn't invited, but because I don't *want* him here, especially after the move he made on me on Monday.

Downstairs, the music is still incredibly loud and I stop in the hall, glancing all around the house in an attempt to pinpoint Darren. I scan the living room, but he is not there, so I march into the kitchen with my eyes sharply narrowed. I am pissed off at him being here *and* for ruining my moment with Jaden, even if he doesn't know it. As soon as I step foot inside the kitchen, I spot him.

Leaning back against the counter with a beer in his hand, Darren looks almost out of place. He is a college sophomore and we are all high school seniors and even juniors, so he doesn't exactly know anyone. The stubble he is suddenly sporting makes him look much older than the rest of us too, and his brown eyes flicker over to meet mine when he notices me enter. "Oh, hey," he says casually, smiling as if he is oblivious to my rage. "I was looking for you."

"What are you doing here?" I spit, walking across the kitchen toward him. Will remains behind at the kitchen door, watching from afar, unwilling to get involved. I can't blame him. Darren isn't his problem; he is mine.

"Looking for you," Darren repeats with the roll of his eyes. He takes a swig of the beer he has helped himself to and then pushes himself away from the counter, stepping toward me, swinging the keys of his truck around his index finger. "I felt bad after what happened the other night."

His reply still doesn't exactly explain why he has decided to show up here tonight, but at least he does have some sense to realize that he was wrong on Monday to use my vulnerability to his advantage. "So you should," I mutter, folding my arms across my chest and giving him a challenging stare.

"No," Darren says, shaking his head at me. "I felt bad for you."

My eyes widen in surprise, taken aback. "Me?

"Yep," he says, taking another chug of the beer, finishing off the remainder. He tightens his fist around the can, crushing it and then carelessly tossing it behind him onto the counter. I hear Will sigh from the doorway. "I felt bad that you've shut me down one too many times, because now I'm pissed off at you, so I wanted to let you know that we're done. I was good for you, but you don't see it, so I'm not wasting my time with you anymore. I don't even want to be friends."

Someone clears their throat from behind me, and when I

glance over my shoulder, I see Jaden is standing by Will's side at the door. He is closing up the top buttons of his shirt, and his expression is hard as he studies Darren intensely with narrow eyes. I don't think he appreciates the interruption either, especially when it's by my ex, of all people. "Is there a problem?"

"No, Jaden Hunter, there isn't," Darren answers smugly, pivoting around me. He takes a few steps forward so that he is directly between Jaden and me, and then he shrugs. "At least not for me. You, however ... Well, I'm guessing you have a lot of problems right now with the Holden thing. I'm surprised you're even here, actually."

"What Holden thing?"

My lips part wide as the color drains from my face. There goes that sickening punch-in-the-gut feeling again. *Oh, God, no.* Darren is unaware that I have yet to tell Jaden the truth, so now—intentionally or not—he has really put his foot in it. A long silence ensues as the music blares next door. The atmosphere thickens as confused glances are exchanged. Jaden is staring at Darren, awaiting an explanation, but Darren is thinking. Will looks at me with his brows drawn together and I know what he is wondering: He is wondering if there is something I know that he doesn't, and there is.

Darren glances back over to me, and his blasé, carefree act is suddenly gone. Now there is more to his expression: confusion and surprise, intrigue and amusement as he sweeps his gaze over me. Slowly, his eyes flicker back to Jaden. "Didn't she tell you?"

"Tell me what?" Jaden asks. His challenging expression has softened and his eyes dilate with worry, his forehead creasing. He takes several wary steps into the room and my heart

299

shatters into pieces when his eyes meet mine. He expects an answer, but I can't give him one.

"Jaden," I mumble, scrambling around the center island and pushing past Darren. I stop in front of Jaden, grabbing a fistful of his shirt and gently pushing him backward toward the door, desperate to get him out of here before Darren says something he shouldn't. This isn't how I want Jaden to find out the truth. Not here, not now. "Please just go back upstairs," I beg. "I'll be there in a minute."

"Oh, Kenz," Darren says, and whistles sharply. He shakes his head in disbelief at me, but he cannot hide the pleasure in his voice and the amusement in his eyes. He casually strolls over to Jaden and me, propping his arm against the counter and watching us with a small smirk toying at his lips. "I thought you said my advice sucked, but apparently you've taken it on board. Decided to keep quiet after all, huh?"

Jaden tenses up and firmly stands his ground in front of me, refusing to allow me to push him out of the kitchen. He grasps my wrist and holds it tightly against his chest. "MacKenzie," he says firmly. He sounds impatient and irritated now, and never has he used my full name before. "What is he talking about?"

"Yeah," Will cuts in, moving toward us. He scratches the back of his neck. "What is he talking about, Kenzie?"

Right that second, the back door opens and Holden enters the house, bringing with him a chilly breeze that blows into the kitchen. He has his head kept down and he wipes his feet on the doormat while sliding his phone into the pocket of his jeans. It appears he has been outside for some air, but he has chosen the worst possible moment to come back in. He shuts the door behind him and takes a single step forward, glancing up. That's when he flinches, freezing on the spot as his dark eyes rest on Jaden. Then he looks at Will, and then Darren, and then me. He must read the panic in my expression, because he suddenly looks alarmed himself.

"She's keeping quiet about her good friend over there," Darren loudly states over the music. His face is aglow from a mixture of beer and sadistic glee as he says, "Holden, why don't you come on over here?" He motions him over, but Holden doesn't budge.

"Darren," I say, pulling my wrist free from Jaden's grip and spinning around to face him instead, my eyes pooling with desperation. He can't do this. He can't cause such chaos, such devastation, all because he is jealous, all because I chose to be with Jaden and not him. "Don't," I whisper. "Please. I'm not keeping quiet. I just haven't had a chance to tell him yet!"

"What, Kenz?" Darren says, widening his eyes as he stares back at me with a lack of compassion. "You didn't think your boyfriend deserved to know as soon as you found out?"

Jaden's patience wears thin, because he heaves a sigh and snaps, "Can someone just tell me what the fuck is going on?"

"Maybe Holden can," Darren says. He cocks his head to one side and looks over my shoulder at Holden, who is still paralyzed on the spot over by the back door. Darren knows exactly what he is doing now, and the sickening part is that he appears to be enjoying the power he has over us all. "You're most likely to tell the truth the best, aren't you, Holden? You know, since you were the one that was there that night."

The same terror that was in Holden's eyes on Monday is back again, only this time it is heightened. He looks at me, but he doesn't have the time right now to get angry at me for telling Darren his secret. There are more urgent matters at

301

hand. Slowly, he shakes his head, begging Darren with his petrified gaze not to go any further, not to say anything more. "Darren…" he murmurs, voice cracking.

But Darren isn't going to stop. He doesn't want to. Instead, he steps back and dramatically glances back and forth between Holden and me, feigning shock. "Neither of you are going to tell him? Alright then." He coughs, clearing his throat as he turns to face Jaden again.

My blood runs cold and a numbness sets in as I realize how helpless I am right now. There is nothing I can do to stop the destruction that is about to occur.

"Jaden," Darren says, though suddenly the pleasure in the situation disappears, because he frowns and bites anxiously at his lower lip. "Man, I hate to be the one to break this to you, but…but your parents crashed because of Holden." Here it comes: the truth. There is a split second of complete and utter silence when I close my eyes, shutting out the scene in front of me as everything goes still, when I don't hear the music or my own breathing, but then almost as quickly as it had disappeared, the noise returns at full force, even louder than before. The music drills into my ears at the same time as Will inhales a sharp intake of breath, and then I hear it: I hear Dani's voice weakly whispering, "*What?*"

My eyes flash open again. Over by the door, Dani has appeared behind Jaden and Will, her jaw hanging open. She raises a trembling hand to cover her mouth and her electric-blue eyes flash with pain, crinkling at their corners. Dani is still fragile, and before she can hear any further explanation, she bursts into tears and spins around. My heart feels broken and heavy in my chest as I listen to the sound of her footsteps as she runs for the front door. I hear it open, but I don't hear it shut.

I am forced to look at Jaden. His eyes are wild with confusion and disbelief, but he isn't looking at me. No, he is looking at Holden, staring across the kitchen as rage fills him. He shakes his head fast as his blue eyes narrow sharply, not with aggressive fury but with pained anger. The burning, searing type of anger. "Is this true?" he asks through gritted teeth. "Holden. You were there?"

Holden is focusing on his breathing, but I think he may just collapse. He presses his hands to the edge of the counter for support, his back to us, his head hung low. He wasn't ready to deal with this tonight. None of us were. "It was an accident," Holden feebly states, but his words sound choked as he forces them out of his mouth. "It was an *accident*," he repeats.

"Holden ... " Will murmurs, but he doesn't say anything else. He grabs a kitchen chair and sits down, exhaling.

"What happened?" Jaden spits, demanding an answer. He barges Darren out of the way and storms straight past me, marching around the center island toward Holden. He grabs his shoulder and jerks him back from the counter, forcing Holden to look at him. "*What happened?*"

But Holden can't speak. He can't open his mouth, he can't do anything. All he can do is squeeze his eyes shut and shake his head. He can't give Jaden the answers he needs right now, not in this state, not here, not like this. Jaden has no choice but to let go of him, and he turns back toward Darren and me, his cheeks flushed red. He runs his hand back through his hair, but he doesn't stop walking. He keeps on going, straight on past me, straight out of the door without saying anything else. He doesn't look at me, and that tells me everything I need to know: He is angry with me, and it's at that point that the tears come. They break free as soon as I hear the front door slam, and I know I can't let him go, not without explaining myself to him. My chest heaving, I turn for the door and am about to make a run after Jaden when Darren's cold hand grabs my arm.

"We're done, Kenz. For good," he states. He is sincere now rather than taunting, but he doesn't appear to have any remorse for what he has just done. He tightens his hand around my arm. "And what was it that you said again? Oh yeah. If you keep this from him, he'll never forgive you. Better start working on your apologies, and when it doesn't work out, don't come running back to me."

"You're such an asshole! We've been done for months!" I spit. Yanking my arm free from his firm grasp, I press both my hands to his chest and shove him away from me. He has ruined everything, and I have to be quick to catch Jaden before he disappears. I *need* to salvage this. I leave the three of them behind in the kitchen and race down the hall. The music and the laughter and the voices from the living room echo in my ears. They're still in there enjoying their night, oblivious to what just happened in the kitchen. Jess calls my name as I run past, but I ignore her and reach for the front door, pulling it open. The cool night breeze hits my face, cooling my tears, and as fast as I can, I search all of the cars parked up outside Will's house until finally I spot Jaden storming toward the black Corolla.

"Jaden!" I yell, running barefoot down the porch and across the crisp lawn. The ground hurts my feet, but I don't care. I don't expect him to stay, but I don't want him to leave without hearing what I have to say first. "Wait! Please!"

Jaden stops just before he reaches the car, spinning around

304

so abruptly that my body slams into his. "You knew," he hisses at me. The blue in his eyes is fierce and piercing, pooling with disappointment, pain and fury all at the exact same time. "You fucking knew, MacKenzie, and you didn't tell me?"

"I didn't know how, Jaden! I was waiting for the right moment!"

"There was never going to be a right moment to tell me something like this! You should have just fucking told me!" He exhales and looks up to the sky as though he is attempting to gather his thoughts, and then he glances back down and pulls open the car door to the passenger seat. Already inside and sitting in the driver's seat, Dani is weeping. "God, Kenzie! What the hell were you thinking?"

"I didn't want to hurt you!" I scream at him, before I stifle a sob in the middle of Will's front lawn, hot tears streaming down my cheeks. I didn't want this to happen. I wanted the truth to come from me, not anyone else.

"Just stay away from us right now," Jaden murmurs as he slides into the car, looking back up at me with those eyes of his. The disappointment in them is the worst part. After everything, I have let him down. He reaches for the door, and just before he slams it shut, he says, "You're good at doing that."

33

It is just after 8AM, and I have been staring at Will's ceiling for the better part of an hour. I've been restless, not just because of the uncomfortable blow-up bed on the floor, but because I can't stop thinking about last night, repeating the events over and over again in my head. I'm furious at myself for telling Darren the truth on Monday, but at the time I never imagined it could have turned out like this. I never thought he could be so cruel.

My head feels like lead, and I am not sure how much better Holden will be feeling this morning. Last night, after the Hunters and Darren left, he threw up twice while confessing the truth to a quiet, stunned Will. And it certainly wasn't because of the two cans of beer he had drunk.

The party had ended before midnight, and everything after the horrendous episode in the kitchen feels like a blur. Holden and I had sat upstairs, side by side on the floor in the hall, listening to the music. Neither of us wanted to go back downstairs. I was a mess, and cried until I ran out of tears. Holden had cursed at me for telling Darren everything. I had cursed right back at him for causing all of this in the first place. We cried, and then we yelled, and then we cried a little more. And when we'd both run out of steam we just sat there, numb.

I feel eaten up now, as I am lying here, eyes sticky with mascara, morning sunlight filtering into Will's room. I know it was an accident that night. I know Holden didn't mean for any of this to happen, but I can't help but keep thinking that this is all his fault.

I hear Will heave a sigh, and in a quiet, raspy voice, he asks, "Are you guys awake?"

"Haven't slept," Holden murmurs from the other side of the room.

I didn't know that they were both awake too. Pushing my blanket off me, I prop myself up on my elbows and crane my neck to look at them. Will is sitting cross-legged on his bed, rubbing at his eyes with the collar of his T-shirt. Holden is on the other blow-up bed, lying on his stomach, his chin resting on his folded arms. He is staring blankly at the wall.

"I feel like shit," I tell them, raking my fingers through my tangled hair. The room is far too warm and smells like boy, so I stand up and push open the window, leaning against the ledge as the fresh air drifts into the room. My headache hurts so bad that it is a struggle to keep my eyes open.

"I hate to ask... " Will warily begins, glancing between Holden and me. He leans back against his headboard and pulls his comforter up to his chin. "But what are we going to do?"

Holden releases a muffled groan into his pillow and covers his head. I feel my blood boil as it becomes clear that he hasn't got a plan. The situation may be complicated. It may be a mess. But it needs fixing, and it needs fixing *fast*. Darren's escapade last night wasn't exactly subtle, and I think it's fair to say that none of us have any idea what will happen once this news gets out. I don't see how Holden burying his head in his pillow is going to help matters.

I sit down on the corner of Will's bed, crossing my legs. "Yeah, Holden," I say, looking down at him. "What are we going to do? This is *your* mess." I massage my throbbing temples, then under my breath I mumble, "If you had just told the truth at the time ... "

Holden shoots upright, throwing his hands up in exasperation at me, his dark hair ruffled and his eyes immediately brimming with angry tears. "I already told you! Do you even know the kind of shit I'd get into?"

"Maybe you deserve to get into trouble," I say, my voice matching the volume of his. "If it was your fault you should have just spoken up about what happened. You should have just paid the damn price, Holden, because you don't get to keep this from the Hunters! Because telling the truth is the right thing to do!"

I stare down at him, studying him. He looks mentally drained, but I am not surprised. He has been carrying this burden on his shoulders for over a year now, and the weight of it has only gotten heavier. He is never going to be able to let this go until he tells the truth. Not to me, not to Will, but to the Hunters. It is the only way. After a minute of silence, I state, "We are going over there."

Holden's eyes widen. "What?"

"You are going to tell Jaden and Dani the truth," I tell him. My voice is firm and I am determined to make this right again. I've let Jaden down before, and I can't bear the thought that I may have just done it again. He might not forgive me twice, so I need to talk to him as soon as possible. I need to explain myself, and so does Holden. "They deserve to know exactly what happened, and they need to hear it from *you*. So get up," I say, pushing myself up off the bed and onto my feet, "because you *have* to do this, and you have to do it *now*."

"Kenzie, I *can't*!"

"Holden! Please!" I yell in exasperation, my voice pleading.

"Holden … " Will says quietly with a croak in his voice. "Kenzie's right, so listen to her. If you've done this—"

"Shut up!" Holden snaps. "I know! Okay? You think I don't? You think I don't know that? Because I do! I've had to live with this for over a year!" His voice is raised and he splutters his words, and in all of the years that I have known Holden, I have never seen him like this. So vulnerable and unsure of himself, so weak and so terrified. "Do you know what it's like? Can you *imagine* what it feels like to see them every day? How hard it is when you ask me to be around them constantly? I can barely look them in the eye. It's soul-destroying, Kenzie … And I regret it. I regret it *so* much. But that doesn't make anything better, it just makes it worse! Everything has turned to shit since that night—the football, my grades. I can't think straight … I can't sleep—"

"Holden."

"All because I *did* fall asleep for *two seconds*!"

"*Holden*," I say again, louder. He stops. "It's going to be okay."

Throwing his head back, he blows out a long breath of air and stares up at the ceiling, rubbing his hands over his face. In the silence that forms, Will looks up at me from the edge of the bed, and as we exchange an uncertain, hopeless glance. I know that he too wants Holden to do the right thing. When it comes to a matter this huge, this important, being best friends isn't enough. We want to help him, but we can't protect him.

"We get it," Will says quietly, though Holden is still staring up at the ceiling. "I'm freaking out just thinking about all of this, so I have no idea what it's like for you, but ... but c'mon, Holden." Will sighs heavily and places his hand on Holden's shoulder. "You have to talk to the Hunters. You don't really have a choice right now."

"No!" Holden recoils, pushing himself up onto his feet, nostrils flaring. "It's not just an accident anymore. What if it's homicide? Or ... or manslaughter? Do you know what that means when they turn me in? Jail! For *years!*" he yells, tears now falling down his cheeks. He strides past me to the window, leaning outside to inhale the fresh air. His back is to us, but we can see he is breathing so heavily that his shoulders are heaving up and down. "You guys *know* my parents wouldn't be able to afford a good lawyer, so goodbye football, goodbye college, goodbye future, goodbye to fucking *me!* I know it's the right thing to do, but it's going to ruin my life!"

Neither Will nor I can respond. Words choke in my throat. Holden is right: This is bigger than all of us now. The secret is out, and it had to come out, but it has suddenly changed everything, and now I'm not sure if it can ever go back to normal.

"Holden," I say finally, lowering my voice. "Look ... no one is turning you in," I reassure him, though I don't know for certain. I don't know what is going through Jaden and Dani's heads right now. I don't know what they're planning to do about all of this, and I'm trying not to think about how ugly this could all get. "We're here for you. But right now, the first thing you have to do is just talk to Jaden and Dani, because

310

if you don't..." I pause for a second, my eyes fixated on the beads of sweat around the nape of Holden's neck. "If you don't do this, then I don't know if I can ever look at you the same," I say finally. "You have to make this right."

Holden lowers his head. He is still leaning out of the window, his breathing is still heavy, and there is silence again. "Kenzie," he murmurs, his voice feeble. He glances over his shoulder at me and his dark eyes are heavy and sunken into his face. "Go and talk to Jaden. I am not coming with you."

What? I shake my head at him in disbelief, entirely stunned. I thought I knew Holden. I thought he would do this, not for me, but for himself. I was wrong. He isn't going to. He isn't going to talk to the Hunters. He isn't going to face up to what he has done. Desperately, I look back over to Will again, praying that he can do something, anything.

"Just go," he mouths to me, holding his hands up in defeat. There is nothing either of us can do or say to make Holden change his mind right now, and I can't stand here and waste my time arguing with him over it. Holden may not want to talk to Jaden, but I still need to, and soon.

I give Will a single nod and leave the room in silence, grabbing my things on the way out. My frustration burns the back of my throat, and I don't realize I've been fighting back tears until I stop for a second to look back at Holden. He is still by the window, paralyzed and unrecognizable. I am clinging on to a tiny fraction of hope that he may just turn around and finally agree to come with me, to tell Jaden and Danielle Hunter the truth about what really happened to their parents last August.

But he doesn't.

311

34

I am hunched over the steering wheel, my hands gripping the wheel tightly as I make the drive from Will's place over to Jaden's grandparents' house. I am so focused on the road that I barely blink as I mentally repeat exactly what I am going to say to Jaden when I see him. *If* I see him. Maybe he will refuse to hear me out. Maybe, after letting him down *again,* he has had enough of me. But I have to try, so I am driving over the speed limit as my heart thumps erratically.

It's just after 8:30AM, and at this time on a Sunday the roads are quiet. Luckily, Mom has let me keep her car the entire weekend. Not for my sake, but for her own. Her reasoning is that if she has no access to a car, then she has no access to the shelves of wine at the grocery store.

The short drive to Jaden's grandparents' place feels eternal, mostly because I am filled with nothing but nervous anticipation, but as soon as I pull up outside the house my shoulders sink. The driveway is empty. The car is gone and so is Brad's boat.

I park and switch off the engine. There are so many things going on in my head right now that my steps are off balance as I force myself over to the porch. First, I need to apologize to Jaden. And I need to explain myself to him. And I need to tell him the truth since Holden won't. *Please be here*, I'm praying. *Please listen to me. Please forgive me.*

The breeze blows stray strands of hair across my face as I take a deep breath and ring the doorbell. I stand back with bated breath, waiting. Now that I am standing here, I realize I have no idea what to expect on the other side. Maybe I should keep my distance at first. Maybe it's selfish that I'm even here. They will need time to process everything.

A minute has passed and no one has answered, so I turn around, a sinking feeling in my stomach, and am about to run back to the car when I hear the front door unlock. I freeze.

"Kenzie!" Nancy says as she swings open the door. She blinks at me for a second, but then a beaming grin spreads across her rosy features and her face lights up. "What a surprise to see you here!"

I am taken aback by the fact that anyone has even answered, and I'm so surprised by her reaction that I can't even so much as attempt to smile back at her. Instead, all I can do is bluntly tell her, "I came to see Jaden. Is he here?"

"Ah, no, he's at the lake with Danielle," she says. She leans forward into the porch and nods over my shoulder to the empty spot in the corner of the driveway where Brad's boat usually sits. "They've taken the boat out. They've been gone for a while now, so they shouldn't be too much longer. Would you like to come in and wait? Or maybe you could meet him over there?"

"That's okay. I'll try and find him. It's kind of urgent." *The lake.* I fumble with the car keys in my hands as I turn around, my heart racing even faster. With each second that passes, the more desperate I am to get to Jaden. But then I realize ... Nancy is smiling. Why is she smiling? Slowly, I stop on the porch steps and look back around at her. "Are ... are you okay, Nancy?"

"Yes. Why?" She widens her eyes and presses a hand over her chest, tilting her head thoughtfully. "Oh dear. Do I look ill? I *have* been feeling a little more flushed lately."

"No ... no. It's okay." *She doesn't know.* Jaden and Dani must not have told them. I am filled with the most overwhelming sense of relief. At least Nancy and Terry don't have their hearts broken right now. Jaden and Dani, however, do. Nancy studies me, looking a little puzzled, but I can't be the one to tell her, to explain all of this, so I do nothing but turn away again.

I rush back down the driveway and climb into Mom's car. I start up the engine again and pull on my seatbelt, but I don't set off immediately. Instead, I grab my phone from the center console and pull up my texts with Will.

Going to the lake to find Jaden and Dani. Tell Holden he has one last chance, and if he wants to take it, tell him to get over there too.

And, unsurprisingly from Will, he replies almost immediately. The text reads:

I'll try.

The morning is dull and the sky is full of clouds, though there *is* a sliver of sunshine peeking through. I keep my eye

314

on it as I drive, taking it as a sign that everything is going to be okay. Jaden will forgive me. He'll believe me. He has to, because he's already given me a second chance, and I refuse to waste it. Not now, not after everything.

I drive past the small 7-Eleven where Jaden and I first bumped into each other again all those weeks ago, and I feel another stab of hope. A lot has changed since then, things I never imagined would change. Something happened that night. Something was kick-started between Jaden and me again, and every day since then all I have thought about is him. I just never imagined that it would end up like this. I keep breathing deeply, and then head toward the small parking lot right by the lake.

As soon as I arrive, I spot Brad's boat hooked up to the back of the Corolla, on the loading ramp. My chest constricts when I spot Dani in the car, her arm slung over the wheel and her neck craned as she stares out of the back windshield. It tightens even more when I find Jaden. He's back behind the car, fumbling around with the boat's trailer, ensuring everything is secure, his head down. Neither of them spot me, but it appears I've found them just in time. They will be leaving any minute now, so I pull over into the first empty spot I can find.

I'm not going to overthink this. I'm not going to waste a single second. Grabbing the keys, I step out into the cool, fresh morning air. It's not cold. At least I don't think it is. I can't tell. I feel too heated, my cheeks too warm. I try to remember the words I'd planned out as I stride across the concrete toward Jaden. This isn't going to be easy, but it's something I have to do.

I come to a halt a few feet away from the loading ramp. Now that I'm actually here I don't know how to begin, but thankfully I don't have to say anything at all, because Jaden catches sight of me. He doesn't move or react, just stands there with an expression of mild surprise. His cool blue eyes bore into mine, and I wait, aching for him to do or say something.

"Kenzie," he sighs, finally. I don't like that he seems surprised to see me here—I don't like the thought that he *didn't* think I would try to fix this.

"Can we talk?" I say.

Jaden looks me up and down, studying me thoroughly. Like Holden earlier this morning, he too appears tired. I doubt he got much sleep last night, if at all. His hair is flat and ruffled, and he's wearing an old pair of faded black jeans and the same black hoodie he wore that night at 7-Eleven. Finally, he gives me a single clipped nod and then reaches for the passenger door of the car. "Dani," he says, "take the boat home. Go."

But Dani stares at me through the glass, her expression just as blank as Jaden's. I see a flash of the old Dani, of the Dani from weeks ago, not the happier Dani who's been around recently, the one who has been smiling more often. It's exactly what I was afraid of. I *knew* this news would crush the Hunters all over again. I knew this would send them straight back to square one. I knew this would bring back all of the grief they had been fighting their way through.

"*I'm sorry,*" I mouth to her, but she shakes her head at me, slowly and with disappointment in her eyes. She has lost all of the trust she had for me, and she glances away, revving the car engine as she tows her father's boat out of the water. I stare after her as she disappears down the street, trying to imagine the turmoil that is going on inside her head right now, and only when the car and the boat are completely out of sight do I look back to Jaden.

His eyes are still on me, his hands stuffed into the front pockets of his jeans. He releases a slow sigh and then turns away. He kicks at the ground as he walks, heading over to the empty picnic tables. Slowly, I follow him over, and I slide onto the bench opposite him, the table separating us.

We are both silent, but I can hear the soft roll of the water and the quiet whistle of the breeze. There are families over at the playground. Boats on the water. Kids further along on the sand. But they all feel so far away. Right now, all I can focus on is Jaden. He is upset, and he is angry. It is written in his eyes. Right now, I can't blame him.

"Jaden ... " I say. I don't know where to begin, so I stare at the wooden table. The green paint is chipped and fading. "How are you feeling?"

"How do you think I'm feeling, Kenzie?"

I glance back up at him. I already knew he wasn't going to be okay, but to actually *see* the sadness in his blue eyes hurts me more than I thought it would.

"First, we find out that everything we thought we knew was actually far from the truth, and then we find out that *you* knew and yet you didn't say anything." He exhales and angles his face to the side, his eyes fixated on the water. "It's been a long night, and I *still* don't actually know what happened last year. Where is Holden?" He looks back at me, his jaw clenched. I hate seeing Jaden angry, but he has every right to be. "Because he has some explaining to do."

"I'm really sorry, but he isn't going to talk to you," I admit. *Fuck you, Holden,* I'm thinking. He should be here right now, sitting next to me, looking Jaden straight in the eye. "I begged him to come with me, but he just ... He's scared."

"Are you kidding me?" Jaden's eyes go wide with rage.

"He's a fucking coward, then. How can he ... How can he have lied to us for so long?" He shakes his head fast, glancing up at the dull sky. The muscle in his jaw twitches. "I just need to know what happened. What *really* happened. He fell asleep ... Is that true?"

I swallow the lump in my throat and nod. This is what I didn't want to do—I didn't want to have to tell Jaden what happened on Holden's behalf. Even thinking about it makes me feel sick. "You guys had football camp that week," I begin, my voice trembling. "And football is everything to Holden. You know how desperately he needs a scholarship. He'd been working himself to the bone and he was stressed out about it. He went for a drive later that night to clear his head. I think. God, I can't remember now." I press my hand to my temple and try to think about everything Holden told me that night in my back yard. It feels like so long ago, and there was so much to process that even now I still haven't absorbed it all. "He was exhausted and he shouldn't have gone out. He ... he was just driving, and I guess he dozed off for a few seconds. He swerved and ... he said a car horn woke him up. I guess it took him a moment to come around? He said he saw brake lights but ... he just thought nothing of it and carried on. He didn't know what had actually happened until the next morning." I inhale a sharp breath of air and bite the inside of my cheek. "I'm so sorry, Jaden."

Jaden presses his hand over his mouth and lowers his head. "Why didn't he come forward?" he mumbles under his breath after a moment. "How the hell has he managed to look at me during practice? During games?"

"Because he hid behind me," I tell him. "I think he was glad that *I* was staying away from you, because he got to use my

318

fear of being around you guys as his excuse too. That's why, when we started hanging out again, he panicked, because he didn't have an excuse anymore. That's why he had to tell me. He no longer had anywhere to hide."

"How long have you known?" Jaden glances up at me, his piercing blue eyes fixing me with a pained look. I know how hard all of this must be to hear, but he is holding up. "When did he tell you?"

"Monday night."

"Why … why didn't you tell me, Kenz?" he asks, and his voice cracks. I have let him down. I know it now. The hurt and disappointment is etched into his face as he waits for an answer.

"I was going to, Jaden," I splutter quickly, reaching across the table to grasp his hands in mine. His skin is cold and he doesn't pull his hands away, so I squeeze them gently. "I was *trying* to, but I … I didn't know how or where or when. How was I supposed to tell you something like that? I didn't want to hurt you all over again, and so I was waiting for the right time. It just … didn't come." Suddenly, I think about Nancy again. I think about the wide, sparkling grin on her face when she opened the door before. She wasn't upset, because she doesn't know. "Why haven't you told your grandparents yet?"

"Because I didn't want to hurt … " Jaden begins, but then he stops himself, his words tapering off. Slowly, his face falls as a new realization dawns on him. He is doing exactly what I have done—he is struggling to break their hearts. "Oh."

"That's how I felt about you, Jaden." Maybe he will understand my reasoning now, maybe he will realize that the reason it was too difficult to tell him is because I *care* about him. I squeeze his hands even tighter beneath mine, and even though

319

I am still trembling a little, all I want is to be near him, close to him. "I am sorry I didn't find the right moment. I am sorry you found out the way that you did. I am sorry that I've disappointed you." I feel a tear break free and roll down my cheek, dripping onto the wooden table.

"Ah, Kenz," Jaden says. He slides his hands out from beneath mine and then places his on top instead, his cold, calloused thumbs tracing a pattern over my skin. "I didn't mean to yell at you last night," he says, looking at me earnestly. His expression is softer now. "It was a lot to take in at once, and I *am* been mad at you, but I get it now. I guess I just thought that you were taking Holden's side. It makes sense that you'd want to protect your best friend."

"No," I say, shaking my head. Another tear falls, and then another. "I mean, I do, but not in these circumstances. I am on your side, Jaden. The *right* side. You have already been through so much, and I just needed some time to figure out how to break the news to you, but I couldn't bear the thought of it because ..." *Here it goes,* I think. I have wanted to tell Jaden for a while now. I wanted to tell him last year. I wanted to tell him last night, and I tried to, but I didn't get the chance. And he needs to know. He needs to know where my head is at. I squeeze my eyes shut, feeling the damp warmth of my tears on my eyelashes, and I take a deep breath. "Because I am in love with you, Jaden," I whisper. "I never stopped."

I wait for a moment before my eyes flicker open again. Jaden is staring back across the table at me, his cold hands covering mine, and he seems to be analyzing my expression. Then, he stands up and slides into the bench alongside me, so I turn to face him. He is closer now, only inches away, our eyes locked.

"Kenz, do you know that you drive me fucking crazy?"

he asks, with a small hint of a smile. He moves his hand to my jaw, gently cupping my face, tilting his head toward me. "Because you do. But," he whispers, "I'll take it, because I never stopped loving you either." He leans forward and presses his cool lips to my temple, holding me close to him as I shut my eyes.

Relief floods through me in one huge wave and it is so powerful that it creates new, fresh tears. Happy ones this time. *I haven't ruined everything.* I love Jaden, and he loves me, even after everything that I have done. We are going to be absolutely, entirely okay. It is a bizarre thought. Weeks ago, we weren't even talking. And now we are here together. Everything is out in the open, and after an entire year, we have finally found our way back to what we used to be.

"Promise me one thing, Kenz," Jaden murmurs, leaning back. His hand remains against my jaw.

"Anything."

"No running away again, okay?" With his free hand, he tilts my chin so that he can look straight into my eyes, though I hate the look of fear there is in his. "Because right now, with all of this going on, I kind of need you again."

"I'm here, Jaden. I'm not going anywhere," I reassure him, closing my eyes again and pressing my cheek against his palm. I am never, ever letting him down again. I am here for good.

Just as I'm about to press my body closer against Jaden's, I hear a tremendous screeching of tires against the asphalt of the parking lot. Immediately, my head jerks up and I crane my neck to glance behind me. It is impossible to miss Will's bright red Jeep as he races toward us, skidding to an abrupt halt several feet away. Within seconds, he is frantically rolling down his window, desperately waving me over.

"Kenzie!" he yells, his cheeks flaring red. Something is wrong. "He's going!"

I run over, a sickening feeling building in the pit of my stomach. "Will, what?"

"Holden!" Will says, shaking his head fast. "He's turning himself into the cops right fucking now!"

My heart feels as though it has fallen straight into my stomach and that sickening feeling turns into a painful punch. "Oh my God," I breathe. "No. We should be there!" I press my hands to my forehead and glance back over to Jaden, who looks equally shocked. *Holden is about to throw his life away.*

"If we're fast, we can catch him," Will says.

Quickly, Jaden gets to his feet and grabs my wrist. There is a determined look in his eyes and he pulls me toward the Jeep, his steps quick. "Will, take us over there."

My mind is racing with questions as I climb into the back seat of the Jeep. Jaden gets into the passenger seat, and he has barely even shut his door before Will slams his foot down on the gas. I am so taken aback that I feel as though I am in a trance. I hate that Holden's doing this. I hate that we don't know what will happen. I hate that we're not there with him. I hate that he's alone.

I lean forward, grabbing onto the headrest. "What the hell is he doing, Will!"

Will throws a hand up in exasperation. I don't think he knows what's going on, either. "I was giving him a ride home and I was just … I was just trying to keep pushing him into coming over here to talk with you guys, telling him it would be the right thing to do, and that it would be pretty pathetic if he didn't. He was silent the entire time, and we were stopped at a set of lights on Main when he just said, 'Fuck it', and jumped out!" he explains, his words spilling out of his mouth. "He ran straight across the street to the station!"

Jaden sits there in silence, fidgeting and shaking his head to himself infrequently. Anyone would think he'd be thrilled that Holden is finally facing up to what he's done, but instead Jaden just looks uncomfortable.

I feel sick. Confused. Faint. The police department isn't far, just around the corner, right across the street from Windsor High. We are only a minute away, but every second feels like a minute itself. We need to find Holden. I need to tell him it will be okay. He is doing the right thing at last, but he doesn't have to do it like this. There must be another way. Maybe the Hunters wouldn't want the investigation reopened. Maybe Uncle Matt could help, give him some advice at least.

We turn off Main Street and speed past the school campus. I can see the station on our left, and Will makes a sharp turn into the parking lot. We are in a race against time, so he pulls up diagonally over a row of empty spots. "Go!" he yells.

Please, Holden, no. No, no, no.

I sprint across the lot toward the building and I can hear Jaden close behind me. We *can't* be too late. We have to find Holden. All I can do as I run those final few steps toward the main entrance is pray that he hasn't yet had the chance to speak to an officer. He hasn't even spoken to his parents, for God's sake! I pray that he is still standing in the reception area, anxious and pulling on his hair, that he's not in there going through this alone.

With Jaden by my side, I burst through the main entrance and into the reception. It is silent aside from a phone ringing behind the desk, and my own hurried breathing. Jaden steps forward, glancing around, and the lady behind the desk looks at us expectantly from behind the glass partition as she picks up the phone. Seconds later, Will comes bounding through the door behind us and bumps straight into me.

"Where is he?" he pants, stopping next to me.

There is no one here. There are doors either side of the reception area, and they are both closed, though not for long. The door on the right swings open and a bulky, broad-shouldered officer with graying hair steps through. He stops, surprised to see us standing here, all three of us on edge.

"Is there something I can help you guys with?" he asks, but I am not listening.

I am looking over his shoulder and down the long stretch of hallway behind him on the other side of the door. I am looking at Holden, and I am looking at my uncle Matt. I open my mouth, ready to yell something, but there is nothing I can say. There is nothing I can do.

They have their backs to us as Matt leads Holden down the hallway, and that's it: We're too late. Holden is entering the unknown. Dread consumes me as I watch Matt come to a stop, pushing open a door and motioning for Holden to step inside. I'm not sure if Jaden and Will are breathing, but I'm certainly not.

Holden steps forward, but he casts a quick glance over his shoulder, and that's when his eyes meet mine. They are a dark ocean of every single emotion he is feeling right now. There is the overwhelming worry of the unknown. There is a deep sadness. But there's also something I can't put my finger on, something that I can't quite read. And then it hits me.

It's relief. His eyes have given up all the anger and dread of this morning, and now all that's left is relief. He is facing up to his biggest fear; he is finally doing it. The unbearable weight of the past year is at last going to be lifted.

His swollen eyes travel to Will, and then to Jaden. And, for the first time in a year, they look at each other in exactly the same way. They *see* each other, their own remorse reflected in the other's face. The moment seems to go on for hours, each man looking at the other as though he were staring in a mirror. Then, slowly, Holden gives a single nod, eyes still fixed on Jaden. Slowly, but surely, Jaden reciprocates. Exhaling, Holden finally tilts his head to the floor. That's when he steps into the room, and Uncle Matt follows in behind him, clicking the door shut.

Everything feels the same, even though we know it will be different from this moment on. The phone has stopped ringing, and the lobby feels still and empty once more.

Jaden steps in front of me and his anxious eyes meet mine. I can tell he didn't want this to happen, not like this. Moving closer, he wraps his arms around me, enclosing me in his firm embrace and holding me tight against his body. I feel secure against his strong shoulders, and as my tears break free, I wrap my arms around him too and we fit together, folding into each other. He buries his face into the crook of my neck, his breath warm against my skin, and he murmurs, "I really am going to need you now, Kenz."

I press my face against the soft material of his hoodie, tightening my arms around his torso, and I listen to the steady beating of his heart as I nod against his body, my eyes squeezed shut. "I'm here," I whisper.

And this time, I really am.